DEAD
AND
BLONDE

A MEG DARCY MYSTERY BY

JEAN MARCY

NEW VICTORIA PUBLISHERS
NORWICH, VERMONT

Published by New Victoria Publishers Inc., PO Box 27 Norwich, Vt. 05055
A Feminist Literary and Cultural Organization founded in 1976

Cover Design Claudia McKay

Printed and bound in Canada
1   2   3   4   5   2002   2001   2000   1999   1998

Library of Congress Cataloging-in-Publication Data
Marcy, Jean.
      Dead and blonde : a Meg Darcy mystery / by Jean Marcy.
        p.   cm.
      ISBN 0-934678-98-7
      I. Title.
    PS3563. A6435D4   1998
    813' . 54- - dc21   98-26123
                                     CIP

Dedication: to steadfast friends of all persuasions

Acknowledgments:

Our thanks to the usual suspects who have supported us as the staunch friends they are. In addition to everything else, we are grateful to the Susans (Faupel and Frain) for the author photos for both this book and the first one.

Tom Stringer advised us on gun lore, and Tim Kniest provided helpful material on JCCC. If we mangled any of their facts, the errors are ours.

We salute Left Bank Books and Our World, Too for, in different ways, standing up against the giants and serving our community.

Even with one book behind us, we still don't know enough of the intricacies of publishing to acknowledge adequately the debt we owe to Beth Dingman and Claudia Lamperti, but we know our indebtedness is large. We feel honored to work with them.

As for ReBecca Beguin—we now understand why authors gush about their editors—it's all understatement, folks.

CHAPTER ONE

The shrill sound split the night.

I climbed the walls of a deep sleep, fought off the damp embrace of a tangled sheet, groped for the bedside phone.

No good news arrives by phone at four-thirty a.m. I swallowed to scrape sleep from my voice box, summoning a wary neutrality for my tone. "Hello."

"Meg." One syllable, but stretched and thin.

"Darcy here," I said crisply, my tone belying my confusion as I ran down the list of those who call me Meg.

She wasn't on it, of course. The last time I'd heard her voice, husky and strangulated, in the intimacy of night, we had tangoed these very sheets into a lust-ridden twist. But she'd called me Darcy then, even during the best parts. And I'd never before, under any circumstances, heard Sarah Lindstrom whimper. But recognition clicked in just a half-second before she said, "Meg, this is Sarah."

I was sitting up then, trying to shuck off the clinging sheet. The floor model fan I keep nearby to imitate palm breezes blew a predawn chill over the faded tee I sleep in when I'm not having company. No doubt why I shivered.

"Sarah, what's wrong?" Her first name, the whole question felt lumpish in my throat. She'd never before given me any chances to use a consoling tone.

"It's Viv. She's been murdered. In my home."

Too much, too fast. I raced over it, couldn't make sense of it. The adrenaline rush dizzied me.

"Are you all right, not hurt?" I blurted.

A peculiar sound, maybe an attempt at ironic chuckle, maybe stifled groan. Then, her voice nearly her own, "I found her."

"Jesus."

"Her killer used a baseball bat."

"Sarah!"

"Can you come to my place? I mean now."

"Ten minutes." I was fishing with my feet for the jeans I'd left on the floor. "Sarah, have you called the cops?"

I'm a PI. I think like that.

"Of course," she said, her tone nearly a snap and pure Lindstrom.

1

"I just wanted to make sure you're safe." Damn. Apologizing again. Last time I swore I wouldn't again, ever. No matter what.

"Safe as houses." Bitter. Black bile bitter. Scary bitter. I'd called Sarah Lindstrom many things in the last six months—arrogant, untrusting, picky, and my personal favorite, Ice Queen. But never bitter.

Now a gush of queasiness swept over me. I smelled my own sweat, strong from my anxiety. I reached over for my Reeboks. "On my way."

"You know the address?" Half-embarrassed.

As she should be. Six months and I'd never been inside her house. Patrick was starting to joke that she had a moat around it.

But evidently not one deep enough. I didn't say that. I didn't say, "Yeah, I frequently drive round your block, pining." Instead, I said, "I know."

A beat. But now wasn't the time to go into it. I added a question. "Is Neely there?"

"Yes." A half-beat. "I called him right away."

First. Sure. She would. That's okay. He's her partner. They work homicide together.

If Lindstrom were Patrick, I'd have said, "Tell Neely to hug you till I get there." Not because Patrick is gay. Because he's cuddly and open and can admit when he hurts. But Lindstrom isn't Patrick. "I'm glad Neely's there." It was more than half true. "I'm on my way."

"Thanks, Darcy." The name and the tone said it all. The drawbridge was drawing up again, the one that protected the innermost keep of the castle.

We hung up. I stood, abuzz with swirling energies, higher than from any drug, nearly struck motionless because so many conflicting signals swarmed in my brain. I felt like I had that first time someone had deliberately shot at me.

And I felt this way the first time Lindstrom and I had had sex. I can count on the fingers of one hand the times since and not use all the fingers. Exactly four. Well, on four occasions. Each time we had had our own private orgy. I think about those four occasions quite often. I have them memorized. The look of her. The feel of her. Lindstrom's silken skin. The smell, the taste. The way she moves. The ways. The tilt of her head, the arched brow, the dry and skeptical voice. Even in bed. Certainly afterwards—when we always clashed.

It never started like a real fight, but sneaked up on us from the side. Who's the best candidate for mayor next time? Can a cop march in the Pride Parade? Had Clinton deserved our vote? Just little throw-away asides that got twisted and turned and, above all, blown up: "You don't know what it's like to be a cop." "You don't know what it's like to be a dyke."

The fiery endings, the icy follow-up. Weeks with no calls, no notes, no amends.

Then, having lived in St. Louis for years without crossing paths, we bump into each other. Patrick and I would be browsing in Left Bank Books or having Sunday brunch at South City Diner, and Lindstrom would turn up.

2

Weeks of pouting undone in an instant.

It's not those perfect, chiseled, Nordic features and her tall, lithe, athlete's body. It's something inside her, some elusive spirit that I want to capture and hold. It's—I can't explain it. So this call has jarred me from more than sleep. Neely was there first, but she did call me. Inside the whirl of conflicting excitements is a small gloating hope: I will rush in on my white horse; I will save her.

I yanked off my tee shirt, quickly pulled on yesterday's sports bra and fresh tee, tied my shoes. For a second or two I just stood there, trying to find a thought to hang onto from the dozens dashing about. Take my .38? No. Cops by the squadrons will be there. A homicide in the home of one of their own.

I started moving.

And tripped over a yawning Harvey Milk, who mewed a strong protest. "Feed you later, Harve," I said on my way out.

In the hallway, outside his door, I pushed down a momentary impulse to wake my buddy Patrick. For the last two years he's been the first to know my big news. But I didn't have time. I flew down the stairs, "I'm coming, I'm coming" humming through my head.

I stepped into the dregs of night. I'd parked my Plymouth out front of the four-flat, one of a row of dark brick apartments that run along Arsenal and face Tower Grove Park. In daylight the park is inviting. At night it's spooky. The reliable blue Plymouth fired right up. It turned a hundred thousand miles this February, and for the sake of my finances I needed it to last two more years. Tonight I just needed it to go, go.

Right away I had to wait for a red on Grand. The quiet on this major North-South artery was surreal. St. Louis isn't a city that never sleeps. The city slumps into a light doze in the wee hours, and morning shift changes hadn't stirred things up yet. Even in summer when restless teens are out cruising, the sidewalks eventually fold. Even on a Saturday. A Friday become Saturday.

I glanced down the street but couldn't quite see the temperature sign on the bank. NPR's Ben Able had forecast the mid nineties for today's high. Suffocation in the Midwest, and it was only June 19. Swelter weather had begun.

Had Viv been sleeping with the windows open? Did Lindstrom have her AC on and the windows closed?

What you don't know can hurt a lot, especially if you replace it with what you can imagine.

Viv was Lindstrom's ex. Lindstrom didn't talk about her much, and when she did, her tone was unrevealing. Calm. Neutral. Civil. One of those. The way I tried to talk about my ex. Gay gossip circuits hadn't given me any clues to Lindstrom's split. Viv was an auburn-haired beauty clambering up the greasy pole of some corporate law firm. Lindstrom was racing down the fast track at the police force. A power couple—very closeted, of course.

But that had become past tense two—three years ago. My impression

3

was that they scarcely spoke, let alone did slumber parties.

Of course, you could drive a Mack truck through the holes in my personal knowledge of the private routine of Detective Lindstrom. I knew she liked to be on top—of everyone and everything. Maybe she and Viv had reconciled.

Still, Lindstrom had called me. I was racing to her house, skipping through stop signs with the bravado of one who figures any cops in the neighborhood will be gathered at the murder scene. Murder scene. No matter what else had happened, Viv was dead.

Truthfully, I couldn't get that fact to stick. Viv alive had more reality, even in my imagination.

I pushed the Plymouth east on Sidney. Normally I'd have avoided it with stop signs at every state, Arkansas through California and Mississippi, but at four-thirty in the morning it was absolutely quiet and free of traffic. I rolled through the stop signs with a quick sideways glance. I caught green lights at Jefferson and Gravois and swung a hard left onto Ninth.

I approached Soulard Market, could see its light and bustle, the big refrigerated semis and smaller vans unloading produce for the day. I swung a sharp right into one of the small side streets.

Over the years the French, the Irish, the Germans, the Czechs, the Lebanese, followed by white Southerners, have claimed Soulard. The red brick French houses with mansard roofs and metal stars along their sides have been spruced up but not rehabbed beyond the reach of the working classes. The houses often sit smack alongside the sidewalk or have postage stamp front yards. In February they celebrate Mardi Gras with plenty of noise and hoopla and drag queens. New Orleans it ain't, but anything that perks up the city's pulse gets my applause.

I'd driven by Lindstrom's house before this night. Okay—I really had done a few lovelorn cruise-bys. Not that I'd have had trouble recognizing it now. There weren't literally a dozen cops outside, but there were three cruisers, an ambulance, and two unmarked department Crown Victorias crowding the street in front of her house. The white crime scene van with the familiar blue and gold stripes along its sides was double-parked, nearly blocking Michellene Street. No TV vans in sight. A few neighbors with robes or sweats thrown over night clothes stood in the street and stared as an ambulance pulled away. I realized with relief that I'd missed my chance to meet Viv.

Aside from all the cop cars, Lindstrom's house was typical of the historic neighborhood. Like its neighbors, the red brick house rubbed against the sidewalk; the narrow strip of concrete was filled with uniformed cops.

Lindstrom's house faced east in the middle of a cramped block. A privacy fence of light-colored wood ran down the south side of the house, leaving only a three-foot strip of thin sun-starved grass on that side. The neighbor to the south, a painted brick three-story, was less than five feet on the other side of the fence. At ground level the north side had two feet of sidewalk between it and its neighbor, but Lindstrom's second story actually

4

touched the next door house, creating a narrow covered walkway running between the houses, an architectural feature fairly common to the area. The little tunnel began and ended on Lindstrom's property; the neighbor didn't share access to it.

In the predawn dark the house didn't give much away. Its red brick front was clean and tidy, its shutters and front door freshly painted. Looked good, revealed little. Like Lindstrom herself.

I drove by without slowing, turning onto a side street, and parked. I glanced at my watch. I'd made the ten-minute trip in a record-setting seven. Suddenly I was no longer in a hurry. I sucked in and released a deep breath and pulled myself out of the Plymouth. I locked up because crime scenes attract the unsavory curious as well as the garden-variety gawkers. I walked around the corner.

The small stoop of Lindstrom's house was off-center nearer the north side. By the time I walked to the front of the house, a cruiser was pulling away, and there were only three uniforms idling on the front sidewalk. I walked up to the closest one. "Hi, my name is Meg Darcy, and I'm a friend of Detective Lindstrom's. She asked me to come over. Okay if I go on in?"

I tried for a smile, but I'm not sure if it came off. The oldest one pulled out his walkie talkie and called to someone inside the house. He was less than four feet from the front door. Boys and their toys. There were two different exchanges before he nodded at me and pointed at the front door. As if I hadn't seen it. I felt the cops' eyes on my back as I climbed two steps. My heart was thudding, but not from their stares.

When I pushed open the heavy front door, I felt the sharp bite of the AC. One question answered. I saw Neely loitering in the hallway, leaning against the stair banister.

"Hi." I offered him my hand. I was surprisingly glad to see him, but unsure if he'd remember me from the Brooks' case.

"Hello, Meg." A good detective. "Good to see you again."

Even though it was predawn, Neely looked well-pressed and combed, as always; the only sign he'd been called out in the middle of the night was the heavy, dark beard stubble. He was a small man, a decade older than Lindstrom. I'd never learned why she was the senior partner, but they seemed to work well together.

I noticed we were keeping our voices low. From upstairs I heard louder, casual voices and heavy footsteps. The crime scene techs I assumed.

"How long have you been here?" I asked, still monitoring my voice.

"A little after midnight." He looked down at the watch on his right wrist. He sighed. "Four and a half hours or so. I'm glad you've come. She's not doing so well. She won't talk to me at all."

I searched his eyes. Did he think she would talk to me? I couldn't believe that Lindstrom had told him we were lovers. I seriously doubted that Lindstrom had even revealed to him that she was queer. Perhaps he just assumed we'd been friends since the arrest in the Brooks' case last December.

"In the living room." He pointed across the hall to an open doorway.

I walked into a long room with cool green walls. It was sparsely furnished with pieces that looked expensive. I didn't have time to notice details because Lindstrom paced across the floor. She was walking away, but there was nowhere to go so she came back. She was in summer weight tan pants with a creamy long-sleeved shirt, a rusty smudge on her left cuff. I didn't think my heart could speed up from the pace it had set already, but suddenly I felt like I had a startled colt corralled in my chest, smashing against confining rails. Each time I saw her afresh, without the hangover of our latest quarrel, I experienced meltdown.

Just now her face was a study. Her jaw was set, her brows bunched over narrowed eyes; both fists were clenched. She bisected the oriental rug, turned and crossed it again. The room, though large, looked too small for her rage.

"Sarah?" It sounded odd from my mouth.

She started and stared at me. For a moment she clearly didn't know why I was standing in her living room. Then she traveled back from wherever to here and now.

"Oh, Darcy—you're here. What a mess!"

I walked toward her, wanting to gather her up in a hug. I knew Neely and who knew what other cops were about; still, even heterosexual friends get to hug for comfort. But as I approached her, she suddenly dropped onto a brocade sofa. She sat with arms and legs crossed, creating an effective defense perimeter. "Damn, damn, damn," she chanted, nodding her head emphatically with each word.

I've used such language over parking tickets. But I had no doubt she was suffering. Her whole body was charged, like a benched player who just wants a chance to release energy into action.

I sat on the edge of the farthest cushion.

"I want to get whoever did this," she said. Each word was a promise.

"I understand, Lindstrom, but right now—"

She turned the full force frost on me, her eyes blue ice. "No, you don't."

My life was spared. A short, African-American woman came down the wooden stairs and walked into the living room, peeling off her latex gloves. She stuffed the gloves in the pocket of her white jacket and rubbed the powder from the inside of the gloves onto the tail of the jacket. A crime scene technician, I assumed.

"Johnson here?" she asked.

"No, in the kitchen," Lindstrom said.

The tech went back out into the hall, and we both sat stock still listening to her steps into the kitchen which evidently ran along the back of the house. In the unnatural quiet we could hear her voice clearly. "All done, Detective Johnson. I'll have the photographs for you by eight. Max is taking the sheets to serology. I need to do elimination prints."

"Just a sec." We heard a chair scrape across the tile floor and then his heavy steps, back down the hallway. Johnson was a tall, stoop-shouldered

6

man with mahogany skin. His short, tidy natural was shot with gray, and his eyes were heavy lidded as if he hadn't had a good night's sleep in months. He looked unhappy to be investigating a homicide in a co-worker's home. I wasn't sure if the hardness around his mouth was always there, or just for this case. He was at least six-foot-two and thick. His stance in front of us was intimidating. It was too much for me; I stood. Lindstrom stayed put on the couch.

"Meg Darcy." I extended my hand.

"You're a friend of Detective Lindstrom's?" He shook my hand.

"Yes."

"Good, I'm glad you're here." He turned to Lindstrom. "Sarah, we need to know if we will have to get any other sets of elimination prints." His baritone was scratchy, but not as hard as his stare.

"No, I live alone."

"Frequent guests, family members?"

Lindstrom shook her head. "No, just Vivian. My folks were here about three months ago. Mom was in my room. I don't think there has been anyone else in there."

"Well, we probably won't need them anyway. If we get a set we can't trace, we'll get your mother's then."

Lindstrom nodded. Her fists were still clenched, but her face was going slack.

Johnson shifted his considerable weight. "Why don't you go with Meg, now? Get out of here and go get some sleep."

Lindstrom looked at me, and I nodded. As easy as that, Johnson had settled several momentous negotiations. The power of heterosexuals is astounding. I rag at Lindstrom for being too closeted, but I had no will to let Johnson see our decision-making processes at work, to let him in on the potentials for either closeness or rift between us. Still, because I, too, believe actions can fix things, I would have liked to quiz Neely before we left, but I suspected Johnson was right and that Lindstrom needed to get away from the crime scene.

We got up and walked through the kitchen to the back door. As she passed, Neely reached a hand out to Lindstrom, but she waved him off and strode out the door. Outside, I paused, unsure. I kept my eyes from her face; I had some sense that she needed to rearrange it, that a social mask had slipped in response to Neely's gesture or to her leaving the house where Viv had died.

"Your car or mine?" I asked to fill the silence.

"I need to leave my car for the crime scene team. They haven't looked at it yet," she said. This was worse than I had imagined. I led her to the side street where I'd parked.

"They suspect you?"

"Of course I am a suspect. She was murdered in my house." She stopped and glared at me. "In my bed."

My years as an MP in the army sometimes come in handy. I had virtually no external reaction to the last three words. My internal reaction was considerable. I had assumed that if Lindstrom were rekindling her marriage she would have at least phoned me. I took a deep breath and unlocked the passenger side of my car. I grabbed the fast-food bag from the seat and threw it into the back. Three uneaten fries fell onto the seat, and I scraped them onto the floor. Well, if she thought she was coming to my place and just falling into my bed, she had another think coming. I would, if necessary, take her somewhere, drive her all the way to the farm in Nebraska that her parents still worked, but there was no way I was taking her to my apartment.

I was whipping right along with that, rebuilding my fort, when she pulled on one of the back belt loops of my jeans and tugged me out of the car.

"It's not what you think," she said to my back, her voice low.

"How do you know what I think?"

"You aren't as good a poker player as you imagine." A jibe but not her usual dry tone.

"How come I usually win?"

"You've never played against me."

She was standing right behind me. I could feel the heat of her body. She placed her hand lightly on my shoulder, just brushing my neck. For a terrible second I imagined I smelled the stain on her cuff, fresh and sickly sweet. I ducked away just a bit. She stepped back.

I turned. In the shadowy side street our faces were hidden. "Let me take you home," I said. I heard the small tremble in my voice.

"No. Just drive. I want to be moving." Not meeting my eyes.

I wanted to enfold her then, offer comfort, hold her tight. Not because she was helpless and hurt. Because she was being so damned brave. But she was as antsy as an adolescent, shifting her weight.

"Drive," she said. I nodded and walked over to my side and slid in.

CHAPTER TWO

She slipped into the passenger side with her usual effortless grace. How she moves her body is a subject on which I've whiled away hours when I've pulled desk duty in my office at Miller Security.

A Plymouth Horizon doesn't offer the luxury of distance between the seats. Just sitting there forced intimacy, but we both rolled down our windows, inviting the night's distractions, letting some of our intensity out. In the past we'd made the world fly apart in firecrackers. You'd think it would have been easy to reach across that small dark of the Plymouth to take her hand. But she was beating her knee with a clenched fist. I was mesmerized by the cuff with its small blot that looked merely inky in the dim light from the nearest streetlight and the faint beginnings of dawn.

"Just go. Let's move," she said.

I pulled from the curb into the remnants of night.

"Do you want to talk about it?"

She didn't answer. She was staring out her window, her hair stirring in the artificial breeze of our movement.

I knew she'd heard. But, we were in front of the Anheuser-Busch brewery before she started talking as if into a Dictaphone.

"I got home just before midnight. Eleven-fifty or so. I was supposed to be off at eleven, but we had just finished a case, and I wanted to clear the paper work." She stared straight ahead, but I could tell she wasn't seeing the brewery as we passed it. "The house was quiet. I figured Viv was asleep, so I fixed myself a sandwich. Read the paper. I went upstairs and as soon as I hit the top step, I smelled it. The blood. So I went into my room. She was still warm."

I stole a look at her. Her blonde hair was mussed, her jaw clenched. Tears were running down her cheeks. I tried to see into the back seat, but gave up—I'd never find the box of tissues in that mess. She ignored the tears or simply wasn't aware of them.

"I saw a partial footprint on the rug. The mattress was pushed halfway off the box springs where she had struggled. Viv's purse was dumped on the floor. I checked the rest of the house, just to be sure, but there was no one there. I called Neely at home. He said he'd come, but asked me to call the department right away so there was no delay to explain. Then I checked the windows. Her killer got in through the first floor bathroom window. The first cruiser got there at the same time Neely did." She looked down at her own long hands. "And now the hell begins."

I'd turned on Arsenal without much thought and now turned left onto Gravois just because it was familiar. "What track did Johnson's questions take?"

She sighed and laid her head back against the headrest. "I wasn't doing too well. All the dead bodies I've seen, all the investigations I've worked—it all went out of my head. Or rather, crucial parts of it escaped me. I managed not to contaminate the scene, didn't step on the footprint, but I sure couldn't give Johnson a coherent account. Neely had to tell him Viv used to live with me. For a minute there, I thought I would be able to keep our relationship a secret—that's how stupid I was. So, once Neely told him we lived together, I knew it would all come out. Still, I wasn't able to give him a sensible report. So he had to waste time coaxing answers from me."

I hesitated. I wasn't sure how she would react to my questioning her. I wasn't sure about my own motives either. I stared at my knuckles, white on the grimy blue wheel. I could feel the red creep up my face as I thought about the last time we'd made love. She'd spun me like a top but pulled back when I tried to reciprocate. Maybe she'd already been anticipating a reconciliation with her ex. How did Viv come to be murdered in Lindstrom's bed? Before I could frame a question, Lindstrom shifted in her seat to face me.

"Viv's current lover, Kathleen Clawsen, is an abuser. She beat Viv up Thursday night, and Viv had finally had enough, and she was scared. So she came to me. I was the only one she knew who would take her in and protect her from Kathleen. But I didn't protect her. Kathleen hunted her down and killed her for leaving. Murdered her because she ran to me."

Lindstrom sounded sure of herself. As if she had seen the whole thing on videotape. My mind whirled. Viv was running to Lindstrom? Lindstrom had clearly said 'Viv's current lover.' Did I believe Lindstrom wasn't Viv's current lover? Shit. I couldn't figure out what was happening. And it all suddenly seemed more important than it should have been.

I scrambled to find a less loaded question. "Has Kathleen been arrested?"

"No, Johnson says he'll go question her as soon as he is done at the house."

"Was there something at the scene that implicated Kathleen?"

"Not yet, the fingerprints, blood, and trace evidence will take a while to process, but she'll crack when Johnson questions her." Lindstrom shook her head. "She's a damn coward. Like all batterers."

Sounded like the smart homicide detective hadn't quite returned. Lindstrom was jumping to conclusions. Partners and family members are always the first suspects, most likely to murder, but Lindstrom had Kathleen convicted on what sounded suspiciously like a jealous guess to me.

"How big was that footprint?"

"I didn't have a ruler, but it looked a little large for a woman, but not impossible. No bigger than my shoe I'd guess."

"What kind of questions did Johnson ask?"

"He wanted to know all about Viv, of course. Her family, her work, money."

"She had a fair amount of money, I assume."

"I don't know exactly anymore, but she was probably worth five-hundred-thousand or so."

Half a million. That was considered rich in my social circle.

"Who inherits half a million?"

"I really don't know, anymore." She rubbed her hand over her face and looked at her lap. "When we bought the house, she changed her will. I got the house and about half the money. The other half went to her sister."

"Your house belongs to Viv?"

"No, we bought it together. When we broke up, I refinanced. Viv got considerably less than her share of its worth, but she insisted she was happy with that. She was always generous with me. She probably didn't tell Kathleen that."

"How did Johnson react to the lesbian relationship?"

Lindstrom wrapped her arms around her chest and held herself. We had argued in the past about the relative merits of being out, so I had an idea that being outed to her coworkers in this brutal way made her feel like she was spinning apart. "He was respectful, on the face of it. God knows what he thinks or what he'll say. He seemed surprised that a woman would abuse another woman, but he didn't dismiss it or argue with me. He just asked what they fought about and if Kathleen had ever hurt her before. But he seemed as interested in learning about Thomas as about Kathleen."

"Who is Thomas?"

"Thomas Aubuchon, Viv's ex-husband."

I was startled to hear that Viv had been married to a man and surprised that Lindstrom spoke calmly about it. I was also nastily curious. Had Lindstrom been involved with Viv while she was still married? This didn't seem the time for that particular question. "How long had she been divorced from Thomas?"

"Six years."

"An acrimonious divorce?"

"No, not really. She and Thomas remained friends, of sorts. Business partners anyway. Thomas didn't kill her."

I promised myself to pursue Thomas later. I decided to get back to Kathleen. "Did Kathleen know that Viv was at your house?"

"I don't know. I told Viv not to tell anyone, just to completely disappear for awhile. I was going to go to her house tomorrow, no, today, to get some clothes and things for Viv. I guess she must have told someone."

"Do you think she called Kathleen? Maybe she was considering going back?"

"No. She really was convinced that was over. But Viv might have told a mutual friend."

"Or maybe Kathleen just figured Viv would run to you for protection?" I kept my voice level. I'm a detective. Lindstrom was a crime victim, like any other crime victim.

"Maybe. But jealous people aren't rational."

A silence. I had time to notice we were passing Soulard Market. Even at this early hour, the market itself was busy, seemingly endless streams of people winding in and out of the brick building. Burly men unloading crates of produce from Florida, California, and Arkansas. Around the market St. Louis's first rush hour of the day was grinding toward the brewery and the industry along the river.

Lindstrom had never really told me much about her former lover, Vivian Rudder. And I had never missed the information until now. "Tell me about you and Viv."

"We were together six years, and I guess we took one another for granted. I'm always working impossible hours at the department. She worked too much, too. Sometimes we wouldn't see one another for two weeks at a time. But we always took off together twice a year. We'd go to San Francisco, or New Orleans or Montana. I was happy. I had no idea she wasn't until I came home one night and found her packing." Lindstrom shook her head at the memory. "It was really the only all-out screaming fight we ever had. She blamed me because she felt stifled. She had to have some time away. I knew she wasn't ever coming back. She wouldn't admit it, though.

"She had already met Kathleen. Kathleen fawned on her. Hung on her every word and followed her around like a pup. Kathleen couldn't believe that a beautiful attorney would be interested in her. When I met Kathleen, I couldn't believe it either. She has no class at all. She's like a moose at a dinner party, always putting her foot in it. And so insecure. At first I thought, Great, let Viv have two months with this woman. Then she'll be begging me to take her back." Lindstrom sighed. "Except it didn't work out that way."

Lindstrom's voice dropped. "After the breakup I didn't see much of Viv at all. She just disappeared. Viv got all the friends in the divorce, so I didn't really hear about her. Turns out she wasn't in touch with our friends either. That went on for about eight months. Then out of the blue she starts calling me. Always from work. We had lunch a couple of times. About the third time she tells me she is worried about Kathleen. She tells me Kathleen is very jealous. Always checking on her to see how she spends her time, who she talks to. She'd been forbidden to talk to me. Forbidden." Lindstrom spat out the word. "Her story scared me. Kathleen sounded like a typical batterer to me. But I know Viv, if she felt like I was pushing her to leave Kathleen, she'd have shut me off. So I tried to get her to call Donna. Remember Donna Purcell?"

I remembered Donna Purcell. Donna has worked with battered women for years.

Lindstrom continued, "Viv did finally call her. I think she went to see Donna once, but it didn't help. Viv kept thinking that Kathleen was just a little insecure and they could work through it. She never told me Kathleen was actually hitting her until Thursday night. When I got home from work, Viv

12

was there. She still had a key to the house. Her arm had fingerprint bruises, and her hip was black and blue. Kathleen had kicked her. Viv was down on the floor and that drunken asshole kicked her." Lindstrom's voice went up, then choked off. She took a breath and continued, "Kathleen killed her because she found her at my house. Kathleen was insanely jealous of me. Viv said Kathleen was always wanting Viv to compare the two of us. She found Viv at my house and assumed that Viv was cheating on her." Lindstrom slammed the side of her fist into the door. "Viv was just trying to get away. She wasn't even interested in me anymore."

I breathed in warm, humid exhaust fumes and tried to forget the pictures in my own mind of Viv murdered in Lindstrom's bed. I wasn't Kathleen. "How was Viv killed?"

"Kathleen beat her to death. Left the bat right there. She was a mess, Meg. You could hardly recognize her face. The medical examiner's investigator said it looked like all of her ribs were broken. It must have taken a long time to beat her that badly." Lindstrom ran her right hand over her face.

I reached over and grabbed her left hand. "She would have blacked out, Sarah. She wasn't awake that whole time."

She shook her head, but held tightly onto my hand. For the first time since we'd initially made love in my apartment months ago, I felt like Sarah Lindstrom needed me.

I was driving through Tower Grove Park by that time. Lindstrom's lids were sagging, and her normally iron spine was melting. I parked on Arsenal and asked her if she were ready to go upstairs and get some rest. She nodded slowly, and the tears started again.

On the climb up the stairs I hit the panic button. We'd never spent a whole night together. Suddenly I felt pushed toward something huge. Not that I had sex on my mind. To my amazement I could actually stand near Lindstrom without fantasies of ravishing her. But the next step was inexplicably bigger.

I was hurrying to sort it out, when she said, "Darcy, I'd like to be alone. I mean sleep separately. Do you mind?"

Relief. No other name for it. I wouldn't have to decide what to offer, what to repress. No hassles over how to touch her. No need to invent consoling phrases.

I murmured assurances and let us in. Harvey Milk greeted us. I sat Lindstrom on the couch and went to find her a tee shirt to sleep in and a spare tooth brush. Then, while she was in the bathroom, I fed Harvey and got sheets for the couch. I heard the shower running. When I walked back to tell Lindstrom the couch was made up for her, I found her already in my bed, her face buried in the pillow. I picked up Harvey and settled on the couch for a short nap.

CHAPTER THREE

I slept hard, but snapped awake when Harvey butted my chin with his head. I sat up, rudely pushing him aside. Why I'd been sleeping on the couch came back to me like a punch. For a cowardly moment I wanted to fall back and sleep this Saturday away. But there was no help for it. I was awake.

I pulled on the jeans I'd worn to Lindstrom's and padded barefoot to the kitchen to start the tea. I stripped the couch of the sheet and blanket. In honor of Lindstrom I decided to fold them and put them back in the linen closet.

How long would Lindstrom be staying? Certainly until the crime scene investigation was complete. Even then I wouldn't want to rush back to a house where an ex-lover had been killed. I thought about Susan, my most recent ex, and shuddered at the brief image of her horribly beaten as Vivian had been. Maybe Lindstrom wasn't really over being dumped by Viv. I could hardly imagine how searing it must have been to find her beaten to death in the sanctuary of Sarah's own bed. I could push the image of Viv, murdered, from my mind. Lindstrom wouldn't have that luxury.

I had wandered back into the kitchen for my tea when I heard Patrick's knock on the door. He uses his own pattern of raps so I'll know who it is. This morning he was fairly loud. I was surprised he was off on a Saturday.

"Shush. Lindstrom's sleeping," I said as I opened the door.

Patrick's blue eyes widened. He knew my lust for the Ice Queen. Despite the fact that he's my best male friend—or maybe because of that—he's a bit skeptical of Lindstrom. Or jealous. He disapproved of what he saw as Lindstrom's using me. Turning me on and off. He thought I should find a nice girl and get married. Give Harvey another mother. And incidentally, that he should find a nice boy and we could live side by side in urban heaven. Never mind that neither of us would last six months in this idyll; it remained one of Patrick's favorite fantasies that he and my wife would exchange recipes.

"You're on again?" Incredulity over curiosity.

Instead of motioning him in, I stepped out. "Let's go back to your apartment." I was whispering.

He arched his eyebrows but shrugged and turned back to his apartment next door. I followed, sipping my tea. I glanced at my watch: noon.

As soon as we were inside Patrick's little entry way, he turned. "What's all the melodrama for?" He loves melodrama.

"Let's sit down." I walked past him and settled on his couch. His two

14

.

Siamese cats, Oscar Wilde and Quentin Crisp, pranced over to greet me. I set my tea on the coffee table to have two hands free for petting.

Patrick was making impatient noises. He was standing too close and looking pickle-faced.

"Don't grill me. I'll talk." It was my last joke for nearly a half hour. With few pauses I recited everything that had happened since Lindstrom's four-thirty call. Partly it was a way for me to process what had happened.

Patrick was glued. He's a great listener. He has perfect instincts about timing nods and ahhs and questions. When I finished my recital, he asked, "Do the police suspect Lindstrom?"

"Oh no, I don't think so." I spoke with certainty. I looked at him looking at me. His face was open, no craft hidden. He wasn't teasing me.

"She's one of theirs," I added. I heard the sound of it. "They *know* Lindstrom." I stretched out know for emphasis.

He was running his long fingers over his blond hair. The hairline is rising a bit from his forehead, and his solution is to keep it all cropped short à la Gertrude Stein, though that's not the comparison he'd use. I think he's handsome, but mostly I love his face because he's dear to me.

"Do we know Lindstrom?" stretching out the *know* in imitation of me.

"You mean do I know her?"

He shrugged.

I thought about it. I'm one of those people who believe that each and every one of us is capable of murder, even the late Mother Theresa. If you pile on enough hypothetical *ifs* about stressful circumstances. If by capable, you mean potentially capable. But even as a private investigator, I see enough hypotheticals played out to know the odds aren't even. We aren't *equally* capable.

Just on the surface there were enough arguments against Lindstrom's being a suspect to make my first answer reasonable.

Against that were two facts: Lindstrom was Vivian's ex-lover; Vivian was killed in Lindstrom's bed.

How well did I know Lindstrom? In the past six months we'd had sporadic sex but had not become either real friends or real lovers. I admired her, was electrically attracted to her, even idly wished I'd been able to interest her in being a buddy. But I couldn't say I knew her passion or understood her concepts of loyalty and retribution.

I knew Patrick much better. And, frankly, loved him more. I would never say he couldn't kill someone. I could imagine circumstances where he might, though his essential gentleness was one of his most appealing attributes.

"I suppose it's possible," I conceded at last. "But I really don't think so."

"Because?"

I shrugged. "She was just too horrified by what she found." I glanced at my watch.

"Who do you think did it?" Patrick's faith in my detecting abilities is one of his most endearing qualities.

I'm sure I looked blank. I was blank. So far I had only been reacting to

Lindstrom's suspicions.

"I don't have a theory. Lindstrom may be right. Viv's ex, Kathleen, had a motive."

"Means?" Patrick knows the lingo.

"The cops have the bat down at their forensics lab. A woman could wield a bat as a weapon.

"Opportunity?"

I shook my head. "Don't know."

"How about the other ex? The husband? Why isn't he on Lindstrom's short list?"

"Good question. I imagine the cops will have some questions for all those folks."

"Including the Ice Queen."

I nodded. "Yes. The investigation will be hard on her, I'm afraid, with every step reminding her of what she wants to forget."

He touched my shoulder. "Give her a hug for me."

I wasn't sure I dared, but I nodded assent. "I need to get back. If she wakes up, she'll have no idea where I am."

"Do you have stuff for lunch?"

I shook my head, and we both laughed. Patrick is familiar with my shortcomings as a hostess. "I'm not sure what Lindstrom will want. We'll probably go out." I eased my way toward the door, promising to keep Patrick posted. He was wary of Lindstrom, sure that she was the wrong woman for me. But he also has a big heart for the hurting.

I slipped back into my apartment. All was quiet. Harvey was curled up on the couch taking a nap. I headed to the kitchen. More tea.

I was just punching the microwave buttons when she said, "It's late."

I turned. She was still wearing my tee shirt and her broad shoulders and greater height made it ride up dangerously close to her pubic hair. The blonde hair on her head was rumpled, and a red streak on her cheek bore silent witness to a pillow's wrinkle. All of this was the stuff of daydreams, but all I felt was "God, here we go; another day." Which meant we had another hill of misery to climb—she as the struggler, me as the unhappy observer.

"You deserved some rest."

"I didn't really sleep. Just dozed." She shrugged. "Is that tea?"

"Like a cup?"

"No. I'd like some coffee. Good coffee." She peered around the kitchen and looked at me as though she, too, knew of my shortcomings as a hostess.

"There's a St. Louis Bread Company around the corner on Grand."

"Perfect." She disappeared back into my bedroom. I had time to sit on my couch and consider. She looked as though she were trying to reassemble herself: Sarah Lindstrom, St. Louis detective, who didn't let you in to see her furnishings. Who didn't let me in.

The shower didn't take her much longer than it would have taken me, but when she reentered the living room, her results were more impressive.

16

Maybe it was the classy clothes. To my relief, she'd rinsed out the spot on her cuff.

I was encouraged by her posture and tone. She seemed more her old self. But she wasn't over it. Just signaling that she could walk across the street without being hit by a car. A part of her mind was free to function on daily business.

We agreed to walk the short distance to the Bread Company despite the battering heat index. We moved slowly, though, like invalids just testing their legs. Only June 19 and already St. Louis's wet blanket of heat threatened to suffocate. We didn't talk, and I found the silence comfortable despite the tragedy we weren't discussing.

We paid close attention to our food—a sandwich for me, a salad for her. Her eating was businesslike; she was consuming fuel. As a cop, she'd eaten thousands of meals like that. But seldom would she have held so much emotion at bay.

When we were down to crumbs, I said, "Tell me about Vivian."

"What about her?"

"What kind of law did Viv practice?"

"Corporate. Loved swimming with the big boys and knowing she was smarter than most of them. She didn't like to live that way all the time, though. Her folks are…" Lindstrom paused, searching for a word. "Her dad sort of measures life that way. They're more materialistic than Viv. She liked being comfortable but didn't think money meant happiness. But she admired her dad—went into business law because he is a businessman. She and her friend Colin sometimes went to parties—she had a collection of dresses for those, but she found that amusing. Didn't mistake society and glitter for real life." Lindstrom looked into her coffee cup and then out the window.

Lindstrom sighed, "She was a smart woman. Too smart to stay with Kathleen. I'm sure she was going to break it off this time. Kathleen probably sensed that, too. That's why it was all or nothing. You know the control thing. 'If I can't have you no one will.'

"She said she wanted to be married to one person her whole life, but truthfully, she got bored easily. Her relationship with Thomas was the longest romantic relationship she had. Mostly because it was harder to get divorced, I think."

"Could she have been seeing someone else, besides Kathleen?"

"No, I asked her. She said she was leaving Kathleen, but wasn't involved with anyone else. I think it was true. If she had been seeing someone else, I think she would have gone to her lover's instead of my place." Lindstrom shifted in her seat. I guessed she was feeling crowded by this conversation.

I struck before she suggested a move. "I think you ought to stay at my place a few days."

She looked at me, not surprised, but she said nothing.

"Do you want me to go over to your place and pick up some clothes for you?"

17

"I need to go back." Her voice was firm, but she didn't look eager.

All the same, she was a big girl who presumably knew what she needed. So I said, "I'll drive you over."

"Let me call Johnson." I understood. It was a necessary courtesy—and maybe something more—to check with the detective in charge of the investigation before reentering the crime scene.

She used the pay phone by the restrooms.

"Johnson says I can go in, and I can have my car back." Her voice was still even.

We drove back to Soulard in silence. I thought again how I'd feel if I had returned home to find Susan murdered in my bed. It was too absurd. I couldn't make a start.

Lindstrom directed me to the back alley lined with dumpsters and trash cans which led to her small parking area with an extra parking space. The backyard was deep but felt closed in with the privacy fence on one side and the old stone garage at the back of her property. A big forsythia, its spring blossoms gone, spread by the garage's corner. To my surprise, the grass in the backyard needed mowing. The back porch was bigger than the front— three steps up to a ten foot by four foot wooden floor with a balustrade of thin spindles.

I pulled my Plymouth alongside her Toyota.

"Where did Vivian leave her car?" I just spat it out without considering its effect.

"She took a cab over. Kathleen had hidden Viv's car keys." Lindstrom's voice tightened at Viv's lover's name.

The sidewalk to the house was old, smooth bricks. Marigolds bordered the path. The porch was freshly painted in light olive with a pale peach stripe and white trim. Very arty. The yellow crime scene tape hung from post to post. Lindstrom, despite her height, agilely ducked under it. I followed. Another tape blocked the door. That she yanked down. I supposed she'd cleared it with Johnson.

She wasn't saying anything, and maybe it was my imagination, but she looked like she'd rather be flogged than to walk back into that house.

CHAPTER FOUR

We walked into her kitchen. It was large and high-ceilinged. The old cabinets had been ripped out. Light blond ones had been installed. The tall, narrow windows let in considerable light; the shutters matched the wooden cabinets. A butcher's block stood in the center. The terra cotta tile floor gleamed. There were two saucers and a glass in the sink. Lindstrom had eaten a snack, then gone upstairs. We both stood a silent moment staring at those dishes.

"Sarah, why don't you tell me what you need from upstairs?"

We both realized the crime scene hadn't changed—except, of course, the body had been removed.

"No, I need to go. Come with me." Her voice had tightened two more turns.

Beyond the kitchen, I had a brief impression as we walked down the hallway that, off to the left, was a den, and then the living room. Clean and uncluttered. No magazine stacks teetering. But Lindstrom was taking me up the light wooden stairs too quickly for me to notice much.

The upstairs hallway was narrow with a faded blue Oriental rug lying over the polished pine floor. Some framed photographs—arty studies of blossoms—hung on the wall. There was a door to our left, a hallway table, another door. As we passed the first door, Lindstrom gestured with her left hand. "Guest room."

The next door was slightly open. She paused, and I saw the deep breath, the shoulders straightening. I wanted to give a reassuring pat, but I hesitated too long.

She stepped in, and I followed. I knew we were seeing different scenes. I had never seen Lindstrom's bedroom before. And I had to take it in. From the doorway we were facing a dark mahogany bed. Not queen-sized but full-sized. It had been stripped of its bedclothes, but the mattress had large splotches of blood giving the room a salty, slightly fetid odor. We both froze for an instant, staring. I pulled my eyes away to do a quick survey. Behind us to my right was an old-fashioned dresser with an oval mirror. A few gee-gaws were scattered on top. The opposite wall had a bay window with a narrow cushioned window seat in light green. In the U of the bay window was a small round table covered by a full-length cloth in the same color. To my left was a chest of drawers with an interesting array of compartments, completing the mahogany set. A few splatters of blood had made it that far.

19

Many more splatters had hit the wall behind the bed. Without seeing the body I knew how vicious this beating—this bludgeoning—had been.

I was breathing shallowly. It took me a moment to hear Lindstrom. She wasn't crying, but she was fighting something. I wondered if that smell would ever go away. She walked forward and opened a large closet. She began pulling clothes out, still on their hangers, and handing them to me. She worked quickly, but she was making choices. She thrust the clothes at me like a surgical nurse slamming scalpels and clamps into a doctor's palm. Then she yanked a small cloth satchel down from the top shelf.

She stood before the chest of drawers. White fingerprint powder clung to its surface. "Damn!" she said, looking at the blood. She pulled a handkerchief from her jacket pocket and used it to touch the porcelain knob pulls. She threw underwear into the satchel: briefs, sports bras, crisp plain white handkerchiefs. Sweat gathered on her upper lip.

Abruptly she was through. Deliberately she let the handkerchief drop. "They took a rug from there," she said, pointing to the bedside. "Had blood on it and the footprint." I looked at the empty spot. "The bat she used was against the wall." She stared at the bloody wall. "Propped it there after she finished."

"Only one footprint?" The question popped out; it had been bothering me since she first told me the story.

"Yes. She either wiped her shoes really well on something she had with her, or, more likely, she saw the print and kicked off her shoes, and then stayed out of the blood."

"The killer was thinking then, not just crashing around in a rage."

"In this day and age, even idiots know about evidence. They see it on TV every night." Abruptly Lindstrom shook it off and walked back to the closet.

"Shoes," she said and stuffed two pairs of loafers into the satchel. "Let's go, I can buy deodorant."

She shut the door behind us and looked at me for the first time since we entered the house. "Is your offer of a place to stay still open?"

"You bet."

"Johnson says they may come back to check some more today or tomorrow."

I lifted my brows. Had they got the evidence they needed or hadn't they? St. Louis isn't New York City or L.A.—and now, post OJ, we know L.A. is seldom like the movies either. "Crime scene investigations are rarely done by purists, I guess."

"Johnson says they're being very careful. Have to be with a cop. Cops looking after a cop," she said.

"What do you think of Johnson?"

"We've never worked together, but his rep is good. They say he's honest. He seems comfortable with himself. He isn't burnt out. He doesn't hate everyone yet. He was very careful with me last night."

"Careful?"

She looked tired. "Courteous. A little afraid of how I might react." She searched for more words. "Kindly maybe. 'Take it easy,' he kept saying."

"Easy for him to say," I said too recklessly.

She looked sharply. "Well, he doesn't know me. I was sure right away Kathleen had done it. Murderous bitch."

I flinched. I hated it. I'm not the kind of feminist who believes women are innately morally superior. I knew the dirty little secret that some lesbians batter their spouses or lovers. But I still hated having the secret out. I especially hate to hear any woman referred to as a bitch.

I changed the subject. "What did he say about the footprint?"

"Nothing yet. He didn't have much to offer." She started back down the steps, and I trailed behind, trying not to trip over the slacks I was holding. I have an undistinguished record as a clothes carrier.

We were walking down the hallway, headed toward the kitchen when a thought came to me. I knew Lindstrom was in a hurry to leave, but I put my question into words anyway.

"Is this the bathroom the attacker came through?" I nodded to my left. Under the stairs were two doors. I guessed the first was a closet and the second, the door to the bathroom, directly across from the den.

She gave me a look.

"It's not idle curiosity," I said.

She shrugged.

I shifted the clothes and opened the door. Inside a toilet and sink and shower, a quick impression of blues, greens and lavenders. The window in the outer wall was above my head and looked like a tight squeeze for an adult. It was closed now but had an old-fashioned sash. Easy enough to lift from outside if it weren't locked or painted shut.

Lindstrom was still in the hall. I called out, "Is Kathleen athletic?"

No answer. I rejoined her. A gleam of tears in her eyes, she looked away. "Don't say it. The window was down but not locked." She turned toward the kitchen.

I formulated some reassuring phrases, but I imagined how feeble each would sound to Lindstrom. No excuses. I followed her through the kitchen, thinking her straight posture and broad shoulders gave no hint of her vulnerability at that moment.

On the porch she held up the yellow tape to help me duck under it. I made it all the way to her car, losing only one slithering blouse which she deftly caught with her free hand.

"Let's go back to my apartment and get you settled," I suggested.

We caravanned back. There wasn't a spare parking place behind my apartment, so she parked on Arsenal.

I can't explain why I again had the jitters as we climbed the stairs to my second-story apartment. But I felt as though I was on a train that was moving fast. We weren't talking either, none of that social chatter that cushions or brakes.

As I turned the key and motioned her through my door, I thought about the few times we'd had sex. Always at the tag end of an evening, usually after a bottle of wine. We'd been as fumbling and as ardent as teenagers. Now, entering in daylight, and unpropelled by lust, I felt solemn and scared.

Usually Harvey greets me at the door but today no sign of his little pink nose. Nothing to cover my nerves as I led her straight through to my bedroom to unload her clothes.

I squeezed my clothes to one end of the closet. She didn't actually curl her lip in disdain, but I figured she felt a smidgen of contempt for my cramped quarters. Or maybe for my wardrobe, as Patrick said later.

"My couch is comfortable for me. Why don't you take the bed?"

I half-hoped she would say we could share the bed. Opening the door. Up to now, we'd had so little really. Just longing and release. I didn't even know what else I wanted, or what I was willing to offer.

She gave me a penetrating look, then said, "All right."

Then there was that awkward little moment. Your guest is going to be there for a few days, and now you're starting this little slice of life. What do you do next?

I actually did clear my throat. "Look. I know a good cleaning outfit. They do industrial cleaning—offices and the like. But they also do special jobs. Cleaning up after vandals or fires mostly. Nasty work. They're expensive, but I could probably get you a deal."

She listened and nodded. "Call them to make an appointment—I imagine by Tuesday Johnson will be through."

"Great." I walked to my desk and flipped through the Rolodex. Miller Security often used Blairs.

"I wonder. Do they paint?" she asked.

I nodded. "What do you want done?"

"Have them paint the walls. Cover the places where they clean the stains. I don't want to see those places." Her voice, which had regained its detachment, wavered. I imagined that she was thinking of looking at those cleaned spots and shuddering. I was thinking fresh paint might suppress the smell of blood. "And ask them to replace the mattress and box springs."

The transaction with Blairs took about ten minutes. I had to explain the circumstances and set it up for Tuesday morning. Lindstrom made several circuits of my living room, pausing to read book titles. Harvey crouched by the couch and glared, his tail twitching. She was making him nervous.

When I got off the phone, I said, "How about something to drink? I've got tea, beer, and soda."

Lindstrom was standing with her hands on her hips, staring out my front windows and into Tower Grove Park.

"You've got a nice view here." Without irony she added, "Too bad it's in a high crime area."

Spoken like a cop. I wanted to snap back that I hadn't found any dead bodies in my bed lately. But that was stress. I was just realizing that the woman of my dreams—rather literally—had moved into my apartment. Probably I'd have to stay on good behavior for days. Like Harvey, I was nervous.

22

I tried to imagine the apartment as Lindstrom was seeing it—through her sharp eyes. She'd seen little of it during the daylight hours. We hadn't been pals here. The veil of horniness hides housekeeping flaws. But now Lindstrom would have a clearer lens to appraise my character in an area in which my shortcomings are many and obvious.

Just off the dark staircase that serves both Patrick's and my apartments, I walk through my door and to my immediate right is a wall shared with the kitchen. To my left, an open area that I call my den—it holds my desk, my Macintosh, and a couple of file cabinets. The den is part of the long stem of the L that makes up my living room. All along that stem are windows that look out over Tower Grove Park, a great perk. The short stem of the L is the wide midsection of my living room where I have low bookcases, crowded with used paperbacks, under those windows which face a neighboring apartment; there, too, I have my couch, a portable TV on a stand, and a couple of overstuffed chairs. All the furniture is comfortable and at least second hand.

Nothing separates the living area from the kitchen. The kitchen is medium-sized, not bad for an apartment with more cabinet and counter space than I need, and room enough for a small oval table that seats four. The bathroom, linen closet, and my bedroom line up opposite the Arsenal side of the apartment. The bedroom is depressingly plain and utilitarian, but the building is old and solidly built. Its walls are thick, so I rarely hear Patrick and the boys bumping around.

Harvey and I call the place home, though. Every now and then I swipe a dust cloth around it, and except for books and magazines that creep out of place, it isn't too cluttered. In my eyes. I was still having apprehensive shudders over what Lindstrom's eyes would see if she could get past her grief and shock about the murder to focus on the mundane details of my living arrangements.

Lindstrom proposed that she make a trip to buy the toiletries she'd mentioned. I offered her the choice of a National grocery or a drug store, both on Grand. I wondered if Patrick were home and if I could bribe him to do a quick cleaning while Lindstrom and I were out. But I didn't have the chance. Instead, Lindstrom said she'd like to go alone, and I murmured the right response.

When she was gone, I raced around the apartment, swiping surfaces with an old tee shirt. Harvey kept twitching his tail like a metronome.

"Relax, Harvey. We're getting a roommate."

I knew very well that if asked, Harvey wanted Patrick.

CHAPTER FIVE

Lindstrom walked in two hours later with a small paper bag just as the five o'clock news was covering the death of a prominent St. Louis attorney found bludgeoned to death in a Soulard townhouse. Police had neither a motive nor a suspect. The house belonged to a friend of the victim's. Vivian's name had been given; Lindstrom's had not. The piece was brief without on-the-scene pictures.

Lindstrom stood in my living room, staring fixedly at the screen even as the local news team flashed forward to a drive-by shooting in north St. Louis.

Lindstrom had called me at four-thirty a.m. We were scarcely over twelve hours from that call, but the newscast seemed surreal to me. How could either of us be standing in my living room watching this account so calmly? Why weren't we rending our clothes, shrieking protests?

I swallowed hard, dredged up a comment. "That was pretty low-key."

She kept her eyes on the screen. "Johnson kept it sketchy. He doesn't want it out that it was a cop's house, as long as he can prevent it."

We watched the weather in silence. More humidity tomorrow, typical for June 20. The Cards were in a slump; the latest Muny Opera was a success.

I glanced at Lindstrom. Tears were running down her face.

I didn't know what to do. "I'm really sorry, Sarah."

She swallowed, her eyes still on the TV.

"Is there somebody at work you can see to help you deal with this?" I was thinking about the psychologist or whoever the police are sent to after shoot-outs.

"I don't need a therapist. I need to see Kathleen locked up." Her voice was strong and cold. She pulled away from the television screen; her eyes were red-rimmed, but she was no longer crying.

"Don't you think Johnson is the one to handle this?"

"While I was out, I stopped by the station to talk to him."

That explained why it had taken her two hours to buy a comb and deodorant. I hadn't wanted to pry. "So, what did he say about the case?"

"He hasn't arrested her. He won't even tell me if she has an alibi. He's shutting me out. Just like the rest of the department will after it gets out Viv and I were lovers."

"Has he questioned Kathleen?"

She sighed. "Yes, but he won't tell me anything. Neely wasn't there.

24

He'll probably shut me out, too. He probably hates me. Finding out this way that he's been working with a dyke all these years."

I suspected Neely had already figured that out, but I kept that to myself.

"He didn't act like he hated you last night, Lindstrom. Both he and Johnson just seemed concerned about you. About how this would affect you."

She deflected it all with an impatient shrug.

"Well, if he can't get it out of her, I can. I can scare it out of her. She's as cowardly as all bullies." Lindstrom's chin tilted upward.

It sounded nineteenth century to me. All honor codes and challenges to duels. Who knew the funny little pictures about love and justice Lindstrom carried around in her head? She seemed intent on riding her charger over to Kathleen's to give Vivian's lover a caning.

"Not a good idea, Lindstrom." I hoped I was brisk.

"Will you go with me? I need a witness."

A plethora of bad possibilities bobbed up on my inner screen. I was a reluctant second being dragged to a duel. I was the PI about to lose her license for intimidating the citizenry. I was the non-entity watching Lindstrom's passionate fealty to her ex.

I was maybe Lindstrom's friend.

"You don't need a witness. You need a restraining order."

The look she shot back was so angry I was instantly convinced that, although she was clearly capable of my murder, she was innocent of Vivian's. I was a boulder in her path. A disloyal boulder.

She shrugged and started moving to the door. Despite the day's terrible weight, she still moved with the lithe grace of an athlete.

"Wait. Not so fast." I followed after her.

She didn't slow down till we were downstairs.

"Your car or mine?" I asked.

"You're always joking."

"Not always." But I was stung. "I really am sorry, Lindstrom. Much more than I have words for."

She weighed it. "Me, too."

"Did you still love her?" We were standing in the pocket-sized lot outside the apartment. The straight couple who currently lived below me struggled by with Saturday's groceries.

She gave a loose shrug. "I don't know. It doesn't matter. I did. And I found her dead in my bed after she'd sought protection from me." She tightened her lips to stop the quiver creeping into them.

I heard the guilt. And thought I understood it. If the love had faded, all the more guilt. Maybe. Or maybe I didn't want to hear how dear Vivian had been to her.

"You feel okay to drive?"

She nodded, and we trailed round the house to her Toyota. In the park across the street teenage boys played soccer. They were white, black, and Asian.

25

Lindstrom drove as I'd anticipated—a balance between aggressive cop (too fast) and cautious Norwegian (always checking her mirrors). Her broad, long-fingered hands on the steering wheel looked capable. I couldn't look at them without imagining their touching me. I looked away.

We had said too much to carry the conversation into the car. So we drove in silence for several blocks. Traffic thickened as the city started its Saturday night. We were a good two hours from complete darkness, but people were already on the move, on the way to movies and dinner. And death. On a normal June evening in St. Louis someone was out to kill, someone else to be on the receiving end of that statistic. And other someones, like Lindstrom, to be caught in the web of tragedy by being the friends and relatives of victims or victimizers.

That's the kind of mulling over that dampens enthusiasm for a Saturday outing. If you had any to start with. I wasn't looking forward to our mission. I was almost sorry I had agreed to come with Lindstrom. Maybe if I hadn't, she would have run out of steam. Or maybe she would have gone and beaten Kathleen to a pulp. It was the last thought that impelled me to go. A silly notion that I could keep more bad things from happening to Lindstrom.

A flashy black sports car with a closely shorn white teenager at the wheel pulled next to us in the left lane. Rap throbbed from it as though the car were a boom box. The song's theme required repetition of "motherfucker." When the light changed, the car charged forward, "Sex Man" on its plate. "I'll bet," I said, but Lindstrom was gathered up in her own world.

On I-70 as we approached the Old Cathedral, I could see crowds of red-shirted Cardinal fans walking up Walnut, headed toward Busch Stadium. A Cubs game tonight meant a large crowd. That old rivalry persists no matter what the standings.

Lindstrom pulled us into the parking garage of one of the downtown towers. Part of the rent for these high rises goes for security, and Lindstrom flashed her badge under the nose of a gray-faced white man in a loose-fitting uniform. He looked unhappy to deal with any irregularity but more unwilling to challenge a cop, and he motioned us through the striped crossbar.

Vivian Rudder and Kathleen Clawsen had been sharing a condominium on the seventh floor. The elevator was quiet and roomy and smelled of polish. We got off onto thick carpeting of an impractical creaminess. Had I been with Patrick, I'd have whistled my appreciation. But Lindstrom didn't look impressed. She looked focused.

She marched us down the hallway to a thick door. She rang the bell. The peal was muffled on our side.

We waited. She rang again. We heard a loud noise like someone's clattering through hockey sticks. Suddenly the door flung open.

Kathleen Clawsen was nothing I expected. She was shorter than Lindstrom and tousled. Not just her hair. Her dress twisted to the side. Runnels of recent tears had smeared her eyes and mouth. She looked an especially sad-faced clown.

"Sarah!"

It was just a loud exclamation. I couldn't read joy or alarm or grief or surprise. But I smelled the whiskey.

"Security usually calls up. Why didn't they call up?" Her voice was mushy, and I understood the smeared appearance. Under the mushiness was grit, laid down by two packs a day since her sixteenth birthday.

Of course she looked thirty years past that now. Maybe she cleaned up good. In the foyer I saw the hockey sticks in the form of an umbrella stand she had knocked over on her way to the door.

"Oh, Sarah, we've lost her," she said in a quavering alto that predicted the face-crumpling crying which followed immediately. Simultaneously she grabbed the cloth of Lindstrom's jacket and pulled her across the threshold.

I saw Lindstrom's face and jumped in behind her. She shook her arm to loosen Kathleen's hold and walked past her into a generously-sized living room done in lush peaches and creams.

Kathleen sloped after Lindstrom. "Horrible, horrible," she sobbed.

Lindstrom's face kept freezing into deeper layers. Any Lindstrom I presumed to know was masked by tight-jawed fury.

Kathleen wasn't noticing nuances. But when she did realize Lindstrom was not responding at all to script, Kathleen whirled—well, a shaky attempt—and demanded of me, "Who are you?"

"My partner," Lindstrom said in a voice of shears.

Oh, oh. I stood straighter, not sure if I were imitating a cop or a more-than-occasional lover. Either pose invited trouble.

Kathleen merely blinked and lost interest. She looked around at table tops, found her drink, walked forward carefully, and reclaimed it.

"You're drunk," Lindstrom said. She made it sound right up there with child abuse and Satanic torture.

"So should you be. Gawd, Sarah." Kathleen was still proceeding under the assumption that she and Sarah were comrades in grief.

I'd heard Lindstrom tell the story, but seeing made believing hard. Why would Vivian have abandoned Lindstrom for this woman? The ironic effect of that question was to raise doubts about Lindstrom. I pulled in a lungful of air with grounding deliberation.

Lindstrom reached out and took Kathleen's glass. Lindstrom was using both her height and sobriety to intimidate.

"Where were you last night, Kathleen?" I'd never heard Lindstrom interrogate anyone but me, so I couldn't swear that this wasn't her normal professional voice.

"Whaddaya mean?" Kathleen took an awkward step back and perched her behind somewhat precariously on the arm of a peach couch that faced its twin on the other side of a huge oval glass coffee table. The table made me nervous for her. Not a good furnishing to have for someone of unsteady pins.

"I mean where were you?" Lindstrom pressed.

"Don't treat me like a cop."

"Where?"

Kathleen rummaged around in her cellar. "I had dinner with friends. I watched a movie. I fell asleep." She slowed it all down so that it would sound precise and sober. But nothing shaved away the mush of too many whiskies. She was a middle-level administrator at a fair-sized hospital. What did she say to her staff friends on her morning afters?

Then, as an afterthought, the sort so many suspects impulsively add, she said, "I told the nigger."

I hadn't thought Lindstrom could stiffen more. "Tell me now."

"No!" She'd been pushed enough.

"What time was the movie?"

"I watched it on the VCR."

"Who were the friends?"

"I want a lawyer." She turned and gave me a smug look. See? I'll put that copper in her place.

"Their names, Kathleen."

"Jody Faircloth and Tori Helbraun." Kathleen rose and walked around to the front of the couch and sank into it. She leaned forward and opened a small bronze casket and extracted a cigarette. She pulled a lighter from her skirt pocket and lit it. She had a practiced stylishness. The acrid smoke hit within seconds.

"Their addresses?"

"Gawd, Sarah. I really told that other guy. The cop."

"I want to know. Tell me."

She did and rambled off into an explanation of how this couple had been longtime friends. I tried to measure Kathleen's feet against Lindstrom's. Kathleen's looked smaller to me, but I couldn't swear to it. She was starting to comment on the House of India's excellent service when Lindstrom cut in.

"What did you hit her with?"

"What?"

"What did you hit her with?"

Kathleen looked at me, appealing for protection against this rudeness.

"What did you use?" Lindstrom's voice didn't raise; it tightened. I didn't like her much.

Kathleen was a woman in a fog down the bottom of a hole. Her life sloshed around her. I know why we feel sorry for the victimizers, the perps. And why we hate them. I was hating her now because she was pathetic and not like me and because she was like the me I've had moments of being scared I might become.

"My fists." A croak. The small hairs stood on my nape.

"What else?" I heard Lindstrom's smugness.

"Nothing, nothing." Kathleen was pulling in more smoke, holding it in, hugging her chest with crossed arms, the cigarette kept up close to her face.

"What else?" A thin-bladed knife this time, slicing closer.

"Just my fists." She leaned forward and stubbed out her cigarette. "Oh, Viv, I'm so sorry." She let her head loll forward.

28

Lindstrom was on her in a second, grabbing her shoulders, shaking her. "Cut that crap! You beat her, you killed her." Abruptly Lindstrom let go but stood before Kathleen, towering over her.

"No! I hit her Thursday. She ran away. She sneaked out."

She looked to me, back at Lindstrom, down to her lap. She reached past Lindstrom's leg toward another cigarette. Lindstrom grabbed and held Kathleen's wrist. "Why did you do it?"

"She was cheating on me."

"You imagined it."

"She could be a slut. You ought to know."

"What?"

"She cheated on you. I guarantee it."

For a moment I feared Lindstrom would teeter over the edge. But she released the wrist. Her finger marks were white on the light skin till the blood rushed back. Kathleen rubbed the wrist and glared defiance.

The words were out of my mouth, silken and smooth, before I thought. "Did she throw it up in your face? Is that what made you angry?"

She looked up, startled to find me still there. "I didn't. I hit her Thursday. I'm sorry. I didn't kill her."

"If you make us prove it the hard way—" Lindstrom said. Her jaw was so set I was surprised her mouth moved.

I used the soft pedal again. "It was a crime of passion. I know how it feels to be jealous. Tell me what happened."

"I hid the keys, but she sneaked out after I fell asleep."

I stayed soft. "That was Thursday. What happened Friday? How did you find her at Sarah's?"

"Nothing. I went to work. I had dinner with friends at the House of India. I decided to ignore her. She'd come back. She had before."

"Did you call friends to find out where she was?" I asked.

"Yeah. A couple."

"Who told you where she was?" I squatted down to her eye level.

"No one knew."

"When did you think of Sarah?"

"Don't know. Yesterday afternoon. Drove by. Couldn't see anything. Went to dinner."

"You drove by my house?" Lindstrom made that a federal crime.

I glared at her and turned my sweet self back to Kathleen. I had a notion. "Did you call her there? Talk to her?"

"I called. She wouldn't answer. To hell with her." Suddenly the words hit. She looked away. Her voice got huskier. "Gawd, the last words I said to her…."

"Did you drive by again? After dinner?" I was coaxing.

"No. I went home right away. I was asleep by eleven."

"What movie?" Lindstrom was curt.

The question nearly threw Kathleen. She scrambled around for an answer. Finally she said, "That old one. *Murphy's Romance*."

29

"When and where did you rent it?" Lindstrom again.

"Didn't. It was Viv's."

Lindstrom swallowed. She looked away. Kathleen regarded her with interest. She reached out and touched Lindstrom's jacket sleeve. "I didn't do it. Swear to God, no way I did." Her voice was still raspy, carrying with it twenty years of rye and tar mixing, but she sounded nearly sober.

Lindstrom looked back to her. I could see the tug of war.

"If I prove you did this—"

"You won't." Kathleen realized it was a bad choice. "I didn't. Wouldn't."

"You got drunk, you went too far." Lindstrom clipped off the words, but she wasn't as sure. I could tell.

So could Kathleen. "I'm not saying another word to you. Without a lawyer. Except I'm sorry about Viv. You ought to be, too." She was rallying now.

"Did Viv have any enemies?" I asked.

"Now that's a sensible question." There was spunkiness to that. A spiritedness more attractive than sodden wretchedness.

I waited.

"Her ex." I thought she was being sarcastic toward Lindstrom. Maybe Kathleen saw it. "Her husband," she added.

"Why him?"

"He never let go of her. He was still trying to pretend she would come back to him. Maybe she called him. They got into a fight."

I didn't answer. "Who else?"

She drew a deep breath. "Probably a burglar, don't you think? Money for drugs."

"Most women are murdered by their intimates."

"Like ex-lovers." She reached around for a cigarette. Lindstrom made no objection. Instead, she walked away, thrust her hands into her pants, looked broodingly at the woman who had so inexplicably bested her at love.

"Who else? Enemies at work?" I pressed gently.

"Talk to Colin. Little fag." She waved her cigarette with Bette Davis hauteur.

Fags and niggers—who knew the depths of her charm to real intimates?

I suspected that a sobering Kathleen wasn't going to be a more helpful one. "Thank you, Kathleen. Can we get back to you if we have further questions?"

She gave me a groggy smile and sank back into the peachy cushions.

Back in the car Lindstrom rested her chin on her hands which were gripping the steering wheel tightly. "She's lying."

"Probably. Wouldn't surprise me."

"You know how it goes. The beatings just get worse."

"I know."

A silence grew. Lindstrom tightened her grip on the wheel. "I wanted to hit her."

30

"I know." I didn't add that this knowledge had scared me. We need crap detectors, but we don't have them. Hunches, experience, common sense, intuition, whatever we call our guesswork has to do.

I guessed Kathleen might be telling the truth about the important parts. I knew that I didn't know the complete Sarah Lindstrom.

CHAPTER SIX

Neely called my place at nine-thirty that Sunday morning to say that Lindstrom was wanted at the station. Lindstrom talked with him about fifteen minutes, then left with a terse, "The Lieutenant wants to see me."

She came back to my place two hours later looking bruised. Her eyes were dulled, her shoulders slumped. It wasn't hard to tell that her time at St. Louis's Clark Street station had frayed her.

I handed her a cup of coffee and followed her into the living room.

"Have they found anything yet?"

"Neely says Johnson doesn't think a woman did it. Johnson thinks it's too brutal."

"Did he get anything out of questioning Kathleen?"

She sighed and set her cup down on top of the Sunday *Post*. "Neely wouldn't tell me much about how that went. The Lieutenant was really angry that I went over to Kathleen's yesterday. He ordered me to stop interfering with the investigation. Told me if I didn't take a vacation and leave it alone he'd put me on unpaid leave."

"Johnson has convinced him that Kathleen didn't do it?"

"I don't know. I think the Lieutenant's keeping an open mind on who did it. At least he told me he doesn't think I did it. But he can hardly afford to have a raging lesbian threatening the citizenry, can he?" I moved to touch her, but she flinched away. "It's over, Darcy. I've busted my butt for nine years, and my career's in the toilet."

"Surely that's an exaggeration, Lindstrom. There are gay cops."

"Not out, not detectives, not with their ex-lovers murdered in their beds." She groaned and sank onto the couch, putting her hands over her face, her elbows on her knees. "It's all over the station. I could feel it when I walked in. Everyone was staring at the dyke. Next, they'll be laughing. I'll be a dirty joke."

I'd made a different career choice at least partially so I wouldn't have to be in the closet. I would have hated the inevitable feeling of being ashamed of myself. Now I couldn't think of a more horrible way of being outed than what Lindstrom faced. But this didn't seem the time to point out the folly of wanting to be a cop in the first place. We both studied the rug.

"So, are you on vacation?"

"Yes."

"I guess a couple weeks in P-Town is out of the question."

She didn't even smile. "I'll tell you one thing. They can't keep me from using what I know. Johnson can do the official police work. I'll find the evidence to nail her to the wall. I can give it to him. Let him get all the glory, just so she doesn't walk. It will be my last act as a St. Louis cop."

Obviously the stress of talking to the Lieutenant had sent us back to Kathleen as the only suspect. I knew I had to keep Lindstrom from burning her bridges. If she wanted to quit the force, fine. But I had the feeling once this was behind her, she'd find she could and would go back to the police department, if she hadn't been fired for insubordination in the meantime.

"Why don't you let me check around and ask the questions? You should really lie low. This could blow over if Johnson wraps it up quickly." She stared at me. "What else did Neely tell you?"

"Nothing really. There were no fingerprints on the bat. Kathleen managed not to drop her purse at the scene." She paused and looked up with pain in her eyes. "Neely was embarrassed to be seen talking to me."

Had she looked into his eyes and seen only her own fears? I didn't think she would hear that interpretation if I offered it. Instead, I asked, "Would he help you? Would he get us information?"

"Probably. Unless it gets really bad and there are direct orders not to talk to me. He's a good cop—loyal."

I thought she was right, and my guess was he did have a large portion of loyalty to Sarah Lindstrom as well. I had seen them work together before. "You don't think he'd guessed?" She looked back at the rug and shook her head.

After a long pause she volunteered, "He might have known, but we never talked about it. Before Vivian and I broke up, he usually asked about her. And he was very nice to me around the time he learned she had moved out."

Suddenly, Lindstrom stood up. "Look, thanks for trying to help—No, I'm sorry. Thanks for helping. You've been great, but I can handle it from here. You don't need to get involved in this mess, too. I don't want to take anyone down with me."

I stood, too. "Lindstrom, don't be an ass. You are not Clint Eastwood, and this isn't the movies. You aren't dragging me anywhere. I'm merely saying I can ask questions and see people that you can't if you want to keep your job."

"I don't think a private dick will solve my problem."

I took a second to remind myself that she was still the Ice Queen, and it was probably a traumatic childhood that had left her so warped. I tested and rejected several responses to 'private dick.' "Lindstrom, if you are absolutely determined to die alone on this one, you can. All I'm saying here is that there are other choices." She glared, and we both thought she was going to walk out, but she didn't.

I pulled out a small notebook, my favorite weapon in the private dick business. "Okay, did Vivian tell anyone else that Kathleen was abusive?"

"I doubt it. Vivian acted like I was the only one she'd told. She said she couldn't spend time with any old friends unless Kathleen was with her. They socialized almost exclusively with Kathleen's friends."

"How about family, was she close to them?"

"Yes, they were pretty close. But I don't think she told them that Kathleen was hitting her."

"How well do you know them?"

She paused and dredged up an almost-normal grin. "We spent holidays with them. They liked me a whole lot better than they liked Kathleen. Viv let that slip."

"Anyone there with a motive to kill Vivian?"

"No one else had a motive. Kathleen killed her. She was the only one with a motive."

"What about the sister who inherits?"

Lindstrom raised her fine blonde eyebrows.

I kept my mouth firmly shut.

"Ruth? Oh, Darcy, forget it. Besides, unless Viv changed her will, I've got as much motive as Ruth."

Even more, Lindstrom was the most recent dumpee in addition to inheriting half of Viv's money. I kept that thought to myself.

"Just leave the Rudders out of this, Darcy. They didn't do it, and I don't want you bothering them."

I counted to ten. Well, I meant to—I actually got to seven before my mouth shot open. "Lindstrom, I'm not all that sure Kathleen did this. I need to know all kinds of things about Viv in case it wasn't Kathleen." I didn't add that Lindstrom needed to get a grip on her control issues and leave me the hell alone. Silence reigned for several beats.

"Will the medical examiner be able to tell that some of Viv's injuries were from Thursday night?" I asked.

Lindstrom took a moment. Calling up the image of Vivian's many injuries obviously pained her. Finally she said, "Maybe. It depends on if she were reinjured in the same places."

"Do you know who any of Kathleen's former lovers are?"

"You think she battered them as well?"

"I'd bet on it. Most abusers don't change themselves; they just switch victims."

I questioned Lindstrom about some people I wanted to talk to, beginning with Viv's ex-husband. Lindstrom looked up Thomas Aubuchon in my white pages and copied down the number in small careful numbers. "It wouldn't help for me to call Aubuchon for you. Thomas and I never got on very well."

Lindstrom didn't know any of Kathleen's former lovers, but she did know Kathleen's best friend's name. I wrote that down, and we went on to discuss Vivian's friends. Vivian had two that she might have talked to about something personal. One was Colin Lanier, a friend of many years who worked with Viv at Collins, Cobb, and Vahey and who often served as Vivian's escort to high-powered parties. Lindstrom tried to call Colin, but his machine was on. She left a message and my phone number. The second friend was Amy Scott, who had been Vivian's best friend since their prep school days together at Mary Institute. Lindstrom called her. I could tell Amy was not eager to talk to me from Lindstrom's end of the conversation, but Amy agreed to see me for a few minutes after her tennis lesson. Lindstrom gave me careful directions to the tennis club.

"What are you going to do while I go talk to these people?"

"I need to pay my respects to Vivian's parents. Her mom will be expecting to see me." Lindstrom looked down at her hands. "How can I face her mother and tell her I didn't protect Viv when she came to me for help?"

I reached out to touch her face, but she turned away. I walked to my desk and rifled through a drawer and found the spare key to the apartment in case she got back before I did. Lindstrom wasn't going to let me touch her. Fine. I could pretend she was just another client.

***

The tennis club that Amy Scott belonged to was in a western suburb. In St. Louis, north is black, south is white, west is wealthy. I fiddled with the radio on my way out 44 but was unsatisfied with any of the Sunday afternoon choices. I rolled down all four windows on the Plymouth and tried to think convertible.

At the gate the uniformed security guard merely looked bored when I told him I was a guest of Amy Scott. So much for my anxiety about being denied admission because my seven-year-old Plymouth was dirty. The asphalt parking lot was smooth, and the lines freshly painted. I left the windows down on the Plymouth. No reason to come back to a scalding hot steering wheel here. The manicured lawn of the country club was hedged with forsythia to disguise the fence, and severely pruned rose bushes bordered the walk.

I located the tennis courts by listening for the thwack of racquet against ball. Only one court was in use on this blazing hot Sunday afternoon. Amy wasn't quite finished with her lesson, so I had an opportunity to watch her in action. She practiced returning serves to a man who had been hired for his skill at teaching tennis, not at inspiring fantasies in the young-marrieds of Ladue. He was short with thinning white hair and scowled as if he had a toothache. He was gradually increasing the difficulty of his serves until Amy was returning less than half of them. Finally he served one in the perfect spot, and she shot it back, nearly clipping his ear. He laughed and called out, "Good, Mrs. Scott. You're returning better. We'll work more on it on Thursday."

Amy Scott thanked him and picked up a thick white towel and ran it over her face and neck. Tennis in the middle of the afternoon in June requires even the rich to sweat. I caught her eye and smiled at her. She nodded and pushed her racquet carefully into an outsized bag before walking over to join me.

She was blonde, tanned, and trim, a perfect model of the youthful Ladue matron. Lindstrom had told me Viv was thirty-six, and a close-up view confirmed that Amy was, too. She led the way to a few tables under a yellow canvas awning. None of the other tables were occupied. It was hot enough that most of the country club's business was inside. We introduced ourselves and ordered iced tea from the middle-aged waiter.

"Thank you for agreeing to meet me."

"Sarah told me it was important and that it wouldn't take long." So much for establishing rapport.

"Tell me about Vivian Rudder." I pulled out my notepad and gave her some business-like eye contact.

"What do you want to know?"

"What had been going on in her life recently?"

"The same as usual, I suppose. Work kept her busy."

"What was the name of the firm?"

"Collins, Cobb, and Vahey," she snorted as she picked up her glass.

"What kind of firm is it?"

"They do corporate law, protecting copyrights and contracts and such. Viv and I had a marvelous two weeks in Hong Kong two years ago. She had to fly over there to threaten to sue somebody. They never did it, of course. All talk. Viv was good at it. All C, C, and V's cases are settled over brief-cases and whiskey."

"Anyone there in particular she had problems with?"

"The attorneys never get any courtroom drama, so they have to fight among themselves. Lawrence Jeffries was a perennial pain, but none of Vivian's work problems would have ended that way."

"What were she and Jeffries fighting about?"

"Not fighting, competing. Vivian loved it. She wouldn't play tennis or bridge with me, but she got fiercely competitive about her job. Jeffries had gotten a partnership, and she'd been passed over, and she wasn't going to let something like that happen again."

"Anything else in her life troubling her?"

Amy stared hard at the green and white of the tennis court and pressed her thin lips together.

"What was her relationship with Kathleen like?" I pressed. There was a pause while Amy frowned and searched for the right words for her best friend's lover.

"Kathleen didn't fit in exactly. I don't think Vivian would have taken her in at all except I think she felt a bit sorry for her."

"How so?"

"Oh, I don't know exactly, but the woman's social skills…"

"Kathleen comes from a different background from Vivian's," I offered.

"Yes, she does. But that's not all. She just smothered Vivian. Kathleen was so grateful for her friendship. I told Vivian she needn't take another roommate. She should have settled for a less expensive place."

I sat back. Surely Amy Scott couldn't be that naive. Did she think Vivian and Kathleen lived together to save money on the rent? Or did she just hope that I didn't know that Vivian was a lesbian?

"Sarah mentioned that Vivian saw less of her other friends since she and Kathleen lived together."

"Yes, I guess. I'm not sure."

"Did you see less of Vivian?"

"Somewhat. We both have hectic schedules."

The past tense still wasn't coming naturally to her. "Did Vivian tell you she was having trouble with Kathleen?"

"No, but Thomas did."

"Vivian's ex-husband?"

"Yes. He said one night when he brought Vivian home, Kathleen started a fight as soon as he and Viv walked in the door."

"With fists or with words?"

Amy bit her lip, but just shook her head. Either she didn't know or couldn't bring herself to say. I decided not to push it. I already knew that Kathleen hit Viv, and it looked like it wasn't as much of a well-kept secret as the average batterer hopes.

"How long had Thomas and Vivian been divorced?"

"Six years. They were married for seven. They remained good friends. Thomas is a saint. In fact, they still owned property together. Divorcing him was the biggest mistake of her life."

"How long after the divorce was it when Vivian and Sarah became… roommates?"

"Vivian moved out of Thomas's home and moved in with Sarah." Amy looked at me a moment and sighed. "Vivian thought she was happy with Sarah. Certainly happier than with Kathleen." It obviously troubled Amy to think of Vivian's love life after Thomas. I wondered how she and Viv had worked this out in their friendship.

"Why did they break up—Sarah and Vivian?"

"Vivian fell in love with Kathleen. God knows why, but she was besotted." Amy sat down her glass with a thump and looked at the thin gold watch on her arm.

"Just a few more questions," I inserted smoothly. "What happens to Vivian's money—did she change her will after she left Sarah?"

"No. She didn't. She'd talked about it, but hadn't gotten around to it yet. Ruth, Viv's sister, will get half the estate, and I suppose the other half will go to Sarah."

"Will Viv's family try to challenge that?"

Distaste spread across Amy Scott's face at the idea of the Rudder family drawn into a legal brawl with a dyke. "I would be very surprised if they did."

I decided to push her a bit. "How did they feel about Viv's being a lesbian?"

She glanced nervously around. She could hardly believe I'd said that aloud at her club. "Really this has nothing to do with Vivian's death. None of the Rudders murdered her for money or any other reason. I'm sorry, but

37

I have to go now. This is going nowhere." She rose and turned to march off to the club house. As she bent over to pick up her bag, I quickly handed her a card. I stood and watched as she stomped across the brilliantly white gravel. Before she pulled open the door to the clubhouse, she dropped my card into a spotless hunter green trash receptacle.

CHAPTER SEVEN

I hopped onto 40 and headed east into Clayton which is just outside the city limits—directly west of Forest Park, a buffer between the city and Ladue. While not as high on the social register as Ladue, Clayton is still the kind of place that has hand-lettered, white wooden street signs, and homes that run two-hundred-thousand and up. Clayton's attitude irritates me. For one thing parking is impossible. The city does its best to discourage average St. Louisans from drifting across its borders. The city of St. Louis is not a part of St. Louis County, which disrupts the efficient government of both city and county. So Clayton has a jail and a court building and enough bureaucrats to run a small nation. Clayton is also home to a large financial district full of the kind of people who make money by shuffling money—or representations thereof. I cursed the traffic around the Galleria shopping mall. I fumbled with my cell phone till I reached Viv's ex-husband. A visit from me wouldn't interrupt his Sunday puttering he said.

The house that Thomas Aubuchon and Vivian Rudder had once shared was more modest than I'd expected. It was a smallish two-story red brick on an undistinguished street. The front yard was neatly clipped but unadorned by either bush or flower. He answered my "hello?" with a call to come to the back yard where I found him assembling a gas grill. Thomas didn't stand to meet me but stuck his head further into the base of the grill and waved at a green and white webbed lawn chair. He had the stringiness of a fourteen-year-old boy. His strength was in his hands; his shoulders were narrow. Aubuchon's brown hair was thick and unruly. His snug Levis revealed long thin thighs; sockless feet were narrow in his battered deck shoes.

His voice echoed out of the black metal pan. "Would you like a soda or a beer?"

I was mainly interested in getting his head out of the grill so I could see him while we talked. "Yes, please. A soda if it wouldn't be too much trouble."

"It's in the fridge. Bottom shelf. That door goes right into the kitchen." I turned to look at the green, wooden door behind me. There seemed little else for it. "Do you want one, too?"

"I'll take a beer, thanks."

When I returned with our refreshments, he was attacking the legs with a Phillips screwdriver. I put his beer on the grill box where he had his tools and screws and parts of various shapes and sizes and returned to my assigned chair behind him.

"You kept in touch with Vivian after your divorce?"

"Yes, we remained friends." His voice echoed from inside the grill.

"How often did you see her?"

"Once a month or so. Sometimes more."

"Do you have any idea who might have killed her?"

He laid his screwdriver down, lining it up precisely with a round wooden handle for the grill and picked up his Michelob. He twisted off the cap and put the cap down on the grill box as well.

"I can't really imagine it. I can't think about someone beating Vivian to death. It must have been a break in, money for drugs or something like that."

"I know it's difficult to think about, but almost all murder victims are killed by someone they know, usually by someone close to them."

"That kind of thing didn't belong in Viv's life. Violence like that—maybe that's an ordinary part of your life—of Sarah Lindstrom's life, but not of Viv's." His voice broke, and he ran a shaky hand over his mouth. I realized that I'd been assigned the green and white chair so that I couldn't see his face. I walked around the grill box and his paraphernalia and squatted directly in front of him. His eyes were red and swollen. Vivian's death had been hard on her ex-husband. He didn't look up at me, but accepted this intrusion. "She was an attorney. A corporate attorney. A nice woman. She had it all before Sarah Lindstrom." It sounded like there was more to that sentence, so I just listened. He took a deep breath and went on shakily. "This has been tough for me. Viv and I were still close. No, I don't know of anyone who might have killed her."

"Why was Viv sleeping at Lindstrom's house the night she was killed?"

"Do they know where Sarah Lindstrom was that night?"

"Do you think she had a motive?"

"She was the most recent one to lose Vivian, and that breakup was not friendly." I would have loved to know how Viv and Sarah's divorce really went—my sense was somewhere between Lindstrom's version and a motive for murder.

"What about Vivian's relationship with Kathleen?"

"Viv didn't talk about it much. They had their tense times."

"Viv told Lindstrom that Kathleen beat her up." Amy Scott had said he knew. I was inviting him to comment. He went on fiddling with his screwdriver and finally picked up another leg to attach to the grill. After a pause I realized he wasn't going to respond at all. "Did Vivian say anything to you about Kathleen's hitting her?"

"No, she didn't mention it." He paused. "But I think I knew it."

I waited. When he didn't continue, I nudged. "How so?"

"I was taking her home one night. We'd had dinner after work. She said she had to be home by seven-thirty. We were running a little bit late—maybe fifteen or twenty minutes. When we got back to their apartment, Kathleen was steaming. She and Viv went back to the bedroom. I heard bits and pieces of Kathleen's calling Viv names, accusing her of sleeping with me.

40

You know, Kathleen was always afraid Vivian was going to come back to me. Homosexual relationships aren't as stable as marriages. I thought I heard a slap, but I don't know who slapped whom. I called out to Vivian, but she stuck her head out—said she was okay and told me to go home." He told the story carefully, controlling his emotional response.

"How long was it before you saw Vivian again?"

"Oh, I'm not sure. Probably three weeks or a month."

"Did you ever see bruises that Vivian couldn't explain or any other signs of abuse?"

"No, but I expect Vivian was probably leaving Kathleen when she went to Lindstrom's. She probably would have come to me, but I was out Thursday night. She'd have been safe with me." The last with a deep bitterness.

"So you didn't know Viv had gone to Lindstrom's till after you learned about her death?"

His eyes shifted in that taking-evasive-action mode of the inexperienced liar. The pause grew; he changed his mind. "Viv left a message on my machine that Friday morning."

"Telling you she'd gone to Lindstrom?"

He nodded. "Asking me not to call her at Kathleen's and accidentally stir things up." His voice slid around a tug of emotion. "Viv said she'd be safe there." At Lindstrom's. Grief and a sense of betrayal worked his face. He swallowed hard.

"Did you go by to see her?" I swallowed to keep my own voice steady.

He shook his head, studied his feet. "We were supposed to have lunch, but she canceled it. I had plans to be out of town, so I left earlier. I went to Branson to see about our property there."

"Whose property?"

"Viv's and mine. We bought a motel down there when we were married. Since Branson has suddenly become the big country music attraction, we decided to hold onto it for an investment rather than sell it when we divorced."

"And you managed it together?"

"No, we've got a couple that lives there. They do the day-to-day managing. But we go down twice a year or so, make improvements, see how things are going. Viv relied on me to make the decisions about the motel."

"How much is the motel in Branson worth?"

"Oh, I'm not sure. Sort of depends on the market at the time, I guess. I'm not looking to sell it."

"Will the motel go to her family?"

"No. I have rights of survivor. It belongs to me after the estate is probated." A few seconds ticked by before his eyes registered his understanding. "You're thinking that's a motive to kill Viv?" He sounded more surprised than hostile.

"You haven't remarried?"

"No, I've never found someone I loved as much as I loved Vivian when

41

I married her. I'm not willing to settle for second-best."

"Was being a lesbian just a phase for her?"

He looked up at me, and I gave him my best 'we're all just heterosexuals being honest here' smile. He finally put down his screwdriver and said, "Yes, I think so. She didn't form lasting relationships with women like she did with me. She went steadily down hill. First a cop who ignored her most of the time, then a drunk who slapped her around. I think she felt unworthy, like she didn't deserve me, so she found others who would degrade her. She just got to taking the feminist stuff too seriously. They made her think she couldn't be happy with a man."

There was anger in his voice. This wasn't something he'd read in a book about what happens when your wife turns queer. Thomas Aubuchon had worked out these theories from his own pain.

"What about Viv's other assets, besides the motel? Who inherits?"

"Her sister, Ruth."

"Do you know how much that will be?"

"No. Viv was good with money, a smart investor. I imagine she would be in the six figures."

I thought it telling that Lindstrom had been certain about how much Viv was worth, and Thomas, with whom she still owned property, was so vague. Even more telling that Viv hadn't told Thomas the whole truth about her will.

"Has Detective Johnson been by to talk to you?"

"No, no one from the Police Department has contacted me. I thought that's who you were when you first called."

"If they think Kathleen killed her, they will want to know about the fight you overheard. Thanks for taking the time to talk to me." I handed him my card. "If you think of anything else, call me."

He glanced at the card. "I thought your name was Darcy."

"It is." I pointed to my name in the small print. "My partner's name is Miller. He owns the agency."

Thomas Aubuchon nodded and looked at his partially finished grill. "I don't know why I bought the damn thing. Vivian always did the barbecuing." He finished his beer and fell silent. I found my way back to my car and headed out.

Thomas Aubuchon didn't look like a good prospect for replacing Kathleen as chief suspect to me. A slim financial gain clearly hadn't moved him to kill Viv in the years they had been divorced. The only way I could see his hurting Viv at all was if he had lost all hope of recapturing her, and, oddly, even after her death, he seemed still to cherish it. Even so, his Branson alibi would need checking.

***

A glance at my watch told me my stomach wasn't lying. I wasn't sure how long Lindstrom would be at Vivian's parents, so I grabbed a burger at Jack In The Box. Amy Scott hadn't been forthcoming. If Vivian's best friend

42

wasn't spilling beans, would Kathleen's? Probably they didn't see her as an abuser. We're all capable of fabulous denial if our investment is heavy enough. Nothing ventured.

After I finished my burger, I tried to wipe the grease from my fingers, not much luck. I still left sticky fingerprints on my cell phone.

I got a recorded baritone: "L.C. Reidy's residence. Leave your name and number after the tone."

I was just giving my name and my request for a call back when the baritone picked up. "L.C."

I started over and identified myself.

"You're investigating Vivian's death?"

"Yes. I'm helping."

"Are you the one that upset Kathleen?"

"I've talked with Ms. Clawsen. I hope I didn't upset her. Investigation is a process of elimination."

A snort. "She didn't do it."

On slender evidence I was realizing that L.C. might be female. Maybe four packs a day had embellished these tones. "Can I talk to you?"

"What for?" Not so much belligerent as obstructionist.

I imagined L.C. won confrontations just by provoking her opponents' withdrawals.

"Because I'm irresistibly drawn to pain-in-the-ass butches."

A silence, then another snort. "Well, you're different."

"Takes one to—"

"Come on over tomorrow after work. Have a brewsky." She rattled off an address and hung up. It occurred to me why Kathleen needed few social skills.

***

When I got back to the apartment, Lindstrom was sitting at my small kitchen table. Her ramrod posture was back, but she was pulling pensively at her lower lip. I tried, but couldn't quite remember her smile. The heat of the day had crept into the room. Lindstrom hadn't turned on any fans or the AC units attached to my bedroom and living room windows. I turned them on. She didn't feel at home here, and, seeing her there at my table, I felt less at home myself.

"How are Viv's parents doing?"

Harvey came in and leapt lightly onto the table. I thought about shooing him off, trying to pretend he never got up there. But if Lindstrom were going to be living here, she would figure out the laxity of the house rules sooner or later. Truth is, I settle for keeping him off the table only during the moments I'm actually shoveling food into my mouth. Lindstrom ran an idle hand over his ears.

"They're in shock. I didn't tell them Kathleen killed her. I thought they might be able to absorb that better later. I'll tell them after she's arrested."

"Are the arrangements for the funeral settled yet?"

"Yes. The visitation will be Tuesday and the funeral Wednesday. Viv's two aunts are coming in from California."

I told Lindstrom about my visit to Thomas Aubuchon's home.

"He always wanted to hang on to Viv. He never really let her go," she said.

"What do you mean?"

"I think in the back of his mind he thought she'd get over her 'lesbian thing' and come back to him."

"He seemed angry."

"Sometimes. You know, Viv always wanted to get rid of that property they owned together. He insisted they would lose too much. They made money on it, but I think he kept it mostly to have an excuse to keep her tied to him."

"I talked to Amy Scott, too. I wondered what you thought of her."

Lindstrom's attention had wandered, and she was staring at the red and gray pattern of the table. "Oh, huh? I'm sorry."

"What did you think of Amy Scott?"

Lindstrom's blue eyes flicked left, then right, as she tried to recapture Viv's best friend. "Mostly I thought she was a snob and a bore. I didn't spend much time with her. We both preferred it that way."

"Didn't her attitude make you nuts?"

"Which attitude?"

"She hated the fact that Viv fell in love with a woman."

"Yes. She was uncomfortable with that. I think she thought that Viv would have been happier in a more conventional relationship. But she was good to Viv. And Viv seemed to enjoy her company."

I looked into Lindstrom's steady gaze and couldn't see the fire there. Where did this woman hide her righteous anger? I feared she would be devastated by being outed at work. If she wouldn't identify homophobia as an attack on her, how would she defend herself? I decided now wasn't the time to go wherever that thought would lead and suggested dinner instead. Surprisingly, Lindstrom agreed with some enthusiasm.

We walked to Pho Grand. It was the first time Lindstrom had eaten Vietnamese, and I was pleased that she took to it immediately. The restaurant is one of my favorites, the food lighter and more subtle than most of the Chinese cuisine that is available in St. Louis. We talked mostly about food over dinner. She rued the fact that she had absolutely refused as a child and an adolescent to learn to cook from her mother. She had seen it as a trap rather than a survival skill. She said Vivian had taught her to cook many of the basics, but Vivian couldn't teach her some of the wonderful things that Lindstrom's mother had done with pastry. We compared notes on favorite meals. A safe topic.

When we got back to the house, Lindstrom picked *Tales of the City* off the shelf and was soon lost in it. I booted up my computer and entered my notes from the day's interviews and Lindstrom's observations about Aubuchon.

For an hour or so an illusion of cozy coupledom hung over the room with the big sounds being the taps from my keyboard and Lindstrom's turning pages. I noticed that Harvey had deigned to lie on the couch within petting distance and that Lindstrom had taken the hint.

Just as I was about to suggest a cup of tea and a check of the late movies, Lindstrom yawned and announced that she thought she'd turn in early. I couldn't protest. After all she'd spent a day with her ex-in-laws, and my guess was she hadn't had very much sleep since Viv's murder.

When she disappeared into my shower, I searched my book-shelves. Not a thing to read. Nothing in the magazines stacked under the end table. I clicked on the TV and started surfing. Harvey moved to my lap when I put my feet on the coffee table. "Looks like you and me and Barbara Stanwyck, kid," I told him. He purred approval.

CHAPTER EIGHT

Monday morning, I heard Lindstrom back in the shower and pulled myself out of the twist of sheet and afghan on the couch. My kinked back and neck told me I had slept in the same cramped position all night. I brewed a pot of coffee in deference to Lindstrom's morning preferences and set out a box of Cheerios. So much for gracious hostessing. If she wanted a better breakfast, she could check into the Adam's Mark. When she came out of the bathroom, I notified her that breakfast awaited and ducked into the shower.

I grabbed the last clean towel out of the cabinet. Monday. I had an appointment with a potential client this morning, a man from a large St. Louis firm that could provide many hours of work for us if he decided to sign on. Walter and I weren't big enough yet to put off that kind of client. Monday. I would see L.C. Reidy today. My heart lifted as I realized I would be spending several hours on my own—away from Lindstrom's tangle of grief and anger. I had a tiny spasm of guilt, then I let it go. I needed to be away from her a few hours, and since my skills as a grief counselor weren't doing the job, it couldn't hurt Lindstrom to have a break from me, either.

When I came out of my bedroom to claim my portion of the Cheerios, I found Lindstrom on the phone. She hung up as I was slicing my banana. I noticed she had washed her bowl and spoon and put them in the dish drainer. Maybe I could get her to wash the towels.

"I'm going into the station. Johnson wants to ask me some more questions about Vivian," she said.

"Did he say anything about what direction they are heading with the investigation?"

"No, I talked to Neely. He just said that if I were available, Johnson would like to know as much as he could about Vivian."

I told her of my plan to see L.C. Reidy that afternoon. She nodded slowly, guarding her response.

"Any hints?" I asked.

She looked away from me—rare for Lindstrom to avoid a direct gaze. "L.C. is Kathleen's buddy."

I nodded, waiting for more. But she knew I was skeptical of Kathleen's guilt. I felt Lindstrom's self-restraint. She might accept my help because her supervisor wasn't giving her a choice, but she didn't trust me to investigate this murder with her passion.

She shrugged, dismissing me. The shrug caught me unawares.

Sometimes the way she moved, some tiny thing, swept over me like a fire storm. But her eyes were remote, keeping me at arm's length. "Do your best," she offered.

Okay. Fine. A different fire crawled up my neck. But I turned away, hiding my fury. She was too sad. I couldn't shake her. I fussed with a phony search of my pockets for my keys just to cover. Then our goodbyes were brief. I wished her luck with Johnson, and we headed out the front door.

***

Our office is on Gravois in the same neighborhood Walter grew up in. Downtown, the street begins as Twelfth, becomes Tucker (a former mayor) for a stretch, then turns into Gravois, which slashes diagonally through south St. Louis heading toward Little Rock. Some blocks of Gravois retain the small town feel of the old white European enclaves where tidy brick stores belong to neighbors, not chains. Miller Security is in a corner brick in a row of such small businesses and next door to a rival agency. Just down the street a block, Hardees and other national fast foods crowded out old diners and mom and pop stores. I didn't like the smugness the traditional neighborhood sometimes represented—stranger beware—but I did like the smaller scale, the particularity of a distinct place fighting off corporate impersonality.

Still our shop reflected the times. We didn't have to do divorce cases to earn our daily bread. The perception that crime is ever-growing and increasingly random kept us busy providing security services. We weren't getting rich, but we were able to give our receptionist, Colleen, a raise every year.

As usual, I entered from the rear, passing a bathroom with a shower on my right and a tiny kitchen on the left. My office was next on the right, followed by a spare office that various temporary operatives could use when working cases. Both these offices had sturdy secondhand furniture and plain white walls. Walter's office on the left was larger but hardly lavish. Colleen and I had talked him into a new desk and client chairs on the grounds that it might help business if we looked like a prosperous place. Walter had snorted and procrastinated, pointing out that most of our business came through his neighborhood contacts: local cops and union mates and Korean War buddies and parish pals who now ran construction companies or managed machinist shops or owned insurance agencies. When he finally followed our suggestions, Walter drew the line at carpets, saying the linoleum tile he'd put down when he'd first rented the building he now owned was still good for another twenty years. "I'm afraid he's right," I told Colleen.

After the spare office, we had a storage room with wall to wall shelving. In this room we stored all manner of electronic security equipment. Across the hallway was the open reception area where Colleen reigned. I almost always walk up to her desk to say good morning before starting my day. She fills me in on messages and appointments, and I try to exert the Darcy charm on a young woman who is, for mysterious reasons, a bit wary of it. Colleen remains a tad aloof for a three-person operation. Walter hired her two years ago on a strictly temporary basis. A mature twenty-three, she's

47

from an Irish family that lived and breathed union organizing, and loyalty is something she believes in. But to her, loyalty does not include permissive mollycoddling of either Walter or myself or our various and ill-sorted friends and customers.

Colleen sits behind a lovely old oak desk given to Walter by a furniture store owner in lieu of cash payment. There are two plastic-seated folding chairs and an old orange love seat for waiting. Neither my uncle Walter nor I bother to bring in magazines. If you wait at Miller Security, you'd better be able to entertain yourself. Colleen doesn't consider chatting to be part of her job description. However, if Walter happens to be in when you arrive, you're likely to be greeted more warmly by Mike, Walter's mutt. Mike is poodle and something and something else. He never knew a stranger, and he seems to understand his kibble supply is somehow dependent on the odd lot that graces the waiting room. So he licks hands and wags tail and tries to compensate for the general lack of hospitality on the part of the two-legged staff. Walter summoned him from under a dumpster last winter in an effort to reunite an old woman and her lost dog. Mike was the wrong mutt. Since then, Walter and he have been inseparable, which has led to Mike's familiarity with several south side taverns.

My office is a more or less square space with a secondhand gray metal desk. The surface is reasonably clear, only a couple odd stacks of 'I'm going to get to it soon.' The initials 'R.J.' are scratched into the top, a previous owner's attempt at immortality. Two metal baskets hold stacks of 'to be filed next week.' The Macintosh and printer sit on an old school table I picked up at an auction. The client chairs are scarred oak and look suspiciously like bar chairs to me.

When I got in that morning, Colleen and Mike were already hard at work. Mike was entertaining what I assumed to be a potential client. Colleen was ignoring both.

"Morning, Colleen. An appointment for me?"

Colleen looked up from the letter she was typing—single spaced on plain paper—obviously a personal one. She looked blank.

"Is this gentleman here to see me?"

"No. He came with the man who's talking to Walter."

"Any coffee made?"

"There's probably a cup left. We're out of milk, though."

I sighed. "When is the guy from Creedman's coming in?"

Colleen consulted the tattered red spiral notebook that serves as our appointment book. "Ten-thirty."

"I'll wait, then. Could you make a fresh pot about ten-fifteen?"

Colleen just nodded as she returned to her letter.

In my office I fired up the Macintosh and stuffed yesterday's *Post* in the trash and pushed the closest "soon" pile to the middle of the desk. I filed and tossed and put in the "file next week" pile all but a reminder to buy my mother's birthday present. That I stuck in my pocket. Self-satisfied with fifteen minutes of hard labor, I checked my e-mail and sent a message to my pal

Patrick at the bookstore where he works.

The man from Creedman's Manufacturing was pleasant and seemed impressed by the security setup and staff we could provide, but was unwilling to commit. I educated, flattered, and smiled until noon. He wanted to meet again, so I set up an appointment for Walter and me to come to the plant on south Broadway.

I didn't drop the smile for a raspberry until I heard the door of his Park Avenue thunk shut.

"Damn. No sale yet. Now we have to go a-courting to his house."

"Um," Colleen remarked unsympathetically.

"Walter still in?"

"No, he and Mike went out for lunch."

"What are you doing for lunch?"

"I brought leftovers."

"I guess I'll go out and get a burger, then." I frowned, trying to test my taste buds for the fast food flavor of the day.

"White Castle?" Colleen suggested.

"Belly bombers?" These hamburgers aren't loose meat; they're liquid meat, poured onto the grill and resulting in a patty the size of a half dollar. Grease and onions—great cuisine.

"They've got a sale on bags of ten. I'll split with you."

"What about your leftovers?"

"We'll split those, too."

So after a magnificent repast of belly bombers and bean salad, I found the strength to make it through a second 'soon' pile. Several calls and a teary complaint about a deadbeat dad later it was four o'clock.

I still felt a little guilty about spending a day away from Lindstrom and her grief. Worse still about the relief of not having to step carefully around her sad, angry edginess. Even sharing my shower was starting to wear on me. So far she didn't seem to notice that I was trying to help her. Even paying clients say "thank you" now and then.

***

L.C. Reidy's place was a neat brick house on a tree-shaded street in Dogtown, a working-class neighborhood near the zoo. I parked the Plymouth behind her small black pickup truck in the driveway, got out, and smelled the barbeque. As I was walking up the front walk and admiring the neatness of the place, that gravelly voice called, "Come round the back!"

I followed the concrete around the side of the house. Standing at the end of the walk was L.C. Reidy.

L.C. was my idea of a stone butch, even though she didn't actually have a pack rolled into the sleeve of a white tee shirt. Her tee shirt was a light-blue pocket tee, and her Levis were a medium blue, not pre-worn. And she was carrying her cigarettes in one hand. She was a smidgen shorter than me, broad-shouldered, with Marine Corps posture. She was in her mid-fifties with her black hair winged by white and cut short in a modified D.A. Her face was broad and swarthy, her eyes a muddy brown.

Those eyes raked over me. Not sexual but speculative probing.

"You're the PI?"

I confirmed it. She waved me round to a tidy back yard. In a back corner was a small patch of tomato plants, neatly tied to stakes. Flower borders were weed free. The brick patio was swept clean. Two white Adirondack chairs sat near the grill and a heavy picnic table.

Another woman sat in one of the white chairs.

"This is Martha," L.C. announced. "Have a seat." She walked on to the picnic table and opened a cooler.

Martha and I exchanged smiles and nods. She was a faded blonde, somewhere in L.C.'s age group. She wore a crisp sun dress.

"Have a beer," L.C. said, approaching and proffering a Bud.

I figured a refusal wouldn't go down well. "Thanks," I said. The chipped ice was still sliding down the can.

The muddy brown eyes were hard to read, but the crinkle around them looked friendlier. L.C. popped her own can and perched on the table top, sneakered feet on the seat.

"Darcy here is investigating Viv's death," L.C. announced, as though she hadn't already told Martha. It wasn't high caliber acting.

"She didn't do it," Martha said, turning light blue eyes toward me. She was lightly made up, and her voice was soft.

"Have you known Kathleen a long time?"

The question seemed to take them by surprise, and Martha looked to L.C. for advice. L.C. considered the trick angles, then rumbled, "Over the years."

I tried to look respectful. "How did you all meet?"

L.C. decided to misunderstand me. "Martha worked as a clerk where I banked. One payday I just asked her if she would mind if I spent some of that dough on her." L.C. looked sly.

Martha looked as demure as she could hearing this line retold for the hundredth time.

I smiled past her to L.C. to show my appreciation for L.C.'s bait, butch to butch.

"That was twelve years ago," L.C. added.

I whistled my appreciation, more sincerely. This looked to be a second or third marriage for L.C., but twelve is nothing to sneer at.

I sipped my beer. Maybe a more specific question would work. "Who was Kathleen's partner before Vivian?"

"Oh, that would be Carrie Fox." L.C. said the name like a secret joke. I hadn't noticed her drinking that fast, but she rummaged around the cooler for more beer. She offered me one.

I shook my head. "I'm fine just now. How did Carrie and Kathleen get along?"

"Well, that Carrie is a pistol, you know. Pretty hard-headed. Wouldn't you say, Mama?"

Mama would. "Yes, she is. I don't blame Kathleen for losing it. Carrie could say the most provocative things." She looked at me wide-eyed, then pleated her skirt hem with her fingers. I'd say that pretty thoroughly established Kathleen's credentials as a long-time abuser.

"Mind if I have that beer?" I asked, tipping the remains of the first into the grass on the side away from L.C.

She found another can and brought it over. Our fingers touched as she handed it to me. There was no electricity. "Carrie isn't a bad person. She just ran around too much."

"Way too much," Martha chimed in.

"I'm not looking to hang anyone," I said, popping my beer.

I decided to scoot my foot a little farther out on the ice. "How did Kathleen guess that Viv had gone back to Lindstrom's? Had Viv gone back before?"

They were carefully not looking at each other. L.C. watched the tomato plants grow up another millimeter. Their spicy new greenness stirred a tingle in my nostrils. I put a finger to my nose to block the sneeze.

Finally Martha said, "Viv stayed in touch with all her exes."

"How did Kathleen like that?"

L.C. shrugged. "What could she do?"

Beat the shit out of Viv. But I let it pass. "I got the impression that Kathleen resents Lindstrom more than she dislikes Thomas Aubuchon." I took a swig of the beer. The can's surface was iced sufficiently that my fingers hurt if I held it, but the beer itself had started a trickle of sweat down my back.

L.C. studied me. "Viv's wounds were fresher from the breakup."

Wounds? From Lindstrom? "You're saying Lindstrom hit her?"

L.C. shook her head impatiently. "Nah. You know, she was cut up from the breakup."

"But Viv left Lindstrom."

"Don't matter. She was still upset. Naturally that bothered Kathleen."

"She wasn't afraid Viv would go back to Lindstrom?"

"What was there to be afraid of?" L.C. lit another cigarette, enjoyed a long pull.

I took it personally, felt the little flare of heat that warned me temper, temper. Easy. I needed to be the PI, not the knight defending m'lady's honor. I lifted my beer can and sipped to gain a minute. I tried for the tone of the jaded professional when I asked, "How did Kathleen find out Viv was at Lindstrom's—if Kathleen wouldn't expect Viv to go back there?"

L.C. shrugged, took another deep drag, exhaled slowly. The smoke curled like a lazy hawk circling.

"I think Viv called her," Martha said.

Kathleen's version to Lindstrom and me had been different. L.C. looked uneasy. She shifted her weight on the picnic table and coughed.

"I heard Kathleen called Viv," I said.

"Maybe that was it." Martha retreated quickly.

"But sometimes Viv would call Kathleen to see if the coast was clear," L.C. interjected with an amused snort.

"Coast was clear?"

"You know. Sometimes Kathleen had a few too many brewskies. They'd tiff. But next day Kathleen's sweet as honey."

The old, old story. I nodded. "When did you find out Viv had left?"

"Kathleen called Friday night to see if we'd seen or heard from Viv yet."

"She hadn't talked to Viv by then?"

"Un-uh." L.C. seemed caught in a straddle over whether to relax into amusement or stay wary.

"Was Kathleen still upset? Worried? Mad as hell?"

L.C. looked sly. "Well, you know." But I didn't.

"She was afraid Viv might be hurt somewhere. An accident or something," Martha interjected.

Or bleeding from Kathleen's boot. "She sounded hurt? Angry?" L.C. was sitting on something. I looked at Martha. But Martha wouldn't play. She watched her fingers pleat her skirt.

"Was she driving around, trying to find Viv?"

"Nah. No way." L.C. again. Positive.

"What makes you so sure?"

"I was talking to her on the phone."

"When?"

"Friday."

I suppressed a sigh. "What time?"

"About ten-thirty. The news had just gone off."

"How long did that conversation last?"

"An hour or more. I nearly went to bed without her," Martha said.

Lindstrom had arrived home at eleven-fifty p.m. she'd had a snack, gone upstairs, discovered Viv's body. Still warm body. Just maybe Kathleen had hung up the phone and dashed over to Lindstrom's house on Michellene.

"Was Kathleen still mad at Viv?" I nailed L.C. with my best MP warns a drunken G.I. stare.

L.C. was out of practice. She blinked, opened another beer. "Yeah, but it was just the liquor talking." Something was shifty there, hidden under the words.

"She made threats toward Viv?"

"She was blitzed, that's all." An exasperated croak. "Fell on her ass right while we were on the phone." L.C. looked relieved, her terrible burden lifted. Now I knew the worst.

"She was too drunk to drive."

"Ain't we all been?" She growled, not sure if she wanted to hate me for prying out her secret or to be women-of-the-world buddies.

I swallowed another mouthful of beer. I was starting to taste the metal of the can. "I can't deny it. But lots of folks too drunk drive anyway."

"But she fell asleep on me. I heard the phone drop to the floor. I was asking if she was all right. She picked the phone up. I was telling her to calm down when I heard her snoring in my ear." L.C. shook her head, but it was mock dismay. "She couldn't get up; she just fell asleep on the floor while we were talking."

I wondered how Lindstrom would take this news. Neither of us would trust L.C. for an alibi, but my reading was that L.C. didn't realize she was giving one. She'd been trying to cover up Kathleen's drunken rage.

"Chances are, when all's said and done, this will turn out to be a botched burglary." L.C.'s pronouncement sounded practiced. But I was hard pressed to name another motive for Viv's murder.

"A terrible thing," Martha said and shook her head sadly.

"It wasn't Kathleen. I hope you find who it was." L.C. said, standing up with surprising steadiness. "If you think of some other questions, get back to us."

I can outmaneuver a bum's rush, but I thought I had what I'd come for. "Thanks for the beer," I said. I stood, too. "Looks like those are going to be some good tomatoes."

CHAPTER NINE

Back in the Plymouth, the beer sang in my blood. I drove home carefully. Traffic was light for a June Monday. Rush hour had wound down early.

The Toyota was parked out front. I pulled into my spot in back and hurried up the stairs.

Lindstrom had on Channel 9's *The News Hour*, but she snapped it off as soon as I entered. I noticed Harvey had perched on her lap, keeping a keen eye on the stranger, no doubt. He jumped down and sauntered over to me for a pet, attempting to disguise how quickly he'd succumbed to Lindstrom's charms.

I quickly summarized my visit to L.C. and Martha.

"Of course they stood up for Kathleen," she said.

"Of course. But I don't think L.C. knew when Viv was killed. How could she? I think she was trying to hide how drunk and how angry Kathleen was that night. But that came out. If Kathleen was that sodden by ten-thirty and passed out by eleven-thirty, there's no way she could have killed Viv."

Lindstrom's blue eyes looked like ice chips. She didn't like a syllable of it.

"Lindstrom, I know it's hard to believe. But I think maybe Kathleen didn't do this." Saying the words took guts. I was afraid she'd hear disloyalty.

"L.C. would lie to protect Kathleen," she reiterated.

"I don't doubt it if she knew the right lie to tell."

I saw her climbing down. She was too good a cop to let her feelings override the facts forever.

"Viv told me L.C. is an abuser," she said, her best last shot.

"Somehow I'm not shocked."

She sighed elaborately. "I don't suppose we can pin this on her."

It was her first joke.

***

We walked to South City Diner. St. Louis heat often dips and swells in early June. We were ninety-four degrees and rising today, the humidity keeping step. But so far we hadn't yet had a week or more of 'scorchers;' the heat hadn't set into a concrete wall, so the evening passed for a pleasant summer's night. Teenagers of all hues cruised by with their car radios roaring rap. The young gay crowd at Mokabe's coffeehouse filled all their outdoor patio. When we turned onto Grand, the street and sidewalk hummed with summer sounds of cars, pedestrians, conversation.

Our stroll was silent. From the outside it probably looked like an easy companionability; Lindstrom was not up to small talk, and I was letting her lead this dance. I was afraid of introducing a topic that would crumple the calm facade.

She was stunning enough to turn heads as we pressed our way through crowds. A week ago I'd have floated beside her, carried by the vanity in being seen with her, electrified by a casual brushing of our arms. Now I felt curled inside myself, afraid to touch, afraid of wanting to.

When we reached the diner, Lindstrom vetoed the sidewalk tables. Instead we took a booth at the back where the air-conditioning was losing its battle with the heat of the day and the heat of the kitchen. As we passed by the booths on the right of the room, a thin man in his thirties with his long light brown hair twisted into dreadlocks frowned at Lindstrom. In her self-absorbed state she didn't notice him, but I took the seat facing the restaurant so I could keep an eye on him. He had the complexion and sharp features of a European-American, but his tee shirt bore a green, red and black-striped Africa with the logo 'African by birth' above the continent and 'Proud by choice' below it. He spoke to his companion, a dark-skinned teenager, and the teenager turned and stared at us. I stared back, and he turned around quickly. I didn't recognize either of them so I was sure it was Lindstrom they were eyeing. Had she busted the guy in dreadlocks?

A twentyish woman with several piercings brought our menus, and we studied them a moment. As Lindstrom asked me what I recommended, the glare pair looked at us again. We decided on sandwiches, light in response to the weight of the wet heat of the evening.

Lindstrom described her day at the Clark Street station and what she was able to learn about the investigation from Johnson's questions. She said that Johnson had seemed interested in the domestic violence, but also inquired into Lindstrom's vulnerabilities and enemies. She said a couple of officers had approached her with awkward condolences and others had busied themselves to avoid seeing her. She had been a St. Louis cop for nine years, always completely closeted. She couldn't imagine any reaction from other cops other than scorn.

"Being a cop is different, Darcy. It is a society unto itself. We're so dependent on one another."

"Like the Army."

Lindstrom just shook her head. "I can't do my job if they don't trust me. I should quit before it gets so bad it endangers me or someone else. Maybe I'll go to the State Police. Drive a cruiser alone all day."

"Why would you go backwards? The State Police have got to be as homophobic as the city cops."

"It's not about homophobia, damnit, Darcy. This isn't some political speech, this is personal."

"Of course it is about homophobia—why else would your fellow officers lose the trust you earned? You're the same cop. Just as trustworthy as

55

you were the day before Vivian was murdered. The only reason not to trust you is their own fear and hatred of gay people." I stopped before I shot out "of course it's political, you dumb shit."

She held my eye for a long minute. Then our much bejeweled waitperson was back setting heavy china on the table and signaling the bus girl to refill our glasses of iced tea. Lindstrom started her sandwich in her businesslike way.

"Okay, but it is more than that, too." She put her sandwich down on her plate. "It is about having a murder committed in my home, having one of my family killed."

"Victim instead of avenger?"

"Yes. I'm suddenly a different sort of person to them."

"But you're still a good cop. It won't take them long to figure that out."

"Everything I do will be under scrutiny."

"It wasn't before?"

She watched me watching our watchers. "Are they leaving yet?"

"Who?"

"The guy in the dreadlocks and his buddy."

"I didn't know you noticed them."

"It's my job to notice things."

"Yeah, they're leaving now. Who are they?"

"The older guy is a snitch. Not mine. He thinks he was done dirty by the department."

"Prone to violence?"

"Yes, but it won't be one of us he hurts. Violence trickles down. He'll rough up a woman or his younger buddy and think of himself as a man." She dismissed him with a flick of her long fingers over the salt shaker and finished her sandwich. "So maybe I'll become a PI. Is it all it's cracked up to be?"

"Sure, car chases, setting traps for bad guys, and shoot-outs under the Arch."

"What do you do when you aren't chasing bad guys through cemeteries?" She referred to the case that had brought us together—however together we were.

"Mostly business security. Corporations, manufacturing plants, medium and small businesses."

"Selling equipment?"

"We don't actually sell much. We recommend the type and amount of equipment, consult, set up security guards and night watchmen, design internal security for retail businesses."

"Just you and your uncle?"

"And Colleen and a few part-time operatives as we need them. Colleen is full-time; the others are more or less freelancers."

"You like it?"

"Most days. I meet interesting people. Make a small dent in the forces of chaos."

56

The irony wasn't lost on me. Here we were, having had dramatic sex four times, and just now getting around to the how-we-feel-about-our-jobs conversation. My therapist would have something to say about that if I were still seeing her.

Lindstrom looked disconcertingly long into my eyes again. Her tone shifted just slightly. "How long have you and Patrick been friends?"

For some reason the question seemed to take more weight than the previous ones about my work. "Four years. We've been really tight about two years. Since my best friend moved to Seattle."

She nodded as if confirming a hunch she'd had.

The waitress came, took our plates, and left us a bill. Lindstrom picked it up and looked at it.

I decided to jump in head first. "Why was Viv in your bedroom instead of the guest bedroom?"

Surprisingly, a smile twitched across her face. Did she think I was jealous? Before I could correct it, her face sobered, and she answered. "She was frightened. Scared and upset. She felt safer in my bedroom. Thursday night I sat with her until she went to sleep. Friday night I wasn't home when she went to bed."

"Did she go to work Friday?"

"No, she stayed home. My place, I mean." On that note the detective ended the questioning by getting up and leaving eighteen dollars on the table. I followed her out. The walk home was silent.

***

"I know this is ridiculous. I think I'll shower and go to bed," Lindstrom announced. "I haven't been sleeping much."

Perversely I was annoyed she was going to bed early. I didn't want to entertain her or tiptoe around her justifiable glumness. But I didn't want to be rejected either.

"Mind if I take some magazines in to read?"

I made the polite response and watched her disappear with the latest crop of weeklies and monthlies I subscribed to. She left with the freshest issues of *Newsweek* and *Ms*. Like most Americans I oversubscribe and underread. I dug around in the end table pile and found newish issues of *The Advocate* and *Utne Reader* for myself. TV didn't seem a good idea. I sat on the couch, stretched my legs.

Harvey Milk came over, spraying his usual froth of white hair. He's a short hair, but that means nothing come spring. He pranced about and leaned into my chest. He made sure he was between me and the magazine until I met his attention quota. Then he curled in a feline ball on my lap and let his purr subside to a quiet drone.

I had moved on to thinking of the inconvenience of house guests and how I'd need to launder the towels soon when Lindstrom emerged from the bathroom. She had borrowed my terry cloth robe.

"Good night, Darcy. Thanks for everything."

"You're welcome, Lindstrom."

***

Two hours later all the iced tea I'd consumed at the Diner was having its predictable effect. I swung my legs off the couch, tugged down my tee shirt over my boxers, and headed toward my bedroom. The door opened with only a small creak. I slid in and stood a moment by the door. The reading light and the bathroom night light were off. But the bedroom's window shade was at half-mast, and the security light from a neighboring apartment sent a slice of urban moonlight across half the bed. Lindstrom was lying still, facing toward the window, a sheet pulled over her hips. She had the bedside fan turned to low—for the white noise or to stir the stale air-conditioned air or both I didn't know, but for the first time I thought we might live amiably together, sharing a guilty secret.

I slid into the bathroom. That door closes with a loud click, but I risked it and flicked on the light. In this old apartment the door is tight and heavy enough to muffle the flush. I waited for the whole process, using the time to examine my face in the mirror, looking for I don't know what, signs of character. When I heard the last gurgle, I shut off the light and carefully turned the handle.

I stood in the doorway, getting my bearings again. I heard a sigh. She'd moved a bit; the shaft of light showed her blonde hair bleached white. Her long body lay curved in a S.

The second sigh, deeper it seemed, made me bold. I walked to the window side of the bed, squatted down, peered at her face. Her eyes were open, two pools of black ice. I thought their shimmer might be tears.

"You okay?" Dumb question.

"I keep thinking I can replay it, and this time I save her." Her voice came from someplace I'd never heard before.

I reached out to touch her cheek, to run just two fingers from the high cheekbone to the firm jaw line. I felt the wet.

Even then I felt ashamed to feel the rage of jealousy that spurted up, the demons that whispered "she loves Viv still." No wonder Lindstrom was so attached to Kathleen as a suspect. Jealousy can tip the balance. I pushed back, told myself to get over it, to just look at this woman in pain and—and what? I moved my hand to stroke her head gently, trying to remember how my mom, Betty, touched me when I was a kid.

"I know, babe, I know," I lied in my best mother's voice.

She sighed again, something that came deep from her gut, as though she were expelling whole dragons.

I leaned forward in an awkward crouch, putting my cheek next to hers, pulling her into my shoulder, continuing the stroking motion.

"Darcy, it feels like I didn't love her enough." She struggled to explain it to me, her voice raggedy.

"You did, Lindstrom. She didn't die from a lack of your love."

I sort of crawled onto the bed, easing myself into the space beside her. I held her, felt the shudders running through her body. All the reasons I

58

wanted to touch her came back to me. I kissed her forehead gently, her eyes, her wet cheek. "Oh, Sarah, I'm so sorry, sorry," I whispered.

But my body was singing. I started trembling all over till even my innards shook with it, like a high school virgin about to give it all away.

"Darcy, I can't. Not now." Appalled. Horrified.

I rolled away. I lay, teetering on the edge, longing for the simple switch that would shut down all the roiling motion in my body's molecules. I was alive; I was humming. Just one touch from her—right there—would explode me, end it in a moment.

I borrowed a voice from some more rational person. "I'm sorry. I didn't mean— I'm sorry."

But she was swinging out of the bed, sitting up on the shadowy side. "Damnit, Darcy." She sounded completely normal, completely Lindstrom, as though she were criticizing my driving or my politics.

I wanted to say, "I just love you so damn much I can't help it," but some sterner voice scoffed at that puny excuse. And that L-word scared me. So far we'd managed to avoid it.

I stood on wobbly legs, walked to her side. She was bracing her arms on the bed, head down, like a player benched for a stupid foul.

"I'm sorry," I said. "That was really dumb." Trying to own up.

Maybe she heard my insincerity, the large part of me that felt no honest regret. She didn't respond.

I heard myself sigh. What a fix. I'd started by wanting to console her, to soothe her to sleep. Now we were as awake as if a three-alarm fire had raged here. A heaviness started to settle in, tamping down all those lively hormones. I couldn't think how to penetrate the awful silence. We were swaddled by shame, anger, grief.

I was arranging the details of my suicide when Lindstrom's voice pierced the gloom. "Do you have any good tea?"

"Good?"

"Strong. Earl Gray. Irish Breakfast Tea."

"I think so. Betty gave me a variety tin for Christmas."

We trailed out to the kitchen. I turned on the stove light. We were not looking at each other. I rummaged around, found the tin, offered it to Lindstrom for a choice. She took the Earl Gray. I pulled out two mugs, filled them with water, stuck hers into the microwave. Harvey, on cue, sauntered in to save us from our silences. First, he twined round my ankles, then he strolled to Lindstrom. She bent to stroke him, to offer him her attention and regard.

I was starting to weigh what it meant to be jealous of a cat when the dinger sounded. I handed her her tea water and started mine.

I cleared my throat. "I just wanted to offer you comfort. I hated to see you lying there, in so much pain."

She looked at me then, a slow and thoughtful appraisal. "Ah well, you certainly distracted me from that."

No clues. Was she laughing at me? Was she outraged?

I couldn't think of another thing to say. I stared into my tea.

"My mother says that if tea were alcoholic, she'd be a certified drunk. It's what she always turns to in a crisis," Lindstrom said, her voice calm, even friendly.

I nodded, stupefied.

She sipped her tea. "I'm taking this with me," she said and touched my elbow as she passed me on the way back to the bedroom. "Good night, Darcy."

I watched Harvey follow her.

CHAPTER TEN

I overslept.

It had taken me forever to get to sleep. Had there ever been a time when Lindstrom had wanted me, had reached for me in lust? I couldn't call up those images. Last night just lying beside her had melted the fillings in my teeth, but her rebuke had shamed me. At least one part of my brain had figured out that I'd made an ordinary, human mistake and Lindstrom had stretched from her grief to forgive me. Another part of me was still too embarrassed to face her. Ever again. I listened intently, but didn't hear any noise from the bedroom. Surely she was gone. I stretched full length and felt a shiver down my legs as the sleep kinks ran out. I stretched again and groaned. If she were still here, I'd give her plenty of warning I was coming. My feet hit the floor with a thud.

I could see she wasn't in the kitchen so I wandered in. Her note was on the fridge, anchored by a tin cat magnet.

> *I'm going to my house to open it for the Blairs. Then to the*
> *station to see if the Lieutenant will assign me other duties. I'll touch*
> *base here—the visitation is tonight.   —Lindstrom*

The printing looked like that of Mike Hansen, a boy I'd sat behind in trig class long, long ago—small, evenly spaced, legible.

The tone of her note reminded me of her attempt to deflect my explanations and apologies last night. She clearly planned to forget it had happened. Good enough for me. With that bolstering thought, I made up my mind to go to Lindstrom's place on my way to work.

I saw that she had put down Harvey's morning kibble. No wonder he hadn't wakened me.

I called Colleen to tell her I was going to be still later. After a fast shower I was out the door. For a June 22 in St. Louis this was a lovely day— the sun bright, the humidity low. The crisp in my collar might last till noon.

When I got to Lindstrom's, I had to park in the alley itself. Her Toyota and Blairs' blue work van filled the small parking space. The yellow police tape was down. Lindstrom was sitting on the edge of the porch, her long legs stretched out before her. A bottle of Heineken's sat beside her. She was in faded jeans and a yellow tee shirt.

Unsmiling, she watched my approach. Her look reminded me of men I serve summonses on when their child support is overdue. But she asked, "Want a beer?"

"Too early for me," I said.

If she heard the reprimand, she ignored it. "The Blairs are go-getters. One man and two women."

I nodded.

"Johnson dropped by."

I raised my eyebrows.

"The footprint on the rug—actually a partial print—looks like a man's. Could be a big-footed woman like me, of course."

She examined her tennis shoes carefully, as though the answer to this question might leap out. She had the big hands and feet of a basketball star all right. My lust stirred.

She looked up at me. "What do you think, Darcy? Did I do it?" Her blue eyes startled me every time.

I ignored the foolish question. "What else did Johnson say?"

"You know the entry was through the bathroom window. Whoever did this slit the screen. Quietly. The screen was bent in, so the killer probably left through the door. I thought the window was too small and too high for entry. I was wrong." Her tone was bitter. She pulled her legs up a step and leaned over them grasping her ankles. She looked up bleakly. "What difference does it make, right?"

"What's Johnson's thinking?"

"He isn't saying much. He just pulls a mask down. Behind that mask is a man who doesn't like queers I think."

"Uh," I said helpfully. I was thinking Johnson probably blamed Lindstrom for handing him this mess. If she hadn't done this or that, yada, yada, yada…

"Excuse me."

I looked up for the source of the pleasant contralto. Jeannette Rico, looking both pert and efficient in crisp, short-sleeved uniform coveralls, stepped by us, carrying empty paint cans and rags in a thin-skinned trash bag. She gave me a half-smile as she passed. Once upon a time Jeannette and I had dated for an intense summer. The breakup had been amicable enough to allow us to stay civil.

She had curly brown hair, worn full and flowing down to her shoulders. Her self-belted coveralls emphasized a waist and hip line that was many a straight male's dream. Not exactly my type, but I'd forgotten that once. Now I met her half smile with my own and raised it. I saw a flicker of acknowledgement as she passed to stow the trash in the van.

Lindstrom and I fell silent. When Jeannette came back by, I said, "How's it going?"

She paused on the step. "Come and see."

I looked at Lindstrom.

"Go ahead," she said. "Once today is enough for me."

I followed Jeannette into the house, through the kitchen and hallway, and up the stairs. Watching her move was still a pleasure to me.

"How's it going with you?" I asked, a slight hoarseness creeping in.

"Fine. With you?"

"Oh, good."

When she reached the upstairs hallway, she turned and gave me a smile. "That your main squeeze?"

"No. A friend. I'm sort of helping investigate." I felt a blush start.

"Sounds complicated." She regarded me carefully for a slow moment. "This was a nasty one, Meg."

"For Lindstrom, too," I said, tilting my head to indicate downstairs. "Her ex."

"Hmm," she said, a small grunt. She led me back into the bedroom.

Bert Blair, a handsome, stocky fellow in paint-splattered coveralls, greeted me when I entered. He was busily painting a new coat of mint green over walls that had been scrubbed clean. Jeannette introduced the other woman, a young blonde, pale and petite, as Sandy McKnight. Sandy was working on cleaning and polishing the furniture. The bloody mattress was gone and a new one, wrapped in plastic, was propped against one wall.

I noticed Sandy kept an eye on Jeannette's responses to me.

I had had only a brief look at the blood-splattered but empty room. The clean-up had progressed enough that I felt my recall fading. Not so easy, I suspected, for Lindstrom. I complimented the work force on their job, gave Sandy a naughty wink just to confuse her, and walked back down the stairs.

I looked around and turned back into the bathroom under the stairway. It dazzled with the polish the whole house had. Given Lindstrom's work hours, I figured she had to have maid service of some sort. I peeked behind the shower curtain, spotting fixtures and a loofah sponge. The screen was missing, and the window closed.

I returned to the porch. "Are you just having the screen replaced or putting in a new window?" I was behind her.

"Isn't it a little late for a new window?"

I sat down beside her. "You're still here." My voice sounded carefully neutral to me.

"Ah, well," she said with a shrug.

A silence extended into heaviness. Finally, without looking at me, she asked, "Did you date that woman?"

"How did you know?"

Maybe it was a chuckle, the sound in her throat. "Your face had a look."

"A look." I watched her profile.

"It occurred to me that I don't know anything about your dating history, except for Healy." She referred to Patrick. "Whenever I see you, you're with him." She sounded cross.

"We're friends. We're together a lot because we aren't dating. Anyone else, I mean." I could have left bad enough alone, but something pushed me. "You haven't been keeping my phone ringing off the wall."

Lots of debris swirled around in that little tornado.

"Your phone only takes calls in?"

Touché.

"Seems whenever I call you're always busy," I said, still resenting those occasions when Lindstrom had blandly put me off.

"I am busy. I was. Ask any cop's wife."

"I'm not a wife," I snapped.

She stared at me as though I'd called her a foul name. Maybe it was my tone and not the words which shocked her. I just seemed to keep stepping in it, although I didn't mean to.

She pulled in a deep breath. "No one's asked you to be."

Well, damn. That was true and was that what irked me? I didn't know what I wanted to be with her—not yet, not clearly—and somehow that was her fault. Wasn't it?

The silence stretched, and I, for one, couldn't think of anything in the world to fill it.

Nor could she for a long while.

"The visitation starts at four," she finally said flatly.

"Okay." I wasn't sure. Did she want me to go with her? I sneaked a sideways glance, couldn't read her. I risked being swatted. "We could meet at my place at three and go together. If you'd like the company."

She waited two beats. A small sigh I barely heard, a gruffness in her voice when she said, "Yes, I'd like the company."

She sounded distant and distracted again.

All the sparks raised by Jeannette Rico and Lindstrom's jealousy of Patrick had died quickly, smothered by her grief for Viv.

I said my goodbyes and turned away, feeling the weight return to my shoulders.

One step forward, maybe five back.

***

I parked in back of the office. I didn't see Walter's car. This morning, like most others, a gray blur flashed out from under Colleen's desk and attacked my pant's leg with merry yips.

"Hey, Mikie," I said and reached down and pried the little poodle off. "How many customers do you scare off with this routine?"

"Oh, they like it," Colleen said dryly. "Walter tells 'em he's a miniature Rottweiler. Good image for security work."

The gray poodle was dancing around me, begging for more attention. I bent and roughhoused a bit.

"Am I the only one in the office working on his manners?" Colleen asked the file cabinet.

"She is, isn't she, Mikie?" I gave him a final pat and stood up. "Walter's out?"

"Just for fifteen minutes. You have a client waiting." She snapped her fingers, and Mikie ran to her.

"I do?" My mind raced. I hate missing appointments or being late.

"A drop-in. She's been waiting about ten minutes."

"She have a name?"

Colleen supplied it and a brief sketch of the client's problem. I squared my shoulders and started down the hall, relieved to let Viv Rudder and the grieving Lindstrom slip away.

***

I was well into my day when Colleen told me Colin Lanier was on the line.

"…Sarah asked me to call," he was saying, a little doubt creeping into his voice, cluing me that I'd been unresponsive.

"Yes, thank you, Mr. Lanier. I'm hoping for some background from someone who knew Viv really well." An invitation to dish if ever there was one. Would he play?

He let the pause grow, then said with impressive dignity, "I'll be more than happy to do anything to help find Viv's murderer."

Corny words but absolutely sincere delivery. I was glad he wasn't one who'd be inclined to seduce me.

I'd assumed we'd do lunch in Collins, Cobb, and Vahey's privately catered dining room or have a drink at Adam's Mark or Mike Shannon's. Instead, he said he was brown-bagging it in Smith Park, a little pocket park downtown, and would be glad to meet me at 4th and Chestnut. He said he'd reserve an end of the park bench for me.

Traffic was irritatingly slow on Gravois, but downtown it lightened. I whipped along 4th under I-40 and past the parking garage for Busch Stadium. The sidewalks were crowded with tourists and employees looking for a quick lunch. The day was gleaming—bright blue skies, air clear and clean. My parking goddess smiled, and I snatched one of the three meters in front of Boatman's Tower. The digital clock there read 12:30:47. Right on time. I grabbed the large Coke I'd bought on the way, fed the meter, and crossed to the Adam's Mark.

I spotted Colin Lanier as I looked down into the little park across the street. He was tall and lean and wearing clothes whose labels I wouldn't recognize. He'd taken off his suit coat; it was lying neatly across his lap. His posture conveyed relaxation without slouching. His sandy hair, perfectly casual, picked up gold from the sun. He looked like a *New Yorker* ad, except a decade older, about my age.

When I descended the few steps into the park, he turned at my approach and took off his dark sunglasses. As usual, I'd forgotten mine and squinted up at him as he rose to greet me. He'd tugged the silk tie down just an inch or so and unbuttoned his collar. If you like pretty blonds, he was probably the most gorgeous man I've ever personally touched. He smelled good, too.

"Meg Darcy?" We shook hands.

"Yes."

We sat down, our backs to the ostentatious entryway of the Adam's Mark, angled to face each other. He put his sunglasses beside him.

"No lunch?"

I held up my Coke.

He brought up a small brown bag from his other side. Peeked in, just like I do, as though a delightful surprise might have found its way there, pulled out a hefty sandwich. "Good. Then you can help me with mine. Unless you don't do roast beef?"

His manners were smooth. Not to accept would be churlish. My mother Betty has a more gracious style of giving way to generosity, but I did my best imitation.

"Good," he said again, and pulled out a small, pearly penknife and deftly halved the sandwich. His fingers were long, the nails manicured. I knew if I'd attempted the same maneuver lettuce would have hit the pavement. He passed my half on the sandwich paper, used the brown bag as his plate. He divided a small packet of chips for us, then reached to his other side for a small bottle of water for himself.

His smile was a radiant production, and I wished Patrick were there to enjoy it. "Bon appétit," Lanier said.

We chewed. My attention was fully claimed by rare beef, red onion, black olives, sprouts, romaine, and something saucy.

"Hmm," I contributed.

"Nice, isn't it? I'm a lucky man. Jeff makes a mean sandwich."

That put it right out there. I supposed Lindstrom had made a full introduction, which could save some dancing around.

"Do you often come here for lunch?" I couldn't imagine he did. Bird shit doesn't go well on gray wool.

"No, but it is such a fine day. Our work requires us to do a fair amount of lunching with clients." He gave me the full court look. His eyes were beautiful, not really blue, a gray. Impeccable manners kept him from saying he didn't want to be seen with me in the usual places. "How about you? Does your work allow you to get out?"

"If you count driving through fast food places." I sounded too whiny. "Really, it depends. Some days I can do what I want. Taking lunch outside is a great way to relax."

"I like a little alone time. Especially now. Viv and I used to lunch together sometimes. I'm already missing her."

"Lindstrom said you were close."

He put his sandwich down. "She was my best friend."

I was caught mid-bite. I swallowed too fast, swigged some Coke, choked. No matter. He was looking at the red flowers across the middle of the park.

"I'm sorry for your loss. Good friends are a precious commodity."

He looked back to me, nodded. "Thanks." He paused, took a breath. "So how can I help you?"

"We're trying to think who might have a motive to kill Viv. I've heard the competition inside Collins, Cobb, and Vahey is, to say the least, keen."

"Cutthroat lawyers, eh?" A slight chiding.

I shrugged. "Tell me it isn't so."

He gave me a half-smile. "It isn't so. Viv had just lost a round. She had a motive to kill, not vice versa."

"Was she in real trouble?"

"No—she was just used to things coming easily, from childhood on. But sometimes the partners like to remind us not to take our blessings for granted. She'd have bounced back."

"She wasn't deeply depressed?"

"You aren't suggesting suicide?" He looked horrified. How dumb was I?

"No. But I'm trying to understand Viv."

"She was incredibly smart, incredibly lovely, incredibly funny in a sometimes too sarcastic way."

"Sarcastic enough to make enemies?"

"No. Too smart for that." He regarded me carefully. "The girl liked to dish. But she chose her audience carefully."

He started wrapping his unfinished sandwich. Reluctantly I followed suit with mine.

"No company enemies, then?" A last check.

"No company killers."

"What about her private life? Was she worrying about being outed at work?"

He shook his head. "No. Her marriage to Thomas was good cover. So was our ostensible dating. Besides, wouldn't that be a motive for Viv to kill someone, not vice versa?" He said it gently, as though nudging me to the point.

"Did you know she'd taken refuge at Lindstrom's?"

"Yes. She called me to cover her story that she wasn't coming to work on Friday because of the stomach flu."

"Did she tell you about the beating?"

"The bare minimum."

"Your best friend?"

I saw how a pretty face looks when annoyed. "Look, Viv was embarrassed. It was hard for her to admit..." He searched for the word.

"That she'd married an abuser?"

He nodded. "That she'd made such a colossal mistake."

"But her track record wasn't so good, was it? Two failed relationships." I was doing the gentle nudging now.

"But entirely different. Aubuchon was probably a mistake, but a different kind. A college sweetheart. A big man on campus, ambitious about business success, emotionally not inaccessible. I'm sure he looked a good prospect. She didn't realize until after she married him that he was a bit controlling." He sank into a pause.

"And?"

"She outgrew him."

"How?"

Lanier shrugged. "Aubuchon's a decent enough fellow, but he's dull. And not as smart as Viv." He caught it, added, "As Viv was," and looked so

67

sad I wanted to pat his arm. A breeze ruffled the trees on the south side of the park, and a semi blared at an unwitting tourist.

"You think he might have killed her?"

"Once upon a time. When they first broke up. You know—that first jealous rage. He couldn't believe she'd left him. He was sure he could convince her it was all a mistake. Maybe when he first found out Viv was falling for a woman. But in recent years Thomas had moved on to wishful thinking."

"That she'd come back?"

He nodded, thinking better of my acuity now. "Never would have happened."

I'd told myself that I had to ask the Lindstrom question, but I was torn between feeling like a wart hog and a justified inquisitor. I wanted to know all Colin Lanier knew about the Rudder-Lindstrom union, but my motives weren't pure.

"What was Viv's life with Lindstrom like?"

"What does Sarah say?"

I nodded, appreciating his style. "From a disinterested observer."

"Hardly that neutral. I like Sarah a lot. But Viv was my friend."

"Understood. From your point of view what was their relationship like?"

"Nearly perfect." He gave me the half-smile again. "Two smart, two lovely, two ambitious people, going after the golden ring."

"How did Viv go from being Mrs. Aubuchon to Lindstrom's partner?"

"She shed Thomas, and shortly thereafter, maybe even during the shedding process, fell for Sarah." He looked at me. "Sarah makes a powerful first impression."

I felt the small flush, not caused by the sun. "Their relationship was good?"

"Even best friends are on the outside looking in. It seemed perfect. They enjoyed each other. They enjoyed good food, good clothes. They believed in achievement."

"So, what happened?"

"To understand Viv?" His tone was martini dry, but he gave anyway. Maybe it was a cautionary tale too good to resist. "Lawyers trying to become associates work brutal hours; cops work brutal hours. They just didn't tend the garden they shared. Viv felt neglected. She liked living with a cop—that dangerous edge thing. But she didn't like feeling neglected."

"Did Lindstrom see it coming?"

Lanier smiled the rueful version of his half-smile. He had plenty of credibility for explaining how good-looking, fast-track yuppies lived. "No. Sarah was surprised. Amazed really. Angry. Hurt. All the fun feelings."

"Would she kill Viv?"

"You ask?" He had that I-misjudged-you tone.

"I don't know the Lindstrom who was living with Viv."

Lanier sighed. "No. Of course not. The answer is no. She's too good a police officer and—"

He paused, and I nearly shook him. "And?"

"And, I think, from the outside looking in, Lindstrom had fallen out of love with Viv, too. Quietly, while no one was noticing." He shook his head. "Of course, maybe I'm projecting my promiscuous, gay male perspective on it."

"How long have you been with Jeff?"

"Ten years. Faithfully."

I was impressed. I hadn't a clue as to Jeff's power of holding a spouse aside from his ability to make a wickedly tasty sandwich, but on looks alone, Colin Lanier probably had to fend off daily temptations from others.

"Explain Kathleen Clawsen."

"God, that I could. I think Viv wanted that pop of danger. Certainly Kathleen's erratic enough to convey that. Once she got Viv's attention, she certainly didn't neglect her. She smothered her."

"Would Kathleen kill to keep her?"

He looked at me. I couldn't imagine looking in the mirror every morning and seeing his face. I thought he was a nice guy, but how could I trust my judgment? Even as a dyke, I could feel his appearance swaying me toward liking him.

"Yes, I think she would," he said. "But that doesn't mean I think she did. I'm not just playing the cagey defense lawyer. I think it would be convenient to blame Kathleen—convenient and possibly wrong." He regarded me carefully. "I suppose you're considering a random burglary or overheated crack addict?"

I looked up at the silver curve of the Arch. "Oh, yes."

"I haven't given you much help."

"To the contrary, you've given me lots to think about."

And he had. All the way back to Miller Security I thought about three golden children—smart, pretty, ambitious—who had risen rapidly in their respective careers, who'd had every door open easily to their smiles, who were used to winning—Colin, Viv, Sarah. Given the world she was used to, did I really have a ghost of a chance?

CHAPTER ELEVEN

Miller Security may not be in the homicide investigation business, but to do any business on the south side, where Irish, Italian, and German traditions are strong, means attending a good many funerals. Vivian Rudder's parents had chosen a modern brick funeral home in Olivette near Creve Coeur where they lived.

I had been relieved when Lindstrom arrived in a summerweight navy and white trouser suit. At least I wouldn't be the only one not in skirt and hose. I'd pulled on a light tan linen suit that still had some pizazz. We drove through a fast food spot for Cokes, promising ourselves dinner later.

On our drive to Olivette, Lindstrom caught me up on the Blairs' work at her house. Incredibly they'd finished. Not surprisingly, she was reluctant to say much about their work. They were fast; they were good. She didn't much care. I considered asking again if she'd see a police counselor, but I decided against it. There's no point in trying to buck up someone who is appropriately grieving just because her gloom pulls you down.

We arrived at the funeral home just after four. I followed Lindstrom in. The sleek rooms inside were spacious and rich: silky couches, heavy drapes, lush carpets. I was reminded of classy hotel lobbies.

Lindstrom introduced me to the assembled Rudders as a friend of hers. Papa Rudder was tall, balding, portly, a picture of executive assurance. His cologne greeted me. His handshake was manly; his eyes gray and dry. Maybe he was secretly torn apart. He looked through me in the way men of his generation often dismiss women.

Mama Rudder was handsomer than I'd expected. Her eyes were red-rimmed. She gave Lindstrom a full frontal hug and me a weak smile but firm handclasp. Viv's younger sister Ruth was a redhead like her mother and sister but with lighter highlights. Tears still seeped onto her cheeks. She was glad to see Lindstrom, but looked frostily at me. Her husband was tall, well-tailored, darkly handsome. His manner was bland. He struck me as just as dismissive as Mr. Rudder but with a contemporary polish.

I was defensive. Mrs. Rudder wanted to keep Lindstrom by her side and, as I read it, Sister wanted to know if "friend" was a euphemism for someone who'd stolen Lindstrom's affections. Maybe I was the reason Viv had left reliable Lindstrom and taken up with uncouth Kathleen. For the first time I felt sympathy for Kathleen Clawsen. The Rudders would be formidable in-laws.

70

Mrs. Rudder led us over to the closed casket. Over two dozen full sprays surrounded the pearly rose coffin. On top pink roses cascaded down; a magenta ribbon said daughter in gold. Above, in a bronze-colored eight by ten frame was a studio portrait of Vivian. Her lovely, heart-shaped face was recognizable, but her shoulder-length hair was wrong. It was blonde, nearly Lindstrom's color. I felt myself frowning and looked at Lindstrom. She and Mrs. Rudder were whispering in choked voices. Viv's sister Ruth was daubing her eyes again.

I stared at Viv's picture. Maybe the photographer got the color wrong. But it was the kind of photograph that screams expense—a portrait by a studio photographer, not a Sears special.

Viv and Lindstrom didn't look much alike to me. But I'd made love to one of them. Suppose Viv's killer broke into Lindstrom's house, expecting to find Lindstrom in bed; he crept into a dark room and attacked a sleeping blonde woman. He bludgeoned her with a bat before he got a good look at her. If he were in a rage fueled by hate, he wouldn't have noticed his mistake—and, even if he did, Viv would be dead. Now what? Does he say, "Oh, sorry. Wrong victim" and call it quits? Or does he stick to his original target and come after Lindstrom?

My pulse accelerated. I saw so clearly what might have happened. I wanted to rush Lindstrom outside, explain it all. I looked at her, so tall, so strong, so fine, talking quietly with Mrs. Rudder. I drew some steadying breaths. Don't panic, Meg.

Don't spread panic either. Think about it. The crackhead theory may be right.

We stood there an uncomfortably long time before other visitors began trickling in. Mrs. Rudder kept Lindstrom beside her. I dropped back and found a vantage from an embroidered love seat across the room. I had plenty to think about. Still the evening crawled by as such evenings do. After the first gush of visitors and an hour on their feet, the Rudders began to spell one another at the casket and used two aunts from the maternal side as a relief team. The immediate family made a joint appearance casket side only for the more important guests, many of whom were Mr. Rudder's business associates. Lindstrom was cut loose fairly early and came to join me on the love seat.

"Want to go?" I asked. Her face had achieved that whiter shade of pale.

"Un-uh. I want to see who shows up."

I nodded. It's a cop thing. Murderers don't always return to the scene of the crime, and hit men don't always attend visitations. But it's true you can learn about the deceased during final rituals, especially if you have a key to the players. For my part, I thought it was just possible a stalker after Lindstrom might show up.

The room we were in was large enough to accommodate four silky couches besides our love seat. In addition, six rows of padded folding chairs offered more seating. Opposite the casket a wide archway opened into a slightly smaller anteroom with three more couches and no sense of crowding.

This suite of viewing rooms was for the large crowds, and the crowds came.

Funeral wear isn't black anymore. Even the next-of-kin get by with their Sunday best, and visitation visitors are often drop-by casual. But Vivian's mourners were definitely upscale. The rooms filled with clusters of mourners in pastel colors, speaking in vanilla voices.

Lindstrom was able to identify the major family members. We guessed at Mr. Rudder's business associates by their behavior. Some of these guys couldn't wait to put the emotional stuff aside to form groups to compare golf scores or stock market ticks. Their wives were dispatched on the condolence missions to the grieving mother and sister.

Amy Scott came in a navy and white suit that reminded me of Sunday school. Mrs. Rudder clung to her, and for several moments they stood, Amy holding both Mrs. Rudder's hands. I couldn't help but wonder if Amy were thinking that Viv's death could have been avoided if she'd have stayed where she belonged, with Thomas Aubuchon. I sneaked a look at Lindstrom, who didn't seem to be seeing Amy at all. I couldn't sit anymore. I got up and wandered off in search of the women's room. I stretched it out, but I was surprised to see Amy Scott heading toward the door as I returned. Surely one's best friend ought to stay longer at the visitation. As she pushed by me, she averted her eyes and busied herself finding keys. I considered forcing her to speak to me, but decided evil done at a visitation might count double.

When Kathleen Clawsen showed up, she was supported by two well-dressed younger women. All three were in dresses and heels. No dykes here. The support was entirely moral. Clawsen wasn't teetering. Vivian's sister and brother-in-law were on casket duty at the moment and greeted Kathleen with restrained civility. The chill nearly caused me to shiver, and I was all the way across the room. I glanced at Lindstrom. Her jaw was set. But she looked more sad than angry.

Mr. Rudder detached himself from a male circle and collected his spouse from the wives' auxiliary. He steered her past us through the archway and through a door that closed after them. A private hideaway for grieving families no doubt; most funeral homes have them. There you can sob away or sneak a cigarette or even a short snort without losing public dignity. I was torn. Kathleen wouldn't be anyone's favorite daughter-in-law, but she had been Vivian's last chosen partner. On the other hand, if she were an abuser—which she was…

I was tripping through this tangle when I noticed that L.C. Reidy and Martha had arrived. L.C. was clean and crisp in the first polyester I'd seen that evening. She was so butch that I knew ten more years of leather wrinkles would render her gender switched to a passerby. Martha was pretty in pink. Again Ruth and her husband delivered the greetings. L.C. and Martha stared a long time at Vivian's picture. When they detached themselves, they gravitated toward Kathleen and her escorts.

"Who are the women with Kathleen?"

"Jody Faircloth and Tori Helbraun," Lindstrom said.

I nodded. Guessed right.

I don't know if phone calls had been made or not, but there was a sudden surge in the dyke population. No, I can't always tell by looking, but there were signs. Women arrived in couples or friendly trios. Some butches steered their femmes by the elbows. It's the nineties, and you can if you want to. I wondered what would happen if the butches joined the circle of suits Mr. Rudder had abandoned. Others may not have worn ear studs or walked boldly or stood with their hands jammed into their pocket, but they did walk directly to Kathleen, or, in other cases, to Lindstrom. I found myself being introduced as a friend a half-dozen times and getting the same speculative stares Ruth Rudder had given me.

I edged away just to keep an eye on the big picture. Some women were brave enough to move from Kathleen's group to Lindstrom's or vice versa, but there was a certain amount of hostile staring from both camps. I was reminded of junior high when girls fight intensely over best friends.

The presumably straight were mostly oblivious, though some younger clusters looked, then nudged. The younger set—late twenties, early thirties—were more gender integrated. I smiled as I saw here and there a husband put his arm around his wife's waist. Never fails when there's a lesbian alert. Makes me feel powerfully seductive. On my own I might have winked at a young matron, just to stir the pot, but I behaved myself out of respect for Lindstrom.

A new group arrived, all in dark suits, male and female. Gucci shoes and bags, ties and scarfs. Fellow attorneys at Collins, Cobb, and Vahey I bet. After a short stay beside the casket, they reformed a circle of seven. Colin Lanier detached himself and walked to Lindstrom. They hugged. He held Lindstrom within his arms while he whispered into her ear, then leaned back. They gazed at each other silently a long moment, looking sexy and intense. I took special pleasure in knowing they were both queer and not the perfect couple hets might imagine. Call it petty.

I also thought Lanier was gutsy to join Lindstrom's group. Not many straight boys would be that self-assured whether the women were straight or lesbian. I looked back to his attorney's group. They weren't obviously watching, but I wondered if one or two might not be adding a hash mark to his file card. And no one else was joining him to console Lindstrom.

Perhaps Lanier's loyalty to Lindstrom was a last straw, but Kathleen's group moved out en masse. They didn't huff, but there was a certain set in several jaw lines. L.C. Reidy glanced over her shoulder, and I gave her a discreet finger wave, probably losing my butch credentials on the spot.

As if by magic, Papa and Mama Rudder reappeared. I was impressed. If our government had such accurate intelligence sources, we'd all be in big trouble. Bigger trouble. Eventually Lanier excused himself from Lindstrom's circle and went to greet Vivian's parents who were now taking their turn in the casket rota.

Lanier didn't tarry long before rejoining the Collins, Cobb, and Vahey clique. I was beginning to like this guy. His manners were sensible as well as smooth. I looked at my watch. We were creeping toward eight and closing time. Visitations used to stretch to nine, but some powers that be decided to have mercy on the exhausted grieving.

Then, at last Thomas Aubuchon entered. He was by himself and looking wan, his skinny frame inside a loose summerweight gray suit. I figured the parental Rudders would fall upon him, but they melted away quickly, and the two aunts jumped up to receive him. He'd seen the snub, of course, and perhaps the Rudders didn't care. He gave the aunts the merest of greetings. I knew from experience that he was no champ of social skills.

He stood in front of the casket a long, long time, staring at Vivian's picture. Finally he turned and surveyed the crowd, panning it deliberately. His gaze held Lindstrom, then moved on. He recognized me, too, but not happily. He shoved his hands in his pockets and played with the change there, continuing his visual search. Whatever or whomever he was looking for eluded him. He rolled his thin shoulders in a shrug and turned away, exiting as he came, unattended. My loyalties were with Lindstrom, but I felt a tug of pity for him. He hadn't a clue.

I was thinking I didn't know many straight men who did when Neely walked in. He's a short, slight man, impeccably groomed even if his suits are cheap and his work hours long. He has the dark hair and pale skin of the black Irish. He spoke briefly to the aunts, stood, head bowed, a further moment before the casket, then turned and scanned the crowd more quickly and less obviously than Aubuchon had.

Lindstrom saw him coming and excused herself from the women who had surrounded her.

She and Neely met midway in the room. Would they embrace I wondered. They wondered, too, I guess. They stood a moment, then Lindstrom put her hands out and spoke to him. He clasped her two hands and held her eyes with his. He spoke softly, his face unsmiling. Lindstrom wasn't smiling either, but she still looked glad to see Neely. Or more relaxed. A cop thing.

They stood there a long while, talking quietly. While they conferred, Detective Johnson came in. It wasn't till then that I realized the room had been all-white. It was a reminder of what I take for granted, what I don't notice.

It wasn't just his brown face that attracted attention now. His tall, thick figure was imposing, his frown intimidating. I was beginning to think his frown permanent. I wondered if his spirit ever lightened. His head thrust forward, rounding his shoulders. He gave the aunts a curt nod and stared down at the casket.

Mr. Rudder came up to join him. Johnson said a few words, then turned away. He walked directly toward Neely and Lindstrom, and I heard the rasp of his voice even though he was speaking quietly. He disengaged quickly and walked past me into the anteroom, where two knots of visitors stood. Like Neely, he could survey a crowd unobtrusively. He turned and came back. He surprised me by stopping next to me.

"You're Darcy, right?"

"Yes, we met—"

He cut me off. "How's Lindstrom really doing?"

I looked at him. His brown eyes and mustached mouth gave me no clues. Was he concerned or checking up on her?

"She's still in shock, I think." I thought that would cover her bases.

"You encourage her to be careful."

"Meaning?" I smiled to show friendly.

He didn't smile back. "The killing was vicious. There was a bloody shoe print, big size, like a man's on the rug beside the bed. The perp cut a screen to get in. But nothing was taken except some cash from Ms. Rudder's handbag, which was in the room. And none of the people who knew Ms. Rudder was there wear that shoe size...except her husband and Lindstrom."

"Her husband knew she was there?"

"He admits she called him," Johnson said. He sounded annoyed to give information he hadn't meant to give. I didn't annoy him further by revealing that Aubuchon had already given me a version of this story.

"When?" I pressed my luck.

"Friday morning. To cancel a lunch with him. He thinks she was wearing a black eye." He paused. "He was right." He put an admonitory forefinger to my right bicep. "But Clawsen didn't do the murder. And so far Aubuchon's alibi is checking out. So ask yourself the big question."

"Who was supposed to be the victim?"

He didn't nod; he just drew his eyelids down in acknowledgment. His round cheeks were starting to slide into jowls. His face gave nothing away, nothing that counted. "So do you know Lindstrom well enough to be a good influence?"

I shrugged. "I'll try."

"Try hard. Because someone nasty's out there."

Somehow having Johnson agree with my notion of who the perp might be—someone after Lindstrom, not Viv—made me feel worse, not better.

"She'd dyed her hair blonde, you know. Vivian Rudder," I said.

We exchanged a significant look.

"Tell Detective Lindstrom to take extra care," he reiterated. He gave me a curt nod and departed.

I doubted that Johnson and I would ever be personal chums. He seemed weighed down and made wary by too many years in homicide, maybe too many years seeing the young arrested or murdered. But in his gruff way he seemed to care about Lindstrom, though he obviously didn't know her well. Even if I counted as her significant other, there wasn't much chance of influencing her behavior. How could I broach this theory to Lindstrom in a way that would promote the right response from her? Wasn't Neely a better messenger to send on this errand?

I looked across the room, saw Lindstrom's signal that she was ready to leave. She paused before the coffin for a last long look at Vivian's picture. I stood behind her, trying to numb out so that I could be strong for Lindstrom. More than ever, finding Viv's murderer would be doing a favor for Sarah.

Outside, the asphalt parking lot radiated heat up through the thin soles of my 'dress up' shoes. There were few cars left in the lot so my eyes were immediately drawn to L.C. Reidy's black pickup parked beside a tan Park Avenue. L.C. herself leaned against the driver's side door, smoking and squinting. She was squinting at me. I touched Lindstrom's arm; "I'm going to go see what she wants."

"Huh?" Lindstrom, normally as watchful as a cat, was lost in a labyrinth of grief.

"L.C. Reidy is over there, looks like she has something on her mind. I'm going to go see what it is."

"Okay." She nodded absently and headed toward her Toyota. As I got closer, L.C. drew her mouth down and glared. She had been waiting for me, and it clearly wasn't to offer condolences. Martha waited patiently in the passenger seat of the truck.

"I thought investigators were supposed to be impartial. Fair."

"What's wrong, L.C.?"

"Rumor has it that you and Sarah are a couple."

How could other people possibly be surer of that than I was? I shook my head. "Not so's I'd noticed."

"Well, it's not hard to see whose side you're on. You just gonna help her pin this on Kathleen? Is that what you're trying to do?"

"No, as a matter of fact, not. It doesn't help Lindstrom to frame Kathleen."

"It does if your girlfriend killed Viv."

"She didn't."

L.C. barked in a sort of laugh and ground her cigarette into the asphalt. "You're whupped. You think just because she's a cop, she can't be jealous?"

"Come on, L.C., there's a long way between jealous and beating someone to death with a baseball bat." I thought but didn't say that if Lindstrom were going to batter someone to death it would probably be Kathleen for hitting Viv. I looked into L.C.'s brown eyes. For some reason, I wanted this woman to approve of me, to recognize that we were on the same side in the gender wars. "We'll find out who killed Viv. That will be the best outcome for everyone."

"Yeah, sure. Just tell your girlfriend to leave Kathleen alone, or we'll have to see about teaching her some manners."

I narrowed my eyes. Did she think I would whimper when threatened? The temptation was to throw out my chest and out-butch her. I turned and looked at Sarah, staring straight ahead through her windshield. Slamming L.C. wasn't going to keep Sarah safe or avenge Viv.

"Look, L.C., Kathleen and Sarah both loved Viv. Aubuchon, too, I guess." I softened my tone. "Sarah overreacted—"

"Him!" Disdain curdled her voice. "How naive are you?"

"You know something I don't?"

She snorted. "Don't get me started."

"Have you got something to tell me that would help this investigation?"

She dug into her polyester jacket for her smokes. "He's your typical man. He wanted Viv under his thumb."

I thought about it. Everything I'd learned so far suggested that Aubuchon was a wimp compared to, say, L.C. herself. "Would he kill her?" was what I asked.

She peered at me through the curling smoke. Her chuckle was a smoker's rattle. "How else could he keep her to himself?" She nodded a curt dismissal and turned to her pickup.

So L.C. had another theory, remarkably like Lindstrom's earlier theory about Kathleen. Or maybe L.C. was just blowing that smoke into my eyes—whatever would turn our attention from Kathleen or settle some old scores.

CHAPTER TWELVE

By the time Lindstrom and I were in my car heading back to the city, most restaurants were closing their kitchens. Lindstrom looked drained.

"Want some coffee?"

"I want a drink." Her voice was sharp. She had more snap than showed on her face.

"Any place special?"

"No—just not your friendly neighborhood blue collar bar."

I was a little offended. I shut up and drove. Traffic was heavy. June invites all the cruisers to be out and about. The air was seductively soft if you didn't mind an occasional jolt of exhaust or the intrusive throb of rap from nearby vehicles.

I was turning over in my mind an argument about why dykes were no more likely to be mugged or hit upon in a blue collar bar than in a yuppies' establishment when Lindstrom spoke. "What did Johnson have to say?"

"That you should be careful about your personal safety."

A long silence. "That's all?"

"Basically. He seems to think a man did it."

"So Clawsen's off the hook." Her voice scoffed.

"She isn't a saint, but maybe she didn't do it." I risked a glance. "Unless she hired somebody with a large shoe size."

She was staring out the side window, her right cheek resting against her hand, her elbow on the window ledge.

"Somehow it was easier if I could flat out hate Kathleen."

I couldn't think what to say. She had lost Viv to Kathleen. To blame Kathleen for everything had made sense. But the evidence said something else. I didn't know how to offer real comfort.

I let several silent miles slip by before reopening the conversation. "What did Neely say?"

She took so long to answer I realized I'd asked a personal question. I amended it. "About the case."

"What Johnson said." A sigh escaped. "Do you have anything to drink at your place?"

"Yeah, sure. Patrick brought over some whiskey last Christmas. Mom brought some rum."

"Don't you buy anything for yourself?" A slight amusement.

"Maybe I've got some vodka."

"You're not in A.A.?"

"No. I don't drink much. My uncle Walter does. It discourages me."

"Ah."

A cop response. Cops believe more in sociology than social workers do. They just take the negative view, see all the pathologies, little of the hope.

I thought I understood. PIs are much the same. "So, did Neely tell you to watch your butt?"

"Around the department or on the street?" Bitter.

"Well, either."

"Well, both," she mocked.

That left me little to say till we reached my Arsenal Street apartment where we climbed the stairs wearily.

I found my meager stock of liquor at the rear of a bottom cabinet. "Hm. Acquired a little dust while in the cellar."

Lindstrom didn't respond. I set the array before her: rum, vodka, Johnny Walker Red, Jack Daniels black label. She opted for Jack Daniels. I found two squat juice glasses, and I poured us each a double shot neat. We sat at the kitchen table.

I approached mine warily. To me whiskey is like an unstable dog. I love its color. But it bites without any warning bark. Tonight I had to admit I liked the woozy warmth spreading in my stomach and sinking downward.

To my astonishment Lindstrom drank hers in two swallows and poured another. I guess my face told all.

"No halfway measures," she said. But this time she just took a delicate sip.

"No. It's just that I can't do that."

"Ah, well. Practice." She didn't put much spin on it, though. Her battery was dry. For her this must have been the evening from hell.

"Do you want something to eat?"

She did attempt a smile. "No thanks. I just want to finish this and go home."

I'd passed hunger an hour or two ago, but I thought the smell of greasy onions could change my mind. Lindstrom did look past reviving. The Jack Daniels hadn't done the job.

"Is going back to your place such a good idea?"

She shrugged. Her face looked sadder. What she said was "Have to sometime."

I wanted to kick her for leaning on the cliché to tamp down her emotion, but I changed the subject. "Thomas Aubuchon didn't look real welcome tonight. I'd have thought the Rudders would embrace him."

She shook her head. "No. They blame Thomas for not being man enough to keep Vivian." A wry grin followed. "I was a better man than he was as they saw it. Viv and I didn't argue with them. Their little fantasy got us what we wanted—more acceptance, fewer tensions."

"Papa Rudder looks like an asshole."

"That is not an illusion. Funny, he's controlling in a strong-man kind of way. I mean he didn't beat them, but Daddy's word is pretty much the law. Thomas manipulated Viv by being, or seeming, weak. She didn't marry her father, but she didn't do a whole lot better." She finished the second glass.

I had been taking companionable sips. Now she poured another shot for each of us.

"When did Viv dye her hair blonde?" I asked.

"I don't know. A month ago maybe. I got the idea it was to please Kathleen, though Viv denied it. She had beautiful auburn hair." Her voice was wistful, but for the first time I thought she accepted the past tense she was using, grudgingly, but at least acknowledging its reality. She swallowed half her glass.

"The creep who murdered her might have thought it was you." I sipped more. I could see how you might come to think you were floating in a warm bath.

She looked confused. "I'm a head taller."

"She was lying down."

"Her I.D. was in her purse."

"That was after. He didn't look there first."

I had used *he* without Lindstrom's objecting. No Kathleen Clawsen at all.

She put an elbow on the table, rested her head on her hand. "I don't want to think about it."

"I don't blame you. But I think you ought to stay here for a while."

"Look, Darcy, if I don't go back now—" She started strong, but her voice cracked on the way. She didn't cry, but I saw how big was the pit gaping before her, a deep one with a dozen different fears writhing like vipers.

"You can't drive."

"Call a cab." She stared at the tabletop. She sounded like a petulant teen.

"If I drive you, will you let me stay over a few nights till we get a better picture of what's going on?"

She pondered it like a trick question. Finally, "Okay."

"Good. Have a drink on me while I get some clothes."

"What about my car?"

"I'll drive you back to pick up your car tomorrow."

All I wanted was a light windbreaker so that I could stash my lightweight .38 in its pocket without a big fuss. When I came back to the kitchen, I put down fresh kibble for Harvey. Despite the fabled curiosity of cats he'd slept through our entry and kitchen conversation.

"Ready?"

I was impressed. She stood and walked by herself and went down the stairs stiff-legged. She slumped into my Plymouth and complained about the cramped legroom. I ran through the White Castle. Lindstrom shook her head no.

She carped, "That won't cut your alcohol level."

"No, but it will make me a sweeter person," as I magically made four belly bombers disappear.

80

I pulled into Lindstrom's alley, then her parking spot. The Blairs' cleanup crew had left on a porch light. We sat a moment, staring at the house.

"You could sell it."

"Maybe. I'll see."

I couldn't imagine wanting to stay there. But stubbornness was a big part of Lindstrom's character.

"Now or never," she said and got out. I followed her up the narrow walk, her tall, lithe frame lit by the porch light. I'd had those fantasies about following her into her house some summer night. I couldn't find one now. That was all a thousand years ago.

There was a dim light over the kitchen sink. The smell of fresh paint was strong.

"Want a drink?" she asked.

"Sure." I took the easy way out.

She went into the hallway and brought back a bottle. I couldn't see the label. She carried two glasses—smaller than old-fashioned glasses—and half-filled them. "Better not switch. But I've got Scotch if you want it. Cheers." She tossed back her drink.

"This is fine," I said. I brought the glass to my nose, took a tiny sip. Whatever it was didn't like White Castle's belly bombers. "Lovely."

"Do you want the guest room or a couch?"

"The couch. I want to be downstairs."

She nodded and disappeared. I wanted to follow her up, wanted to go before her, checking. But I held back. She was a big girl, a cop. Most of the demons she faced I couldn't protect her from. I thought I heard a muffled trip on the stairs. But nothing more.

I tried my drink again, just a tongue dip. No. Too sweet maybe. I poured most of it into the sink. A sodden PI is not much of a guard dog.

She was back in five minutes. Her voice was thicker when she spoke from behind the stack of pillows and blankets. "The couch in the TV room is longer. Besides, if you can't sleep, you can watch a bad movie."

I followed her. The TV room was narrow. The foot of the couch faced the TV. Two walls had white built-in bookshelves with generous cabinet space below. On the outside wall a TV stand sat before a fireplace. Opposite the couch a computer sat on a desk that lined up with a file cabinet to hold the printer, and a reclining chair was angled for TV viewing. Without windows the room was claustrophobic or cozy, depending. I chose to think of cold winter nights in front of a small fire.

Lindstrom made up the couch by spreading a sheet and leaving two fat pillows and a blanket. Her eyes were red-rimmed, her focus vague, but her hands steady.

"I'm sleeping in the guest room," she said. "Now or never" took her just so far.

"Lindstrom, if you need me for anything, just call out."

"Sure, Darcy. Thanks." She patted my shoulder as though it were I who needed support.

I waited till I heard her reach the top of the stairs. Then I made a quick tour, checking the front and back doors and every window. I stared quite awhile at the bathroom window. Status restored but not improved. I peeked inside the lavatory cabinet, the one under the sink. I pulled out Comet, some anti-mildew stuff, a hefty Liquid Dial refill bottle and arranged them along the window ledge. It would take an amazing B and E not to knock those into the shower.

Back in the TV room, I stripped off my shirt and shoes, but left on my sports bra, pants, and socks. I didn't want to feel defenseless. I fixed the sheet so I could slide into it like meat in a sandwich, put my .38 on the floor close at hand, and arranged the pillows. I slid into the sheet halves and listened for the strange sounds of the house.

Quiet. Not even a clock ticking. My ears strained. I wished for Harvey or a good watch dog. I thought about what had happened here. The All-American nightmare. I thought of Lindstrom, upstairs, confronting that nightmare.

I stretched and wriggled, trying to let fatigue and whiskey sink me. The strangeness of the place—even the smell and feel of the buttery leather of the couch—tweaked my nerves. I concentrated on imagining Harvey's steady purr beside me.

Sometimes when I'm asleep, I can feel myself sleeping, can know I'm enjoying it. Two winks into this sleep, and I was an anesthetized patient.

The insistent 'breep, breep' of the phone that reached down and scooped me out of the dark pit, jangled my nerves. I was both instantly awake and still groggy. I grabbed the gun and jumped up in a smooth motion, my free hand brushing my eyes. A sharp thumping inside my skull reminded me why whiskey never pays.

I saw the phone on the corner of the desk. The 'breep' had stopped.

I went out into the hallway. A dim night light sent its faint beam along the stairway. Lindstrom came out of the hallway shadows to stand at the top of the stair. Her blonde hair was tousled. She wore cotton pajama bottoms, nothing on top. She stood there unselfconsciously, an athlete who'd stood naked in a thousand locker rooms. I was struck by lust, the warmth spreading like whiskey, my heart jolted. The look of her bare shoulders, her breasts perfect and smooth, locked me to the bottom stair. I wanted to look at her for hours, just so, then touch her, just so.

"Who was it?" My voice was gruff. I hoped she'd attribute it to tension of a different sort.

"No one. A breather." She couldn't quite manage a dismissive tone.

I said nothing. I couldn't tell where her eyes were. Mine were all over her greedily. I pushed a scolding voice aside. I stuck my snub-nosed .38 in my pants pocket. "Are you all right?"

She shrugged. "My number's unlisted."

Of course a dedicated breather could sit up half the night spinning out random numbers till he got lucky. But other possibilities intruded.

"Is your number written on your phone?"

"Yes."

"Is it in the bedroom?" She would know which one I meant.

"Yes."

I hadn't noticed. But maybe Viv's killer had. Who knew how much looking about he'd done after the crime? We both thought about it.

She sat on the stairs, her long arms hanging between long legs, a posture of despair, her face down. "Damn, Darcy. You think it could be him?"

"Maybe not. Who else might know your number? The Blairs' crew was here, lots of cops. Every woman rising fast in her department must earn some grudges from the guys she passes. St. Louis is a conservative place. Probably some guys just hate the idea of women cops." I was jabbering.

"Gee, thanks. I feel so much better."

Her sarcasm was better than despair. I moved up the stairs. The faint light was like moon glow around her shoulders. But I couldn't keep my lust pure. Other brain lobes kicked in, the one that wanted to protect her and the one that wanted to make her feel safe and the one that wanted to figure out who made the call.

I sat beside her, not touching her. I stole a look, then looked down the stairs. "Was there a number on your caller ID?"

"Yes. The prefix was 481. I'll track it down tomorrow."

"Okay. Maybe it was whoever killed Viv. Maybe we have to assume he was after you."

"You sure know how to make a girl feel good." She couldn't squeeze her voice dry, though.

I pretended she had. "You noticed." Then I slapped her nearest knee in a hearty, comradely fashion. "So let's brainstorm a list of people who hate your guts."

A silence. Then, ruefully, "Enough to kill me?"

"You sound like we have to winnow from a list of thousands."

"I do have enemies in the department. Like you said. And outside the department some ex-friends who sided with Viv. Maybe an ex-girlfriend before that. I'm not a saint, Darcy."

She shifted her position, and her arm brushed mine. The electric tingle was instant and adolescent. I let my dirty mind off its leash for a moment, imagined how she might be, reined in the loping beast. "We all have laundry lists." My voice was throaty. What did she think? Could she sense all the little hairs of my body bristling beside her?

"Sure. Can you name someone who's ready to kill you?"

I took the question seriously. At first it seemed an easy "no," but there might be some guys who were upset because Miller Security had fouled up their larcenies—and a few had gone to jail.

"I might manage a few. Saints collect grudges, too."

She laughed. I knew it grew out of her edginess, but it was a sweet sound anyway. We exchanged quick smiles, and I rode the exhilaration. If I started touching her now—

But her mood had shifted, too. "All right. The street scum. That's a long

83

list." This was Lindstrom. Her shoulders squared, her head up, the curt dryness to her voice. Touch her and be electrocuted.

"So, can you make a list of those?"

"Some are watching TV at Central Missouri Correctional."

"Fine. Those you eliminate."

"Some are back on the street. Some never left."

"Right. So you'll review those cases."

We were all business, her vulnerability hidden, my lust tucked away.

"Sure."

"Will you tell Johnson about tonight's call?"

"Ah—that. He'll think I have the heebie-jeebies."

"Why not? It's scary."

"I'm a cop."

"Right. They never pee their pants." The lust was sneaking out again. We'd turned toward each other to banter, and I was thinking how absurd I was, fighting to keep my eyes on her face. It all ran together, my wanting and my scolding. I was pissed, too. She sat beside me with none of the modesty that implies sexual context. Had she forgotten? Or maybe for her it was over.

"Sure. But they never talk about it," she said.

"Johnson looks saner than that. Plus, he's got to know how it feels to be an outsider."

"Black men are just as capable as white men of resenting women." She leaned against the banister.

"You don't trust Johnson?"

She shrugged. I looked away. Our little brain chips are programmed. The light and shadow playing on the motion of her shoulders and breasts were trip wires. I wanted to sniff her skin.

"I don't know him," she said.

"Tell Neely."

"Ah, he's as bad as you."

"Meaning?"

"He worries, he fusses."

"I'm not a fusser," I said. I tried for a mock-defensive tone, but it landed at my feet with a thunk.

She reached across and ruffled my hair. "Sure," she said. It was affectionate and dismissive. You don't ruffle the hair of the one you're itching to rut with.

I was pissed and aroused, and the whiskey was coming back to pound the back of my head. I glanced at my watch.

"What time is it?" she asked.

"Three." He must have called at two-thirty.

"Can you go back to sleep?"

"Dunno. Can you?"

"Ought to try." She stood up and offered me a hand.

I took it. I was stiff from sitting cramped on the stair, and my head swam a moment as I stood.

If I kiss her, she will irretrievably know that I am more concerned with my gonads than with her vulnerability. Or I'll find out she's lost interest—our budding romance trampled by Viv's murder and its aftermath. It was scary.

"You'll go with me to the funeral tomorrow—today?" she was saying.

"Yeah. You bet." Maybe the whiskey had left a permanent gravel in my voice.

She patted my shoulder. "Thanks."

I had no where to go but down. "Good night," she called after me.

Back on my couch it took me only three hours to replay every second of our encounter and to rewrite it with happier endings. Masturbation would have helped, but I was lovelorn and wanting the real thing. Just as the red display of the clock announced the morning, my lids drooped, and my twanging body relaxed. I had a wonderful erotic dream in which we both talked dirty and did things to match.

I awoke a little after nine Wednesday morning. Lindstrom was stirring around the kitchen; I smelled the coffee. I stretched and groaned. I felt like a woman who's had good sex and wants more.

"Ah, you're up. No, not quite." Lindstrom was smiling from the doorway. She'd added a tee shirt to her p.j.'s.

"Is that coffee?"

"Yes. How do you like it?"

"Splash of milk."

She disappeared. I pulled on yesterday's shirt and started folding bed clothes.

"It's funny, Darcy. There's a lot I don't know about you." Her voice from the kitchen was cheerful and flirtatious.

"No shit," I said to myself.

CHAPTER THIRTEEN

The rest of the morning was pedestrian. We weren't cheerful. The phone call and the funeral hung like clouds of past and future. At the same time we were trench buddies. It was companionable. We repeated the businesslike portions of our night time conversation, and I got Lindstrom to semi-promise to tell someone at the department about the phone call. We drove back to my place; she gathered up her clothes and headed back to Soulard in her car. I showered and drove to Miller Security.

"And who are you?" Colleen said.

"Your boss. Don't get snippy, missy."

"You've got a stack of messages."

"I'm leaving at three. Funeral."

She looked at her watch.

"I know. But think, Colleen. No one goes to a funeral for fun."

"Did I say anything?"

I poured my own coffee and hid in my office, attached to the phone and the computer, the main tools of my trade. I tried to keep the brain cells aligned to tasks and away from bare-breasted police detectives. My success was modest.

***

At three-thirty p.m., after a dash back to my apartment, I showered again. The day's increasing humidity had left me soggy. Harvey was meowing as I toweled off, complaining about neglect. I agreed but hadn't time to correct it. I looked at my closet. Patrick was right. I did need to invest more there. I pulled on the classic navy pants, found a clean white shirt, chose the red, three-quarter-sleeve, unconstructed blazer. At least I'd be patriotic.

Lindstrom was punctual. She had still another navy and white outfit, contemporary but principled. Her face was solemn, the occasion weighing on her. She told me briefly that the phone number from last night's breather call was a pay phone near Concordia Cemetery.

After that, it was a quiet drive to the Episcopal Church. The service was new to me. Not many South Siders are Episcopalians. Lindstrom and I sat together in a pew behind the Rudders. Colin Lanier sat on the opposite side of Lindstrom. Then a woman attorney, beyond her, Thomas Aubuchon. The service was tough for him. He shed tears and sobbed noisily twice. I tried not to be judgmental. Lindstrom was biting her lip, taking controlled breaths. I wondered if Thomas's way wasn't better. The Rudders were poised, constrained.

I let myself float above the service and sneaked some looks back. I spotted Kathleen Clawsen; incredibly, she was veiled and in black. Later I heard some choked sobs that I assumed came from her. Again Faircloth and Helbraun sat beside her. I couldn't see more without causing comment and a neck crick, so I drifted back above the music and the homily. I didn't want to think about Viv lying bashed and bloody at Michellene or cleaned and cold in her coffin.

I thought about Lindstrom till, the homily over, the final procession beginning, she clasped my hand, tugging hard. Abashed, I squeezed back, purifying my mind. I saw Johnson at the back. His eyes didn't acknowledge me.

We were farther back in the parade than I'd expected. Lindstrom accepted my offer that I drive. She was glum, a hand shielding her eyes.

The Rudders buried their daughter in a modern cemetery, the headstones all flat for mowing. I'd thought they'd choose the more traditional. But this way the walking was easier to the grave side. My fingers sought Lindstrom's, and we stood, hands clasped, two rows behind the Rudders but still on the vividly green artificial turf the undertaker provided.

Near the end Kathleen Clawsen, who had elbowed her way closer to the Rudders, began a keening cry. Her friends soothed and suppressed. I saw Thomas Aubuchon, a mere few feet away, look around, wild-eyed and edgy. He looked guilty of everything: unmanliness, mass murder. By my side Lindstrom stiffened. I squeezed her hand lightly, meaning to reassure. She returned it but then let go. It felt like rejection. It was petty to mind. The sky was blue, cloudless. I was alive.

As we walked to her car, I sensed a sea change. Lindstrom was less burdened. I've seen it before. Maybe the real grief starts only after the funeral when the business is over, and the real solitude begins. But also truly the funeral ritual sometimes lifts the first stone from the heart.

***

The afternoon heat began to close in on us as we were driving back from the funeral through midtown. I could barely hang onto the steering wheel. St. Louis's rush hours are nothing compared to those of New York, Los Angeles, or Calcutta. Unfortunately, I'm not the kind of person who can work up any sense of perspective or gratitude when stranded for thirty minutes on Route 40. The sun was streaming in the back window, and the orange needle on the temperature gauge was creeping upward. If we didn't start moving soon, I'd have to turn off the air conditioner in order to prevent the Toyota's engine from overheating.

I glanced over at Lindstrom, who had lost all remnants of her ramrod posture. She was slumped against the door, trying to get as much of her body in front of the air-conditioning vent as possible. I glanced at all the rolled up windows around us and felt grateful that Lindstrom had insisted we take her car to the funeral. The Plymouth would have been an oven just now.

87

I was glad to have the funeral behind us, but I was a little at a loss about where to go from here. Probably from now on Lindstrom was going to need my skills as a friend much more than she needed a PI. This might indeed be one of those cases that only the police can solve with their inside information on Lindstrom's cases and their more numerous personnel to track down suspects. But it was important that this case get solved soon; I had the sense that Lindstrom couldn't really go back to living her life, couldn't begin to forgive herself, until Vivian's murderer was brought to justice.

When we arrived Lindstrom went upstairs to change clothes, and I flopped on the couch in the den and kicked my shoes off. As I lay back and put my feet up, I wondered if there were any possibility we'd share the guest room that night. Last night had reawakened all my not-so-latent desires for Sarah Lindstrom. Despite my funeral clothes I couldn't keep a grin from sliding across my face. In a moment she came down the stairs looking considerably more cheerful in blue cotton shorts and a tee-shirt from Run, Jane, Run, a fund-raising event for Women's Self Help.

"I'd like to go home, tend to Harvey Milk, and pick up a change of clothes, and get my car," I said.

"Great, on the way back let's stop at the grocery store and pick up something to fix tonight. I'm tired of eating out. Just let me check my messages and get the mail, and I'll be ready."

The first voice on the machine was remarkably like Lindstrom's. "Sarah, honey, I'm just calling to check on you. I know the funeral is today. Are you okay? Your father is worried about you, and so am I. Call me. We'll be glad to come if you change your mind. Take care, honey, and call right away. I'm so sorry."

Lindstrom glanced at me. "Mom and Dad still live in Nebraska. I'll call her after dinner." The next message was a male voice.

"Sarah, sorry I missed you." The voice sounded mechanical, as if generated by a machine. The emotional tone was ambiguous. Was he sarcastic? I looked at Lindstrom but saw no light there. She rewound it and hit the message button again. "Sarah, sorry I missed you."

"Do you know who that is?" I asked.

"No, I don't recognize the voice."

"I don't like the sound of it. If he really wanted to talk to you, he'd have left his name and number. Take out the cassette so we don't lose that message."

She pushed the button on her caller ID box—it showed "private," which meant he'd blocked the caller ID. "Oh, Darcy, forget it. It's probably some damn reporter. I don't want to have to record a new message."

I reached over her arm and popped open the lid of the machine and pulled out the mini-cassette. "Have you got a blank tape or do we need to buy a new one?" She sighed and rummaged through a cabinet drawer until she pulled out a new tape. I plucked it from her fingers and put it in the machine.

"Hi, you've reached the home of Sarah Lindstrom, super-cop. She's too busy cleaning up the streets of St. Louis to answer your call right now, but if you'll leave your name and number, she'll put you on the list of suspects." Lindstrom laughed but hit the rewind button and recorded her own, more somber "at the sound of the tone" message. I pocketed the other mini-tape.

"Have you ever gotten a call like that before?" I asked.

She shook her head.

"I wonder if it is related to the hang-up from last night," I said.

"I doubt it. I get hang-ups all the time. Wrong numbers, people trying to sell stuff. Who knows? It's nothing to worry about, Darcy."

"Last night you knew better." I didn't want to taunt her with being scared. I wanted her to be scared, so she'd take care of herself.

She looked away. "Don't make a federal case out of it. In the middle of the night things are spookier."

"Don't dismiss this, Lindstrom. I'm here in broad daylight, and listening to this guy sends shivers down my spine. My gut tells me that call is not about aluminum siding."

She puffed out her cheeks, blowing out air. "What do you want me to do?"

"Call Johnson. Tell him about these calls."

"All right. I will." She didn't move.

"When?"

She glared at me. "Don't push it."

"Don't procrastinate."

We were ready to push and shove. Her eyes were flint, but she was pale with worry. Change tactics. I softened my voice and said my worst fear. "I think he means he missed you Friday night, Lindstrom. You were his target, not Viv."

She stared at me. I couldn't read her mind, but her face showed a tug of war was going on. I pitched in to help one side. "You've made enemies over the years. And, not to put too fine a point on it, your enemies are likely to be from the killing class."

She looked away and gave the middle distance a good stare, then squared her shoulders. "All right. I'll call Neely."

I nodded, afraid to say more. I eavesdropped as she made the call, reached him, and in succinct cop fashion reported the two phone calls.

CHAPTER FOURTEEN

We were silent on the way to my apartment. I was designing, and reject-ing, ways to keep Lindstrom safe. I suspected she was having a mighty bat-tle with her feelings about Viv's having been killed in her stead.

I picked up the *Post Dispatch* Patrick had thoughtfully put on the kitchen table. The follow-up article on Vivian Rudder's murder had moved back to page four. Incredibly, the *Post* still wasn't publishing Lindstrom's name in connection with the murder. Someone was doing Lindstrom, or per-haps Johnson, a big favor.

The heat had built up at my place despite the pulled shades and opened windows. I shrugged out of pants, shirt, and blazer. I pulled a clean pair of cotton pants and a tee-shirt and a work shirt out of my closet. I stuck under-wear, my clothes, and Kate Allen's latest in a gym bag. A quick trip to the bathroom for my toothbrush. I tossed my funeral clothes in the hamper and stepped into a pair of shorts. When I came back into the living room, Lindstrom was stroking Harvey. She had won him over completely.

"I think we should stay here, Lindstrom. It's only a matter of time until he comes back to the house."

She shook her head. When she spoke, she was fighting tears. "I won't be chased off. I'll stand and fight. You should stay here, though."

I could see this argument was going nowhere, and I didn't want her to pursue the idea of cutting me out, so I picked up my bag and said, "Let's go."

"Wait a minute. If we walk around in terror, or fussing at one another, this pervert wins. Let's just live our lives. Be careful, but not give him that power over us, okay? Let's just have a normal evening."

Lindstrom was either pretty smart or the Queen of Denial. I wasn't at a good distance to see which. I conceded. "A normal evening it is."

We drove separately but stopped together at Schnuck's on South Grand. The evening's heat was intense. The blast of the store's hyperactive air con-ditioner smacked us rudely, but after an initial shiver, I welcomed it. We grabbed a bottle of wine on the way to the checkout line where we had a brief, though subdued, struggle about who was paying and agreed to split the bill. Outside the sky was wearing the yellow pre-storm colors of a St. Louis gully washer. Not that we have gullies, but I've seen flash floods in Forest Park. The temperature had dropped, and the wind was rising.

We dashed for our cars. The Plymouth's steering wheel was still hot. As we drove, a few fat drops plashed down but stopped by the time we reached the house. We ran for the kitchen, and for a minute the mysterious caller's menace fell away.

We immediately started food prep. Lindstrom rummaged in her spice cabinet and talked to herself while she made the sauce and put water on to boil. I washed and cut vegetables for the salad. Soon the kitchen smelled good, and I began to imagine this house as a home and not a crime scene. Lindstrom cooking was a revelation. She hummed and muttered measurements and actually smiled once or twice. It occurred to me that to see Lindstrom only at work—or in bed—was not to know her at all. Maybe there was something really possible between us. Something more than lust and sarcasm. I shook my head. Was I really imagining domesticity with Lindstrom?

I decided I'd risk a first date question. Somehow in the scramble of our sex and bickering we'd never done that basic lesbian ritual.

"So, Lindstrom, when did you come out?"

She looked over her shoulder at me and frowned. "I told my parents I was gay when I was nineteen. I was in college and was talking to them about changing my major to law enforcement. I'd been majoring in business. They kept telling me that being a cop would be too hard for a woman, and I just blurted it out." She shook her head at her younger self. "It's okay now, but both Mom and Dad had a tough time of it for a while. No matter what you've read about permissive Scandinavians, a lesbian daughter wasn't part of their world view. But they both love me very much. We worked through it. After telling them, I never cared about anyone else's knowing or not knowing, really." She sighed. "Until now."

I didn't argue with her. Of course she cared. If she hadn't cared if her co-workers knew that she was a lesbian, it would be common knowledge. She'd have had a picture of Viv on her desk and been inviting Neely over for family barbecues.

A distant rumble of thunder told me the storm was still building.

She turned the heat down under the sauce and folded her arms across her chest. "They can't fire me for being gay, but I know I won't be able to work in the department. Things will go wrong, and I'll be blamed. People will snicker or grow quiet when I'm around. It just won't work. Hell." She pressed her knuckles against her upper lip. "Damn, Darcy. All I've ever wanted to be is a cop. A cop, a detective, head of the Homicide Squad, and when I'm too old for the department, teacher at the Academy. I wanted to die of a heart attack at seventy-two teaching some nineteen-year-old how to cuff a violent perp."

"Lindstrom, you need to get back to work. Just go back and do your job. I'm sure it will be tough sometimes, but hell, the half of the force that has any brains probably suspected you were gay long ago. The other half needs an opportunity to grow up. This is the nineties. You'll do your job, and all the dykes and fags still in uniform will finally have a hero."

"I don't want to be a hero. I want to be a cop."

"Of course, you want to be a hero, that's why you want to be a cop. You just imagined being a hero would be easy."

She glared at me for a second, then snorted. "Who appointed you philosopher for a day?"

I decided not to respond in kind. "You're a good cop. Just do your job. That's all they pay you for." I turned and went back to slicing mushrooms. A sharp crack—the ceiling splitting?—made us jump, then laugh with relief as we realized what it was: the storm was right over us.

Ten minutes later we were eating the first meal either of us had tasted in days. Over dinner I described the rainy afternoon I came out to my mom, Betty, and her subsequent activities in PFLAG.

After dinner we brought our glasses and the remainder of the wine into the den. We sat on the couch and finished the wine over Lindstrom's first ill-fated romance with a ROTC soldier in college. Midway through her story I heard the rain start, accompanied by timpani rolls of thunder. The TV den felt snug and cozy.

The evening had had a quiet, anti-climactic feel to it. Despite the menace of the phone call, we'd built a fort of sorts from the ordinary: preparing a meal, comparing coming out stories. Sitting close to her on the couch felt comfortable; for once Sarah Lindstrom's presence wasn't electrifying me. I was close to her without experiencing meltdown.

When she rubbed the back of her neck, it was easy and natural to reach out with my left hand to rub her neck and shoulders for her. The muscles were knotted and tight but gradually loosened as I kneaded them. The right hand was required to do an adequate job. I felt the first betrayal in my fingertips. Touching her skin was undermining the fort's foundation. Every touch was wired. I frowned, trying to hide the giddiness that swept through me. Was Lindstrom oblivious to the voltage charging between us? As if to answer, she sighed and leaned back against me.

"That's good. Very good."

Could that be an invitation?

She smiled and touched my hand lightly with her first two fingers. I leaned over and kissed her, trying to be gentle and suave. She didn't slap me. Outside another rumble of thunder grumbled overhead.

She kissed me next, not really looking at me, and our hands began to explore, pushing aside clothing. I know she touched me, but I scarcely noticed. My fingers had a mission of their own, to trace every inch of her. She was firm and soft and every bit as passionate under the ice as I remembered her, melting the protective shield she'd worn since Viv's murder. She whispered "Darcy," and I eased her down onto the creamy leather.

Always before she'd been the one initiating our couplings. I'd be aching to touch her; she'd keep her distance till, when I least expected it, she'd reach for me. Any proud resistance I'd planned collapsed, erased by my longing.

Now I was afraid to breathe, afraid to shatter the spell of it. She was all magic, every inch of her, the soft, the hard, the smooth, creased, outside, inside, salty, sweet. My fingers danced; my mind raced to follow them. She turned her head, clutching me to her but hiding her eyes. Unbidden, the upstairs bedroom flashed in my mind. Uncleaned, bloodied. I shut my own eyes, pushed it away, opened them, let my fingertips focus on the slippery flesh, led my mind back to her: cheekbones, collarbone, breasts, belly. Still, moving. Parts of our clothing scritched across the leather couch. A sharp jolt—compassion for her vulnerability, her griefs, her loss—struck at me. I shoved it back, behind the fingers that sought. Oh, there, yes, her thighs affirmed. Dry, wet. Viv's name shouted in my ears. I looked at the woman twisting under me, beside me. Her eyes were closed.

"Who am I?"

"Oh, Darcy," she answered. Voice strange, strangled, impatient, familiar. Squeeze, release. Push, slide. Close, open, close.

I concentrated, thrusting aside all the horrors of the last few days, shutting away all the doubts of the previous months, intent on the heat we were creating, blotting out everything, past or present, but the focused tracing by my fingers.

Either seconds or hours later the phone rang.

We jumped as we had from the earlier thunder crack. Lindstrom's face drained of color. We peeled apart quickly, fumbling with our clothing as though caught by a spying eye. She pushed me aside and rushed to the phone on the desk. I stood up, still rearranging my clothes.

"Hello?" There was a silence of a few seconds, and Lindstrom clenched her fist. "Who is this? Don't hang up." But the caller obviously did. She shook her head and put the receiver gently down on the phone.

"It was him." She finished buttoning her shorts.

"What did he say?"

"He said, 'Do you know who I am, Sarah? Do you know who I am?' Then he just hung up."

"We have to tell Johnson. Get him to put a tap on the phone."

"It wouldn't be admissible unless he knew he was being recorded."

"Lindstrom, admissibility isn't the point. We need to catch this jerk so you'll be safe. He meant to kill you, don't you get that? Now he's going to torture you before trying again."

"You're not a cop, Darcy. There is no use in knowing who he is if I can't put him behind bars forever. This isn't the wild west where I can go out and eliminate this asshole because he irritates me. We need a good arrest and solid evidence."

"Okay, then let's help Johnson get it by telling him about this call."

"I will." She sighed and leaned back against the couch. Rain knocked at the roof. I reached out to touch her, but she shook her head. "No, Darcy. You have to go home now." The Ice Queen was back.

"What do you mean go home? You surely don't think I'm going to leave you alone, at his mercy."

"I'm not at his mercy. I'm a big girl, and if he comes in here, it'll be his blood on the walls this time. I won't have you here. I can't protect you." She stood and handed me my overnight bag.

"Call Johnson first," I stalled.

"I'm going to the station to make a report, and you're going home. I'll call you tomorrow." She stepped around me when I didn't move out of her way. She was out of the room in two strides. I followed with my bag.

"Lock up after me," she said, turning away.

She was out into the storm before I could protest further. I stood on the back porch watching sheets of rain drench her as she ran toward the Toyota.

"Damn" was my only editorial comment. I closed and tested the door. "Damnit, Lindstrom," I said quite sternly. I watched her Toyota disappear into the night. Then I hunched my shoulders and plunged into the pelting rain.

Even the short dash to the Plymouth soaked me. My skin stung from the rain's ferocity. A glance in the rear-view mirror showed my hair slicked down like a seal's pelt.

My insides swirled with enough chaos to match the storm: Lindstrom had thrown me out of her house. Was she throwing me out of her life? Why hadn't I just stayed put? Why didn't she trust me? Had she ever truly cared for me? Was she really in imminent danger? What could I do to protect her? Enough questions to script a soap opera, and with every beat my heart pumped out a new one, half-formed, anxiety-driven. I was spinning apart.

Slow down. Deep breath. Think, Meg.

Another slash of lightning lit Lindstrom's back yard.

Lindstrom was on her way to the Clark Street station. I couldn't believe even a determined killer was hanging about on a night like this. Bad guys look after their creature comforts. Unless this one was really bizarre. Suppose this guy was an authentic monster, as cunning and as cagey as my worst nightmare? Would he drop by after the storm—persist on the theory that Lindstrom would let her guard down?

I shuddered. That set off a series of shivers. My clothes were pasted to my skin. I doubted that the temperature had dipped below the 60s, but I was definitely chilled—body, mind, soul. I felt naked and weepy. Hardly the white knight on a charger protecting the proud princess. The too proud princess.

I could try to roust Walter, get him to watch the castle while I raced home for my .38. Or I could call Leroy Vergis, another operative we hire from time to time. Or I could play the odds. Unless the menacing caller was staked out nearby, chances were he wasn't going to venture from his lair till the storm passed. I eased the Plymouth out of the alley at a crawl; even full steam ahead, the wipers were inadequate. I snaked around the block, studying parked cars for signs of life. The goose bumps were thickening on my arms, my body's futile attempt to raise the heat. I glanced toward my back seat. For once no stray sweatshirt to use as a towel.

I turned the Plymouth homeward. Just past eleven and the streets were nearly empty; the storm had scoured traffic from the Soulard neighborhood.

When I crossed Jefferson, the storm was slackening. I could now see every other swipe of the blades, and the thunderous din on the car roof no longer suggested going over Niagara in a barrel.

Sometimes I think the Plymouth heads home like a horse to the barn. I parked next to Patrick's colicky but treasured old MG. I braced for the run to the building. Inside, I raced up the stairs like a woman demented—to find a startled Patrick staring at me. Irritatingly, though his short, thinning hair was dark from damp, his white shirt still looked crisp and his Levis dry.

"Meg! You look like something Harvey dragged in."

"Save the compliments, Patrick." I fished for my keys.

"No, you look terrible. I mean, are you all right?" Usually Patrick has the gift of suave, but his floundering betrayed concern.

"Come with me, boyo, and throw down some kibble for Harvey."

I kept walking and talking as he trailed me into my apartment. I peeled off my tee shirt as I walked and tossed the soggy knot on the floor. "I am cold and starving. Can you fix something to eat while I take a quick hot shower?"

If I'd asked Lindstrom that, she'd have given me a debate. Patrick heard my tone and said, "I know you don't have fresh bread" while turning back to his place.

"Not even moldy," I called after him as I tugged at my pants. They were clinging like a girdle—like I imagined a girdle. I started the shower, finished peeling out of my clothes, and gave myself over to the welcome cascade of warmth.

In my bedroom I searched for socks, tee shirt, briefs, jeans, sweatshirt. Warm and dry were the only requirements. I'd left the snubbie .38 till last. Carrying it doesn't give me a thrill. I wish I lived in a world where outsmarting bad guys was enough. I was strapping on my nylon shoulder holster when Patrick stuck his head in. "Your repast is served. What's that?"

"You know what it is." Patrick is truly averse to guns, even small ones. Like some people are to snakes he says. Like some people are to queers, I say—a learned response that can be unlearned.

Tonight I said, "I think Lindstrom is in danger."

Patrick's ears twitched, at least metaphorically. I did just the headline news about the caller and his threats. No details about Lindstrom and me till the end. Which made my being kicked out into the storm a surprise ending. "So I need you to pack up that repast. Sorry I didn't mention it."

Maybe I looked as pathetic as I sounded to my own ears. Meg Darcy, great PI, can't stand her ground. Meg Darcy, great lover, suddenly a total loser. But all he said was, "Give me five, and I'll be ready with the sandwiches packed and the coffee into a thermos."

I was too twitchy to wait idly, so I followed him into his apartment where he disassembled two plates of midnight snacks with a presentation worthy of Duff's and repacked them into a small but perfectly designed picnic basket. Instead of wine, he put in the thermos plus two mineral waters. Patrick has a gene for sandwich making. Despite my glumness my appetite reasserted itself as more than a craving for food.

"Won't the police guard Lindstrom round the clock?" he asked.

"You'd think," I said wearily. "But what have they got to justify a round-the-clock-surveillance besides a tape with ambiguous threats?" I shrugged. "If the cops show up in force, I'll come home."

Something flickered in his eyes, but all he said was, "Let me grab a sweatshirt, and we're off." He handed me the picnic basket.

"Who's this 'we'? You aren't going."

"Meg. Don't be silly. Look at yourself. You aren't in shape to take on a killer."

"This isn't about fashion, Patrick."

"Oh, funny. You look drained."

"You know I don't like to involve you in my work."

"That's a bad B movie line. You're playing the husband. Cut it out." He disappeared into his bedroom and came back with a Wash U sweatshirt and two narrow trays of tape cassettes. In the interval I'd had time to consider marching back alone into the storm and maybe into Lindstrom's icy stare. Patrick's company offered comfort.

"All right. If you won't play the perfect, stay-at-home wife."

"Wife is okay. I don't do doormats." He was checking for his keys. "Anymore," he added with quiet conviction. I tried to guess if that was about Mark or Bob, but I was too anxious to think it through.

CHAPTER FIFTEEN

Outside we found the storm tapering off. The whole outdoors was deliciously air conditioned. I'd stopped back by my apartment to grab dry towels. I used one to wipe my driver's seat and two to sit on. Patrick tucked his gear in the back seat after making his usual complaints about a resale shop on wheels. The tidiness issue is a deeper divide than gender most of the time.

The drive back to Lindstrom's took only seven minutes down Russell. We rolled our windows down. I needed the windshield wipers only on the lowest setting. Sometimes a storm like this one cools us down for a day or two; sometimes within hours the humidity creeps back. St. Louis weather is interesting as in the Chinese curse "May you live in interesting times."

Rare for us, Patrick and I didn't talk much on the ride. I don't know what his thoughts were, but mine were down to the basics: Drive, see that Lindstrom was all right, stay awake. Alert was more than I could stretch to.

I turned into the alley behind Lindstrom's house. The rain had slowed to intermittent drips.

"I'm going to check the perimeter," I said.

"What do I do if the killer shows up?" Patrick asked.

"Honk like blazes."

I was nervous enough to pull the .38 for my tour. My movements I kept slow and careful. Staying awake was suddenly no problem. Even the hair on my forearms was tense. The brick pathway was slippery from rain. I stepped onto the grass, also slippery. The night was quiet, without the summertime bustle of Soulard on a dry weekend. The drops off the trees sounded magnified like the indoor fountains of the Botanical Gardens during their orchid show.

I stood before the porch for a moment, studying the shadows before moving onto it, testing the door. Still locked. Ditto the window from the kitchen. I moved off the porch, made a decision; I'd do the north side next, where Lindstrom's house butted up to its neighbor with a small narrow walkway cut under Lindstrom's house, a brick tunnel, typical of this part of Soulard, wide enough for just one to walk through. I stood outside and built my courage. Then I used a trick that serves me well when I arrive late at a movie. I stepped into the pitch black walkway, stood still, closed my eyes, counted a fast sixty, then ten more because fast was cheating. I opened my eyes and could see in the dark. But not much. This walkway was designed for creep shows. I inched forward a distance I could normally cover in five or six strides, saw the light at the end of this tiny tunnel, Michellene's street light.

I checked the cars parked along the street, could already recognize a few neighbors' vehicles. All looked empty, locked up for the night.

I walked to the other side, where Lindstrom had a strip of open side yard. This was the side Viv's killer had used to enter the house, but nothing was moving there now.

I rejoined Patrick and answered his inquiring look. "Seems okay. Feed me."

"Yes, miss," he said in his best *Upstairs, Downstairs* mode.

I didn't talk again till I finished the apple that followed the crusty bread, fancy cheeses, crisp veggies, and Patrick's inspirational sauce—all of my sandwich and half of his.

"Patrick, you're a god."

"It's been said." He's a bit smug about his culinary skills and who can blame him? Lavish praise is a small price.

He handed me a mug of steaming coffee. "Regular tonight and extra strong. I figured you wanted the jolt."

I nodded, sniffed. Hazelnut, my favorite. "You are divine."

He grinned, stretched his long legs sideways, hampered by the Horizon's limited space. "And what does m'lady wish for after-dinner entertainment?"

The Plymouth has few amenities. In winter the heater was adequate. In summer the air-conditioning consisted of rolled-down windows. Its below-par radio I'd replaced with a radio-tape deck, my one concession to hours spent in the car. Tonight we had two trays of Patrick's cassettes to choose from.

"You choose," I said. "But it needs to be soft."

"Scare off the killer?"

"Wake the neighbors."

Miller Security does more surveillance than you might suppose given our business clientele. It's one way to find out who's heisting the tools or who's selling industrial secrets.

But it is a job I hate. If you entertain yourself too well, you'll miss what you're watching for. If you don't, the hours crawl.

Having a partner helps. You can keep up a sporadic conversation. You can spell one another. There were no fast-food places or all-night bars close enough, so when the time came I took Patrick into Lindstrom's yard and told him to pee behind the forsythia bush.

The night was settling into one of post-storm coolness. The air smelled clean with a nearly springtime freshness. We left the windows down but were glad of our sweatshirts. Minutes before midnight, just as Patrick was raising the issue of why *Bound's* lesbians stirred less furor than the women in *Thelma and Louise*, Lindstrom's Toyota slid into the slot next to me.

She didn't look my way once. Her profile was all I got as she slipped from her car. The roof blocked her face while she locked up. "Lindstrom," I said, weakly I admit. Just like in junior high, I could tell she was going to snub me. She marched up the pathway, shoulders straight, head high, and disappeared into the house. We watched as light after light flicked on inside.

"What spell rendered us invisible?" Patrick asked.

And speechless. I just sat there, cheeks flaming, totally humiliated. How could she? Why would she?

I was way too mad to cry. Good thing because tears just then, in front of Patrick, would have necessitated violence—her murder, my suicide. I sucked on that fantasy a minute before I recognized the batterer's world view and spat it out with an audible choke.

"Okay?" Patrick asked solicitously. I knew it was a measure of his caring that he asked such a stupid question.

I was scalded. Burned by the return of the Ice Queen.

I jumped from the front seat and climbed into the back, rummaging frantically in the debris, raising a cloud of dust and two dead french fries from the floor. But I found the el cheapo cell phone Walter insisted I carry.

I punched in her number, listened to the answering machine through the beep. "Lindstrom, pick up."

Nothing.

"Pick up, damnit."

She did. "Why are you and Healy parked in my driveway at midnight? I told you to go home, not invite a party here."

My teeth were in the way of my tongue. I had too much to blurt out. I took a deep, steadying breath. "Lindstrom, be sensible. We're here to keep watch. We're here to protect you."

Patrick made no pretense of not listening. He hung over the seat, giving me a big thumbs up.

"A PI and a civilian protecting a cop? Isn't that backwards?" So cold the syllables clicked.

"Don't be an ass, Lindstrom." I knew my mother Betty would have said that vinegar was no way to catch flies. At least I'd toned it down. My impulse had been to say, "Don't be a prick," but respect for Patrick restrained me.

"She hung up." I hadn't thought she could top waltzing by without recognizing my existence.

Astonishment gave way to fury. I dialed again, nodded my head through her machine's message, waited again for the beep, and yelled, "Lindstrom, we aren't leaving. You can sleep tight because we will be here." I punched End.

For several moments what passes for silence reclaimed the night. A breeze through the trees sent a shower of raindrops down from the leaves. Romanovsky and Philips crooned a lullaby. My breathing rasped. A distant dog barked.

"Something tells me Uncle Patrick is missing a chapter."

I said nothing. To say I didn't want to talk about it would be a lie. I wanted to tell him in minute detail how unfair and wrong and arrogant Lindstrom was being—and rude besides. But all the right words jammed up. Images of junior high returned. Seventh grade. My buddy Nancy Flowers waltzed right by me in the cafeteria, side by side with MaryLou Winchell, on their way to sitting at Julie McInerney's table. To capture the exact nuance of that snub, I'd have to be Jane Austen, but the broad swatch of passion unleashed I'd recognized finally in high school's required *Macbeth*. Lady Macbeth had her reasons.

I was following all these curlicues of thought—though thought scarcely described the gush of feelings roiling inside—when Patrick spoke in his best, most patient therapist's voice. "What's going on, Meg?"

"I'm in love with a woman who doesn't love me."

"How do you know she doesn't?" Patrick said gently. We both ignored the historical fact that he himself had charged Lindstrom with that precise indifference on previous occasions.

"She doesn't act like she loves me."

"Tell me."

I gave him a brief but frank account of the last few days, this time not omitting the night's lustful groping. "Then she kicked me out." I tried not to squall, but found no way to pronounce those words and squeeze out all the whine.

"Meg, Meg." Gentle chiding. "She's not rejecting you. She's scared. Someone she loved has just been murdered, and she feels responsible. She couldn't bear to risk anything like that again, so she had to push you away. She's too entangled in grief and fear to be tender. You have to wait."

He was saying what I didn't want to hear, and he had the credibility of a gay man who'd lived during the plague years. He knew all about death and fear rudely shoving aside love and sex.

I shook my head, denying his truths.

"Wait till this is over. Give her time," he said.

"When this is over, she'll go back to being cold and utterly self-sufficient." All right. Whining.

"Mmm," he said like the doctor who hears something really juicy at the end of his stethoscope—juicy and deadly. "If that's the essential Ice Queen, why do you want her in your life?"

"Patrick, that's too therapeutic." I hate a good question.

"You want to save her, have her grovel at your feet, swept up in a tidal wave of gratitude?"

"Are you forgetting the part where she swears to be my love slave forever and to obey my slightest whim?"

"In other words, you want to be in control of this relationship?"

"Yeah, like that. I want to top." I knew the term from reading Kate Allen. My own sex life was more vanilla than I cared to admit.

"And you think Lindstrom doesn't?—want to be in control I mean."

Well, of course. We knew that. Before Kate Allen, I'd have said Lindstrom was a born BA for boss ass. "Sure, but—"

"Suppose your ex had been killed in your apartment? Wouldn't you be feeling vulnerable and wanting to hide away safely what's most precious to you?"

"You mean me?" A disbelieving croak.

"Yes, yes."

A silence fell while I chewed on it. I was neatly boxed. Maybe Lindstrom was unworthy of my affection. Maybe she was worthy—and cared enough to worry about my safety. Maybe Patrick was right, and she was too heartsick with guilt and grief to welcome my love. That L-word again. It had slipped out... "I love a woman who doesn't love me." Did I?

A cool breeze touched my head like my memory of Betty's fingers when my forehead and cheeks were feverish. I let the night sounds creep back into my awareness. The drips from the wet leaves were irregular, not like the pulse of faucet drips. Every now and then, a small quiet breeze orchestrated a xylophone cascade of water, scattering drops onto the roof and windshield. The scent of flowering bushes mingled with the alley's dumpsters. I leaned back into the seat, pushing against the floorboards to unkink my legs. My eyes stung from unshed tears. My head hurt from tension.

Did I?

"Well, hell," I said flatly.

"Oh, sure, be philosophical about it."

I made a face.

You'd think we'd said enough, but we rehashed it two or three times till we wore it out. Patrick is even more sympathetic than Betty. But, I've stopped apologizing for his being male; it's his cross to bear. He's a champion listener and soothing clucker. I soaked it all up like warm, soapy water on tired, achy feet.

Finally we wound down. I did another tour of the premises but didn't walk onto the porch. I didn't want Lindstrom to mistake me for an intruder. The clouds raced overhead, and from time to time moonlight created shadows that moved if we stared too long. I've been urging Walter to buy some of those army goggles that improve nighttime vision by a kazillion. He hasn't seen the need.

The coffee Patrick had brewed was bad for the peeing situation, but good for the nerves. We were both jangled and alert till three. By three-thirty Patrick was stifling yawns, and the intervals between wisecracks grew longer. Every now and then I'd sent him around the block to stretch his long legs. Now I suggested he recline his seat, just to rest a bit. He did without even a feeble protest. I looked for an old fifties fave tape whose songs I knew from Betty's collection. I turned it low and sang along. The lyrics were trite but easy to recall.

Twice I saw a police cruiser go by. Each time their lights warned me of their approach, and I ducked down till they left. They didn't get out to check the extra car.

When it came time for me to check around the house again, I slipped out quietly. The house was still lit up. She had her own night watch. Silly, of course, she in there, us out here, all of us holding a strange memorial vigil for Vivian Rudder. Thinking of Vivian prodded me awake, and I made my tour briskly.

In the next hour the sky lightened slowly into sunrise. I was surprised to find myself shivering slightly. Patrick snored softly, a fact I promised myself never to tell him.

At five real daylight came, and the first neighbor walking a dog. Shortly after I hallucinated and saw Lindstrom in Levis and a Rams tee shirt walking down the pathway with two coffee mugs. I shook my head, and the vision came closer. I slipped out quietly, not closing the door, and met her a third of the way. Even after what was probably a restless night, she looked brand spanking new in the soft morning light. A closer look revealed some puffiness around her eyes.

"I keep forgetting you aren't easily discouraged," she said.

She handed me a mug; it was steaming hot, and a sip told me she remembered how I liked it. "Do you want me to be?"

She looked away, studying the much peed-upon forsythia by her garage. "Ah, there's a question." She let her eyes rove over my face and past me to the Plymouth. "Did Healy go home?"

"He's asleep," I said, lowering my voice.

"Umm," she said, and turned back up the pathway. I followed meekly. When she reached the porch, she sat on the top step. She looked up at me, her eyes in a squint. "You can sit."

Several juvenile retorts rushed forward, but a grownup squashed them. I sat down beside her. Our upper arms brushed, and the tingle flew through the total circuitry. Maybe it's body physics, not body chemistry. Or her molecules dance round mine, creating upheavals. She leaned away a bit, as though she'd felt it, too. I was obliquely, absurdly flattered. Her movement away felt more like compliment than rejection.

"Were you able to sleep?" I asked, emboldened to be personal.

"I was well-guarded, wasn't I?" Her tone was wry, but underneath it ran a weariness.

"Did it help?" I told myself I wasn't fishing for compliments.

"Some." She sipped from her mug. "The problem isn't just what's out there. Going to sleep isn't much to look forward to. I don't want to keep finding Viv, over and over." She puffed her cheeks out with air, let it slip through pursed lips. "Not to whine."

"Of course not."

She glanced at me, smiled ruefully. "You really are pushy."

"Umm." I looked into her eyes. Sleep deprivation aside, despite puffiness and red rims, they were a startling blue. I'd once accused her of Paul Newman's industrial strength contacts, but she'd said "Norwegian DNA."

"Did you come out to pick a fight?" I asked.

"No. To say I know you were trying to help last night."

Not exactly an apology. The 'trying' was patronizing. Still, for Lindstrom, pretty good.

"We didn't catch the caller. But he didn't come back either. Like that old, old Boatman's Bank ad about there being no sharks in the Mississippi River."

She looked at me blankly.

102

"Probably before you left Nebraska," I said. "Maybe we succeeded in scaring him off."

"Ah." She nodded understanding. "Maybe. But you and Healy can't keep up a vigil every night. We need to catch this creep. Keeping me safe is only half."

"But an important half—to me." There. I'd said it.

"Darcy, I just feel so—so weird right now." She gestured, spilled some coffee on her knee. The uncharacteristic awkwardness touched me as much as her tone.

"Okay, okay," I said defensively. "I want to catch him, too. But not by using you as bait."

"Who's better? We know he's picked me."

"Is that what Johnson says? Neely?"

"Johnson says I might want to visit Nebraska. He agreed with you about the phone tap, by the way. A tech will be over today to install it. Neely says I can live with his family."

I felt disappointed. I wasn't the only white knight on the field. But I bit that back. "Sounds good to me."

"For how long?"

"Till somebody catches this guy."

"Most murders aren't solved—if there's any mystery at all attached. Not to mention how long the South Side rapist has gone on."

I nodded. I'd give up my next raise to catch that predator. But she hadn't deflected me. "I saw two cop cars drive by last night in a slow trawl. That's adequate only if this garbage cooperates by breaking in on schedule."

"Department resources are stretched thin."

"Mine aren't. Let me move in—just till this creep is caught or we're pretty sure he's discouraged."

"I'm afraid you'll get hurt."

"Two against one. I'll watch your back, you watch mine."

A longer silence. "I'm afraid you'll—" She shook her head, pulled in a deep breath. "I really can't handle romance right now."

"Romance?" My best scoff. Inside I hurt. I could smell the minty scent of her morning soap, feel the warmth of her leg through her Levis when she shifted on the step. "Don't flatter yourself that you're irresistible. Me, I can switch it on or off like Philip Marlowe or Sam Spade." I've never strung two bigger lies together in my life.

"Who?"

"V.I. Warshawski? Kinsey Millhone?"

She was looking at me as though I'd grown an extra nose. "Cops never give PIs recognition," I said.

"Darcy, if you stay here, you can't do drugs." She spoke softly, as though breaking bad news to me gently.

But I'd heard her assent. "What *do* you read?"

"You can bring Harvey."

Oh, yeah, sure, the floating fur ball would be welcome. "Can't. He's a

103

one-apartment cat. Besides, he'd miss Patrick."

"Healy can't come. Maybe to dinner. No more overnights."

On his behalf I nearly sniffed; in truth, I knew Patrick would commit murder himself to live in Soulard.

I was starting to grin, hearing the escalating playfulness in her voice, till she said, more soberly, "And when it's over, you have to leave and go home."

"Oh, I'm outta here," I said meanly. Just like I'd told Nancy Flowers 'I don't care, I don't care.'

"And if it gets too dangerous, you'll leave?"

"Negotiable." Easier to believe than a flat out lie.

She examined me for trustworthiness. A mote of skepticism crept into her eye.

"A deal?" I stuck out my hand, forcing the issue.

"You're on good behavior."

"In intimate circles I'm known as Meg Good Behavior Darcy."

"Ah, yes." She gripped my hand hard.

CHAPTER SIXTEEN

I don't know how much he'd overheard, but Patrick's timing was perfect. He emerged from the Plymouth with exaggerated stretches and yawns and sauntered up the path toward the porch.

"Meg, I told you not to let me sleep in."

He and Lindstrom regarded each other with their usual wary civility. They kept their complaints for my ears.

But not all their zingers. "Glad your guard duties didn't interfere with your sleep," Lindstrom said.

Patrick handled it with aplomb. "I knew Meg had it covered. She'd wake me if I needed to run for the police."

That fragmented into several pieces of shrapnel like a hollow-point. What was Lindstrom, chopped liver? I didn't know what they were so edgy about. I put a heavy foot in and changed the subject to breakfast. Lindstrom excused herself. She had a brunch date with Mrs. Rudder and Viv's sister Ruth. Lindstrom didn't look happy about it. "I'll call you this afternoon," she promised.

A nugget of worry made me want to stay till she left. Thinking of her alone and vulnerable in the house, in the shower, was scary. But I didn't want to push too hard. Our new arrangement was fragile. I told myself she was safe here in the daytime.

Patrick was starting to fidget, so I said my goodbyes, and we crawled back into the Plymouth, which he was now calling Motel 6.

"Where to?" I asked. I was feeling buoyant, relieved. I was running on high, the exhilaration of winning a big concession from Lindstrom swimming in my veins.

"We're here, why not do Soulard?" Patrick asked.

I headed the Plymouth toward Lafayette two blocks away. We could have walked it, but I didn't want to leave my car at Lindstrom's as though I had a right to one of her parking slots. The fine points of our agreement weren't yet clear. The parking goddess blessed me; I found space right on Lafayette.

Soulard Farmer's Market, a huge brick building, takes up two city blocks between 7th and 9th Streets. Nearly one hundred-fifty different vendors hawk their products from the sides of the concrete walkways that run from the inside of the building through the outside stalls, producing some of the noisy confusion of a stock exchange. If you pause even a moment to appraise the oranges or bell peppers, a seller pushes you to buy. You can buy flea market items and tee shirts and handicrafts, but the point of the market is its fresh produce. The smells tantalize: flowers, fruit, fresh bread, coffee, spices, veggies.

As usual we did our preliminary tour up and down, just checking out the day's offerings. Next we headed for the small stand run by an Asian family selling miniature doughnuts. I bought a dozen. Then we wandered back outside. Saturday is the busiest day; the doors open at six a.m. But even a weekday like this Thursday offers a peek at the city's diversity: a black kid on a bike swooping over the bricks; an elderly white man with his net bag for shopping; a young Asian couple with a baby stroller; a black family with two teens and two toddlers; two middle-aged white men with canvas bags full of produce. These last two elicited a look between Patrick and me.

"Brothers," he said. He'd run across the street to the corner of Lafayette and 7th where the St. Louis Bread Company has a small outpost. I chose a bench that put our backs to the later stages of rush hour traffic on 7th, all charging toward downtown. Instead, I wanted to people watch, a far different pleasure from the tedium of surveillance. The sun was bright; the sky a vivid cloudless blue; the after-rain crispness was melting from the air. In an hour we'd be muttering about St. Louis humidity.

"Here's your hazelnut," he said, handing me the takeout cup.

"What did you get?"

"Dark French roast."

I offered him the doughnut bag. "These are health food if you eat them after staying up all night."

"Hmm," he said around his first one, "So I've heard."

We munched contentedly. He didn't have to be at the bookstore till one. After years of obsessing about being on time, my character was collapsing. I was going to be late for work just because I was larking about, and I didn't care. Seemed to be happening often these days. Maybe Viv's murder had put that into perspective. Being alive and having people to love was more important than slavish obedience to a clock. Could Lindstrom love a woman who occasionally blew off work?

"Patrick, we ought to do this more often."

"That's what we always say, Meg."

I scrutinized him. "You know, you might go with that Bruce Willis stubble look."

"Think so?" He rubbed a testing finger under his chin. "I dunno. Might attract Demi Moore."

We ambled speculatively over a few more celebrity lives till we finished the doughnuts. Patrick leaned back and closed his eyes, enjoying the sun beaming on our backs. I studied the market's impressive brick edifice.

"How old is this place?" I asked idly.

"The market started around 1799. It's probably the oldest public market west of the Mississippi."

"They don't know?"

"I don't think the *Post* was covering it." He opened his eyes, sat up. His newest thing is St. Louis history. "This is one of the oldest parts of the city." He sipped coffee.

"Wow," I said to encourage him.

He nodded. "Soulard had a fruit orchard here. His widow Julia Soulard donated it to the city; she said the land had to be used for a public market."

He knew I liked it when women got mentioned in history—and not as kindling for stake burnings.

"So this building is French?" I studied it, trying to notice details.

"No, no. Actually it's based on some Renaissance hospital in Italy."

I whistled appreciatively. "How do you remember that?" He looked sheepish. He dug a crumpled pamphlet from his jeans. "I saw this brochure in the market and read it while I was waiting for our coffee at the Bread Company."

I hooted, but not too long. I didn't want to discourage him from learning and teaching me historical tidbits. "But you haven't mentioned the most important fact about the market, have you?"

"It's on the National Registry of Historic Landmarks?"

"The market master is a woman."

He knew which way to jump. "So that it explains it," he said admiringly.

"Yes, it does," I said.

"Want more coffee?"

"Even I may have hit my hazelnut limit after last night."

"Well, what did we learn from our watch?"

"That a police patrol car made two swings past Lindstrom's home."

"That's good, isn't it?"

"Means they care. But obviously if this nut case doesn't operate on their schedule, it isn't sufficient."

"Is he a nut case?"

"I don't know. We don't know anything for sure." I stretched my legs, thought a bit. "You know if Vivian's ex, Thomas Aubuchon, were really clever—and guilty—he could be creating a terrific diversion to cover his tracks."

"Wouldn't he have to follow through by killing Lindstrom?"

"Not necessarily. Sometimes nut cases fade away. Or at least the police never know for sure what happened to them. Like Jack the Ripper."

"You think Aubuchon did it?"

"Don't know. The police are checking his Branson alibi. Maybe we'll know for sure soon." I studied my tennies. I had grass stains from my midnight patrol. "I think Lindstrom is the original target; Viv was a mistake."

He said nothing for a moment. "Horrible for Viv, but also horrible for Lindstrom. I hope you can catch the bastard."

I had no doubt he was sincerely and deeply moved. Even *bastard* is strong language from Patrick. He might have reservations about Lindstrom, but his heart is too big to leave her outside. I squeezed his arm. "I hope somebody does," I said and realized it was true. She was in too much danger for me to waste energy worrying about who rescued her.

I sketched in the broad outline of our agreement that Lindstrom would let me stay with her at night. "So will you look after Harvey for me?"

"You know I will," he said warmly, and a little sadly.

He didn't have to explain. He'd miss me as I'd missed him during the Ray fling. In four years we've grown close. Sometimes our love confuses us with its surges of jealousy and affection. But not now. I touched his arm again. "I'll miss you, too."

"How long will this take?" He looked away. "You don't know, of course."

I shook my head.

"Stay safe, Meg. Harvey needs his mother."

A shadow had passed over our sun. We put our trash in the nearest receptacle and returned to the car. On our way home we discussed cat antics, trading old stories. When we reached Arsenal and parted at the top of the stairs, Patrick announced he thought a short nap would fill out his sleeping requirements.

Inside my apartment I swooped up Harvey, to his disgust. "I'm gonna miss you, buddy." He released a shower of white hairs to punish me for my forcing intimacy on him. I put down fresh kibble, stripped out of my clothes, stepped into a hot shower. I'd decided to go on with my day rather than trying to recapture sleep. In my twenties pulling all nighters was easier, but this morning I was still pumped up.

***

A good investigations firm turns away more business than it takes. Lots of people in trouble think a private investigator is what they need because they watch too much TV. Most of them would be better served by a good criminal lawyer, a confessor, or divorce proceedings. So I spent what was left of the morning turning away three hopeful clients and made an appointment to see the fourth that afternoon. After getting off the phone, I sat at the computer and typed up notes from my encounter with L.C. Reidy and Colin Lanier. These weren't going to lead us to our killer, but good paper is as important to a private investigator as admissible evidence is to a cop. I sketched a map of Lindstrom's house with rough dimensions and marked how the killer had entered and where the murder had taken place. Then I looked in my Rolodex and called Vista Security, who often subcontracts for us on residential set-ups. Phil Nelson agreed that he could meet me in Soulard late this afternoon. Phil and his partner are expensive, but they do very good work. Lindstrom needed the best.

At twelve-fifteen Colleen told me Detective Lindstrom was on the phone.

"Hi, how's it going?"

"I've been better. I wanted to let you know that I talked to Johnson. He has an officer looking through my old cases trying to figure out some likely suspects."

"Great, I think it is likely to be someone connected with an old case. I've called our subcontractor about a security system for the house."

"I don't think that is necessary. Those things are such a pain. The department is always responding to false alarms."

"Yes, it is necessary. If for no other reason, it acts as a deterrent. Better he should see the signs and the wires and decide not to break in than you should have to shoot him."

"I guess. It will probably be expensive."

"Yes, it will." I let the silence hang a moment. "Phil will meet us at your house at four."

"You'll be there?"

"Sure."

"I'm not going to buy a bunch of unnecessary bells and whistles."

"Okay, just the basics. Phil is good. He won't try to sell you things you don't need."

"Did you tell him what was going on?"

"No, not in detail, but I imagine he watches the news. He'll probably put two and two together."

She huffed into the phone. Being the crime victim was a painful change for Lindstrom. I tried to think of something reassuring and came up empty. "Okay. See you at four," she said.

"I'll be there." It was a relief to hang up the phone.

On my way out the door I explained to Colleen that I'd be sleeping at Lindstrom's house for a while. I gave her the phone number and told her about the appointment with Phil Nelson.

I then drove to the main public library on Olive with its bas-relief stonework urging me toward lofty thoughts and descended to the basement and the more mundane. I figured that our stalker was connected with Lindstrom's work, and since Johnson was already perusing case files, I would take a peek at what had gotten Lindstrom's name in the paper in the last year. But an hour's search proved fruitless.

CHAPTER SEVENTEEN

Phil was already at Lindstrom's when I arrived. I had to park on the street. He and Lindstrom were looking at the outside windows when I walked up. Phil was a portly white man with receding brown hair, but he topped Lindstrom by a few inches. She was still looking subdued, but the old charge raced over my skin, and I couldn't stop my automatic grin. Luckily, she was staring at the kitchen window frame and didn't notice me until I got my face arranged. We walked around the house and talked about locks for the windows and even new windows. We placed motion detector lights mentally, and I insisted that one be installed at the back of the covered walk between the houses.

Phil explained that the system would be wired to an office on Chouteau through the phone line. She could have a couple of choices about what to do if the alarm were tripped. In one set-up, the security company called her, and if they couldn't reach her, called the police. In another they called the police immediately. He advised a sign in both front and back proclaiming the property protected by a security system and stickers on the doors. Deterrence, he said, was the first issue. Lindstrom nodded vaguely. She clearly didn't believe signs and stickers were going to deter Viv's killer. Lindstrom asked questions about how sensitive the system was and how difficult to disarm. I asked Phil about security cameras at both doors, and Lindstrom objected. She didn't want the house to look like a prison. We went back and forth a few times and finally settled on an oscillating camera hidden up under the roof of the back porch. It and the video display in the kitchen would be removed as soon as our killer was arrested. The front door was right on the sidewalk and a less inviting place to break in anyway. We made a date for Phil and his partner to install the system the next day.

When Phil finally left at five-thirty, Lindstrom looked up at me and shrugged. "They installed the phone tap today. Try to remember that all incoming calls are being recorded."

"Can't you turn it off?"

She shrugged. "I'll probably forget."

I sighed. So much for phone sex. Back to work. I pulled out my pad and pen. "Who hates you enough to want to beat you to death?"

She took a deep breath and sat down, too. "It's hard to know which ones really blame me. Some of them I'm sure. Some of them blame their attorneys. Some their mothers. A good many of the really sick ones are still locked up. I don't know if either of these guys is out yet, but I've thought of a couple of potentials."

I raised my eyebrows and waggled my pen to indicate I was ready.

"My first year on the force, I arrested a white guy who beat and killed an eighty-year-old black woman on the North side. He wasn't all that smart, but he was one very angry young man. It took six of us to take him down, and he told his lawyer that I was the one who broke his ribs in the struggle."

"Did you?"

Lindstrom frowned at me. "Darcy, he had savagely beaten a defenseless old woman to death. Six of us were on top of him just trying to get him cuffed. I don't know if I broke his ribs, but if I did, I'm not sorry. He would have killed me if he'd had the chance."

"What was his sentence?"

"Fifteen to twenty, but if he behaved himself, he'd serve about a third of that."

"His name?"

"Gregory Page. He was twenty when we busted him eight years ago. He went to Jefferson City."

"I'll want to go there—see his file and talk to people who knew him. Can you help with that?"

I could see Lindstrom at war with herself. She could barely stand to help a private dick 'interfere in police business,' but with her own safety on the line she needed my help. Should she cross the line and actively help me investigate? Or should she sit back, have faith in Johnson? In the end, I'm sure she saw helping me as a way to be active rather than passive. It mattered less that I was a private investigator than that she do all she could to bring Vivian's murderer to justice, and quickly. "Yes, I'll call and set it up. When do you want to go?"

"Tomorrow." It would be perfect. Not only would I get the information right away, but because Phil had pushed other jobs aside, he and his partner would be at the house all day, installing a camera and lights and wiring contacts to windows and doors. Lindstrom would be safe while I was gone.

She glanced at her watch. "I'll have to call in the morning."

"Thanks."

She nodded.

"Who else is on your list?"

"Terry Ray Krebs beat his wife to death. His conviction was voluntary manslaughter. I'm not sure whether that was the prosecutor or the jury. She was in bed with another man when he started beating on her, so her life wasn't worth even murder two."

"Did he threaten you as well?"

"Right after the guilty verdict, when they were leading him out of the courtroom, he lunged at me. Tried to bite me."

"Bite you?"

"Yes, his hands were manacled, so he couldn't use his arms. The violent ones often come at you with their teeth when they are cuffed."

111

I shook my head. She lived in a strange world. "Anything else from him?"

"No, nothing after that. I just remember the look in Krebs's eye when he was coming for me."

"Who do you think is our man?"

She sighed and put her chin on her fist. "Probably Page, then Krebs."

"Are you going back to work soon?"

"I talked to the Lieutenant today. He wants me to come in tomorrow. He says I should just get back in the saddle."

"Sounds like good advice. If he'll back you up, you can make it work."

Lindstrom shook her head. "I just don't know. I talked to Neely this afternoon. He says most of the guys are okay about it. But you just don't know; there is so much macho on the force. Some guys only know they are okay because they aren't women or fags."

I'm sure this was true, and yet there had to be room in the world and in the St. Louis Police Department for growth. "But that's not how you define yourself. You must know you can't let them define you, or you never would have made it to detective as a woman."

"It will be too hard. I just don't want to do it." Strangely, in her tone I heard some of the old Lindstrom grit. Whatever her stance, she was stubborn.

"So quit. You're a smart woman, you'll find another job." I could see I'd said the right thing—the steel in her jaw was coming back and her spine straightened.

"Don't think I don't know you're trying to manipulate me, Darcy."

"I have to go back to my apartment to pick up some things. What are we going to do about dinner?"

"Why don't you bring back something when you come?"

Lindstrom rummaged in a drawer and pulled out a house key without comment. It took me a moment to realize we were now officially roommates.

I must admit I was a bit relieved that she didn't want to come with me. I like living alone, and I had a feeling I was going to be short on solitude for a while. So it was with a lighter heart that I rambled back out to the Plymouth and across town to my place.

When I walked into my apartment, Harvey greeted me warmly.

As I sat petting Harvey, I realized I'd rather stretch out on my couch than pack for my sojourn at Lindstrom's house. I rolled my head forward and back, stretching my tight neck muscles. I pushed myself off the couch. I knew at this point I was too tired for a nap. If I slept now, it would be hours before I woke. So I shuffled into my bedroom and looked dispiritedly at the disarray.

All my favorite shirts heaped beside the bed waiting for me to have two free hours to spend at the laundromat. I wondered idly if Lindstrom had a washer and dryer. Wouldn't hurt to take them. I grabbed my olive green duffel and stuffed it with the shirts and the underwear and socks from the basket in front of my dresser. I opened the gym bag I'd packed the night before and added an extra pair of underwear and my good sneakers. I rummaged through the closet shelf and found my second hand Nikon and the zoom lens. I sighed as I zipped the gym bag closed.

Was I ready for this move into Lindstrom's? Probably not. I couldn't imagine Lindstrom and me cohabiting peacefully, even when both of us weren't on red alert listening for a killer. We could barely get through an evening without a clash of some sort. Staying in the same house was going to call for reserves of patience I wasn't sure I owned. And I chafed as I imagined her critical gaze on me constantly. I stripped the sheets off the bed and wadded them in with the dirty clothes. If Lindstrom did have a washing machine, I might as well get all the good from it I could.

On my way out of the apartment I dumped the last of the already-old milk, put fresh water in Harvey's bowl, and closed all the windows. Then I doubled back and called Pho Grand for two orders of spring rolls, curry beef, and lemon-grass chicken to go.

It was seven-thirty by the time I picked up the take-out and headed for Soulard. The smells made my mouth water. When I got to Lindstrom's house, I left my bags in the car and carried in our dinner. Lindstrom had made iced tea, and we ate from styrofoam containers with little conversation to grace the meal. Lindstrom looked as tired as I felt, and neither of us was inclined to pretend this was a date.

After a longish silence, Lindstrom sighed again. "At least it's a little cooler after last night's rain."

I thought about all the ways I knew to complain about the humidity. Before I could decide between "the air's too thick to breathe" and "it's not the heat, it's the humidity," she spoke again. "You know, he can't have been too smart—when he killed Viv, my car wasn't even in the driveway." She didn't have to explain who *he* was.

"Either not too smart, or he hasn't been stalking you long enough to know what you drive."

"But there was no car in the driveway."

"No, but he could tell someone was home—lights and so forth. He probably watched until Viv went to bed."

"I can hardly stand it that someone killed her instead of me."

I was silent. There didn't seem to be anything to say to that, and Lindstrom was radiating don't touch me signals.

"We'll catch him, Lindstrom. He won't get away with it."

"That's not good enough," she snapped and pushed away from the table. She stomped up the stairs, ending the conversation.

I cleared and wiped the light oak table and tied off the white garbage bag. I took it out to the dumpster in the alley and grabbed my bags on the way in. After I dumped them in the door, I found the door to the basement and located the washer and dryer. I decided not to start my wash now in case Lindstrom wanted a shower. I'd wait until she was in bed. So far, living together wasn't exactly a slice of chocolate cake.

I wandered into the den and found the Cardinals behind in the sixth

113

inning. I watched three outs, then stuck the snubbie .38 in my pocket, and got up to walk around the yard again. Inside the house just felt too cut off from the street. The air conditioner's hum covered almost all the street sounds. Thursday night was fairly quiet on Michellene street, and I jumped when I heard Neely's voice from the passenger side of an unmarked police car.

"Hi, Meg. Sorry to startle you. How are things going?"

"Pretty quiet right now."

"Are you staying here?"

"Just for a while. Safety in numbers."

"I think it's a good idea. We'll be driving by as much as we can." He looked like he wanted to say something else, but instead he sat back and waved the driver on.

I wished I knew Neely better so I could ask him how Lindstrom's co-workers really felt about her violent coming out. When I returned to the back porch, Lindstrom was sitting there, iced tea in hand. Her eyes were bloodshot and red rimmed. I sat down beside her.

"See him anywhere?"

"No, but Neely just drove by."

She nodded. "Sorry about earlier. I know catching him is all we can do now. I just wish I'd have been home to prevent it."

"I know."

We sat in silence a little longer.

"The Cards lost." She drained her glass. "What time do you want to get up in the morning?"

I thought about the drive to Jefferson City. "Six, okay?"

"Yes. I'll set my alarm. But I can't reach anyone at the prison for you until nine."

"That's okay. I need to go into the office first anyway."

"Well, I'm going to bed. I'm beat."

"You know, Lindstrom, you can wake me up if you need to. I'd be glad to talk awhile if that would help."

She sighed. "I don't know. I hope I'll sleep. Good night."

She left me alone with the humid night.

CHAPTER EIGHTEEN

Jefferson City Correctional Center, formerly Missouri State Prison, is the oldest prison west of the Mississippi still in use. With its original white stone wall and many stone buildings, the prison has a brooding authority missing from modern brick facilities. In the mid-nineteenth century, when Missouri was still frontier, the 'Walls' as JCCC is known, had held only a couple of hundred men. Now close to two thousand were incarcerated there.

Fifty or so were in the yard as I pulled up that Friday afternoon, exactly a week after Vivian's murder. Dressed in gray work shirts and pants, most of them stood around smoking, waiting for time to pass. Several stared at me. A few played basketball under the watchful eye of two brown-shirted correctional officers ready to stop the game if fouls turned into fights. The guard on duty in the shack fixed me with an inquiring look and grunted when I told him my name. He ticked me off the list on his clipboard and pointed to the building I needed.

As I entered its waiting room, I wished for the tenth time that Lindstrom hadn't presented me, by implication, as a cop. There was probably a secret handshake I'd muff. Or someone would ask me where I went to academy. I picked up a two-month-old *US News and World Report* to flip through. There were five aluminum and plastic chairs around the perimeter of the waiting room. I chose what looked like the cleanest of the lot. The smell of disinfectant and stale air made the institutional green and tan walls seem closer than they actually were.

Finally at twelve-forty-five a young man came out from one of the offices. He was in civilian clothes, a brown summer suit that looked like he had worn it once too often between cleanings. The crease had melted away over his thick thighs. He offered me his hand and introduced himself as Pete Dyer of the public relations office. Dyer showed me into his office with its gray metal desk that was a duplicate of my own at Miller Security, but slightly newer. I wondered if R.J., whose initials were scratched into my desk, had worked at the prison. Always before I had imagined him as a creative spirit caught in mid-level bureaucracy in City Hall.

"So, Officer Darcy, you need to see the files on Gregory Page and Terry Krebs?"

"Yes. Detective Lindstrom explained to you that they are suspects in a homicide?"

"She did. I've pulled those files out." He laid his hand on two thick olive green folders. One was considerably thicker than the other. "Why don't you look through these, and I'll check back with you in about thirty minutes to see if I can answer any questions you may have."

I looked at the six-inch stack. "Make it an hour, and you've got a deal."

"Can I get you a cup of coffee or a soda?" The idea of coffee made in a prison didn't appeal. I had a vision of their mixing saltpeter into the grind. "A Pepsi would be good, or a Coke. Whatever you have."

He left, and I pulled the stack toward me. Page, prisoner number 501678, was the one who had beaten the old woman to death. His was the thick file. He had come to JCCC under the order of Judge Thomas Galbreath, who had sentenced him to fifteen years in June of 1987. I looked at his mug shots in the upper right hand corner of the page. They were grainy black and whites, front and side shots.

Dyer came back into the office with my Pepsi in a can and a glass of ice. When he found that he couldn't do anything else for me, he excused himself.

I hoped I wouldn't be put in a position of trying to identify Gregory Page based on these pictures. I could tell he was white, but his features were flat and didn't look as if they represented a real person. His hair was light and unruly, his mouth was drawn in a tight, angry line, but his eyes looked scared. I tried to imagine that first hour of his incarceration—being processed from a free man into prisoner number 501678.

As I read Page's history, I felt hate's cold hand on my skin. Gregory was not a man I'd like to meet. Although I wanted to get up and walk away from the violence and bigotry screened in bureaucratic language, I sat still and read. Lindstrom's life might depend on it. When I finished, I hefted the file back onto Dyer's desk and stood up to stretch my back. It was one-thirty, so Dyer would return soon. I'd just have to ask him for some time. I settled down next with Terry Ray Krebs.

I read the file on Krebs, taking a few notes and shifting uncomfortably in my chair. The next time Dyer returned, I was finished with the files.

"Good, good. Did you find everything you needed?"

"Yes. They were a good start. I'd like to talk to some staff and inmates that knew Page and Krebs."

"You could certainly talk to some of the staff." He pulled the files toward him. "Let me just see which building they were in." He flipped through the files, then he was on the phone. Soon he had someone lined up to see me, and we were on our way toward the cafeteria. As we passed through the hallways, we walked by dozens of men. Some in the brown guard uniforms, some in prisoner gray. Most of the prisoners were young, and prisoners and guards alike squinted at me as if I smelled of the outdoors. Their glances, some quickly averted, some boring into me for seconds, pinned me to a mattress. They didn't shout or whistle like construction workers or like *Silence of the Lambs*. This was all quiet and completely disquieting. Before we reached the cafeteria, I was staring at the floor. Determined to hold my own, I pried my eyes upward.

The cavernous room, smelling of cardboard, produce and grease, was empty save for a man in gray work shirt and work pants sweeping with a large brown push broom. Dyer seated me at the end of a long table. I realized after he'd gone into the still-clanging kitchen that the table hadn't been wiped off. I picked up my elbows and sat back. Soon Dyer reemerged with a fifty-ish man in a faded blue work shirt, jeans, and heavy black shoes.

"This is Dennis Moore, one of our civilian employees. He works in the kitchen and knew Terry Krebs." Dyer sat down with us and looked at the table. Clearly, even though I was supposed to be a cop, I wasn't to be trusted alone with the help. Dyer's appointment for the afternoon was to watch me. "Dennis, this is Meg Darcy. She's a St. Louis police officer here to investigate a crime. They suspect Krebs may have been involved."

"Thank you for agreeing to talk with me, Mr. Moore." He nodded politely. I tried to think of how Lindstrom might conduct this interview. Unfortunately, the only time I had seen her question someone else, she had not been at her best. I suspected that I would soon be exposed as an impostor by my failure to ask cop-like questions or to ask questions in a cop-like way. "Did Krebs work in the cafeteria a long time?"

Moore didn't lift his head when he spoke. "Yes, he did. Terry Ray worked here the whole time he was in, six years."

"What did he do?"

"Terry Ray was an assistant cook. Best I've ever had. Mostly we hire from outside for cooks, but Terry proved himself. He was good, and reliable, and very clean."

"Did he ever mention his crime or the arresting officer?"

"Just to say that he wished he'd never done it. His wife wasn't the first woman that'd done him wrong. All the way back. His mother, um, had what you'd call a bad reputation, too."

"He mention any women cops?"

There was just a slight hesitation before he said, "No, not that I remember."

I paused, then decided to push him. "How about a cop named Lindstrom?"

"Terry had some feelings about police officers, most of the boys do, but he didn't blame anybody but himself for his trouble. He is a good man."

"What were his plans for when he was paroled?"

"Terry Ray'd worked it all out. He'd written letters to lots of appliance repair places in St. Louis. One of them promised to give him an interview. I wrote him a letter of recommendation saying what a good worker he was. He'll do all right. He's going to put it all behind him."

I thanked Dennis for agreeing to talk to me. He hadn't once met my eye as we talked. I wondered how much to credit the fact that he liked and trusted Krebs.

I asked Dyer if he had any inmates that were friends of Krebs or Page that I could talk to. He explained that prisoners retained the right not to be required to answer police questions unless they were a material witness to a crime. So any cooperation we received would be voluntary. I told him I understood. We returned to Dyer's office where he settled me with a second Pepsi and went off in search of a someone willing to talk to me.

Thirty minutes later, Dyer returned. He hadn't found anyone at all who knew Page who was willing to talk. The man who had been Krebs's last cell mate agreed to answer some questions.

We had to walk to one of the newer brick buildings where we met Krebs's cell mate in a tiny windowless room across a battered school desk. Victor Roberts had a winning smile and a lovely head of hair. It was curly brown and long enough to brush his shoulders even pulled back in a pony tail. He stood as I came in and looked me in the eye as he offered his hand. "Afternoon, Officer Darcy."

"Thanks for agreeing to talk to me, Mr. Roberts."

"Call me Victor, please. Actually, thank you for rescuing me from another afternoon of making license plates." We both laughed at the triteness of his occupation.

"Do you really make license plates?"

"Yes, ma'am. From eight in the morning until three in the afternoon. Maroon for your car, black for your truck. White if you're a municipal or state car. I make 'em right here at J Triple C."

"Sounds like a pretty boring job."

"You got that right. The career opportunities do tend to be limited. Which was why I was so happy when they wanted to talk to someone who knew that worm Krebs. What's Mr. Clean done?"

"We're not sure he's done anything at the moment. We're trying to get some information about him to see if we should pursue him as a suspect."

"Suspect in what?"

Out of the corner of my eye, I caught Dyer's minuscule head shake. He thought I shouldn't tell Victor anything. I was thoroughly tired of the prison and its *1984* atmosphere. "Someone has beaten a woman to death and is sending threatening messages to a cop."

"Phew. Bad stuff. I can't say I ever thought Terry Ray would kill again. I figured he didn't have the balls for it really. He only killed his old lady cause he caught her in the act."

"What do you mean?"

"Essentially Terry Ray was your basic ass-kisser. He'd always try to figure out who had the most marbles and kiss up to him. He was an institutional man all the way. Prissy. Liked straight edges and clear rules."

"Did he ever mention any police officers?"

"Not to me. Just in general, I guess. He'd have made a good cop in some ways. He sure believed in right and wrong. He was a little rigid." Victor gave a short laugh at his understatement.

"What did he say he wanted to do when he got his parole?"

"He had his whole life mapped out. He was going to find a job at a TV/VCR repair shop, get a small apartment within walking distance of his job. And he was going to meet the perfect woman when she brought in her

TV for repair. They were going to get married, have a boy and a girl, and live happily ever after. And his wife wouldn't work."

"She wouldn't work?"

"Yeah, his last wife met her boyfriend at work." He grinned at me.

We talked some more, but no matter how I asked it, Victor Roberts did-n't know if Krebs had a grudge against a cop or anyone else for that matter. I thanked him for his help, and he went back to his license plates fairly cheer-fully.

When we left the claustrophobic room, Dyer said he'd call Probation and Parole and get Page's and Krebs's current addresses. He said it as if it should be the last thing I asked of him. We returned to his office where he made a call, and five minutes later I had the faxes in hand and was being shown the door.

The drive back to St. Louis was long and hot, but I was grateful for the solitude. I thought briefly about stopping at my apartment for a visit with Harvey and perhaps Patrick, but felt guilty about spending more time away from Lindstrom. As I pulled into her driveway I noticed a blue and white 'Security by Vista' sign hugged the sidewalk in the back yard. She was sit-ting on the back porch, drinking coffee.

"Hi, I see by the sign Phil Nelson has been here."

"Yes, they finished up about an hour ago." My eyes followed her glance up at the black camera in the right hand corner of the porch roof. We went inside, and she showed me the alarm panel at the back door. I quickly mem-orized her code, and we set it and unset it a couple of times for practice. She said she had asked Phil to set up the alarm so that it didn't ring at the police station until Vista cleared it with her. We looked at a semi-circle of the back yard in black and white on the video monitor. Lindstrom seemed low, like Viv's death was again weighing her down. I got a glass of tea from the fridge and told her about my visit to JCCC.

"They're both on the loose, so we can't really eliminate either of them at the moment. I think I'll see Page first, just because he should be easy to find at the halfway house. Page was not a model prisoner. He was moved several times the first six months he was at JCCC in response to multiple fights. Page was brawling with every African-American prisoner he came across. After his sixth or seventh serious fight, he shaved his head and began hanging out with prisoners suspected of being members of Aryan Nation. Eventually, his Aryan Nation buddies got him a lawyer, and she got him released to the halfway house.

"Both Krebs and Page are back in St. Louis, but they are with the pro-gram according to the records at the prison. Krebs's last cell mate didn't like him, but mostly because he was a suck-up. He sounds like the least likely to me, maybe too good to be true. He took classes and passed his GED and fin-ished a small appliance repair course. He saved his money, collected his good behavior time, and received parole the second year he was eligible. He's been out since March."

Lindstrom shook her head. "Who knows? It may be neither of them.

Johnson is still looking at my files. Maybe he'll come up with something."

I hesitated, "Lindstrom, might this be something related to your private life, instead of work?"

She frowned at me. "I don't think so. I'm pretty sure I'd know it if someone I knew was angry enough to beat me to death with a baseball bat."

CHAPTER NINETEEN

Saturday, June 26, I woke on Lindstrom's den couch feeling cramped in body and mind. The drive to and from Jeff City, the lack of activity since, left my unstretched legs kinked up. Had I been home last night, Patrick and I would have taken a walk in Tower Grove Park. Had I been home last night. Already I missed Harvey's wakeup calls. If the first meows don't work, he settles on my chest and kneads and purrs till I open my eyes.

I was on the downward slope to feeling sorry for myself when I remembered that it was only a week since Lindstrom had awakened me in the early morning hours to inform me of Viv's murder. Whatever my complaints, they were bound to be smaller than Lindstrom's. I sighed and stretched. I heard a noise in the kitchen and realized Lindstrom was already up and about. I stretched again. I'd have sworn I slept on full alert, but I hadn't heard her come down the stairs.

I was still lying there, gathering my resolve to leap up, when she came padding into the room in a Corn Huskers tee shirt and khaki shorts and bare feet. She carried a steaming mug.

"Ah, you're awake," she said, the smile more in her voice than on her face. "What?"

"That explains it—" I said cheerily. "How you tiptoed by without waking me." I leaned over and admired her feet—large as befits a tall woman but shapely and as yet ungnarled by life. The skin was white with blue and pink tints, the nails unpolished and evenly clipped. I'd never attended to them much before, beyond a teasing tickle, and I vowed to make amends if we ever—when we—broke out of this prison.

"So we're in trouble if this creep comes in his stocking feet?" She managed a jocular tone but just. Her mood wouldn't bear much weight.

"That coffee for me?" Not graceful but she probably wouldn't mind the clumsy style if I changed the subject.

"Maybe. I put milk in but no sugar. I keep forgetting what you like."

"I'll put a post-it on the cabinet." I was hurt she hadn't yet memorized that detail but not prepared to pout about it. I reached for the mug. "You guessed right this time." I glanced down at her feet. "I never figured you for a barefoot girl."

She looked at her feet, too, and wiggled her big toes as though testing the temperature or texture of a mud puddle. "I'm a Nebraska farm girl. My feet are no strangers to grass."

"I guess I thought you wore cowboy boots all the time."

"Ah, yes—boots round the clock, spurs everywhere, even to bed."

The remark lay there a moment too long, too flirtatious and dangerous to touch, too awkward to call back. Her face said she hadn't been flirting. She was surrounded, constricted by grief. Every remark became a delayed-action bomb.

"The coffee's excellent. What brand?" I rushed in with the mundane to rescue us.

"Schnuck's gourmet," She shrugged. "The Irish creme I think." She tried a wry smile. "I'm surprised you didn't know."

I was flattered. I'd impressed her with my familiarity with exotic coffees—like QT's French vanilla cappuccino.

But she was moving along her own line of thought. "I notice after the times we've been together," she said, pronouncing the words delicately so I knew she meant when we'd had sex, "you seem to memorize all the details about me, what toothpaste I use, how I take off my shoes."

The blush didn't crawl but raced to my cheeks. I tried to bluff it out. "Well, sure, I'm a PI. Observing details is my game." No need to mention I wanted to swallow her whole, absorb her every cell into my being.

"Colgate tartar control toothpaste?" I couldn't read her. Irked? Amused?

"A definite clue to character."

She arched a single brow. I hate people who can do that.

"A touch of vanity," I explained.

"Ah. Vanity," she mocked. "What a surprise." But her tone told me that whatever she was defensive about, it wasn't vanity. She looked into my eyes a moment, then turned away. "I had a bowl of cereal. I have bagels in the freezer. Any of that useful to your breakfast?"

We hadn't yet discussed that essential piece of domestic routine. I was disappointed we weren't breakfasting together. But I said, "Cereal is fine," and sat up, putting my legs over the side.

She paused in the doorway. "There's really quite a bit you don't know about me, Darcy." Her tone was rueful, but rueful about what wasn't clear. That I didn't know? That what I didn't know would be disappointing or painful to me? To her? And I felt condescended to. She was a complex, worldly woman beyond my simple comprehension. Before I could puff up indignantly, she added, "I think I'll shower while you're eating." In that simple statement I thought I heard her saying she'd feel safer in the shower with me in the house. My defenses collapsed; all my concern for her vulnerable state flooded in. But she was gone, climbing the stairs.

I finished my first cup of coffee, removed the sheets from the couch, and folded them neatly, a concession to Lindstrom's tidy house, and pulled on yesterday's clothes. I crossed the hall to use the downstairs bathroom, then returned to the kitchen. I poured another cup of coffee, contemplated Raisin Bran and Special K. I considered searching the freezer for the bagels, decided to buck up and do bran. I was chewing my way through a bowl when she rejoined me—crisp and cool in caramel trousers and safari-style camp shirt. I suppressed a whistle. I was there to serve and protect, not ogle.

"So you're off to Clark Street station this morning?" I asked.

She nodded and poured a cup of coffee for herself. Black.

"I told the Lieutenant I had old paperwork to catch up on. But I'll take another look at the files for Page and Krebs. And I'll fan out to some other cases, too, just in the hope something will stick out."

I nodded back. What she sketched in for her day's program sounded vague, but in an investigation lacking clear leads it was the sort of wide net even cops have to fall back on. As a way to spend her day, she'd probably find it more satisfyingly proactive than patting the hands of the grief-stricken Rudders.

I told her I'd start my day at Miller Security, after a quick stop on Arsenal to shower and change. Then, if I could get away, I'd start trying to track Page and Krebs.

As grim and frightening as our motivation was in this case, these topics had a workaday familiarity to both of us. We're always tracking down people who wish to stay hidden. A kind of companionable ease settled on us. By the time we left, I was tempted to peck her cheek. But I didn't lest I break the spell.

As soon as I slid into the Plymouth, the shirt started wilting. One of those St. Louis days. When I pulled the Plymouth into the lot behind the office, I saw Walter's Oldsmobile.

When he started Miller Security, Walter kept it open all day on Saturdays and till eight or nine on weekday evenings. He was hustling business, and he wanted to make it easy for clients to drop in. But the boom in security and investigative services has allowed us to go nine to five and strictly weekdays as far as keeping the office open. Walter is now considering Saturday half-days and part time help to assist Colleen, but he never makes a sudden move on business matters.

Walter is the kind of guy who goes to the office on Saturday because he's comfortable there. It's like other men go to the barber or a bar except Walter is more a loner. Walter is my dad's step-brother. When my dad split, Walter stepped up his role as uncle. He's a Reagan Democrat who disapproves of Betty's hippie sympathizer past and presently nonconforming views. He's a Catholic who feels keen guilt over the vows he doesn't always keep. He's often predictably a good hater.

He's also unpredictably complicated. I don't know if he loves Betty from family duty or personal fascination. But he's been more than generous with her kids, especially me who's tested all his limits. I'm a woman doing a man's work; I'm a lesbian denying that women need men as sexual partners. For heaven's sake, I've been a gay in the military.

Still he's given me the opportunity to work for him and to learn from him. He's indulged me on the issue of flex hours. I was about to test his patience again.

Despite Colleen's and my attempts to spruce up his office, he keeps the space cluttered. Unfiled folders occupy every surface, often weighted down by cameras, binoculars, electronic equipment that ought to be in our storage room. Walter creates disorder faster than Colleen cleans up. That he perpetually grumbles about 'this mess' as though he hasn't made it isn't his most lovable trait. This morning I found him with his big feet up on his desk. He was in khaki work clothes as though he were on the way down to the plant. His beefy body strained the cloth. His fair skin was more than usually red; maybe a nip to put a glow in his cheeks. His once red hair was a faded rust now with blondish gray making inroads. He was chewing on a cigar his doctors warn him not to smoke. Mikie was perched on his lap. The hyperactive poodle sat up to wag a tail at me but resettled on dad's thighs.

"Mornin', Walter," I started.

He squinted his blue eyes. Once they were as clear and sweet as cornflowers, Betty says; now they tend toward red-rimmed and narrowed. And often calculating except when he looks at Mikie; then he's daft.

"What brings you here?" Both tone and content sounded gruff. Walter is the sort of man that the phrase 'bark worse than bite' was coined for. Still it's tiresome having to decode everything. I made my pitch. I brought him to speed on the history. I told him I'd be staying at Lindstrom's during the night. I described it as protective surveillance. Furthermore, I wanted to lighten my daytime load, so that I could actively pursue the leads we had.

"For how long?" he asked.

I stared at him. He waited. He doesn't win a lot at poker. But he can stay in a game a long time, make small advances. He personally is one of the best surveillance men around if he doesn't relieve the tedium with a drunken binge. It's a big 'if,' and to get around it, he assigns other operatives to the task.

I wanted to answer him "Till this fucker screws up," but I said instead "Till this creep messes up." Somehow stronger language makes me sound more determined, but he doesn't believe in equal opportunity swearing.

"That could be a long cold wait in a hot July." I am to notice that he cleans up his speech for me.

"I know."

"What's in it for us?"

I couldn't answer that one. Walter knows I'm a lesbian, but he cannot pronounce the word. He certainly doesn't want to know that my gonads dance like fairies to Irish bagpipes over Lindstrom. He hasn't Betty's interest in my romances.

"She's a friend. She's a cop, too."

He likes loyalty to family and to friends. Secretly maybe more to friends. He likes cops. Many cops are his friends. But the police department with its black chief represents Guv'ment and the kind of politics Walter claims doesn't pay off for South Side anymore.

"They ought to protect their own," he said. Vigorous chew on the cigar.

"You're right." I shrug a whadda-ya-gonna-do.

"I don't think you can do this alone. You gotta front and a back and this gal doesn't sound like a real cooperative client. Cops always think they know it all."

"Hmm." I nodded.

He sighed, choked a little on the saliva the cigar was promoting. "Well, try it. Maybe if Leroy gets done with that Stephano job, I'll send him over to sit with you a couple of nights."

"Thanks, Walter." I got up and headed for the door.

"Are you carrying?"

I showed him the .38 Bodyguard Airweight in the attaché case. He nodded approval. Mikie stood balanced on Walter's thigh and barked a good-bye.

I went to my office, consulted my calendar, and called Betty to cancel our date. I told her I had an unexpected surveillance. I made it sound too boring to discuss.

Still she said, "Be careful, hon."

***

I sat down and pulled out a scratch pad and removed the notes I'd copied at JCCC. I supposed I could flip coins between Page and Krebs. I could trot back to Walter and seek his opinion. The sound of happy yips suggested that he and Mikie were into some dog and master game. Or I could use my own gray cells.

I considered the options. Terry Ray Krebs had killed a woman. Lindstrom said he'd lunged at her at his trial. The prison staff seemed to find him a good boy, and the woman he'd killed had only been his wife—which scarcely counts in quite a few circles. On the other hand, his cell mate suggested Krebs was a sly one, maybe not as reformed as his paperwork showed.

Page didn't strike me as a deep thinker, one likely to do the basic plotting necessary to finding Lindstrom's home and striking. That might reflect my basic prejudice against skinheads. Still his explosive violence against an old woman suggested he certainly had plenty of rage to expend.

PIs and cops use hunches without relying on them to solve cases. I thought Page would be explosive to handle when I found him. I hate to confess being scared, but the militia folks and skinheads scare me. Krebs would be easy to find; I'd save him as a little reward. None of this represented a heavy commitment to a theory by any means; I just needed a place to start.

I had a work address for Krebs and no phone number. Moving right along, I called the halfway house number where Page was supposedly lodged.

"Yo, Thornby House," a laconic voice answered.

"Hi, my name is Meg Darcy. I'm trying to find Gregory Page to ask him some questions about the information he put down on his employment application."

"Ain't here." I could sense the phone going down.

"Wait a sec! Any idea when I can catch him?"

125

"Nah. He ain't here much."

"Will you ask him to call this number when he comes in?" I pronounced the office number carefully.

"Yeah, right. He's interested in working." Dry.

"You never can tell. Thanks." I hung up.

I could drive to the North side and try a personal visit to Thornby House, or I could stay in the air-conditioning and work through some paperwork for the cases I was shifting over to Walter while I was pursuing Lindstrom's menacing caller. Air-conditioning is about the only thing that makes paperwork more appealing, but I was antsy to start acting. So I pulled out my Wunnenberg's street guide and located Thornby House.

Heat poured out of the Plymouth as I opened the door. I should get one of those windshield-cardboard-screen things, I thought for the hundredth time. I sat down and touched the steering wheel gingerly. I turned the key and yelped as my palm hit the metal top of the gear shift. My next car will definitely have air-conditioning.

On my way up Grand to the North Side, I passed beautiful St. Louis University, the theater district, and John Cochran Veterans' Hospital on my way to neighborhoods that once had been made up of working class white ethnics, but were poor and black since I could remember. In my lifetime the North Side has come to resemble nothing so much as a waiting room for jail or the morgue. Broken glass, gang signs, simmering anger, and hopelessness were all a white person could see. The Fairgrounds neighborhood probably hadn't wanted Thornby House in their backyard anymore than Clayton would. But Fairgrounds was where it was.

Just north of Fairgrounds Park, I found the address. Thornby House was a three-story brick house with a huge air conditioner slanting downward out of a front window. Water dripped from the aluminum back of the window unit forming a mud hole. The yard—full of dandelions and clover—grew over and through the broken sidewalk. Only weeds were determined to thrive in this heat. The tall, narrow windows needed a coat of paint, but the windows in the upper floor were open and real curtains, neatly hung, gave the house a look of home.

The front door was locked, an ordinary, if ironic, precaution. A solemn four-year-old stared at me from the porch to my right as I waited for my knock to be answered. A tall, round-headed African-American answered the door. He laughed and invited me in when I asked to speak to the director. He introduced himself as DeAntony and explained that he was the resident weekend coordinator. The director was Mr. Givens, and he was rarely there before noon and never on Saturday. DeAntony invited me to sit on a wheeled secretary's chair, and he eased onto the split seat of an old green executive chair. The furniture was shabby, but the room was clean and there were motivational posters on the walls. Pictures of grinning men, black and white, were tacked to the bulletin board. A computer generated sign taped to the wall adjured me that 'Personal Responsibility + 100% effort = SUCCESS!'

126

"You called earlier about Page?"

"Yes."

"Well, I imagine the paperwork hasn't made it over there yet, but Mr. Page departed Thornby House Wednesday, June 16."

Departed? "He was released?"

"No, he just departed. Left to go to a job interview his parole officer arranged for him at Bi-State and never came back."

"Bi-State, the bus company?"

"Yep. Washing buses I imagine. They hire a few of our men every year."

"So, is anyone *looking* for Page? Can he just walk off like that?"

"Nobody's out in the neighborhood, calling his name if that's what you mean. A warrant'll be issued pretty soon. If he gets stopped for anything, he'll be picked up. The PO will call his mother."

In a moment, Page shot to the top of my list. His 'departure' from Thornby house was exactly two days before Viv's murder.

"Do you have his mother's name and address—and the name of the person he was supposed to see at Bi-State?"

"I'll look. We have to put down an emergency contact. That might be his momma." DeAntony pulled a bright green folder from the desk behind him and read out Emma Page's address in Wood River, Illinois.

My fingers itched to grab the file from his hands. Instead, I asked politely, "Anything else in there that might help me find Gregory Page?"

"Something's not in here."

I raised my eyebrows impatiently. DeAntony smiled at my obvious restraint.

"Aryan Nation. Gregory Page was a skinhead. Look for a posse of ugly crackers with prison tattoos, and you'll find Page."

"Any idea where I might look for the Aryan Nation?"

DeAntony widened his eyes at me and just shook his head.

"How about a girlfriend?"

"None that I know of. Page wasn't inclined to chat with me."

"Was he close to anyone here?"

A smile lit DeAntony's face. "Nope. Gregory Page was lucky enough to arrive when the house population was one hundred percent African-American. He didn't talk to nobody here. Just grunted and shuffled. Moved on as soon as it occurred to him he could."

"How long was he here?"

"'Bout three weeks. Page was stupid. If I were him, I'd have been gone in a week."

Stupid and violent. "Thanks, DeAntony. Do you want to know when I find him?"

"Not me. Tell his PO. And tell him not to send Page back here."

CHAPTER TWENTY

When I left Thornby House, there was plenty of daylight left to make some calls about Page, but I was thinking of Lindstrom and itching to get home. Whatever 'home' meant in that context. First stop, my place. I headed back to Arsenal. The air felt like a tight skin about to burst; how much humidity could the air hold before the rains came?

I ran up the stairs. As soon as I opened the door, Harvey pranced forward for a pet. Patrick had stuck a note to the fridge. He missed me. He hoped that if I hadn't caught the murderer, I was at least igniting a flaming romance.

"From your lips to Lindstrom's ears." I crinkled the note into a ball to toss to Harvey. "Look, buddy, here's a note from your Uncle Patrick." Harvey pounced on it and gave the paper a few soccer swats across the uncarpeted living room floor. I headed for the shower. I chose jeans and an old cotton tee shirt, both thin with wear. I needed to do a laundry soon. No recycling an outfit during this hot spell. Maybe we'd find time tonight.

I called Lindstrom just to check if she wanted me to stop at the store on my way to Michellene. The machine answered. I identified myself and was starting the next sentence when she picked up.

"Darcy?"

"Yes. Are you screening calls?"

"Yes. I don't want to get caught unprepared."

Her voice sounded tight.

"Makes sense to me. I wouldn't want to be caught off guard by the creep." Calling him demeaning names was a way to diminish his power over my imagination—perhaps over Lindstrom's, too. I shifted gears. "Listen, I called to ask if—"

"I got a note from him."

"A note?"

"Yes. Hand-delivered to my back porch, tucked inside my screen door."

"What does it say?"

"Come over. See for yourself." Her words were clipped. But not quite the old Lindstrom asperity. She sounded dejected, underreacting because she was squeezed dry.

"On my way." I hung up.

I was starving, but I rushed past all the fast food places, embarrassed to even notice I was hungry. I slid through all the state streets between my place and hers and parked the Plymouth by her Toyota and walked up the tiny path to her back porch. I knocked loudly.

She opened the door right away. She was in pre-faded jeans and a new white tee shirt. Her face was stony.

"Tell me," I said as I stepped into the kitchen.

"I went down to the Clark Street station and talked to my boss and to Johnson and Neely. I looked through some picture files, reviewed some old cases, trying to jar loose any memories. When I got home, the note was just stuck inside the screen. I thought it was you or the Blairs or a neighbor."

"Where is it?"

She nodded toward the hallway. I followed her back into the den. She sat on the couch and motioned me down. The note and envelope lay on the coffee table, tweezers beside them.

"Don't touch," she said in her cop voice.

Once I'd have teased her about that. Or flared up. But everything had changed.

I leaned forward to peer at it. No wonder no alarms had gone off about the note. The sheet of paper and envelope were a matched, delicate yellow, very feminine.

Nothing was on the outside of the envelope. Inside the message was block-printed in bright black ink with a bold, thick stroke as though made with a laundry pen.

I read:

Sarah,
    Have you been thinking of me? You've been on my mind. Sorry I killed your girlfriend. I'll make it up to you somehow. Are you looking forward to seeing me?

His printing was A plus perfect—neat, legible, evenly spaced, and larger than I expected from such dainty stationery.

I wanted to rush Lindstrom out of there, hide her away. To cover that, I asked, "He didn't seal the envelope?"

"No. Just tucked the top flap inside."

"Have you seen this printing before?"

"Not that I remember. I didn't notice anything in the files today. Page is nearly illiterate."

I looked at her. Her blue eyes gave nothing away. I didn't like the detachment in her voice.

"He could get someone—a girlfriend maybe—to print for him. Might explain the paper," I suggested.

She shrugged. "Could be. But it would mean an accomplice knowing something about a fairly well-publicized crime."

"You know women who love warthogs, the stupid things they'll do to keep the dick-brain happy." I was angry. Or fearful. I was lashing out at someone. I took a breath. Steady. "Have you called Johnson or Neely?"

She shook her head. "It's only been an hour or so since I got home. I sort of wanted to talk to you."

Lindstrom isn't a 'sort of' person. But she was acting like the deer caught in the headlights. What the psychologists call 'affect' was dimmed down to the lowest wattage. I couldn't tell if she were exhausted or depressed or just intensely wary.

I tried to rally my own optimism. "Maybe the lab will find a print or a fiber. In any case you've got to tell Johnson."

"Vivian didn't have to die." She spoke calmly.

"Don't start that. There's no end to it." I was sharp.

She looked—I don't know—determined and down. Her jawline said "You can't prove me wrong." Her eyes stayed unreadable.

"You don't offer yourself as a sacrifice to right the wrong. We've got to catch the maggoty asshole," I said louder.

"I hate it that she died by mistake." Her voice was too level for the content.

"She died on purpose—his purpose. He's playing mind games with you, Sarah. Believe me, you won't be happier if he makes up for Viv by killing you." I weighed it, took the plunge. "Nor will any of us who care for you."

She stood up quickly, looked away. "I don't want to hear that now."

"That's not a pass. There are lots of ways to care. Neely wouldn't be happy either."

Lindstrom gave the wastebasket a small, scuffing kick. "She came to me seeking safety. I couldn't keep her safe." She shot me an angry look. "You need to get out of here. I'm dangerous to be around."

"You wanted me to come over so that you could yell at me?" I flung my arms in a gesture of frustration. Before she could respond, I added, "You're the one in danger. Get rid of that, and I'm safe."

She gave a dry snort. No stooping to quarrel.

I saw why she hadn't called the cops in yet. She wanted to have this quarrel privately, send me packing, without giving Neely or Johnson a chance to ally with me. "Did the alarm work?"

"Yes. Vista Security called my machine at four-twelve p.m."

"You got home when?"

"Maybe seven minutes later."

"Maybe you ought to change to the system that rings the cop shop directly." She didn't say anything. "Maybe we ought to go back to my place and stay for a while."

"I can't. I'm a cop. I can't jump at every squeak or fear every shadow." She squared her shoulders.

Sounded like whistling in the dark to me. I didn't blame her for being afraid or for denying it to make herself brave. I blamed her for taking chances that were too big.

"Have you looked at the video from the security camera yet?"

She nodded, absently. "Some little girl stuck the note in the door. Nine or ten years old."

"Did you recognize her?"

"No. I don't think I've ever seen her."

"It would be easiest to hire a neighborhood kid. Can we follow up on it?"

"Sure, I'll give the tape to Neely. They'll do a door to door."

I could tell from her tone that she didn't hold out much hope of finding our innocent delivery girl. "Look, I found out today that Page skipped out of Thornby House. You'd be safer someplace else."

"Page skipped? I'll have to tell Neely." She ignored my main point.

We haggled for some time. Finally she called Johnson and got Neely, who promised to send a uniform over to collect the evidence and convey it to a lab. She relayed the news about Page. Then she and Neely argued some. She was fine, thank you, and didn't need to stay at his house or anywhere else. She'd be back to work Monday.

I considered another plea, but she was set against leaving the house. She had all the reasons ready to tick off again, but I suspected the biggest was that she'd been thrown from the horse and had to crawl back on or never ride again. To be a cop, she had to prove to herself she could ride it. But she didn't have to ride alone.

We'd argued ourselves to an impasse. She wasn't budging, nor was I. But life would be tiresome if we had to have the same argument every night. Well, that was a euphemism for what I meant. Every time this vermin poked us by violating her space, it was a war of nerves, and currently he was winning.

We waited for the cop at the kitchen table, tense with each other and straining our ears. After an interminable silence, Lindstrom spoke again.

"I saw Thomas today."

"Aubuchon? Where?"

"At the cemetery."

I tried not to stare at her open-mouthed. She had been hanging around in the cemetery? "Where Viv is buried?"

She nodded and looked down at her hands. "He blames me. He kept saying this would have never happened if she hadn't left him."

"That's a pretty self-centered view of the world."

"All this overwhelming grief seems a bit too much, too."

"What do you mean?"

"I mean Viv left him years ago. He's acting like they were still married when she was murdered."

"Like he never got over her," I agreed.

"I think we need to be paying more attention to Thomas. He knew she was here. He couldn't stand it that she wasn't coming back to him. Maybe he snapped."

"I don't see Thomas as the type to beat Viv to death with a baseball bat, Lindstrom."

Her blonde eyebrows arched, "You'd be surprised."

Before we could finish this conversation, Neely's messenger arrived.

131

The uniformed cop stomped up onto the back porch, full of himself and his maleness. He stood in the kitchen with his hands on his hips and looked around as if he were there to give a traffic citation. I'd never before seen a cop strut so much while standing still. I could almost hear him thinking that he had better things to do than carry notes. I got a paper sack from a bottom drawer, and the cop shook his head impatiently as I dropped the sack trying to get it open. Finally, Lindstrom slid the note into the bag and taped the bag shut. The uniform reminded us to lock the door after he left. He was the kind of man who couldn't connect to a woman's fear in her own home—fear of assault, fear of rape. He couldn't imagine it. Of course, Lindstrom felt vulnerable. She'd been outed as a gay; she'd been targeted as a murder victim. But her real weakness in the eyes of many of the boys was that she was a female—the group God designated as victims. That's how I read this boy. I was in a bitter mood indeed. Shoving his baton up his ass seemed like a measured response.

CHAPTER TWENTY-ONE

When she closed the door on him and reset the alarm, Lindstrom turned to me. She looked pale and whooshed.

"What do you want for dinner?" I asked.

She gave me an exasperated look. "I'm not hungry."

"Probably not. But you look like low blood sugar to me."

A different look. "You amaze me; your expertise covers so many fields."

I rose above it. "Look, I don't want him to have the advantage of surprise and all the calories he needs while we pine away like hostages in a besieged castle."

"That's rather good, Darcy." She was about to say more but bit her lip.

"Thanks, Lindstrom. We could do Chinese or Mexican or fast food or breakfast at Uncle Bill's."

"Why don't you go out and get something? I'll stay here and mind the fort."

"I'd feel better if we went together. Watch your back, remember." I kept my tone light. "We could order out for pizza."

"And throw the delivery boy against the wall and frisk him I suppose." I wasn't sure toward whom her sarcastic tone was directed, but I suspected me. But maybe she wasn't being flip. I had the jitters, too, and until we cracked this case, I wasn't trusting delivery men or utility workers or postal employees who approached the house.

Maybe she was just too weary. She didn't wait for my reply. "All right. Order pizza. Anything. You choose." She turned away impatiently, started filling the tea kettle.

Suddenly I felt crass for being hungry. Here she'd just received a note from the creep who'd killed Viv. Of course, she'd lost her appetite.

"Lindstrom, I know we're smarter than this guy. He may think he's cute, making these calls, getting his little note delivered. But that's a mistake. Maybe he gets a jolt from jangling our nerves, but it keeps us on guard. We aren't going to forget he's out there. We'll be ready for him when he comes."

She gave me a look that said I'd said something intelligent.

"You think?" She arched her brows.

"I know. If he'd kept quiet after Viv's murder, we'd not even know he's out there. He could have sprung a surprise."

She considered. "He still has surprise on his side."

"But not a big surprise."

"I'm trying to take comfort from that." But I saw a little lift in her energy. I pressed further. "While he's playing games, we're pursuing leads."

"Page and Krebs?"

"For starters." I shrugged. "I know that murder cases that aren't solved in the first twenty-four hours are the hardest. Doesn't mean that they're never solved."

She didn't bother to point out again that many are not. And if this guy were not on our short list, our chances would shrink. "Okay. Tell me what you learned about Page."

We settled around the kitchen table, and I talked. Just exchanging information was doing something—in fact, we were doing the most ordinary and generally useful parts of an investigator's job. I saw her pulling back from whatever edge exhaustion and fear had led us to.

After we'd twice gone over my interview at Thornby House, we ordered a pizza from a nearby Soulard bistro that doesn't deliver. But I know Sheri, the manager, and she sent a bus boy. We both met him at the door. His eyebrows said the large tip didn't entirely make up for the .38 I had tucked into my waist band.

After pizza the long evening stretched ahead. Lindstrom was nearer her self-assured norm, but neither of us was calm. We were waiting for him to make the next move. No matter how we tried to shrug it off, to be proactive in our thinking, there was a feeling we were bugs pinned under his scope and waiting on his next poke.

Watching the Cards, playing Scrabble wouldn't be enough to hold us; we didn't try. Our conversations were repetitive, sifting over and over the facts we had. The police hadn't found anything from the bat or the shoe print or Viv's wounds that would be spectacularly helpful. The assailant had worn a tennis shoe that left rows of ridges, rather than a grid. The aluminum bat wasn't new.

"But they're working the case hard?" I pressed her.

"Ah, well. Not so hard as if I were dead." More glum than bitter. Of course. We all know how cops respond to a dead cop. But no department has enough police to prevent every crime.

"Neely and Johnson are still working it?" I asked.

"They are. But it's not their only case."

"Well, it's mine." Okay. Bravado.

She smiled, a tamped-down but authentic smile. "Thank you, Darcy." For once no irony.

I felt a blush ascending, so I stood and paced. "I think I'll go outside and check how things are," I said after two turns.

That started another round of debate. Was it better to stay inside and let him come to us? Should I go alone? Would I scare him off? Should I park my car elsewhere? Could we fool him into thinking Lindstrom was alone?

We settled nothing, but I ventured out into the night, a cop's flashlight in one hand and the .38 in the other. Even with the security camera, I felt better seeing and hearing the yard and surroundings myself. I didn't turn the light on. I stood on the back porch till my eyes adjusted. Clouds swam overhead, shutting off the moon. Humidity thickened the air. I moved slowly, out into the grass, triggering Phil's newly installed lights, taking my time, checking everything, listening to the summertime night noises. Saturday in Soulard. A few blocks away a jazz band ripped through Dixieland; closer by car doors slammed. A shrieking laugh. A cat's mew. I collected them all while probing the garage, the forsythia, our cars. When I got to the tunneled archway on the north side of Lindstrom's house, the flood light was bright at the back of the house, but I needed the flashlight near the front. The beam revealed no surprises: the tunnel walkway was empty of all but spiders above and brick sidewalk below. At the end Michellene looked lively. Neighbors came and left in cars I increasingly recognized. On the south side I used the flashlight again. We—Lindstrom, me, Phil Nelson of Vista Security—thought Viv's killer might have used a hose holder bracket to step on to hoist himself up to the bathroom window. Nelson had removed the hose hanger. The grass alongside the house was thin, but no footprints showed in the dirt. I wasn't looking for old ones; I was checking for new. I switched the flashlight off and finished my tour.

Lindstrom greeted me with a questioning look. Silly because I'd not have entered so calmly if I'd seen any sign of the stalker. But both of us were italicizing everything.

"Take me around the house the way you did Phil Nelson." I wanted to know all the strong points, all the weak points.

She gave me the complete tour, from the dusty attic to the musty basement. Maybe a crime wave from an earlier era was responsible; the basement windows were bricked shut. Windows on the second and attic floor would require an extension ladder. Phil Nelson had wired every downstairs window and door. The house was as snug as we could make it without extra security guards or a moat.

I looked at the clock. Nearly ten. Only ten. A huge night loomed before us. I glanced at Lindstrom and then away quickly before our eyes could meet. I didn't want to be caught pitying her. She looked exhausted, the energy of our search drained away, her face too pale.

"Can you think of anything else we should be doing?" I asked.

"You're the security expert." A frayed edge to the tone.

So I was. I thought. "Do you want us to put guards outside?"

"No, I want that bastard to make his move."

I looked at her. "You need some rest."

"Yes." A matter-of-fact evaluation.

"Lie down and get some sleep if you can. I'll do a tour outside in an hour or so."

"Let me know if you leave." She sounded anxious.

"I'll be all right." Flattered she cared.

"I don't want to blow you away by mistake when you come back in."

Serious. No teasing.

I thought about it. "I'll leave a note on the table. Look before shooting." I looked away. "I don't want to wake you if you're sleeping."

She suppressed a sigh. "Ah, yes."

"Would you sleep better if I were up there or you were down here?" I still wasn't meeting her gaze. I didn't want her to see me seeing victim's eyes.

"I don't think that's what's keeping me awake." She just managed to wring her voice dry. She started for the stairs.

I wanted to reopen the argument about moving to my place, but thought better of it. Seemed too much like poking a sick cat. She was hunkered down in her lair.

"Good night, Lindstrom," I said instead.

If she answered, I didn't hear, but she gave a little nod and a wave of fingers.

I walked into the den and made my bed of sheet, pillow, blanket and crawled on top with my clothes and shoes on and lay there, listening to the sounds of an old house filled with modern appliances that hum white noise, and watching a digital clock blink toward eleven. My own adrenaline surge was long gone and keeping my mind on business required all the habits of Army discipline. In fact, I used the face of a lesbian-baiting sergeant to keep me steamed. When the red numbers announced eleven, I rose and composed a note. "Lindstrom. Gone to walk the dog. Darcy." I had no hope she'd smile, but maybe she wouldn't shoot. I disarmed the alarm system and slipped out into the night.

Eleven on a summer night in Soulard is quite early if you aren't keeping the kind of watch I was keeping. The Dixieland band was bringing it home with gusto, and I wished I were there to join in the stomping. I heard a dog bark and doors slam and saw nothing I hadn't seen on the first tour.

But I stayed outside a little longer than I had to because outside felt like freedom and inside felt like imprisonment.

I thought about Page and Krebs—they were beginning to sound like a law firm to me—and wondered why anyone just released from prison would risk doing anything, even earning a parking ticket, that might send him back to the Walls.

Too soon I was back inside on the den couch, shoeless and cranky. I missed Harvey's conversation. I missed Patrick. I was well onto a list of how the creepo had deprived me of all life's normal amenities when I slid into a light and restless sleep.

I woke at two with that instantly sharp and wide awake start that shouts *insomnia*. I knew I would never sleep again—not that night, maybe never. I pulled on my shoes, added my .38 to my disheveled ensemble, and began another tour, pausing only long enough to scribble times onto my note: 11:00, 2:00.

Outside was markedly quieter now. No band, no barking. I did hear a car engine stuttering to a start down the alley. On Michellene I saw a male-female couple locked in an embrace on the sidewalk three houses down. I hoped theirs would be a happier future. I stared, trying to store their appearance for later identification, but I wasn't given much to work with: lots of denim, lots of hair. On such a hot night, too, I thought prissily, trying not to be envious. Me here, Lindstrom inside, upstairs. No kissing. Not that night. Maybe never.

I kicked at a marigold and finished the tour quickly. Inside, I heard nothing that wasn't old house, modern electronics. I knew I wasn't ready to sleep again. A cup of tea? No. I was too wired. A slug of whiskey? No. A little would increase my paranoia; a lot would incapacitate me. The solution came in one of those swift, clean strokes that cartoonists label 'Zowie!'

I gathered up my duffel bag of laundry. I carted it down into the basement that would always smell like a basement no matter how much whitewash and Lysol Lindstrom used. But there was plenty of halogen light—Viv's contribution Lindstrom had told me, her voice wobbling just at Viv's name. The washer and drier sat up on wooden pallets, and a long, cafeteria-style table offered space for folding clothes. Two navy blue plastic chairs sat alongside.

I'd scooped up some paperbacks for my stay at Lindstrom's just for a sleepless night, but nothing held me to the page. I put in the whites and paced up to the rinse cycle. I kept replaying every particle of what had happened since Lindstrom's call the morning after Viv's murder and told myself I was reviewing the facts of the case. But what it felt like was spinning my wheels. I climbed the stairs and brought back a stack of magazines from the rack in the den.

I muttered through an issue of *Vanity Fair*—a funny Fran Lebowitz piece was buried among hundreds of ads, many featuring emaciated children. I turned to *National Geographic*, comforted by its familiar format and staid prose. I'd finished still another trek by an intrepid woman traveling alone through Australia's Outback when the colored tee shirts unbalanced and *thunka-thunka* boomed through the basement.

I was there in a minute, unsnarling a sodden lump of cotton. In another minute I heard something behind me, a brush of cloth maybe, and whirled, my mind racing to my choice of weapons, the .38 gleaming uselessly on the folding table. Lindstrom stood on the stairs in a plain white tank top and light blue pajama bottoms, her feet bare and her arms extended with a police-issue 9mm pointed toward me. Our indignant "What?"'s sputtered out simultaneously.

And simultaneously we realized what had happened. She lowered her gun, but not her glare.

"I'm sorry if I woke you," I said.

"You didn't." She looked and sounded cross.

"I woke up and couldn't sleep and—"

She nodded impatiently. "You can't be walking naked through the streets of St. Louis," she finished for me, yada, yada in her tone. "God, Darcy, I thought you were being bludgeoned."

I didn't feel compelled to apologize for not being. "Did you get *any* sleep?"

She shrugged. "I dozed."

"Maybe sleeping pills? Just short term."

She glared. "Then he gets in, and where am I?"

"I'm here." I tried to sound steady and strong—and taller than I am.

She blew a puff of exasperation through pursed lips. A beat more while she thought. Then she looked into my eyes and spoke carefully. "It's not that I doubt you, Darcy. But at two o'clock I feel an army battalion couldn't stop him."

"You've watched too many slasher movies."

"I never watch slasher movies." She shrugged again. "Finish your laundry." She turned back up the stairs.

"Can I fix you something—a cup of tea, warm milk?"

"Un-uh. Good night."

I watched her long legs disappear up the stairs. Wouldn't this be easier on both of us if I dashed after her, swept her into my arms, offered the comfort of a warm body? Was I silly, even wrong, to accept her answer to that question? She looked like a woman who needed comforting, but even more like one who didn't want it. All she could think of was him, his next threat, his next move.

I returned to my laundry. In the next hour I watched the clothes toss in the drier. Even the *Geographic* couldn't pry my mind from its own spins: Lindstrom-Viv-him; Lindstrom-Viv-him.

By the time I climbed the stairs, loaded down with clean clothes, I was as tired as if I'd actually exercised that day, but body aches reminded me I hadn't. I stowed my clothes in her hallway closet and fell onto the couch, pushing my shoes off. I stuck the .38, just so, under the couch, pulled the blanket over me, closed my eyes, just to rest them.

CHAPTER TWENTY-TWO

When I emerged from the shower, Lindstrom was making coffee. For a while I busied myself with pouring cereal for my breakfast and setting the table. "No cereal for me," she said.

I knew she wasn't going into work today, that her real return to work would start tomorrow. Long ago, before the note, I had had a day in the park planned—sandwiches from Mangio's maybe, followed by a stroll in Tower Grove. Or a trip to the zoo. Something out in the open, putting a little sunshine into our lives. I'd thought to suggest this casually. Before the note.

But now her face discouraged me. I knew I couldn't count on her finishing her coffee.

"You looked dressed for going out. Got plans for the day?" What I'd meant as casual came out heavy and intrusive to my own ears.

To hers, too, from her look. "Colin and his partner Jeff invited me to brunch with them at Duff's." Her tone was even. I only imagined the sarcastic "What's it to you?" she was holding back. "I'll be all right," she added.

I hadn't said she wouldn't. But she wasn't through.

"You can only do so much to protect me." She sounded as though she'd given the matter lots of thought, most of it carved from her night's sleeping time. I felt guilty for having slept like someone comatose after our two-thirty encounter.

I nodded and tried for a pleasant face. Of course, I didn't mind that she had plans for the day that didn't include me.

As though she'd read my mind, she asked, "You're having brunch with Healy, right?"

So she remembered that most Sundays Patrick and I got together for at least bagels and commiseration about our mostly dateless Saturday nights. I hadn't told her that I'd e-mailed Patrick to cancel this Sunday's affair.

I didn't tell her now. "Sure, but you'd be welcome."

She was all surface and very polite. "Thank you, but I promised Colin." She started clearing away. Maybe I just meant to hang onto her a moment longer. I blurted out, "I thought I'd try to get some leads on Page."

"What?" A staccato snap. She turned on one heel, her face suddenly energized.

I sketched in my plans for calling people who might know about Aryan Nation and like-minded groups. I concluded, "So I might skip my brunch with Patrick."

"Oh, damn," she said.

"Oh, he won't mind. We see plenty of each other."

"No—this thing with Colin. I don't think I can get out of it."

"So?"

"I can help you make calls. I'll leave early."

"Lindstrom, I know how to dial."

She wasn't listening. "The Lieutenant couldn't object to phone calls. Especially if he doesn't know about them." She smiled brightly, the best smile I'd seen since Friday. "Where will you be?"

"I thought I'd go into the office."

"I'll see you there then—about one?"

I nodded. Why wasn't I happy? I wanted to spend the time with Lindstrom. That make looking after her easier. Did I fear interference in my investigation? But I couldn't think of a sensible objection, and we parted company.

***

The day looked broody. Another storm brewing with huge thunder-clouds building in the southwest. In the meantime humidity ruled, creeping into everything. My fresh clothes were a waste. My shirt stuck to my back by the time I reached Gravois.

No sign of Walter when I reached the office. The Cards were at home; maybe he was in the bleachers with some buddies. I walked through the office, making sure I was alone. I stopped in the kitchen and made a pot of coffee, plain Schnucks' brew. Before the pot filled, I'd grabbed a memo pad and brain-stormed a list. You'd think Sundays would be a hard day to do business, but PIs know better. You can catch people at home, and a rainy Sunday was ideal. Some still made it to church, but golf dates and picnics got canceled. By the time it was safe to fill a cup, I had a respectable phone list.

I knew as well as Lindstrom that the cops were better equipped than I was to catch a guy like Page. But, with the exception of Neely and maybe Johnson, the cops were not as highly motivated.

Still, I started with an easy one. I had the Anti-Defamation League on my list. I tried their web site and got a list of Missouri counties where I might find splinters of militia, some focusing on gays, others intent on elim-inating blacks and Jews, several dedicated to the proposition that the U.S.A. was meant to be a Christian nation, and all adhering to guns and violence as a means to impose their vision of the world.

I'm an urban gal. I scarcely remember the names of counties important to my own life. But country people talk about their counties. They're always hauling something to the county seat or visiting someone in the county hos-pital or jail. I had followed the trail all the way to the county fair and to its quilt display when a light clicked on.

Mary Jo Middleton! Of course, she was right smack in the middle of the third county on the list. Mary Jo Middleton had been my immediate superior in the Army. She was a white woman, maybe fifteen years my senior. She had a Southerner's easy charm, laid back and mellow, coupled with a military woman's bluntness when action's called for.

There was a knock at the door. I knew who it was, and, sure enough, there she was, peering in with that cop's look of impatience and, yes, arrogance on her face. I undid the locks.

"What happened? Did Colin not show?"

"I ate quickly and excused myself. What have you found out?"

"Not much yet. I have a few more phone calls to make before we visit Page's mother. And I need to get lunch."

She took the hint. "What do you want? I'll get it while you finish your calls." She was still pumped up, the prospect of investigation allowing her to shake off the night's oppressive weight.

I gave her my order for White Castle basics; Lindstrom frowned but refrained from lecturing and left. I returned to my desk and Mary Jo Middleton. When I called her, she herself answered. She was enjoying a rainy day, sitting on her back porch, rocking, and appreciating life. In her retirement, life revolved around a carefully planned and personally constructed log cabin, built bit by bit, over years of service leave. The cabin, sparsely furnished with just the trinkets Mary Jo treasured, sat amid a hundred acres with its own creek, a small cave, some open meadow, and lots of timber. I outlined my problem first.

She listened with her usual careful attention. When I finished, she said, "Well, you've got the right place. There's a passle of 'em down here."

"Doesn't that make you nervous?"

The pause seemed long. "Things are a little more complicated than CNN's version of the world. I got cousins and second cousins and third cousins. Not all of 'em are on the right side of this issue." She paused again.

"You're thinking they won't shoot their kinfolk?"

She chuckled. "Oh, some would and be glad for the excuse. But even here, where so many talk big and walk big, it's a little more complicated."

"Could I come down and ask questions?"

"God, no." She sounded as shocked as if I'd casually proposed a sexual act.

I paused. "I don't get it. Isn't this a free country?" The idea that some St. Louis streets are not safe for me already stuck in my craw. But small town America? And this, from Mary Jo?

She cleared her throat. "You'd stick out like a sore thumb. And so might Gregory Page. You know folks are getting suspicious of outsiders who come in and claim to be part of the great anti-government, anti-other movement. Since Oklahoma. Now they're more worried about the F.B.I. and, worse, informers."

"So?"

She cleared her throat again. "You haven't lost your impatience I see." Fondly. Or so I heard it. "So, let things unfold. I'll see if any of these pesky branches on the family tree have noticed your St. Louis boy strutting about."

"The thing is, I'm rather attached to the woman he may be stalking. I'd like to find him."

"That's the thing, is it?"

"Yeah."

"Well, I'll try to hurry it along. Since it's more than just truth, justice, and the American way." A dry ha for a signal she was joking. Or gently chiding me.

I asked her for some information I might pass on to the law enforcement pipeline. She named names. Whether she weeded out or left in cousins, I didn't ask. But some of the names were part of her local law enforcement. I wondered if Klanish deputies butted heads with militias who hated any government authority other than their own self-proclaimed common-law selves. I'd save those questions for another conversation. As it was, I had a depressingly long list of people who might welcome a man like Gregory Page into their midst.

"You got any good guys down there?" I asked when she finished.

A small hoot. "Oh, yes. And gals, too. But sometimes the good guys are harder to recognize. Darcy, some day, when this is over, come visit. Bring the lady."

"Count on it."

CHAPTER TWENTY-THREE

Earlier, I'd called my friend Nina, who ran a women's shelter, for leads on the Aryan Nation. I was scrawling notes on that call when she called back. "I've got an Alice whose husband attends militia meetings down in the boot heel. She was a little shy about telling me how he hates black folk but eager to bond over the fact he despises queers. I decided not to destroy the moment by telling her the awful truth in the hope that she'd talk more freely."

"Timing is everything."

"Yes, it is. But, Meg, I'm thinking you better not ride off into the west by your lonesome self because these militia types scare me. If they take on sheriffs, they wouldn't hesitate to chop you to bits."

"I'll be careful."

"Hear me. I'm no runner, and I'm no quitter. But my momma raised me to be smart. Let the police do this."

"I'm just asking questions."

"That isn't a promise."

"Nina—" I started a smart remark, then switched. "Thanks. I'll be very careful."

"I don't want to read in the papers that you've been shot."

"Did Alice say this group was violent?"

"Oh, yeah, they act out all their little spites when they can."

She told me where to find this group, giving me directions into the boot heel. I was Photocopying the directions when Lindstrom returned carrying two sacks of my order. I offered her a share of my belly bombers and fries and a sip of my shake, but she snubbed me. "I already feel like an accessory to a crime, just buying this for you."

"We can't all brunch at Duff's," I said primly.

"As if you wouldn't in a second."

"A heartbeat." I was scarfing my second bomber.

"Should your heart still operate." She picked up the photocopy. "What's this?"

"A road to one of Page's lairs maybe."

She frowned when I explained. "Darcy, this is too dangerous to stroll into."

"You can't impersonate a redneck, a Nebraska farm girl like you?"

"I read too many police journals. These guys don't hesitate to go after law enforcement."

"Are we just going to let the crazies run the country?" My voice rising.

She cocked an eyebrow. "No. But you and I aren't going to tackle them by ourselves. I'll pass this on to Neely."

"Will the St. Louis police send out a posse?"

"Honestly? No. But we'll get in touch with the people who keep an eye on these groups."

"Someone is?"

She shrugged. "I have to believe it."

"All right. Here are the directions to pass on. You call Neely. I'll finish my lunch."

We accomplished our assigned chores within seconds of one another. I was just returning from washing White Castle grease from my fingers when she hung up.

"What's next?" she asked.

***

The sunshine hadn't improved when we left the office to head to Page's family home, east across the river. The clouds were heavy and dark, squeezing damp air downward, not cooling anything off.

Lindstrom whistled as we approached the big oil refineries.

"You oughtta see this at night. Looks like some futuristic city, the *Blade Runner* kind," I said.

"I thought Illinois was all farming outside Chicago."

I couldn't tell if she were joking.

Wood River doesn't offer many challenges, even to the directionally impaired. The humidity spread the stink of oil being refined into gasoline a little further, and small bungalows that made up the blue collar neighborhoods looked a little shabbier without sunshine to light up their trim lawns. We found Emma Page's clapboard house in the middle of a block of similarly modest houses, some with vinyl siding, some with paint. "I went to one of my first gay—well, lesbian—parties here, right after high school," I confided.

"Here at 706?"

"No—in Wood River. I was just out of high school. A women's softball team held the party."

She cocked a brow. "I don't think of you as an athlete."

"Well, see, you don't know all the details." I was maneuvering the Plymouth up to the front curb. The driveway was cracked asphalt. On it sat a shiny red Chevy pickup. On the bumper *It's a Child / Not a Choice* and above that *JESUS* confined by a chrome outline of a fish.

We hadn't called ahead because I didn't want Mrs. Page to have time to confer with her son.

"I think you ought to let me take the lead, Lindstrom. You're way out of your jurisdiction." I tried to be bland. I was concealing a grumpiness about having Lindstrom along at all. I was used to working solo or with Miller Security colleagues who understand a PI's ways.

"All right," she said. "What's your plan?"

I didn't have one mapped out. Winging it often works for me. "For what?" Just stalling.

"Say Page is there."

I thought that unlikely. I thought he was in southwest Missouri playing militia man or in the city hiding out. I was after information, not a collar. "If he's there and threatens us, we go for the local cops. If he's there and isn't threatening us, I tell him to come back voluntarily; it'll go easier for him."

"We don't stomp him with our hobnailed boots?"

"Sorry to disappoint you."

Her lips compressed into a tight line while she thought. "You walk a little ahead of me. I'll have my Beretta ready."

"Yeah, well, watch how you use it." I didn't want to be between her and Page if guns started blazing.

"Don't you trust me, Darcy?" Her blue eyes lit with mischief, the first such glimmer I'd seen in days. Maybe months.

Number 706's sidewalk was edged with impatiens, and two begonias fought for life on the front stoop. The closer we got the worse the paint job on the clapboard. Little blisters of paint appeared unattended.

The short walk from the curb to the front door was the uneasiest part of our journey. I didn't see any twitching of curtains at the windows, but who knew what spying eyes had us in view? I opened the screen door and pounded.

I was just ready to repeat the pound when the door opened. A woman taller than me, not so tall as Lindstrom, stood in the doorway, dressed in white uniform pants and a Garfield tee-shirt. She was maybe in her late fifties, around Betty's age. Her chestnut hair, cut for low maintenance, looked rich enough to be colored, but I saw threads of gray. Maybe she'd started the day with make-up; only a bit of lipstick stayed with her. Her eyes were bluish gray behind rimless glasses. She looked startled by our presence.

"Mrs. Page, Emma Page?"

"Emma Woolsey. I was Mrs. Page."

"Mrs. Woolsey, we're here to ask a few questions about your son."

"I have two sons." Guarded.

"Gregory. Gregory Page, ma'am."

She wasn't happy to hear it. She looked at me and past me to Lindstrom. A small sigh of resignation, a slight shoulder straightening. "Who are you?" The words weren't welcoming, but her tone was merely flat.

"I'm Meg Darcy." I pulled out my billfold and showed her my PI's ID. "I work for Miller Security in St. Louis. We're contracted to the State of Missouri to help locate parolees who've lost touch with their parole officers. This is my partner, Jennifer Slater."

She listened carefully to the first two sentences, but was stepping back before I finished. "You'd better come in."

A small square living room was overwhelmed by faux walnut paneling. But the room was clean and uncluttered with a couple of big lounge chairs and a matching couch with end tables, a TV in one corner, a few geegaws scattered about. One wall had a Wal-Mart landscape. The wall opposite the sofa had a photographic display. A black and white of a young couple dressed in the styles of the 30s or 40s with a small coupe behind them were probably Emma's parents. A studio portrait in color showed a younger Mrs. Page— maybe not Mrs. Woolsey yet—with two boys and a girl. A single mom raising a family. Then we had rows of separate school shots of the kids, culminating in the senior pictures.

"These your children?" I asked, putting as much interest into it as I could and indicating the family grouping.

"Yes. Leon was fourteen, Gregory was twelve, Deana was eight." For just a moment a note of pride crept out. She shrugged. "They grow up too fast. Will you sit down?" Not really welcoming. Resigned.

"Thanks. We will," I said. I picked a chair and sat forward so I wouldn't sink into it. Lindstrom took a couch end. Emma Page Woolsey sank into the other chair.

She glanced at her watch. "I was just on my way into work. One of the other nurses got sick at the hospital, and I said I'd come in early for my shift."

"You work nights?"

"Mostly. It's not bad once you get used to it." She pulled a rueful smile from somewhere. "You aren't here to discuss me. How can I help you?"

"We'd like to find Gregory, ma'am."

"I don't know where he is. We don't stay in touch."

I was considering my next question when she went on. "It's funny. All these years I never heard anything about Leon except that he made A's and was doing great at his after-school job. Greg was in trouble by the second grade, and it never stopped—lies, petty theft, fights. He was like a ticking time bomb, like his red hair set him on fire."

"How did he act at home?" Lindstrom asked.

Emma Woolsey gave Lindstrom an acknowledging nod, "Pretty much the same. From the time his daddy left, Gregory was an angry little man. Maybe even before and I didn't notice."

"Did he fight with his brother and sister?" I couldn't imagine that he didn't, but I asked.

"Sure, till he was big enough to stay away from home. Mostly he picked at me." Her smile was lop-sided. "I know that sounds crazy. Who's the adult here?" She shook her head. "But he liked to torment me. He certainly didn't have any family feeling."

"You raised them by yourself?"

"Pretty much. I know single moms are the cause of everything." She didn't struggle against the bitterness. "I was luckier than some. I had some schooling, and I got my nursing degree a year after Jack left. But I didn't get any help with child care. Take that back. Jack's grandmother helped watch the kids while I finished school."

"I know it's hard. My mother had the same row to hoe."

She looked at me a moment. "I appreciate that. I loved my kids—well,

146

I did till Gregory killed the old woman. After that—I can't say I loved him anymore." She pleated the material on her kneecap with nervous fingers. "It's hard to say that. Anyway, I loved 'em and worked for them, and I was pretty much alone. Then Gregory did that killing, and I got even more alone. Lots of neighbors and so-called friends and even relatives stopped speaking to me. Now I've got my church. They know, but it don't matter to them. But till I started to church all I had were the other two kids. They remembered how it was. So I'm glad you remember how it was for your mom."

She'd taken a long way round, but I didn't mind. I figured the world owed her some listening time.

"Do you live here by yourself now?" Lindstrom asked.

"Yes. Woolsey's my maiden name. After the kids got married, I went back to it."

My ears had pricked. "Did Greg marry?"

A dismissive laugh. "Not him. Leon did, after college. He's in Creve Coeur now. He works for Boeing, a good, white-collar job. Deana didn't do so well. She had a baby and got married in the wrong order." She shrugged. "Wasn't glad, but I'm not ashamed. That baby's one dandy. And Denny—that's the father—he's turning out okay, too."

"Would Greg be likely to get in touch with his brother or sister?"

"Yeah, sure, when hell freezes over." A more genuine laugh. "He won't get any help from any of us. Maybe that's wrong. He's still my son. But I've had too many visits from too many cops over too many years. And it's terrible to say this, but I believe he'd as soon stomp me or Leon or Deana as that old woman."

I agreed. A terrible thing to say, and I wondered how she'd said it so calmly, but I figure she'd had practice wrestling with it.

"Ms. Woolsey, we have reason to believe Gregory is mixed up with one of the white supremacist groups—Aryan Nation or some other militia-type of group. Any idea how that got started?"

We watched a blush creep up her cheeks. "I won't lie to you. There was a time when he probably heard bad things about blacks around here. I was raised that way, and I didn't question it for a long time. Nothing vicious, you know, but the run-of-the-mill insults." She paused so we could help her out.

I nodded, and she continued. "Now I think lots different. Jesus loves us all. I don't have time to judge how other people look or how they live." She said it like a private whisper, not expecting applause. She looked me in the eyes. "And I was way wrong about black people. I know it's some kind of joke about 'some of my best friends are black people,' but Nora Roberts, she's my best friend now. She's a nurse at Alton Memorial with me. Her son is doing time because he was a crack dealer. She's cut him loose, too. We have a lot in common." She glanced at Lindstrom who was moving restlessly; I wouldn't have minded hearing more, but Emma Woolsey had a question of her own. "Will he go back to jail if you find him?"

"Maybe," Lindstrom said, strongly overriding my "I don't know."

Gregory's mother looked at us questioningly.

I jumped into the lead. "Depends how he answers some questions about how he's spent some of his time recently."

"Whether he's committed another crime?"

"Yes."

She didn't ask what.

Lindstrom couldn't stay quiet. "If we can find him, we may prevent another crime."

More shadows settled in Emma Woolsey's face. "I'm sure everyone will be safer if he's back in jail."

Sounded like understatement to me, and I couldn't improve on it. I rose and handed her a regular Miller Security card and thanked her for her time.

CHAPTER TWENTY-FOUR

Outside the wind was rising. Another storm was blowing up. I didn't know if we could make it back across the river before the storm broke. A wish filled my mind. Lindstrom knew nothing of the East side of the region except East St. Louis's bad rep. I thought of staying on this side, hanging out, showing her some of the sights. I could take her to Belleville, introduce her to Betty. Or we could drive north a bit, see Pere Marquette State Park, visit the Village of Elsah. I glanced her way. She still looked energized by being in the active part of the investigation, more like the Lindstrom I'd first been attracted to.

We climbed into the Plymouth; the seats were nearly squidgy with humidity. She spoke first. "Do you believe her?"

"About?"

"He's not in touch with her."

"I think so." Actually I'd been quite convinced.

"What about the brother and sister?"

"He'd be less likely to try to see them, wouldn't he?"

"Maybe." She sounded doubtful.

"Why not?"

"You can visit people to inflict pain on them. He might try to make them pay him to go away."

We looked at each other. "Shit," I said, dismayed it was becoming my favorite expletive. I crawled from the car, the sticking seats clinging like velcro to my clothes.

The wind was really gusting now. I knocked, and Emma Woolsey opened the door immediately. She'd probably been watching for us to leave so that she could jump into her truck and drive to the hospital.

"Sorry to bother you again. Could I just have the phone numbers and addresses of your other two children?"

She creased her brow to a frown. "I don't mind answering your questions. Maybe I owe that to society since I raised Gregory; I don't know. But I've tried really hard to not let him spoil their lives." The more she said, the hotter she got about it.

I tried to deescalate. "I understand. It must be tough for all of you. We'll try not to take up too much of their time. It just crossed my partner's mind that Gregory might try to bother them himself."

I have to say she listened carefully, which is more than most hot-under-the-collar folks can bring themselves to do. And she got it right away.

"All right." She waited quite patiently while I fished my pen from my pants. Then she carefully dictated the information I needed. Only then did she say, "Deana and her husband are away this weekend. His folks have a fishing cabin at Kentucky Lake."

"Would Gregory know where that is?"

"Oh, Lord." She hadn't thought of it. "You think he might bother Deana's in-laws?"

"I'm thinking he might realize the cabin is a place he could hide in during the week. If you could just tell me how to find it, we could ask a local sheriff to check on it."

"It never ends, does it?" Just flat. She was right. The victims of crime include the perp's family. The ramifications just kept spreading outward, waves from a tossed stone.

I waited for her to recover. She gave a tight-lipped smile. "Let me double check." She disappeared from the doorway and came back with a flowered address book. This address she rattled off more quickly, but I caught it on the fly. The wind tugged at my clothes.

I thanked her, perhaps too much. She was ready for me to leave. But when I said at last, "I hope this all ends peacefully, Ms. Woolsey," I saw in her eyes that I'd stumbled onto the right thing.

"Me too; me too. Oh, darn."

Her last words were a response to the fact that the storm broke then, ripping open the sky. A deluge fell upon us in big, splatting drops. I raced back to the car, but it was too late: I was soaked.

Lindstrom laughed. Not a great laugh, more a rude belly laugh.

The rain fell in a delirium.

"Thanks," I said. I tossed the damp notebook her way.

"I'm just always amazed by your bursts of athleticism," she said, shaking the notebook away from her.

I didn't know what she meant. The only athletic things I'd ever done in her presence had been done in my bedroom in cozier times. I didn't think I could use that as my retort. Instead, I nodded toward my notes. "Still usable?"

She checked. "Yes. What's this Stricklands in Kentucky?"

I explained, and she agreed she'd relay that to Johnson and Neely. We talked it over and decided a drive to Creve Coeur to see Leon Page would not be amiss.

***

St. Louis isn't a climate that follows a downpour with a quick dry out. We had to stop somewhere so I could change clothes. I had to pause to think about which parts of my wardrobe lodged where. Seemed to me I had all the disadvantages of living back and forth in two domiciles with my sweetie and none of the advantages. Maybe not even a sweetie.

But while the drive to Wood River had been mostly silent, on the trip to Creve Coeur Lindstrom, while not exactly chattering, stayed alert and fully present. I half-expected her to say, "The game is afoot, Watson."

We travelled west past Ladue, one of St. Louis's most prestigious sub-urbs. Certainly one of the priciest. I figured Creve Coeur was for wannabes, but when I said that, Lindstrom chided me for classism. I told her not to sound like William F. Buckley, and she said who? Her spirits were higher. She seemed a long way from the tense woman who'd confronted me, gun drawn, from her basement stairs the night before. Being out of the house and on the lookout for Page was definitely better than waiting for him to look for us.

We found Leon Page's brick-and-stone house at the wooded end of a cul-de-sac. The doors to the two-car garage were open, displaying a Ford Explorer in red and a BMW in navy. "Where's the white Porsche?" I asked as we slipped into the driveway behind them. A plastic tricycle and other infant scooter toys sprawled over the drive, just like in trailer courts.

"Maybe I'd better ask the questions," Lindstrom said.

"I'll behave."

"Suppose there's always a first time. Are you sharing the umbrella?"

"I'll be round to get you," I promised and ducked out. Of course she used her greater height to take charge of the umbrella, but we clasped waists like members of a potato-sack race and did a quick march up to Leon Page's front steps. We pressed the bell; a dog somewhere, perhaps in the basement, began barking, and before Lindstrom parked our umbrella, a young man who looked middle-aged even in weekend khakis opened the door, a baby in a receiving blanket draped over one shoulder. He was tall enough and of medium weight but without any muscle tone to him. His brown hair was receding from his hairline; his horn rims gave him the accountant's look, even without a pocket protector in his plaid shirt. The baby on his shoulder didn't soften his frosty look.

A young woman's voice called out something I didn't catch.

"I'll take care of it, hon," he answered in a lush baritone that matched nothing else. He patted the baby's bottom. "Mom said you'd be here."

Lindstrom and I exchanged a quick look.

"May we come in?" I used my most adult voice.

"I really can't help you. I've not seen Gregory in years. I don't know anything about him, and I don't want to know." He kept patting the baby's butt gently, but his voice chiseled out the words.

"He hasn't tried to get in touch with you?" I pressed him.

"I said he hadn't."

I glanced at Lindstrom. She had that interested look that resistance brings out in authority figures.

"Mr. Page, we're not trying to harass you. We think your brother may try to get in touch to ask for money so that he can travel from the area." I kept my words sweet.

"He knows he won't get any from me. Or Deana. She and Denny don't have it, and I wouldn't give him the time of day." He shifted the infant, who seemed to be falling asleep on his father's shoulder.

Lindstrom spoke then, her voice as chilly as his. "We're also afraid your family might be in danger. He could use them as leverage to get money from you."

Leon Page looked astonished, as though however much he'd scorned Gregory as a social embarrassment, he hadn't pictured his brother as that kind of threat. "You mean to me or Deana?"

"Or to junior there. I presume Gregory knows where you live." Nothing cuddly in her tone.

Leon stopped patting and shifted the baby to cradle it in his arms. "I don't think Greg would... " He wasn't sure how to finish.

"Stomp an eighty-year-old woman to death?" Lindstrom supplied.

Leon flushed. "We didn't do anything wrong," he said.

"Then help us find him," she said.

"Sometimes siblings know things mothers don't," I suggested.

"Not me. I couldn't stand him. Mom put up with his shenanigans way too long."

"No idea where he'd go to ground? Girlfriends? Buddies?" I kept it light.

He was shaking his head no to everything. But he looked worried. "You know my wife and kids are here by themselves during the day. Can we get police protection?"

I nearly laughed, turned it into a throat clearing. We'd gone just that little bit too far. I choked back a bitter retort—the one about the St. Louis police not even being able to guard their own.

"I wish I could say yes, Mr. Page," Lindstrom said, politely as though they'd not had a verbal tussle. "But take my card. If you hear anything from Gregory, anything at all, get in touch with me. And urge your mother and sister to do the same." She was fishing in a back pocket.

I covered quickly by handing her one of Jennifer Slater's cards. She blinked but kept her face in order. The card simply read 'Jennifer Slater' with the number for Miller Security. I had had Jennifer Slater's false, generic business card made up a few years before. She has a phone number that rings on a separate line into Miller Security and connects to an answering machine that Colleen doesn't respond to until the caller or caller ID reveals who is calling. Jennifer has many careers; her job *du jour* depends on the case I'm working.

"Anything at all, call me," Lindstrom said sternly, fixing him with a laser-beam stare.

"Thanks a lot," I said pleasantly, just to break the spell and turned away to lift the umbrella. Leon Page closed the door.

While we'd been engaged in his scintillating repartee, the rain had stopped, once again having failed to squeeze the humidity from the air. I could feel a new sheen of sweat beginning.

"Some low profile you kept," I said to Lindstrom.

She merely grunted.

***

The drive back to the city gave us plenty of time to dissect Leon Page, even enough to disagree in our interpretations of him. I expected Lindstrom to be more generous. She of all people should appreciate how crimes spread like oil spills across the lives of victims, relatives, friends, hapless bystanders. But she took a cop's narrower view: if you aren't cooperating with us, you're part of the problem.

My stomach was starting to rumble, and I mentioned this fact to Lindstrom. Once again she looked impatient with the regularity of my appetite, especially whenever I mentioned it during an investigation.

"Someplace quiet," she said. I thought Mendoza's fit the bill, and she didn't argue. By the time we pulled into one of the slots along the curb on its south side, we'd run out of Leon Page as a subject. Lindstrom stayed subdued through ordering and eating.

I threw out conversational balls, but she didn't run with them. She looked glum. Finally I asked point blank. "Is something wrong?"

"I hate going home without having caught him."

I had nothing comforting to say. I felt like we'd been on a day's release from jail to do our work, but now we had to go back to our cell. That view made me want to draw out the evening before going back, but Lindstrom was just pulled down by it.

"We could go to my place—watch a movie on the VCR, play with Harvey."

She shrugged me off. "I'm not missing entertainment."

***

She was right, of course, and I had no cure for her blues. In fifteen minutes we were back at Michellene. This time I suggested we try cards or Monopoly or any damn thing as a diversion. But Lindstrom wouldn't play. She called Neely to pass on the information about the Kentucky Lake fishing cabin and the white supremacist spots in Missouri. Then she retired to the living room with a stack of magazines and her silence.

That hurt, and my first response was the adolescent classic "I don't care." Every time I thought about Lindstrom in the old way, something happened to remind me to stuff the feelings down. I wondered if I kept killing off every little twitch of desire, if I'd end up unable to love her at all.

Meanwhile, every two hours I checked what was visible on the surveillance camera and made a tour around the house. Once we had another spate of rain. The rest of the night was quiet. By eleven Lindstrom had wished me good night. I lay on the den couch and ticked off the little we'd learned about Gregory Page's whereabouts that day. I was starting to like him as the most probable suspect. I wished I could believe he was far away in some Missouri woods tromping around with like-minded militia and attracting the attention of, say, the F.B.I. But I wasn't sure he'd left Dodge. Calling him names to demean him didn't shrink his actual I.Q. I thought he might be just smart enough to stay uncaught in the city.

Maybe it was that uncomfortable thought that led to an uncomfortable body. I couldn't find a position that didn't twist or pull some unhappy body part. I did another tour at two and found the night still squishy with humidity. I didn't linger long. Back inside, I took a long, hot shower, and for a few soapy minutes felt clean and free of both sweat and anxieties. Back in the den I fell into the couch, pulled half the sheet over my naked body, tucked the .38 under the couch. Comforted, protected, at least minimally, I let go and fell asleep.

CHAPTER TWENTY-FIVE

Monday morning Lindstrom got up, did thirty minutes on the treadmill, showered, and spared herself fifteen minutes with bran flakes and the *Post Dispatch*.

"What's on today?" I asked.

"Whatever a Monday brings, I suppose. Depends on who shot whom last night."

"Will you work alone?"

"No, they'll assign me a partner, temporarily."

I knew she was nervous about facing the whole homicide department this morning as the rumor mill had had plenty of time to do its work. She didn't relish their sympathy much more than she did their disgust, I was sure. And yet I was at a loss for what to say to her. Her tamped-down mood warned me off addressing the subject openly. I settled for, "Be careful out there," in my best *Hills Street Blues* imitation as she left. I left right behind her. I had things on my mind to look into. For the next eight hours her safety was on her and the St. Louis Police Department.

But of course I couldn't keep her out of my mind even though Miller Security filled my day. Lindstrom crawled into the corners of my warehouse inspection and distracted me during my interview of a new security woman for a local grocery chain. I pride myself on my ability to focus, but Lindstrom was a magnet pulling me toward her. I wasn't even lusting after her—well, not much. By the time Colleen wished me a good evening, I was ready to fly back to Lindstrom.

When I pulled into the slot behind the house, Lindstrom's Toyota was already there. She must have gotten off work precisely at five and driven straight home. I found her sitting in the kitchen, staring at nothing when I came in.

"So how was your day?"

She looked glum. "It felt strange not working with Neely. We had a teen shooting—both victim and shooter under seventeen. It was a long day."

"Who are you working with?"

"Judith Rosero."

I thought that was good news. If the department thought Lindstrom was a crazed lesbian, would they assign her with a woman?

Lindstrom read my mind or needed to relieve hers. "She's one of the worst homophobes. She might as well be handling me with surgical gloves and tweezers. She's obvious in her distaste."

I hated hearing it. I don't believe women are innately superior to men, morally or otherwise. The Judith Roseros prove that women can be as nasty as any insecure male.

"Was the pairing someone's idea of a bad joke or a big hint?" I asked.

She forced a tense smile. "My thought exactly. Her partner's on sick leave, and they want to give her some experience in Area 3."

Area 3 is the North side, mostly poor, mostly black.

"Is she racist as well as homophobic?" The two so often dance.

"Seemingly not. Her partner is black, and I've heard they get along."

I turned it over. "Maybe they think Rosero is educable."

"Maybe, but I have my doubts."

"Is she older?" I asked.

"No, younger. Maybe twenty-seven."

Another theory blown. Or hope. "I keep thinking the younger ones will be more generous of spirit."

"Not Rosero." She made a hopeless gesture with her hands. "At least she's open about it. What makes me crazy are the behind-the-back whisperers."

I nodded. "Look, let's go to dinner. You've had a hell of a day. You deserve a good listener," I said when she finished her report.

"Do you know you are always trying to get me to go out to eat? Some women try to get me in bed. You want to take me out to a restaurant." Her tone was very dry.

I laughed. "I know that says something I don't want to know." I wanted to protest that I was plenty interested in getting her to bed, but I was cautious.

"Maybe some people who are always pushing therapists should see one," she said. Definitely arch I thought.

"I never thought it was an either/or choice, food or bed," I said, primly suppressing the joke about different kinds of eating that rushed to the front lobe of my dirty little mind.

"Hmm," she said and started toward the stairs. "Let me change clothes."

I heard no invitation to follow, so I returned to the den.

She was back in fifteen minutes, her blonde hair wet from a quick shower.

***

She drove us to one of The Hill's most expensive Italian restaurants. "My treat," she said. "After all, you've been guarding me for days now."

I didn't give my best attention to white table cloths and obsequious waiters. Good wine is a loss to me. We each limited ourselves to a glass before dinner. Dinner was very quiet. I tried to get Lindstrom to talk more about Judith Rosero, but her heart wasn't in it. Lindstrom pulled out a gold American Express card to pay the bill.

By the time we returned to the house on Michellene, neither of us had much to say. Lindstrom started on the breakfast dishes immediately and rebuffed my effort to help. When she finished the dishes, she swept the floor, vacuumed, and cleaned the downstairs bathroom. I ducked out. Coping-by-cleaning wasn't something I wanted to watch.

I prowled restlessly outside, wishing we could lure our stalker out into the open. I formulated and rejected several plans. The neighborhood was pretty quiet. I checked that Lindstrom's car was locked, and then I checked mine. I decided a walk would expend some of this anxiety and energy. I stretched my legs out and headed north. I walked a mile toward Busch Stadium in twelve minutes, but it took me fourteen on the way back.

As I walked down Michellene, I noticed a car I'd never seen before. It was a dark blue sedan, parked a little to the north of the house and facing Lindstrom's. I wondered briefly if the St. Louis Police Department had sent someone to do surveillance. I squinted at the plates. I couldn't quite make them out from my vantage point, but they didn't look like municipal plates. I sidled over to the edge of the sidewalk into the shadows and took a few steps forward. There was someone in the car. His head moved. I hunkered down. Beard the lion or go straight for the house and call the cops? I needed at least a make and a plate number. I took a few more steps forward and stared at the plate until the numbers and letters came clear. I repeated them over and over and moved closer to the car. The engine was running. Maybe he was just waiting for someone to come out of another house. I dropped my head and tried to peer in the window. But the driver pulled out into Michellene and accelerated down the street before I could get a glimpse of him. I ran the last few yards to the house.

"Ever seen a dark blue Chrysler in the neighborhood?"

"I don't think so, why?"

"One was sitting outside your neighbor's house a minute ago, pulled off as I walked up to him." I scribbled the plate number on her telephone pad as I talked.

She pursed her lips. "Maybe he just dropped somebody off or something."

"Maybe, but I was walking up the street, and I watched him for three or four minutes. It sure looked like he was just sitting there, staring at the house."

She reached out and tore my note from the pad. "Do you know the make, model, year?"

"Chrysler, a large sedan. I didn't recognize the model."

She dialed and had a very brief conversation. "We'll know in a few minutes."

We waited three and a half hours, and finally Lindstrom called the Clark Street station again. She was redirected to Neely's desk. The phone at his desk rang seventeen times before she hung up in frustration.

She tried again ten minutes later and got Neely. She nodded and said "Yes," and after a couple of minutes she looked up at me and said "Aubuchon."

I could hardly believe it. He would have been my last guess. Well, maybe not my last. But certainly not my first. Lindstrom and Neely talked for twenty minutes, with Lindstrom mostly listening, so I learned very little.

Then she told me, "They brought him in for questioning. As soon as they had run the number, someone thought it would be a good idea to tell Johnson before me, and he told them he'd call me after he talked to Aubuchon."

"Did they get anything? Is he the one?"

"I don't know. Neely thinks maybe; Johnson thinks it's doubtful. They didn't get anything in questioning him. He says he was in Branson the night Viv was murdered and he knows nothing about any calls or the note. He says he was just here mourning for Viv. I think it's him."

"What happens next?" I asked.

"They'll keep investigating."

"Will they put a tail on him?"

"No, not full time anyway. We just don't have the personnel for that. So many cops are on this investigation already."

We rehashed it a few times, but there it was. Nothing much. Just your ordinary lurking-around-in-the-dark-staring-at-the-house-of-the-ex-lover-of-your-ex-wife-where-she-was-murdered-kind-of-evening.

Lindstrom grew more and more sure that it was Aubuchon. I felt she was grabbing at the only alternative to Viv's being killed in her stead. An appealing solution to Lindstrom. It meant she didn't have to carry Viv's death around her neck for the rest of her life.

After our conversation, I felt worse, not better. This case seemed to be going nowhere or everywhere, which was just as bad. Yet the threat was real. The killer was priming himself. The calls, the note, all were warnings. We had to stop him before there was more violence.

CHAPTER TWENTY-SIX

I wasn't getting anywhere with finding Page, so on Tuesday I fumbled through my notebook to find an address on Terry Ray Krebs. For some reason the Department of Corrections didn't have a home address or number, just the shop where he worked. I fervently hoped Terry Ray hadn't gotten himself fired. I found the address—on Gravois, but several blocks northeast of our office. I thought about calling to see if Krebs was at work, but decided I'd risk missing him for the advantage of surprise.

As I drove southwest through the Cherokee and Oak Hill neighborhoods, I considered how I might get the information I needed from Mr. Krebs. Victor had said he was a prissy kind of guy, a rule follower. So maybe I needed to be an authority of some kind—cop? Department of Corrections? I hated the risk of either of these. I was always nervous that I would fall into the seemingly bottomless hole of my own ignorance. And get caught telling a lie. Somehow despite Betty's best efforts I had, at about age twelve, come to the conclusion that the really sinful, ugly part of lying was getting caught. Getting away with it generated a certain buzz. So maybe Jennifer Slater, the ace reporter, would come in handy.

Advance TV-VCR Repair advertised a free loaner VCR with deposit while mine was repaired. The shop was small, occupying half of one of Gravois' tidy brick squares. The other half was rented by Aqua Pets. Outlandish looking tropical fish had been painted on the front window of the latter by someone who hadn't quite gotten perspective in Art 101. Aqua Pets' window was clean, however, which was more than I could say for Advance. The interior there looked dark, but several TVs along the right-hand wall flickered. I pulled my attaché out of the mess in the back of the Plymouth and checked to see I had my .38 and a couple of Jennifer Slater business cards.

The dust on the front window of the shop extended to the interior. Every surface was either dusty or smudged or both. There were odd stains on the blue-green carpet. Two dozen televisions, floor models to kitchen-counter size, were scattered haphazardly over the floor. A shelf of VCRs ran at shoulder height all the way to the rear of the shop. Toward the back I was able to see a short wooden counter. As I approached it, I could see that the back edge of the formica top had been used repeatedly as a place to lay lit cigarettes. Twenty or thirty irregularly spaced burn marks testified to a heavy and forgetful smoker. The only light for the shop, aside from the little sunlight to penetrate the dirt on the front window, was provided by a fluorescent fixture hanging unevenly from aluminum chains over the desk behind the counter. If Victor's description of Krebs as Mr. Clean were accurate, Advance TV was probably closer to hell than JTripleC for Terry Ray.

I could see through an open doorway a smaller room at the back where I surmised the actual repairing work was done. As I peered through this door, a slightly-built man came through it. At first in the strange light all I could see was his white-blond hair.

"May I help you?"

"I'm looking for Mr. Krebs. Terry Krebs."

His head looked small for his shoulders, but his eyes were quick and intelligent. He smoothed the front of his shirt, and I knew I had Terry Ray. Then he touched a small scratch on his jaw line and sighed.

"I'm Terry Krebs. What do you need?"

"My name is Jennifer Slater, and I'm doing a piece for *The Riverfront Times*. I wondered if I could interview you, Mr. Krebs?"

"What's this about?"

The phone rang, and Krebs glanced at it impatiently, but he reached over and picked it up.

"Advance TV." He ducked his head and listened for a minute, touching his upper lip. Then he said "Hang on," and stepped into the back room. He returned in less than a minute. "No, ma'am. It's not ready. We had to order a part on it. Probably have it done Thursday or Friday."

"Are we alone, Mr. Krebs?"

He considered and looked me over carefully.

"Yes, why?"

"Well, the nature of the article is personal—it will be on the treatment of prisoners in Missouri prisons."

"I'm not interested. I really don't want to talk about it."

"But, Mr. Krebs, this will be an important piece, a way to educate the general public about what life is really like on the inside."

"I said 'no.' That's behind me now. No point in bringing it up again."

"Your parole officer, Mr. Jackson, thought you might be willing to participate. I could change your name in the article. No one would know it was you. I've got several sources already, but they are all men who were troublemakers in prison. They were treated badly because they were always in trouble. Mr. Jackson said your point of view might be different."

"Nobody ever beat me, if that's what you want to know."

"Exactly. You did all right because you understood the system?"

"More or less. It wasn't that hard. Just do the time. Do what you're told."

"And you learned a skill at JTripleC?"

Krebs crossed his arms across his chest and looked around him. Despite the dust and disarray I could tell the shop was a busy one. And I could only assume that Krebs was doing pretty well if the owner left him to run the place alone.

"I took classes in electronics. I was already pretty good at fixing things."

Easy does it, Meg. Keep him talking. "Did your parole officer help you get this job?"

"No. The owner's wife goes to church with my mother. I sent out thirty-seven resumés. He was the only one that gave me an interview."

"And things are working out for you?"

Krebs took a few steps back to lean against the room partition. He was still wary, but for whatever reason, willing to talk awhile.

"Are you going to take notes or something?"

"Um, yes. Sure. If that's okay." I pulled my notebook out of my attaché.

"My life is going well since I left prison. I wasn't like most of the guys there. By and large they are losers. Been criminals since they were babies. I knew I just needed to get my life back after I got out." I took notes.

"What is your relationship with your parole officer like? Is he helpful?"

"Mr. Jackson's okay. I only see him about ten minutes once a week. Just to tell him I'm still around, still got my job. He helped me get rent money when I got my apartment."

"Where did you go when you first got out of prison?"

"To my mother's. She lives in Kirkwood. I've got a little place near here. Soulard it ain't. But it's good enough for now."

"How about the police? How were you treated during and after your arrest?"

"Oh, they did their job," he said easily. "No rough stuff. But it wasn't too hard to figure out. I told them I did it right away."

I wondered how Krebs would describe his crime. "Would you mind if I asked what happened?"

"Didn't Mr. Jackson tell you?" He grinned at me.

"Only partly. He said you were found guilty of voluntary manslaughter."

"Woman-slaughter. My so-called wife was fucking another man." His blue eyes never left mine. His lips curved into a tighter smile. "I believed in my wedding vows. Forsaking all others."

Until death do us part echoed in my brain.

Suddenly this shop felt very sinister. Krebs didn't move a muscle. Don't show him your fear, Darcy.

"So, Jennifer, you wouldn't mind if I just called *The Riverfront Times* to verify that you work there, would you?"

"I don't work at *The Riverfront Times*. I'm a freelancer. But they'll buy the story. I've written for them before, and I know what they want."

"Did you talk to anyone else besides my PO?"

"No, are there others you'd like me to talk with?"

"What other prisoners did you interview?"

"One was a man with you at JTripleC. All the others were in Patosi.

"Any from death row there?"

"No. None on death row. All the men I've interviewed are out now."

"How 'bout women? There are women in prison."

"That's a different story. This is mainly to focus on the kinds of physical and emotional abuse that men endure in prison. It's a much bigger problem." I knew I needed to switch back—get control of this interview. "Do you hold any grudges, Mr. Krebs? Anyone you feel bitter about because of the way you were treated?"

"My wife."

The phone blared over the soft sounds of the televisions.

Krebs moved forward to pick it up. I noticed a slight limp in his right leg, as though he'd lived with some pain and made an accommodation. I couldn't tell if he was favoring a hip or a knee. "Advance TV." His tone was perfectly modulated—as if we'd been talking about the Rams.

"Hi, honey. Nothing. Yeah. I'll get off at two. Pick me up here. Thanks."

So Krebs had a girlfriend already. Fast work for a man out of prison for only six months.

Krebs lifted his eyes to me again and smiled. "Are you interviewing cops for this article, Jennifer?"

"Um, no. They probably wouldn't be that helpful on this article."

"Can I see the article when you get it written?"

"Sure. I'll send you a copy as soon as *Riverfront Times* agrees to buy it."

"You have a card? In case I think of some things you should know."

"Sure." I opened my case again. I handed him a Jennifer Slater card

He looked at the card several seconds. "No address?"

"No. If you need to get me—that number is an answering service for several small businesses. They will get me a message right away."

"Where do you live?"

"Florissant."

"Where in Florissant?"

"I'm sorry, Mr. Krebs. I'm sure you understand I don't give out my home address. If you want to get in touch with me, just call that number. Thanks for your cooperation."

"You're welcome, Jennifer."

I turned and tried not to run to the front door. As I opened it, the bell overhead rang. I thought I heard "See you 'round" as I stepped from the shop into the sunshine.

I stood for a moment on the sidewalk, soaking up the brightness and trying to figure out if there was good reason to be spooked.

Either way, I planned to be near enough to see when his girlfriend picked him up at two.

I considered my options as I drove back up Gravois. Krebs had been creepy. Wouldn't anyone be creepy, though, if you knew he or she had killed a loved one? Why did he talk about calling *The Riverfront Times* at the end of our conversation rather than the beginning? And what about his asking *exactly* where I lived? As I sat at the light at Grand, South Side National Bank, an old Art Deco building, cast almost no shadow. Must be lunch time.

I looked at my watch. The car behind me honked. All right, this isn't New York I thought irritably. Some lunch, then I'd cruise around for a location to watch Krebs leave Advance with his girlfriend.

I decided I needed to ground myself, so I made a sharp left through the Amoco first and headed homeward.

Harvey ran to the door as I came in. He never read in the cat rule book about aloof. We had a nice chat and a chin rub. I sniffed his plate and detected that Patrick had given him tuna that morning, so Harve had completely ignored his hard kibble. Why slum when you don't have to? I looked in the cabinet and found another can of tuna. I walked downstairs and hopped back into the car, drove to National, and picked up a tomato, mayonnaise, and a package of brownies—a balanced meal. Back home I found a message from Lindstrom on the answering machine. She'd been invited to a family bar-beque at the home of an assistant district attorney that evening. She'd accepted. Her voice sounded polite rather than regretful.

I called Colleen and told her about Krebs and what to say if he called. She said, "We'll be glad to see you when you drop by."

After lunch I drove back to the Oak Hill neighborhood. I cruised around a bit and lamented my decision to park the Plymouth right in front when I had gone to interview Krebs.

There wasn't a place on either Roger or Oak Hill where I could park and see the front door. So I had to do it on Gravois. If he spotted me, he'd just have to spot me. If he was our killer, he'd already have figured I wasn't Jennifer Slater anyway.

CHAPTER TWENTY-SEVEN

She drove up at one-fifty-five in a fifteen-year-old light blue Chevy. She was either short or slumped down in her seat, as her brown head barely cleared the steering wheel. She neither filed her nails nor read. She waited, seemingly patiently, for Terry Ray Krebs. At two-oh-seven, he limped out of Advance TV, yanked open the passenger-side door, and eased himself down into the front seat. They sat a moment and talked. Then she pulled out into traffic and immediately into a corner lot, turning there to head back north on Gravois. Sometimes the tailing business isn't as easy as on television.

Soon we were back in the Cherokee neighborhood. Low-rent, mostly white by the few pedestrians I saw. She slid up to a curb, and they both walked into a three-story building without a backward glance. Was this Krebs' place or his girlfriend's? I waited five minutes, then walked up to the building. Six black metal mailboxes. Four had blue plastic name labels: Wm. Robke, Luther Mothershed, Beverly Farris, and John and Sarah Vrabec. So, she was Beverly Farris, or she or Krebs was one of the two unknowns. I took a quick look around and then peeked into the two nameless mailboxes. One had a Union Electric bill for Sandi Bidwell; the other was empty.

I retreated to the car and rummaged for the cheap cell phone Walter had provided me. Local information had no listing for a Sandi Bidwell, but Beverly Farris' number was 865-0005. I dialed the number. Seven rings. No answer. Probably Sandi Bidwell then. Or Krebs in the other unnamed mailbox. I sat for a while and considered my options. I could sit and wait—tail them and probably lose them and learn nothing, or I could pick through the garbage.

The dumpster was directly behind the building in a brick alley. No Yard Waste it warned. I gritted my teeth and threw open the lid. I peered over the edge. Only a half dozen bags or so, but the smell was all you'd expect and more. I'd need something to stand on. Or maybe this mission should wait. I looked around the alley again. Two doors down a tire leaned against the back of a garage. That wouldn't hold me. I walked toward the south end of the alley. Behind me a door slammed, and I jumped. No one emerged into the alley so I took a deep breath and went in search of a step ladder substitute. Finally I found an old plastic igloo-style dog house beside a trash can that would do.

The inside of a dumpster in late June is not recommended. The footing was iffy, and the heat and smell enough to knock over a Missouri mule, but in the third bag, I found it. A phone bill for Sandi Bidwell, with her unlisted number printed at the top. I stuck the bill in my back pocket and finished searching the bag. A crumpled note at the very bottom was what I was looking for—

Terry, Gone to the Store. Turn on the Coffee pot, it's already for you.   —Love you, Sandi.

So, Sandi loved Terry. Good luck to you, hon. I hoped she remained faithful to him. I stuck my head out of the dumpster and looked around. No sign of the locals. I skinned my belly on the way over the front, but managed to land on my feet. I carried the dog house back where I'd found it and retreated to the Plymouth.

Sandi's Chevy was still in front of the building, so they hadn't decamped while I was adventuring in dumpster land. I sat in the Plymouth and thought. After a few minutes of wide-ranging images from Sandi's confessing to me that she'd helped Krebs kill Viv, to Lindstrom's begging me to kiss her, I realized the smell emanating from me wasn't going to fade, so I made a snap decision and headed for home. After a quick shower, I grabbed a few extra clothes and patted Harvey on the run. He mearred when I shut the door on his broad white nose.

Back at Sandi's, the Chevy was gone. I returned to the mail boxes. Sandi's was D. I looked in again. The electric bill was gone. A deep breath later and I was in the front door and halfway up the stairs. Two apartments to a floor, D should be on the second floor. The building was in pretty good shape, but there had been some disagreement over colors. The stairs were brown, the banister tan and light blue, and the wall to the left of the stairs was yellow on the first floor and pink on the second. Perhaps the manager just bought whatever was on sale, or each tenant just picked a section and painted. Rush Limbaugh blared from a radio in apartment C. No noise from D. I held my ear to the door in the time-honored PI way. Then I tried the door knob. Locked. I sighed and shifted my weight from one foot to another. I had her number. I could go home and call her. But, for getting information, nothing beat the surprise visit in my book. In the middle of trying to compose a note interesting enough to lure Sandi into meeting me somewhere, I heard footsteps on the stairs. No voices; just one person, I thought. The hall was bare, no place to hide. So I composed my face into a bright smile. It was Sandi. She was anxious at first, as you would be—a stranger at your door.

"Hi, Sandi. I was hoping I'd catch you. My name is Meg Darcy." I stuck my hand out. She shook it. First connection made. Sandi was short, about five-foot two, I guessed. She wore a *This Bud's for you* tee shirt and black knit shorts. She was thin, but I could see the ropy muscles in her forearms.

"Hi, uh, how do you know me?"

"I don't really. I looked you up. I'm interested in talking to you about Terry Krebs. We don't have to go into your place; if you prefer we could talk somewhere else."

"What about Terry?"

"I'd just like to talk to you about him. I'm a private investigator. Miller Security." I handed her my card. "Miller Security has a contract with Missouri Corrections. Mr. Jackson, Terry's parole officer, just wanted me to do a little checking on Terry. Just to make sure he wasn't hanging with the wrong crowd or getting into something that might be trouble later."

She considered it.

"Shouldn't take long. Just a few minutes to go over some names and dates, then he'll get a clean report."

"Okay. Wait a minute. I have to change clothes. I have to be at work soon. We can talk in the hospital coffee shop."

We agreed to meet at the Alexian Brothers' Hospital in twenty minutes. Once at the hospital, I checked my wallet. Two dollars. I'd have to stop by an ATM when I was finished with Sandi. I found the coffee shop, got a glass of iced tea, and settled down to write out the questions I wanted to ask her. Masked with stale coffee and something garlicky baking, the hospital smell wasn't overpowering in the coffee shop.

Right on time, Sandi came in dressed in whites, got a large diet Coke, and sat down across from me.

"Have you worked at the hospital for a long time?"

"Since I was seventeen. I started in housekeeping. My aunt got me the job; she's worked here twenty years. Now I'm in the cafeteria. I make up trays to go up to the patients."

"How did you meet Terry?"

Sandi grinned at the memory and twisted her ring. "I took my mom's VCR into the shop. We talked a long time. So when he asked me out, I just said yes. He was so polite. He's a very good man." She looked up at me. "He's not in any kind of trouble." It was a statement, but not as firm as she'd meant it to be.

"Good. Those cases are the easiest for me. Now I'd like to see if you recognize any of these names. The first is Vivian Rudder."

"No. I don't know her. Are these people who are in trouble?"

"Some of them, some are just accidentally connected to a couple of unsolved crimes. You've never heard Terry mention Vivian or Viv Rudder?"

"No." She sounded sure.

"How about Sarah Lindstrom?"

"No."

"Do you know where Terry was Friday night, June 18? Weekend before last."

She paused and thought. "My aunt and uncle had an anniversary party. I picked Terry up from work, and we went over there."

"What time did the party break up?"

"We left about ten and took my grandmother home. She wanted to go home, and I was tired, too."

"Terry went with you—to take your grandmother home?"

She nodded.

"And then what? Did you drop Terry off at home?"

She looked puzzled for a moment, then shook her head. "No, he was with me. All night."

"Does Terry drive?"

"No, his license expired in prison, and he hasn't gotten a new one yet. So he doesn't drive. Terry hasn't done anything wrong." Slightly stronger this time. She was convincing herself. "He's really got it together now. That thing with his wife was just a one-time deal. Anybody would be that mad." She trailed off.

"Okay, I'm sure Terry's not involved in this; I just want to give his PO a good report with a clear conscience. His apartment is on Gravois, right?"

"No, that's the shop. Advance TV. His apartment is on Spring. Near Gravois." She recited the address, and I jotted it down.

"Thanks, Sandi. You've been a big help. I'll be glad to tell Mr. Jackson that Terry is doing so well. You two thinking of getting married?"

"Um, it's a little soon for that, but we will someday. I know he's the one for me."

I wanted to shout "Please don't" at her, but instead, I shook her hand and smiled. She looked hesitant again.

"What happened on June 18th?"

"A break-in. Some things were stolen."

"Oh, Terry's no thief." She smiled, relieved.

Right. No thief. "Thanks again, Sandi. And good luck."

I left her there and headed to Miller Security.

***

I drove through the Hardee's that's just down the street from Miller Security and bought two large diet Cokes. I wished I could convince Walter that imbibing something non-alcoholic was manly. But except for coffee, which doesn't help in summer, he won't budge.

But Colleen's eyes lit up when she saw the big cups. She's sparing with compliments, though, and didn't overdo the gratitude. Mikie bounced out from under her desk to greet me. A few yips spoke volumes.

"Okay, okay. I forgot your treats. Where's Walter?" I knew if Colleen were pup-sitting, Walter was gone.

"He had that visitation today. Pop Sandvic."

I remembered. Sandvic was one of Walter's Korean War buddies. Had been. A sudden heart attack had felled him.

"Did he say if he'd be back?" I asked, looking over the edge of my Coke. Too syrupy this time.

She met my eyes, glanced away. "He didn't think so. He and some of the guys were going down to the Legion."

To salute Sandvic by bending their elbows at the bar. I looked at my watch. Five after four already. "Well, off to the salt mine," I said pathetically. "You coming, Mike?"

Colleen rolled her eyes at me, but Mike responded to his name and trotted after me down the hall to my office. I sank into my chair and rolled a ball from scrap paper and tossed it to him. He isn't as imaginative as Harvey. He started to chew it up.

Colleen had left a list of calls I was to make before business hours ended, and I started down the list. I was good for three out of five when she buzzed me that Mary Jo Middleton was on the line. Mary Jo reported absolutely no luck with Gregory Page. As far as she could tell, no one new had come into the county in the last six months. Just the usual collection of cousins, in-laws and outlaws. She renewed her invitation to visit and mentioned the added attraction that the corn was really sweet this year. I had just hung up when Colleen stuck her head in the door. "We're leaving." I looked down. Mikie was peeking round her shapely ankle.

"You're taking Mike?"

"I told Walter I'd keep him overnight."

Before I thought of a comment she added, "In case Walter runs late tonight."

"Later than Mikie's bedtime?"

"Yeah, that," she said and gave me a slow smile, slow and rueful.

I took a sip of flat Coke. "Is it your opinion that all the fast-food drinks, regardless of brand, taste like cow piss?"

"I have no basis for comparison, not having done the research you've done." Mischief claimed her eyes.

I grabbed another piece of scrap paper and quickly folded a plane and sailed it toward her. "Zap."

She snatched it as it was falling. "I'll bring some homemade lemonade tomorrow."

"Fresh-frozen?"

"I shall personally squeeze twenty-four lemons. Joey will love *that* for a date."

All the sweeter if Mr. Joey is stymied I thought. I smiled. "Have a lovely evening," I said in saccharin tones.

"You, too," she said more sincerely.

I listened to her and Mike walking to the door, heard her set the locks, felt the office become hollow and lonely.

CHAPTER TWENTY-EIGHT

I was registering so high on the crabby meter that I decided hunger pangs were the cause. I trudged home to Arsenal and tapped on Patrick's door, not expecting much. He works odd shifts at the bookstore, and his eclectic social activities occupy most of his off time hours. Tonight I had some luck.

He swung open the door, a vision in his laundry clothes—frizzy short shorts and an old Pride tee shirt cut off at the arm holes and accidentally dyed a pink by me when I'd once helped him do his laundry.

I whistled appreciatively.

"We gave at the office," he said and closed the door, literally in my face.

"Patrick!" I yelped.

He opened the door. "Who are you?"

"Don't pout, Patrick, I don't sulk when you're busy."

"Liar," he sniffed.

Quentin Crisp and Oscar Wilde pranced over to see me. They forgave me, even if I smelled of Harvey Milk. I squatted for better cat chat, and we ignored Patrick. I'm genuinely fond of his two aristocrats, but I had an ulterior motive. Patrick can't hold a grudge, especially against someone who cherishes his boys.

"Aren't you staying at Lindstrom's tonight?" he sniffed.

"Later. Right now I'm starving."

"I've got some pasta salad. Let's see… " He was heading toward his kitchen. Someday Patrick will figure out that he really wants to be a chef.

I glanced at my watch. "I'll have to eat and run."

"How's it going?" he asked as he began preparing cold chicken sandwiches to go with the pasta salad.

I brought him up to speed on the latest developments at Lindstrom's place, ending with Aubuchon's lurking.

"Is she crazy? I'd be crazy."

"Well, you know Lindstrom. But, yes, in a stoic Norwegian way she's crazy." I wondered if I were being disloyal. Telling Patrick didn't feel like betraying her secrets. Not exactly.

He nodded sympathetically. He might be wary, even jealous, of Lindstrom, but his concern was genuine. One thing he doesn't lack is the imagination to put himself into someone else's shoes.

"Are the police making any progress?"

I told him about Rosero and about Lindstrom's fears that other cops were snickering behind her back.

"Will that affect their investigation?"

"I don't think so. Neely is a genuine friend I think. Johnson strikes me as a straight-arrow bulldog." I saw Patrick's question. "Play by the rules, tenacious. He may or may not like queers—or white people. Hard to tell by his manner. But he's one hundred percent cop."

"I guess that's good." He used his fork to play with the remnants of his salad.

"But Lindstrom has a thousand nagging doubts."

"Internalized homophobia," he said, but sadly, not smugly.

***

Lindstrom was home, Toyota safely in its slot, back porch light on. I unlocked the door, stepped in, and immediately punched in her alarm code. I wondered, idly, if she'd change her code after this was over so I couldn't come in at will.

"Honey, I'm home!"

"Hi, Darcy, how did it go with Krebs?"

I raised my eyebrows at her and dumped my bag, extra clothes, and revolver on the kitchen table.

"How did you know I saw Krebs?"

"Johnson was pulling up to talk to him as you were leaving. He called me to complain about it. He wants to know what information you gave Krebs."

I took a deep breath and tried to keep the defensiveness out of my tone. "I didn't give him any information. Didn't mention you or Viv or anything related to the case. I went in as a reporter doing a story on the mistreatment of prisoners in Missouri."

"You learn anything?"

"Not much. He says he isn't angry at the cops—that his only interaction with police was to confess. He has a girlfriend. He's creepy."

"I'll tell Johnson you haven't soiled the nest. Find out anything else?"

Briefly, I recounted my conversation with Sandi Bidwell. Lindstrom picked up my bag and my .38 and carried them to the den. I followed with my extra clothes. She sat with a sigh on the leather couch and motioned for me to drop my clothes in the chair. I sat beside her.

"This isn't working, Darcy. We're at least seven steps behind him." She turned to face me. "Do you think it's Krebs?"

"I don't know. Like I said, he was creepy. He challenged me about being a reporter, but he didn't say anything particularly incriminating. I think it's still a wide open field."

"That's it, exactly. And I think maybe your being here is keeping him away."

"It didn't keep him from leaving his note Saturday."

"No, but you were gone all day Friday and most of Saturday. Maybe he thought you were gone for good."

"Lindstrom, if this is another fight about my leaving you here alone to do battle with the dragon single handedly, let's just skip it. I'm staying. If it keeps him away, so be it. Johnson and Neely and I will just have to get smart enough to catch him some other way."

"No, listen. I think you should park your car somewhere else, so he thinks you've gone."

I looked down at my hands. Did this make us more vulnerable? Or did it really matter to our stalker? He had to know that the cops were driving by frequently. "Okay, so I park my car somewhere else, and he feels free to drop by, right?"

"I don't know, but flushing him out might be the fastest way to catch him."

I had a picture of the staked goat in *Jurassic Park*. "Okay, I'll move it. Tell Neely we're doing this and to have the cavalry close at hand. Any ideas where I should park?"

"Emmet is close and quiet." She pointed west.

She insisted on going with me, so we reset the alarm and moved the Plymouth to Emmet, a dead end residential street behind Lindstrom's house. The walk back was muggy, and the exhaust from I-55 and Seventh Street burned my nose and throat. Lindstrom went in, and I circled the house. In the fading light, everything looked homey and safe. I walked out into the alley and south toward Geyer. Most folks were at home on a Tuesday evening. Some still in the kitchen cleaning up after supper, some in the back yard piddling with projects or watching the kids and sipping cold drinks. The ordinary motions of lives in progress, while ours seemed frozen, suspended, waiting for the next lash of mayhem. Back in the house, Lindstrom was upstairs. The light was on, but the house was completely silent. I thought of joining her, but lost my nerve and retired to my den.

I slept fitfully on the couch and twice I heard Lindstrom moving around upstairs. At three-forty-five, I thought I heard something, leapt up and grabbed my gun. I slid to the door and listened to the summer quiet. The air conditioner clicked on. Nothing else. Adrenaline pumping, I pulled on my shorts and stepped into my tennis shoes. I walked through the kitchen, left a quick note for Lindstrom, and stepped out onto the back porch. From there, the neighborhood was so quiet I could hear the trucks rumbling on I-55. The grass was heavy with dew and tickled my bare ankles. No sign of an invader anywhere. The motion detector lights were triggered by my progress around the house. I walked back to the alley and stood for a moment by the garage. I heard the door open behind me and turned to see Lindstrom, silhouetted in the kitchen light.

"See anything?"

"No, I thought I heard something earlier, but there's no sign of trouble now."

"Let's go for a walk."

I started to protest. It was the middle of the night; there was definitely out there somewhere a man who wanted to kill Lindstrom. But then I thought better of it. Hell, it was the middle of the night, and honestly we were probably less vulnerable touring the streets of Soulard than closed up in the house. And certainly neither of us was apt to sleep anymore. I stooped to tie my shoes, and we walked.

We talked about Lindstrom's hassles with Judith Rosero and the best way to manage the situation. I encouraged Lindstrom to confront her, call Judith on her attitude. Lindstrom thought she'd wait. She wanted to just get along until things jelled more, until this whole thing was over or she left the force. I asked her if Neely might talk to Judith.

"I'm not asking Neely to solve my problems for me." I silenced her with a hand on her arm. I peered down the street, trying to see my car. The driver's side window was bashed in. Little pebbles of the shatter-proof glass fell inward crazily. As I ran to the car, Lindstrom grabbed at me to stop me. I was a step too fast, so she hissed, "Careful." Just the one word. But he was long gone. I patted my pockets, but my keys were back at the house. Lindstrom watched me a moment, then reached in through the open space that had been window and pulled up on the door lock. I shook my head and opened the car door. In the pool of brightness cast by the dome light, what seemed like a bucket full of tiny glass pieces glittered across the seat and floor of the car. "Damn him," I said, just keeping myself from pounding on the roof. Lindstrom looked around at the silent, dark houses.

"Come on, Darcy. Let's go back to the house and call the station. I doubt if they can get evidence, but we should try."

It was probably the first time in the history of St. Louis that a call on a broken car window yielded a crime scene van, two patrol cars, and a homicide detective. The detective was balding and thick in the middle. Bill Hirsch took careful notes about when I'd parked the car and why I'd found it at four a.m. Lindstrom and he chatted easily. He seemed concerned, but doubtful that this incident would produce any new leads. The vandal had taken whatever he'd used to bust the window with him. Hirsch reminded Lindstrom mildly that this might be random, not linked to Viv. She growled something I couldn't hear at him.

The sun rose, white and impassive, as I stood staring at my car. This was a message, and I thought I understood it: Don't bother to try to fool me. I know where you are and I will strike at will. My will.

I ground my teeth and tried to listen again to Hirsch and Lindstrom. He thought it unlikely that any of the residents of Emmet Street had been up to see the perp, but there'd be a house-to-house later that morning. Hirsch would see to it. Lindstrom thanked him for coming out and spoke to each of the patrolmen and the crime scene tech. It was six-thirty by the time we got back to the house. I was exhausted from standing around watching them do nothing with efficiency. Lindstrom said she was going to work.

CHAPTER TWENTY-NINE

Not many words had passed between us on our walk back to the house. Suddenly the air had whooshed out of me, and the gumption, too. I felt like Lindstrom and I were standing alone against a million shadowy threats—classic victim feelings. The only cure I knew was work.

Colleen gave me a thoughtful look as I stood in front of her desk trying to remember what I was doing there. "You okay?"

"Um, yeah. Lindstrom's at work now."

"No. I meant how are you?" Amazingly touchy-feely for Colleen.

I shrugged. "Okay."

She shrugged back. "Okay. Okay, don't tell me."

I felt a flush start. In my mind it's quite clear that in any relationship with Colleen I'm to be the big sister—the cool, dashing, self-assured PI able to handle any curves the world throws me. I changed the subject. "Walter in?"

"You didn't hear Mikie?"

I nodded and walked back down the hall to Walter's office. Sure enough, a low ur-ur-ur that might pass as a growl emerged, and when I knocked and entered, Walter was down on the floor playing tug-a-rope with the feisty poodle.

Walter grinned up at me like the proud father he's become. "Here's Aunt Meg to get your rope," he warned Mikie.

"Actually, Mikie, I know a good security service that will protect that rope." I looked at Walter, unsure if I should go down to his level or wait for him to come up.

Walter, with some puffing for the effort, grabbed the edge of his desk and pulled himself up. I filled him in. I didn't have to apologize for being late, and when I thought of that, the rush of gratitude nearly swamped me. Walter trusts me to have good reasons, and, if he asks a question, he wants to get information, not to humiliate me.

Now he had some information of his own. "Leroy Vergis is free this evening. He can help you with surveillance at Lindstrom's place."

Leroy is a greasy fellow. He's in his fifties, totally cynical about law enforcement and justice, but competent enough in his work. He also owes Walter big time. I'm not sure of the debt, but I suspect Walter saved Leroy from prison—and not by being a law-abiding role model.

Just now the idea of an extra pair of eyes, an extra gun if it came to that, was reassuring. "Tell him yes. And thanks."

A silence fell. Walter doesn't like silence. Usually he starts fiddling with a cigar, or, more often these days, just resumes his deep philosophical discussions with Mikie. Today his shrewd blue eyes stayed focused on my face. "Somethin' on your mind?"

I told him about the Plymouth.

"Could be street thugs, looking for tapes and a tape deck," he said in a tone that rejected his own suggestion.

"Could be."

"Maybe you should pull out of this case."

I was astonished. I just managed to keep my jaw shut.

Walter pressed on. "Meg, we're just a security outfit. Murder isn't in our line of work." His voice rumbled at one of its lower settings. All those cigars.

"I can't quit this one. Lindstrom needs help."

My voice stayed steady, but inside I flew apart. The temptation to bail out was so strong that I bit my lower lip to seal the words inside. All that had happened to me was a trashed car—not even a thorough job—and I wanted to skedaddle.

"Do you want me to help?"

Of course. Yes. But I couldn't run to Uncle Walter, not all the way. "Leroy will be fine."

"I got a trip planned down to Branson this weekend to meet a theater owner about a security contract." He made a face. "One long traffic jam for the Fourth."

"Why don't you fly?"

His grimace screwed tighter. "Nah. Mikie and I'll drive." He cleared his throat. "But if you need me, I'll cancel the trip."

I heard the words between the spaces. My own throat tightened. I shook my head no. "Could you check on Thomas Aubuchon while you're down there?" I reviewed who Thomas was for Walter and added that he'd picked a fight with Lindstrom and I'd caught him mooning around the house. "I need to know if he really was in Branson the night Viv was murdered. The St. Louis cops asked Branson to check his alibi, so you'd be plowing the same ground twice."

Walter grinned at me. "But we can't just take their word for it, now can we? Guy they sent was probably thinking about his lunch while he was asking questions." Naturally Walter would be more thorough.

I gave Walter the name and address of Aubuchon's small hotel and promised, if humanly possible, to get him a picture of Thomas before Friday morning. One favor wasn't enough. He made another offer.

"Want a different car to drive for a while?" A local rental agency is working off its bill to us by providing freebie rentals. Walter believes in long and easy credit for his buddies, but he likes to foist free rentals onto our operatives now and then just to remind everyone that the debt is being paid.

I thought about it. "I think I'll stay with the Plymouth."

He nodded. "I'll call Buddy, get him to come over and get you fixed up with some new glass, maybe check your carburetor while he's got it."

"I'll need it tonight."

"Sure." He motioned me out. He was handling it.

Outside his office I sucked in two deep breaths. I was amazed to find myself feeling taken care of.

***

The remainder of my Miller Security day crawled by in the slow lane. Patrick e-mailed a greeting. Betty called just to chat. I fiddled with paperwork. Colleen's homemade lemonade was the high point. At four-thirty Lindstrom called to say she had another dinner date for the evening.

"I'll be back by eleven," she promised.

I didn't want to reveal how disappointed I was. "I'll guard the castle." A silence loomed. "Walter has a spare operative he's lending us to help out outside, so we'll have an extra crocodile in the moat."

I could hear her reservations about it shout through the silence. Finally, she managed to ask, "Is this a reliable guy?"

I couldn't say that I'd trust him with our lives. "He's not my best friend, but he's a competent operative."

"I'll pass on to Neely that we've got an extra hand. This stuff doesn't work if all the good guys shoot each other."

She sounded like me—cross about someone else's plans but rising above it.

"Hey, maybe this creep will come after me while you're out; maybe he gets off on hurting you through your friends." I really started that sentence in an effort to be upbeat, though by the time it thudded to its end I felt my foot wedged between my molars, the toe pressing down my throat.

"That's unfair."

"I'm sorry. I didn't mean it the way it came out."

"This dinner invitation is post-funeral stuff. Friends I haven't seen socially in five years want to do their bit to cheer me up. In another two weeks they'll be gone for another decade." She was talking right past my apology and sounding more than a little guilty about her plans. Then, dryly, "Unless, of course, you become a sacrificial lamb. In which case I'll see the whole rotation much sooner."

"Is that a joke?"

"Trying."

A swell of feeling warmed my veins. "Lindstrom, I love you."

Thunderous silence. "Is that a joke?" Her voice very careful, in the same manner you take steps over ice.

"I don't think so."

More silence. "Ah well, maybe you can let me know when you decide."

Ball to my court. Saved by the bell. Ruined by the bell. Colleen was buzzing me on another line. "Damn."

"Don't feel that bad about it," Lindstrom was saying cheerfully.

"I'm getting another call."

175

"Sure."

"I'll see you at eleven." I wanted to say something else, but no words came up, only static.

"Darcy, be careful. No joking. I mean it."

"You, too. Me, too."

A click and she was gone. I wanted to call her back immediately, to prolong the conversation into one of those stretched-out calls of teenage angst, full of sighs and stutters.

Colleen's call was just to inform me that the amazing Buddy had returned my Plymouth, glass replaced, carb goosed, upholstery swept as best they could considering the flotsam swimming in the back seat, and he, Buddy, took personal responsibility but they'd removed the shriveled french fries and cidery apple, did I mind?

In fact, I mourned the apple; it was my deodorizer.

I looked at the clock. Time to go home, but what for? I tried to rouse Patrick, but he wasn't answering his phone or his e-mail. I skimmed over a list of female friends, women whose company I'd enjoy in ordinary circumstances. But not while I was protecting a homicide detective I might be falling in love with. Fallen in love with. In love with, in lust with, in like with.

I decided to solve the immediate problem by staying late to work on paperwork, but fifteen minutes after Mikie pattered by followed by Walter's lumbering roll, I was antsy. I was playing solitaire when I heard the knock on the door. Standing in the unflattering gleam of our security light was Thomas Aubuchon. Beard the lion, indeed. And here he was. It seemed like a stupid-heroine move to let him in when I was here alone, and yet I wanted to talk to him, to get a sense of what was going on in his Viv-obsessed brain.

I walked back to my office and slipped my .38 into my pocket before unlocking.

He began talking the second he stepped through the door. "Why did you turn me in to the cops?"

I stared at him.

"They think I killed Viv, now. What on earth did you tell them about me?"

We stood in the reception area. I decided not to invite him to sit.

"What I told the cops was that someone with your license plate number was sitting in a car, staring at Lindstrom's house at the very time she is receiving some threatening calls and mail."

"I didn't kill Viv. You know I couldn't have. I was in Branson when she was murdered. If I hadn't been, she'd have come to me, and still be alive."

"What possessed you to lurk around the house, then?"

"I don't know." He rubbed his lips with the back of his hand. "I just wanted to put it to rest somehow. I just can't quit thinking about her death. It was so awful. I'm not sure I want to live without her."

"Aubuchon, get a grip, man. You have been living without her. You were divorced years ago. What's your problem with Sarah, now?"

"I don't have a problem with Sarah. I couldn't care less about Sarah Lindstrom. I just want Viv back. Is that so hard to understand?"

"Vivian's not there. Sarah lives in that house. You're going to get yourself arrested for murder if you don't stop acting so stupid. It's no use blaming Sarah for Viv's death."

"I don't blame Sarah."

"That's not the impression you're giving. You told her you blamed her at the cemetery."

"I don't know. Sometimes I think like that."

"Are you calling Sarah?"

"No. No. No. I'm not calling her. I'm not following her. I just came to look at the house last night. That's all."

"Look, Aubuchon. Go home. Get some counseling. You have to get on with your life."

"Will you tell the cops I didn't do it?"

"I don't need to tell them anything. If you were in Branson, they already know it. If they thought you weren't, you'd probably be in a cell right now." I opened the door. His face was showing signs of caving in again, and I didn't want to spend any time patting Thomas Aubuchon's hand, so I looked pointedly at the open door.

I didn't suspect Aubuchon as much as Lindstrom did, but I was glad Walter was double checking his alibi. If Walter came home with a definite "no," I'd cross Aubuchon off my list.

I refused to go to Lindstrom's house and fidget. I made a quick stop at Arsenal to assure Harvey that I loved him most of all the world; meanwhile, I knew his Uncle Patrick was looking after him. I didn't fool him. Harvey knows when he's getting a drive-by hug and not the dedicated attention he requires to flourish.

I found a parking place in the lot beside the Tivoli and picked up a ticket for the seven o'clock show, then treated myself to a sandwich at the St. Louis Bread Company across the street. The movie was an old screwball comedy, and the sparse Wednesday night audience was in the mood to laugh. I found myself joining them with gusto.

I pulled into Lindstrom's alley at five minutes of ten. I saw Leroy on a lidded garbage can in the shadow of the garage. He walked over at a measured pace and leaned his pale face with its white five o'clock shadow down to my window. "She ain't home," he said sourly.

"She's visiting friends. She'll be home later."

"She ought to stay home," he said, still grumpy.

I shrugged. No use to argue about it. I knew what he meant. Stay put, offer a target, entice the guy out. That being cooped up in the place Viv was killed was torture to Lindstrom didn't concern him.

I took him for an inside tour, just in case something happened where he'd need to know the layout. I hated owing him a favor so the whole time I silently reminded myself that he was repaying Walter—and glad to be. Or as glad as Leroy gets. Afterward I sat at the kitchen table scrawling a useless list of things to check on. Whatever good energy I'd acquired during the day was definitely drained away now. About ten of eleven I drifted back outside, sitting on the back porch steps and waiting for Lindstrom. When her Toyota pulled in, I walked to greet her and to summon Leroy from the shadows for an introduction. As usual, Leroy was monosyllabic, and Lindstrom matched him.

Inside, she wasn't more expansive. Whatever moment we'd had on the phone had dropped from memory. Her own face was pale, and for once I saw the heat's toll on her clothes. She looked wilted.

"Long evening?"

"Long day. I think I'm hitting the shower and then straight to bed." She was heading toward the stairs.

"Rosero still a pill?" I called to her retreating figure.

She wasn't going to engage. "Today and every day." She unbuttoned her shirt as she climbed and had the shirttail out by the top step. "Good night."

So much for comparing notes. So much for cuddling.

CHAPTER THIRTY

"For me?"

I was standing in her bedroom door with a steaming cup of coffee. She was dressed on bottom, but wearing only her sports bra. I tried not to stare at all the parts I was hungry to see.

I handed her the cup, and our fingers touched, and nothing that had happened stopped the tingle that sang through me. I looked away, then back. She was still smiling at me as though glad to see me or the coffee. "Thanks," she said.

"How did you sleep?" I asked, trying for Betty's solicitous tone.

She shrugged. "I'm strong. I don't need twelve hours a night."

I nodded for lack of words.

She sipped her coffee and smiled for real. "Hmm. Has Leroy gone?"

"I saw him off. He'll work again tonight, but he has other plans for the weekend. Do you want me to ask Walter for another operative?"

I saw the complicated shift in her face—some disappointment, followed by resolve. "No. We'll handle it."

I liked the 'we.' But I was scared, and somewhat reassured that she was, too. I didn't want false bravado or just bullheaded denial leading either her or me into complacency. I really didn't want us to do this alone. I wanted the entire St. Louis Police Force, the F.B.I., and the Marines on our side.

She nodded and opened her closet to find a shirt for the day. I wanted to linger, but I deferred to her disciplined schedule. "See you downstairs with the bran flakes."

"Honestly, Darcy, I expected you to corrupt me with croissants," she called after me.

Over breakfast our conversation was strictly business. She and Rosero were still partners. She hadn't heard anything from Neely about the leads on Page and Missouri militias. Whenever she got back to her desk, she checked old case files, trying to find other suspects. So far, no luck. Did I have any new ideas?

I sketched a brief account of Aubuchon's visit to Miller Security and offered my thought that possibly Aubuchon was guilty only of wretched grief. She wasn't swayed. But our disagreement about Aubuchon's probable guilt held no rancor. I told her Walter would need a picture to check Aubuchon's Branson alibi. Could she help?

"I don't want to be late to work. I'll look this evening." To an outsider,

179

we probably sounded like a long-wed couple, past endearments and into shorthand. Maybe stock brokers. Or school teachers. That the core of our conversation was murder by bludgeoning, that we were living in the gaze of a private terrorist wasn't obvious. Not for the first time I thought there ought to be more keening and wailing. I knew my therapist wouldn't approve of all the stuffing down I was doing, ignoring lust and fear evenhandedly.

But we finished the bran flakes and were on our separate ways without saying anything more shocking than "Catch you later."

***

When Colleen walked in to find me at my desk, she claimed cardiac arrest and did a jokey stagger. She wasn't so happy that I'd made coffee. Not the usurpation of her rights but my inadequacy in that department. She was better pleased with the danish I'd brought in for mid-morning coffee break.

My day hummed along with all the normalcy I usually took for granted. I'd seldom enjoyed routine calls and paperwork so much. The highlight of the day was when Walter called me in to consult with a new client about security cameras for his warehouse and staff trainings that I could conduct for him. Problem-solving is the icing for our kind of security and investigations firm, especially as increasingly our foot chases have become Internet pursuits. We can't prevent all crime, but we definitely can discourage certain specific crimes.

A current client rang through with a personnel problem. The upcoming Fourth would leave him shorthanded; could I line up a reliable watchman for his medical supply company? I could and did, but it took several calls before I found an off-duty cop who wouldn't be called in for extra duty to cover the VP Fair crowds.

I was just self-congratulating the Darcy charm when Colleen buzzed me that Lindstrom was on the line.

"Darcy, here."

"I got a package. I've called Neely." Her voice was strange. It was taut and abrupt but a a trace of fear ran through it.

"I'm on my way."

"Right." She hung up without a goodbye.

I hung up and dashed out, throwing an abrupt farewell to Colleen as I raced by her desk.

***

I made it to Lindstrom's place in record time. She came out onto the porch, still in her work clothes by the look of her. The jacket and slacks were still crisp. I think she uses magic. "This is horrible, Darcy." She is not given to hyperbole, so 'horrible' got my full attention.

"Was it hand delivered?" I asked.

"No. UPS. My neighbor signed for it."

"UPS. Can't Neely trace that?"

"He's started a trace."

We were walking and talking. The package was on the butcher's block in her kitchen. A small, narrow box lying on its brown wrapping paper. I have to admit it, "horrible" had suggested the grisly—a severed finger, a dead rat. What I saw was a fat Mont Blanc pen, gleaming innocently under the light overhead.

I looked at Lindstrom. "I don't get it."

"It was Viv's. I gave it to her when she was hired at Collins, Cobb, and Vahey." Her voice still sounded like a controlled strangle.

I thought about it. Then I touched her arm gently. "Look, Sarah, this creep took it from her purse when he killed her. Anyone could see it's a special pen. He didn't know it was something you'd given her." I could hear abrasiveness creeping in. I wanted to be patient, but I also wanted her to snap out of it, to think like a cop.

She pursed her lips, trying to stuff down a roil of emotions.

"Listen," I began again. "This is hard to think about. He grabbed the pen out of her purse. Maybe he looked at her ID in her purse. He realized he could torment you with it."

She drew in and released a deep breath. "Is this supposed to make me feel better?" Her voice wasn't under her command yet, but I heard echoes of her normal asperity.

"Yes, it is. Because he isn't all-knowing. He isn't infallible, he isn't Superman, he isn't the devil." I was pretty acerbic myself. "He had to use UPS, didn't he?"

"So?"

"So, he didn't sashay up to the porch this time. Maybe he knows about the alarms and lights and police patrols. And me."

"We're scaring him off." She made it an accusation. I was hard put not to be irritated. We were protecting her. But I understood the tug-of-war. She wanted him caught; she wanted this to end. Right now, standing safely beside me, she wanted it to end. But the dread of calling him from the shadows, of being at risk and maybe at his mercy, was human and strong, and probably stronger at midnight when she was alone in her room.

Before we could get a pointless tiff going, the front doorbell rang. Lindstrom answered it and Neely walked down the hall and into the kitchen. We shook hands manfully.

The usually neat Neely looked as raggedy-edged as Lindstrom sounded. His five o'clock shadow overran his pale cheeks, and the skin under his eyes looked like smudged mascara. He carried a limp jacket over his arm. The tie had disappeared in the mile between downtown and Michellene.

"This is a hell of a thing," he said, meaning, I took it, the whole mess of Vivian's murder and the aftermath. I nodded solemnly. Lindstrom feared his response to her being 'outed' by Vivian's murder, but he seemed the same old Neely to me. I was growing more sure that he was one of the good guys, had done battle with his homophobia and won. Of course, I wasn't his partner.

He bent over the box and peered at the Mont Blanc there and said, "Umm" just like doctors so maddeningly do.

Lindstrom had left tweezers on the block, and he used them to pull the paper loose and study the same bold black ink and square printing of the address. "I wish I could print this legibly," he said.

Lindstrom watched Neely tweezer the package into a brown paper bag for evidence collection. None of us expected prints except those left by UPS workers, but cops get a lot of help from a perp's slip-ups.

"Any luck on the trace?" Lindstrom asked.

"Not yet, but we sent Pulowski to UPS. He'll hold their feet to the fire until they get it." As usual, he sounded cheerful and upbeat as though enthusiasm solved cases. Maybe it does.

Lindstrom nodded.

"How was your day?" He spoke gently, but didn't lay it on thick.

"Ah, well," she shrugged. "I've had better."

"Sarah, I'm asking the Lieutenant to assign a cop to watch the house." He tried to lock her eyes into his, but she wasn't having it.

"We don't have the manpower. The VP Fair is coming up. We'll need every uniform for that." She tapped these arguments out as though she'd already spent time rehearsing them. With a glance she pulled me into it. "Meg's staying with me, and we've got a Miller Security man in back at night." Tap, tap. Two more nails in.

Neely looked at her, then at me. He knew exactly what she was up to. "Good. You can have the security guard in back, our man in front, Meg inside." No way he was going to put down Miller Security or get distracted by a cop versus PI rivalry.

I jumped in to help him. "Besides, this is Leroy's last night till after the Fourth."

Neely wore a look that said, "See?"

She shot me a look that screamed betrayal. "He won't come out if I'm surrounded." Her own ambivalence was lessened by our joint opposition. She'd take on Neely, me, and the Mysterious Him.

"I don't want us using you as bait. We are too short of manpower to set up a good sting. But not so short we can't look after our own." Neely's voice stayed soft, but he was determined. "I don't like the way this slime is escalating. I don't want to take any chances."

She shifted restlessly.

Neely tightened the screws. "I haven't seen my kids in two days, but if you won't take the uniform, I could move in here for the weekend."

"All right. Who've you got?" She wasn't gracious in defeat.

"It'll have to be Warren tonight. Maybe Cressey tomorrow."

The way I read it Neely had come to the house not needing Lindstrom's permission to assign police protection. He had higher police powers behind him. But getting her to give way even grudgingly was better than treating her like a civilian victim.

Lindstrom was nodding at the names.

"Okay, Warren isn't my first choice, but Cressey is coming along. He's young but bright," Lindstrom said.

Neely sent a glance to include me, but his very politeness reminded me to excuse myself. I knew he probably didn't want me to hear detailed evaluations of police personnel.

I meandered down the hall and into my den. My understanding was that Lindstrom and Neely's partnership would resume as soon as they caught Viv's murderer or put the case on inactive status. Neely had requested that meanwhile he be allowed to work with Johnson. I thought Neely cared for Lindstrom and wanted to protect her in the way he best could. Now I figured they had some partnership things to say and that Neely could reassure her about her police career in ways I couldn't.

Maybe ten minutes later Neely left with the pen, and Lindstrom joined me.

She shook her head. "I can't get over that he sent the pen. It's got to be Thomas."

"Why?"

"He knows so much. He knows I gave the pen to Viv. He took it as a trophy."

"I don't think the killer had to be a rocket scientist to figure out sending the pen would hurt you. Your friend in your house."

"Why are you defending Thomas?"

"I'm not. Honest." I shrugged. "He can't let go of Viv. He's obsessed. And he sometimes blames you." I ticked off the points.

"Every week we scrape up the remains of women some guy loved too much to let go," she said. "You're profiling that guy."

I nodded. "Maybe so. But I don't want someone else to slip under our radar screen while we're looking at Aubuchon. That's all I'm saying."

She relaxed a bit. I could see it in her shoulders. Not that she'd changed her mind. "Maybe we should question him."

A rerun of Lindstrom's grief-stricken assault on Kathleen Clawsen didn't sound like a good idea to me, so I deflected. "What about that picture of Aubuchon? Walter's leaving for Branson tomorrow morning."

Lindstrom frowned. "I don't know. Maybe." She walked upstairs. "Let me look."

I sat down on the den couch and stared at the gray TV screen. I considered Thomas Aubuchon. I thought about Page and Krebs.

Lindstrom returned with a large photo album and an old Polaroid of Aubuchon, Viv, and her parents in front of a cabin. Aubuchon's face was the size of a pencil eraser.

I shook my head. "Anything larger?"

She sat and opened the album across our laps. "Somewhere. Viv took a picture of Thomas and me." She looked and sounded sheepish as though she'd been caught consorting with a criminal. "I haven't wanted to look at these," she said, nodding down toward the album and its pictures.

"Want me to do it?"

"I think I know about where it is." She flipped toward the back, then slowed down.

Sure enough. A quite helpful closeup of her and Aubuchon grinning into Viv's camera appeared amid other shots of a ski vacation. From other shots I deduced Aubuchon had brought a date.

"Happier times," I said inanely. I wanted to assure her that if she'd ever slipped up and liked Thomas for just a minute it couldn't be held against her now.

"Not one of Viv's better ideas," she said.

I liked the dryness of her tone and decided to push it. If she started thinking of Viv as a fond memory and not as a constant reminder of guilt, surely that would be an improvement.

I flipped toward the front of the book. "Mind if I look?"

Of course, she couldn't stay out of it. I needed explanations. Right away I'd opened to a page of four shots of Viv in front of some gray body of water. Her hair, still dark red, was cut just below her ears, and she was smiling broadly and looking more like a girl having a good time than a high-powered attorney.

"Where's this?"

"San Francisco. That was our second trip there. We had only three days, but we had a great time."

We progressed through Fisherman's Wharf, the Golden Gate Bridge and some too-dark shots of a group of laughing women inside a bar.Then some of Viv's family for Christmas. "The Rudders accepted you as part of the family right away?" I asked.

"No, there was some awkwardness at first. And Ruth resented me for quite a while. She hated my being a cop as much as that I was a woman. But we grew to love one another over the years. It'll be hard now. I'll probably lose touch with them. They say they don't blame me for Viv's death, but I think they'll have to when it comes out that he was trying to kill me."

Lindstrom closed the picture album and rested her head against the back of the couch. I watched her cry for a few seconds. Her losses were adding up. Viv, Viv's family, her sense of belonging at work, her ability to move through her life without looking over her shoulder. She rubbed her face, but the tears kept spilling over. I touched her shoulder, and she fell against me and sobbed. I wrapped my arms around her. No words of comfort seemed real to me, so I just waited for the storm of emotion to abate. Minutes later, her breathing became more regular, and she sat up. She walked into the bathroom, and I could hear her splashing water against her face.

Later the cop, Warren, arrived and Lindstrom went out to greet him. He turned out to be a middle-aged white man whose face was seamed and whose stomach hung over his uniform belt. He was quietly attentive while Lindstrom introduced him to me, the house, and the general security set up. If he were annoyed that a private security man would be guarding the back of the house, he didn't show it. In fact, he gave no clues to any internal life, but he looked capable of staying awake in his cruiser, which was parked right in front of the house.

"He's within pissing distance of his pension. He doesn't want to get killed before then," Lindstrom said. She must have noticed my look. "That's a quote from Neely."

Lindstrom rarely let a vulgar word cross her lips, and Neely seemed similarly restrained. In public. I tried not to mind that their private chats were less starchy.

Leroy checked in at eleven. I met him and explained the new set up and asked Leroy to play nicely. Then Lindstrom and I walked him around to meet the cop, and Leroy was as silent and wary as Warren. I managed to get Leroy away without his peeing on the cruiser tires to mark his turf.

When I came back in, Lindstrom was still on the couch, but soon she sighed and said good night.

"Want me to come up with you?"

She paused, her penetrating blue eyes searched mine for my intentions. I met her gaze steadily. She sighed again. "No. Stay down here. I haven't been sleeping, so you wouldn't get any rest."

"I could sleep in the other bedroom." The other bedroom, of course, was her bedroom, where she hadn't been able to sleep since Viv's murder.

"Thanks, but I don't think it would help. I am glad you're here, though."

I settled for that.

CHAPTER THIRTY-ONE

The next morning Lindstrom left me a note. She and Rosero had agreed to meet at Dunkin' Donuts two blocks from a scene they were working. They planned to do some personal apartment-by-apartment calls to ferret out possible witnesses to a shooting they suspected had more to it than run-of-the-mill domestic violence. Maybe they would bond over deep-fried dough.

Without Lindstrom to inspire me, I skipped the bran flakes and drove straight to the Bread Company. I splurged on hazelnut coffee with a raisin bagel and bought two pastries to share with Colleen at coffee break. As I headed toward Miller Security, I considered Lindstrom's businesslike note. Maybe she was feeling embarrassed by the tears she'd shed the night before. Maybe getting back to normal with Lindstrom would mean crisp, unemotional communications. I found myself wondering what her daily life with Viv had been like. Had they joked? cuddled? played Scrabble? watched old movies on the VCR? Their vacation pictures looked recognizably human, but vacations are hardly a true sampling. So much of Lindstrom remained mysterious to me, but I didn't have to sort out the complications of Sarah Lindstrom to know that my understanding of her wouldn't be important if he still tormented her. Us.

The rain hadn't left St. Louis shortchanged on humidity. Ben Able said we might top out at ninety-six instead of ninety-four, and even his cheerful voice sounded downcast by it.

Expecting little, I called Leon Page's number. To my surprise he was home. I reintroduced myself.

"Have you found him?" He sounded excited, hopeful.

"No. But I wonder how Gregory supported himself when he wasn't in trouble."

A snort. "Well, he used to bully mom for money. Tried to get it from me. I suspect he peddled grass. I can't prove it."

"Did he ever hold real jobs?"

"He had a pal he worked for sometimes—an auto repair thing. Just a garage at the guy's home. Gregory would help out, and sometimes the guy paid him."

"Know where that is?"

"Not really." Stiffly, as though he were being put in the wrong.

"Would your mom?"

"Maybe."

"If you talk with her, will you ask her to call me? I'd like to talk to that guy."

"Sure, okay." I could hear the dismissal in his voice.

I heard the baby start a good, strong-lunged squall in the background. "I have to go," Leon said.

"Thanks for your help, Leon," I said, and hung up.

I found my notebook and rummaged around in my office till I located the notes I'd made on Page from JCCC. I retreated to Walter's office and used his yellow pages to look up listings under 'Employment' that looked like they might be places that hired day laborers. You never know. I'd read in true crime books that some crooks do sometimes turn an honest dollar in between cons, hustles, robberies, muggings, drug deals, burglaries, and embezzlements.

I was working my way through a list when Emma Woolsey called. As I'd suspected he might, her son Leon had called her to make a PI alert, and she'd called back with the address in Pontoon Beach where the guy with the garage lived.

I stuck my head around the corner and winked at Colleen. "I'm going out."

"Go ahead, I'll stay here all alone and manage the firm."

"And supervise Mikie."

She threw his red ball at me.

***

I stood beside my Plymouth, reluctant to enter the traveling oven. On the way over I'd passed two street thermometers that said Ben Able had underestimated the heat by two degrees, and I bet the heat index was well over a hundred. I was torn between wanting to go to Michellene to be there when Lindstrom got home and driving across the river to Pontoon Beach in search of Joe Griff's garage.

I was already a little uneasy about approaching Griff. If he and Gregory Page were buddies, I didn't want to spend much time with him alone. Taking Patrick along for company might be even more provocative. Patrick can pass for straight, but it puts a strain on him. I could collect Lindstrom and take her along, but the two of us might be too dykey for Griff and have the same effect. The heat added to my problems. Nothing I could stand to wear would easily hide even the lightweight snubbie; I'd have to carry my attaché case and that wasn't designed to win over the Griffs of the world.

The heat was cooking my brain. None of the options looked like winners. What I'd heard from Page's family removed any doubts I might have had that Page thought physical violence was the correct response to life's multiple-choice questions. In the end what pushed me back into the car and directed me toward Pontoon Beach was a simple fantasy that I might return to Lindstrom that night with some small piece of the puzzle filled in, some concrete thing that would take us a step closer to our killer.

I crawled past the exits for East St. Louis, drove off Exit 6 onto 111 and stopped at a tavern, already filling with the after work crowd who gave the

187

stranger a good looking over. I asked directions to Joe Griff's garage. Some clown down the bar called out "Ain't nothing Joe can do for you that I can't, honey," which brought the expected hoots from his pals but which I didn't have to hear, and the bearded bartender, small hoop in his ear, was polite enough. And sober enough to give good directions. I got back on the highway, went two blocks down, made another left and hung on till the end of the road. Sure enough, I recognized Griff's by the dismembered cars in his yard. I guess, despite its recent growth, Pontoon Beach's city ordinances were still relaxed.

The house that sat behind the cars was a small gray bungalow, nearly square in shape and with a roofless concrete stoop. An unattached garage had been transformed into a mechanic's shop, and I saw a dismantled Chevy inside with a shiny Mustang waiting outside for some final tweak toward perfection. The concrete apron in front of the garage had been widened to hold an extra lineup of cars, and I parked well back from the garage, so that I wouldn't get blocked off by someone pulling in behind me. The dread I felt when Jodie Foster approached the house where Buffalo Bill was holding his latest captive assumed a leaden shape and passed up from my stomach to my gullet.

But here I was, and nothing more inspirational than pride nudged me out of the car, carrying the attaché case carefully, as though it held unstable explosives.

The bright sun outside had deepened the shadows inside, but as I moved toward the garage, I saw that two bulky shadows moved and had arms and feet. I tried to see more clearly, but I heard "Can I help you?" before I saw the rough outlines of a man wearing Osh Kosh overalls over naked white skin. His bald head was bullet shaped, shaved close, and his beard was gingery and long but scraggly. His eyebrows were as invisible as Dick Gephardt's. He wore a medium-sized gold hoop in one ear, and a screaming eagle tattoo decorated the opposite shoulder. He was maybe in his thirties, but his fleshy heft and skinned head made him look older, nearly middle-aged. Behind him, his comrade was tall and lanky, wearing long hair and a full dark beard. He looked younger and prettier. I couldn't see his eyes; he wore mirrored sunglasses.

"I'm looking for Joe Griff."

The ginger beard smiled, a small, sly smile. "You found him."

I'd stepped close enough to see the Confederate flag hanging as the centerpiece of the back wall; on the side wall, above the shelves of tools and motor oils and, out of easy sight from the street, was a Nazi flag. I know about war memorabilia, but neither of these boys were WWII vets. Just looking spooked me, so I turned back to Joe Griff. His eyes were porcelain blue, a perfect match for his fair skin and ginger beard, and not really small and piggy. Right now he was widening them, assuring me of his innocence and openness.

"That's a mighty pretty Mustang in your drive," I said. I said it as much to distract myself from my fear, as in any hope of diverting him.

"You makin' an offer?" This from the younger one. He had a soothing baritone, and I bet he was a hit with the ladies.

"No, but admirin' is free, ain't it?" I snapped back, letting the *g* fall to the ground.

"You still believe in a free country?" Griff asked. His own voice was reedy but not really unpleasant if I could hear it just as sound.

I gave him a careful look, but that was just 'how's the weather' talk for him. Small change. I tried to find enough saliva to make a swallow and plunged in. "Emma Woolsey told me I might find Greg Page here or you'd know where to find him."

"You can see he ain't here," dark beard said, wanting to get more attention. Griff sent him a quieting look, just a thin slice, but the dark beard clamped shut.

But Griff saw that an admission had been made. They knew Page. "And why would Emma send you looking for her little boy?"

I hadn't planned it, but a big fib came to me. I waved my attaché case in front of me as though I held gold. "A relative has left the family a pot of money, and to collect his share Greg needs to be notified and to come in and get it."

I let the story lie there, living or dying on its own, no help from me but their own belief system: there's a free lunch out there for a lucky fella.

Griff wouldn't bite; he was too shrewd. But he could take a cautious nibble. "You a lawyer?"

"Excuse me! Watch your mouth."

"Then who?"

I shook my head. "You call Emma and ask her if she sent Jennifer Slater." I hoped Emma would remember the alias I'd given Lindstrom when I was trying to conceal Lindstrom's police connection. Meg Darcy was a name I was afraid Page might recognize if Page were the one who'd been keeping us locked in his scope.

Griff tried a bemused smile. "You ain't a lawyer?"

I shook my head, gave him back a rueful smile. "I might have to take some of their money, but I don't have to walk their walk."

"Not to pry, but how much money are we talkin' here?"

I met those blue eyes head on. Army poker had taught me a thing or two about bluffing, and Walter had honed my skills. "You know I can't tell you. I wish I could. But I ask you to consider if some tight-assed lawyer would pay me to tromp all the way out to Pontoon Beach if a big commission weren't involved. End of speech."

Griff laughed. Not pleasantly but genuinely amused. "Not likely."

"Damn straight not likely," I said.

"I don't know where Greg is," Griff said, probably honestly.

"But maybe for some of that commission we could find out," dark beard volunteered.

Griff shot him a thunderous look. "Zip it, ace."

I kept the attaché case in my left hand but waved my right hand in mock surrender. "Hey, it won't play that way. Greg has to come in and sign for it, and if he wants to split it fifty-fifty with you guys, who am I to object? But I haven't got anything to split with you."

We shared a long silence while Griff considered.

"What's the name of this long-lost relative?" Griff asked, slapping the wrench in his palm now.

"Damned if I know. I'm not overburdened with details. My job is simple. Find Page, ask him to come in." I could feel the sweat trickling down my spine. The air in here was stifling; I couldn't figure how they worked here during hot weather. A small fan on an upper shelf creaked but stirred nothing.

Griff studied my face. I was getting the feeling he was mean but not crazy. I wanted to ask what he'd been doing on the night of Viv's death, but there was no way I could fit it into this episode.

Finally, with a small, resigned sigh, he asked, "How would he get in touch with you?"

I stifled my own sigh, made a deft dip into the attaché case, praying I was delving into the right little pocket. I pulled out a small white card, squinted at it, thanked the goddess. The plain Jennifer Slater model with her special Miller Security number. Oh, the webs we weave to catch deceivers.

I handed Griff the card, which he barely glanced at but tucked into his overall bib. "Not much on it. What's the address?"

I gave a short laugh. "Un-uh. My boss is funny about that. But if Page calls us, we'll find a place to meet."

"No reason for a lawyer to hide his address."

"You think?" I nodded, not wanting to mock him too much. "Well, I appreciate your time, and I hope you get a chance to pass that on to Gregory. At the very least make him buy you a beer, maybe a case, if he comes in to collect." I started to turn away, paused, did a Columbo. "You don't know the last place Greg was working, do you?"

But they were too clever for me. "Shit, no, that boy hasn't worked since he got out of JTripleC."

I climbed back into my Plymouth, started, backed out into the street, drove down a block, stopped, opened the attaché, took out the .38, set it on the passenger seat. I itched to crawl out of my skin. I couldn't shake the dread snaking through my system.

I headed back to the Gateway City, looking forward to the non-golden Arch that signaled home. At this time of evening I was not a lonesome salmon, but the throng was mostly headed east away from the city. I was back on the maze of interstates on Poplar Street Bridge but not yet taking the 44 exit when I looked in my mirror and saw a dark pickup dogging my heels. With great originality I said, "Oh, shit."

Buddy had pumped a little life into the Plymouth, but I knew the boys behind me had more stallions under their hood. Still, a little creative driving might pay off. I hit the gas and panicked two lanes of traffic by crossing sharply into the far right lane. A glance in my rearview told me the pickup had maneuvered one lane over. When it bullied its way into the far right I-70 exit lane, I did a sharp diagonal left. I was lucky; the Plymouth scooted along, not even brushed by the closest semi. I heard honking and tires squealing behind me, but no crashes. I sailed around the curve of the ramp and onto 55 to Memphis and 44 to southwest Missouri. The evening had plenty of sunshine left in it, but I was again at a disadvantage in the play of lights and shadows. Was that my pickup a dozen cars back or some other cowboy?

I kept rolling, and so did the pickup. I pulled into the far right lane again and drove off the Seventh Street ramp, hell for leather. I didn't pause at the stop sign, but dashed into a side street and parked where I had a clear view of the ramp. Three cars later the pickup flew by, and dark beard was steering it. Riding shotgun was a skinhead I'd not seen before.

Maybe Griff had ordered the pursuit, but I bet not. Maybe I chose to believe not so my teeth wouldn't rattle. Griff's calculations scared me more than dark beard's impulsive greed. I started the Plymouth and planned a zigzag route to Michellene that kept me off Seventh.

I passed several dark pickups on the way home, and each time my heart nearly stopped. Maybe dark beard intended nothing more than to find out my lawyer's office. Maybe he wanted to scare me. I won't say 'only to scare me' because terrorizing someone is itself an act of violence, something your whole body tells you even if society pretends it's no big deal.

When I pulled into the alley and saw Lindstrom's Toyota, I nearly cried in relief. For the first time Michellene felt like home, at least home base. I shoved the .38 into my waistband and loped up the walk. I used my key and let myself in the back door. I noticed the fingers punching in the code to defuse the alarm were shaking. "Are you home?" I tried to call out, but my voice box was still creaky.

Lindstrom strode into the kitchen. She'd had time to change into gym shorts and a tank top. She was barefoot. I suspected that if she'd been living alone in a saner time she'd have been buck naked in understandable response to the day's brutal heat.

"Darcy, are you all right?"

"Oh, yeah, I'm bloody hell fuckin' fine." I snarled because before I would cry I'd slit my throat.

She moved closer, used her height advantage to peer down like an entomologist with a particularly juicy bug in view. "Ah well, fooled me. You look like you've been dipped into an especially nasty brine."

I stared at her, stared at my body. My clothes were soaked, and I was shaky, inside and out. "I need a drink," I said.

"Iced tea? A beer?"

"A gallon of water."

She started for the fridge.

"Out of the tap. Please." I started shaking more; her AC blasted me like an Arctic storm. I followed her and reached for the glass she was offering. Our fingers touched, and for once I felt nothing. I paused, took some steadying breaths, and drank the water.

"Darcy, what happened?"

"Just hold me a minute, will you?"

For a half-second wariness flickered across her face, then she stepped close and held me to her murmuring, "Easy, easy," as though I were a shying horse. All I wanted was the strength of her arms, the natural warmth of her body, the comfort a kitten gets from a littermate. I didn't exactly relax into her embrace, but I was steadied by it.

I stepped out of it almost a minute later. "I need some orange juice." I opened the fridge and poured my own and willed myself to sip it.

"Start at the beginning. You smell like hell."

"Flattery won't get you the detailed version." I drank some more, put the glass down. "I'm having a long hot shower. If you want to talk right away, you can join me. If you can wait for the details, make me a cup of hot tea. How did your day with Rosero go?" I was walking toward the hall.

CHAPTER THIRTY-TWO

In the shower I turned on the water to the highest hot and built a cloud of steam before I stepped in. I soaped and scrubbed and rinsed, soaped and scrubbed and rinsed. I stepped out into one of Lindstrom's luxuriously thick towels. No doubt about it, the girl knew how to live. Unfortunately, that took me back to Viv, and a new shudder started. So far Page had been a name and a mug shot attached to a trail of criminal files. Meeting Griff and dark beard had colored Page with a new reality.

I heard a knock on the door and her hand followed holding a cup of tea. I reached for it, and this time when our fingers touched, I wanted to pull her into the bathroom and address several serious personal issues, not to mention exploring why the shiver she sent through me was so pleasurably different from the ones that had sent me to the shower. But I resisted. I was getting too damn good at resisting, I thought, but I passed and said, "Thanks, Lindstrom."

She closed the door on her "Welcome" before the steam escaped.

I pulled on a long-sleeved cotton tee shirt and a loose pair of white shorts with a side pocket in which I could carry the .38. Then I pulled on thick white socks and a pair of tennies with plenty of traction.

I emerged into the real world. Lindstrom was sitting in the kitchen, leafing through a *Time*. She looked at me inquiringly as though deciding whether or not to come take my pulse.

"You look better. Are you hungry?" she said.

"Ravenous."

"What do you want?"

"Calories. Lots and lots of calories, never mind the vitamins."

We decided on Rigazzi's on the Hill. Over flash-fried spinach and pasta in butter and garlic, I told the story of Page's buddies Griff and dark beard. She listened stoically, frowning as I described my maneuvers on the Interstate. I chose not to engage with her. I was sure I didn't want to know what she thought.

By the time I turned down spumoni, not from character but simple repletion, and Lindstrom had ordered a brandy with her coffee, I was ready to hear about her day with Rosero. No way they were going to become buddies; Rosero would wear latex gloves to protect herself against AIDS while riding with Lindstrom if it weren't clear that the Lieutenant would disapprove.

"That means he's taking your side, doesn't it?"

"Not at all. He's seriously annoyed with both of us—me for being a problem, her for being an asshole. His whole philosophy is 'Don't sweat the small stuff.'"

I gave up trying to show her the bright side. Maybe her take was right and not just paranoia. Somehow, despite this tangle, she and Rosero had done a good day's work. They were pretty sure the killing had been drug related after all, and they had some leads that might move them up the food chain to a middle-management dealer. Despite what was going on in her personal life, this news was obviously heartening to her. She wasn't back to the Lindstrom swagger, but I felt her renewed self-confidence.

When we arrived home, I looked at the shadowy yard and missed Leroy on his perch. I hoped his fishing trip didn't reward him too much for this desertion.

We walked up the path without incident, and inside I advised Lindstrom to turn on the motion detector lights. She said they'd be a pain when we did our walkabouts, and I said "I don't care."

Back and forth till she promised to turn them on after the eleven o'clock stroll.

We were standing in the kitchen for this argument with only the sink light on, and suddenly I thought it would be a fine time to kiss her—just reach out and scoop her toward me, gathering up the smell and heat of her in one smooth motion. She must have had motion sensors of her own because she moved away and restarted our conversation about Griff, moving to the stove and sink to refill the tea kettle. She laughed at parts of my big fib strategy. She didn't care for the chase scene, though, and was cop enough to chastise me for endangering others by reckless driving. This wasn't the total admiration I thought the action warranted, and I was a little huffy about it. "Cops aren't the only ones who know how to drive."

"That's not the point."

"Is, too, the point." I was standing up to walk around, out from under her superior stare, when the phone rang, and we both jumped. But it was only Neely, checking in to see how things were going, and Lindstrom took advantage of his call to feed him Joe Griff's name and ask if Neely could get some cooperation in Illinois to find out more about the boy. She gave him a succinct version of dark beard and his younger sidekick and my minimal description of the pickup.

"No, she didn't get the plates," Lindstrom was saying, and I fumed, knowing the cop-to-cop disparagement of civilians who never get plate numbers.

She and Neely nattered on about her day with Rosero. Probably they missed each other, as partners do. I shouldn't begrudge Lindstrom the intimacy with Neely. I had Patrick after all. And Harvey. Lindstrom said she was close to her Nebraska family; she reported calls back and forth that were made after she climbed the stairs at night. But who did she have to hang with in St. Louis?

The answer came back—me.

And we were hanging. But as if by a puppeteer's threads.

A knock at her front door announced our cop date for the evening. We both went to the door, and Lindstrom and I both used the peek hole to examine Officer Cressey, standing crisp and stiff like a new Marine. He was a young black man, clean-shaven, whose baby face invited us to like him at first glance.

"Tell him we already gave to the Boy Scouts," I said.

"Behave. He's one of our sharpest new men." She opened the door.

"Detective Lindstrom?" But even asking a question, his voice sounded older and surer than his face.

"Officer Cressey," she said formally and introduced me as a friend who'd be sharing the watch.

I offered my hand and got a brisk, manly shake accompanied by a cop's appraisal from his eyes. Not unfriendly, but alert.

We walked him around the house, inside and out, and he opted to leave his cruiser out front while he took advantage of the back yard's shadows. Not many cops volunteer to stand post, and I admitted I was impressed when Lindstrom and I walked away. It was eleven, and time for our first walk around. With Cressey there, we could have skipped it, but I like holding the reins. And maybe summer called us.

Music throbbed from nearby bars, and laughter and song joined with tire squeals and a distant siren to play the urban medley. After all the food we'd consumed, walking felt good, and after we'd checked the front of the house, we kept on Michellene and walked on for a couple of blocks, greeting other couples setting out or returning from weekend parties. We came to a stretch where a streetlight was burned out, and in the dark I took her hand, and for just the short block I had enough romance to make me dizzy. We turned and walked back, and in the densest dark I stopped, and we leaned into each other, and we kissed. A cascade of trip-wires fluttered through me, all systems swept up in the bliss of it, for that short-long while we were outside time.

A car turned onto the street, and we jumped apart at the headlights as though impaled in a tabloid's flash. I didn't have time to protest the intrusion before she spoke. "I can't do this—not in that house."

"My place is still open. Patrick tells me Harvey hasn't sublet it yet."

"Believe me, the best offer I've had in—well, you know. But the time isn't right either." She was definitely apologetic. I wasn't sure that was what I wanted her to be.

Then she took my hand again, and we walked onward. "This is very nice," she said.

And it was.

***

When we returned home, both of us agreed it had been a long, long day. I took courage in my hands and leaned forward and gave her cheek a good night peck. The look I got back was too complex to analyze. Maybe yes, maybe no. Maybe she was as ambivalent as I was—two steps forward, three back. Maybe the hand-holding couldn't be improved on.

In the den I built my usual sheet sandwich topped with the blanket but left my clothes on. I set the small clock for one, fearing exhaustion might ruin my internal alarm. I was thinking that sharing my Griff news with Lindstrom had calmed me down. I was thinking that discussing our work and walking companionably might mean good things for our future. I had just reviewed the good kiss, when sleep reached up and grabbed me.

CHAPTER THIRTY-THREE

About five-fifteen my bladder nudged me awake. I walked into the kitchen for a glass of water. I'd staggered the times of my tours from night to night so that an observer couldn't set his watch by me, but I usually didn't make one this close to dawn. Dog walkers and shift workers start early. I figured our boy wouldn't want to be seen lurking about after five. With vague thoughts of catching dawn's early light, I padded back to the den, pulled on my shoes.

I was crossing back through the kitchen when all hell broke loose—an explosion that shook our window panes and jolted my principal organs into overdrive. I fumbled through the locks and flew out the back, the .38 waving at the end of my unsteady hand. Cressey was running toward the steps, his 9mm drawn and his winsome face suddenly angular and strained. Behind me the motion detector flashed on, locking us into the bullseye glare of harsh light. The angry whang of the alarm sounded.

"Down there—maybe two houses over. I'll check. You stay with Lindstrom," he barked and ran off toward the alley, leaving me without argument, but unhappy not to see for myself.

I'd just had that thought when a new roar called my attention to flames blazing up into the night sky and a few thousand rounds of ammunition going with them. Somebody's Fourth of July had gotten out of hand a day early. I headed back into the house to call 911.

Some motion detector of my own worked. I caught a flicker of movement by the garage. I jumped off the porch into a patch of shadow. Then I saw him. I pulled my head back and quickly reviewed the alternatives. Go in the house for a phone? Get Lindstrom? Confront him? The motion sensitive floods lit all the way to the back so if I approached the porch, it was likely he'd see me before I got a better look at him. I had to assume he was armed and a good shot. I decided to go after him. The alarm was already tripped, so Lindstrom was probably talking to the alarm company on the phone. I ran out of the shadow toward the garage, and he took off immediately. He was slender, in dark pants and tee shirt. And fast. I kicked it into high gear, and we raced down the alley. At the other end, he turned right. I was running flat out and hoped he was, too. If he had more speed to burn, I'd be out of it in a minute. He turned down the next alley heading north, away from the fire. I ducked my head and willed my feet to go faster and willed Lindstrom to call the cops immediately. As I turned into the alley, I saw him stop and open a gate. What was he doing? Going into the yard? No—he ran on leaving the gate wide open. As I approached it, I realized why. A one-hundred-pound German Shepherd came barreling out of the yard into the alley. He took a step forward and growled deep in his throat. I stopped as quickly as I could. I had come running into his territory, clearly with nothing beneficial to him or his family in mind. There could be only one interpretation for him. It would take much too long to woo him, if that was possible at all. It would be even stupider to turn and try to run away from him. I'd surely be prey then; he would be on me in a minute. He growled again and lowered his shoulders as if preparing to jump at me.

"NO!" I said sharply.

He blinked.

"No. Go back in your yard." Obviously not a command he'd been taught.

"Sit." As much alpha-dog as I could muster. He stopped growling.

"Sit, boy." He slowly lowered his haunches and looked expectant. I'd have given a month's salary to have a treat in my pocket for him.

"Good boy. You're a good dog..." I walked up to him slowly and veered around to his left and put my hand on his gate.

"Go." I commanded, pointing to his house. He thought this over. Evidently he remembered he wasn't supposed to be outside his fence except on a lead. With great dignity, he stood and walked back into his yard, keeping his eye on me. I gently closed the gate behind him.

"You are a great dog. Tell your momma you deserve a treat and a long run in the park." I looked down the alley. My backyard creeper was long gone.

The smartest thing now was to get the car. I'd never catch him on foot even if I knew which way he ran. By the time I was back to the drive, my sides were heaving and a pain was beginning to make itself felt above my right kidney. I was almost to the car when I spotted Lindstrom standing in the back yard.

"What the hell is going on, Darcy?" she demanded.

"He was in the back yard. I think he set off the explosion. That's where Cressey is."

"Where is he now?" I knew which *he* she meant.

"I lost him in an alley. I'm going to take the car, see if I can spot him."

She glanced at the Plymouth.

"I'll drive. I know the neighborhood."

I shook my head. "You need to be here when the cops come."

She responded by getting into the car on the driver's side and glaring at me until I handed her the keys. She pointed the car north in response to my breathless wave in that direction. I noticed a suspicious lump in the waist of her pants. Uncharacteristically, her tee shirt was not tucked neatly into her waistband. She'd grabbed her Beretta as she dressed. I showed her where I last saw him, and we did a crawl around the surrounding blocks. It was five-forty-five, and the faintest glow was beginning to lighten over the river.

Lindstrom headed toward Soulard Market.

"If he's smart and knows the neighborhood at all, he'll go to the market. It's the only place he won't stick out like a sore thumb by being on foot at this hour," she said.

I nodded. I hadn't thought of the market. Had I gotten a good enough glimpse to spot him again? I wasn't sure. I knew I didn't recognize him. I had an impression of dark hair and a narrow waist. But he wouldn't have had time to change clothes, and I thought I could spot them. Clothes and body shape. I closed my eyes and saw him again standing, opening the gate to let the dog out. He was slender enough to be Aubuchon or Krebs. I'd never seen Page.

"He's maybe five-foot ten or eleven", medium to slender. White guy. Regular haircut. Could be any of our suspects."

"What color hair?"

"I don't know. Dark."

"You tripped the alarm yourself?"

"I didn't disarm it when I ran out. He was in the back—the flood lights were on so any way I approached, he'd see me first. I didn't know if he had a gun or not."

She nodded to herself. "That was smart, Darcy." She pulled up to a meter on Ninth Street and peered into the market.

Large produce trucks were arriving. Men in sleeveless tee shirts and jeans were pushing loaded dollies and unloading crates. As we entered the brick H-shaped building, a man was filling his barrel barbecue grill with charcoal. His sign advertised ribs, pork steaks, sandwiches, and snouts. We walked through an over-sized garage sale with carpets, painted tee shirts, jewelry, and, at the end, fresh hot mini-donuts by the Donut Man, actually an Asian woman. As we passed a bakery, a spice shop and a snack stand, the smells mingled and stirred up my stomach juices. No sign of our back yard creeper.

Then on my right I saw a movement that caught my attention. I grabbed Lindstrom's arm and stood still. The hackles on the back of my neck rose, just like my friend, the well-trained German Shepherd. I sniffed, but all I could smell was produce, fresh and not-so fresh and diesel fumes from the trucks. Lindstrom stepped quietly behind me and toward the hall of the market.

We flushed him several stalls ahead of us. He scrambled up out from under the lift-gate of the truck and climbed over the counter, dumping over a pile of tomatoes, white radishes, and mixed greens. We were right behind him pounding down the concrete floor. Ahead of us, I saw him push down a woman with a bag of melons. Good. Maybe others would join the chase.

"Stop! Police!" Lindstrom screamed. She pulled out her weapon, but we all knew she couldn't use it in this space. He sped on toward Seventh Street. Just before he reached the exit, he veered right and climbed over one of the stands. He paused just long enough to dump a huge pyramid of oranges on the floor and then jumped down outside the building. I decided not to slow down and almost immediately my right foot hit an orange, and I went flying palms and knees first onto the floor. Lindstrom had better luck; she was within two steps of the door before she hit one. We'd lost him.

I called to her, "Hey, come on. Let's call the department, get some more help here." I was panting again, and I hated it that she wasn't. She turned to me.

"Okay. Is there a phone in there?"

I shrugged but walked back up into the building and asked the man who was trying to pick up his oranges.

"She said you was the police," he objected.

"She is, but we need some back up here. The car is all the way up on Ninth." He pointed toward the middle of the market, and I trotted away. I had hoped Lindstrom would come with me to talk to the station. I was sure she'd get quicker results. The man at Schmidt's Meat Market dialed the number for me, and I talked to the dispatcher.

Carefully, I told her my name and that I was with Detective Lindstrom at the Soulard Market where we had chased an intruder. Quickly she informed me that there were three units at Lindstrom's house responding to the alarm there. I asked her to send them here. She said she would radio them immediately. I told her I'd meet them at the corner of Seventh and Carroll.

When I walked back to the corner, Lindstrom was gone. Two cruisers were on the scene in less than three minutes. I explained the foot and car search to a young cop by the name of Hemphill. I showed him the stand our quarry had dumped over and the direction he'd been running.

He turned to his partner and said, "We'll go down through the market on foot. Tell Parkins and Hayes to cruise the neighborhood."

We walked around the market for another thirty minutes, but none of us spotted him. The runner, whoever he was, was still on the loose.

***

Hemphill insisted on driving the Plymouth back to Michellene, and truthfully I was exhausted enough to appreciate it. I hadn't done such flat out running since my Army days. All the pasta and garlic bread were making a doughy lump in my gut. I had a stitch in my side, kinks in my legs, and a general array of aches at key joints. "And you're still a young woman," Lindstrom said when she caught me moaning as I followed her into the back of the car.

"In a very old body," I said. Not only did I hurt all over, my spirits were low. I'd sighted him two, no, *three* times, and we'd still lost him. He'd just slithered away like those lizards that leave their tails behind. Except he hadn't left behind anything that I'd noticed.

I was feeling we'd reached for a ghost who could walk right through us. Whoever he was, he was seeming like the maniacal villain of some scary movie, impervious to ordinary weapons, superior to ordinary mortals. He just kept coming back like Freddie Kruger.

The early sun promised another heat-alert day. Lindstrom was glowing

200

in the light like a Nordic Jackie Joyner-Kersee after a triumphant run. She spared me a glance, saw where I was. "Don't worry, Darcy, we'll get him. He runs on two legs, like you and me."

"Just a little faster," I muttered defiantly.

"Head start." Her tone was serene. I couldn't spoil it.

She and Hemphill compared notes on their different views of the search. When we pulled up to Lindstrom's house, two other patrol cars were jamming the street, arousing the curiosity of a few neighbors. "You know when I first moved in here, some of these people thought having a cop on their street would cut down on crime," Lindstrom said. Hemphill and his partner chuckled. Hemphill double-parked, adding to the jam, and we all climbed out and sauntered over to confer with Parkins and Hayes and Rovelli and Stamps. With effort I learned Hemphill's partner was named Amy. With more effort I learned it was Amy Grant, no jokes please. While I was eliciting this information, Lindstrom was calming down the other patrol officers, all of whom were revved up by the chase and all of whom wanted to help the homicide detective get her man.

Then Officer Cressey reported in. He looked sheepish. Bits of ash smudged his uniform. "The perp must have set up the explosion to lure me away. The householders vow it wasn't their fireworks, and their neighbors say they never have fireworks."

Lindstrom gave him a nod. "You did the right thing, Cressey. The potential harm to civilians was much greater. We're here to protect them."

I could tell he was sifting it carefully to see if she was hiding any superior officer sarcasm inside the speech. I wanted to pull him aside and whisper "Relax. That's just how she talks." Instead, I asked, "What did explode?"

Cressey looked relieved to have a change of subject. "The fire chief says it looked like ordinary fireworks—just lots of 'em. And they were set up to go off in two stages."

"Anybody hurt?"

"A dog got some singed fur. Their garage roof is gone, but luckily nothing else. I got everybody out of the house and kept the neighbors back." He was explaining why he missed the chase.

"Good," she said curtly and turned toward me. "My only regret is that Cressey might have caught him. He looks faster than you."

Cressey and I exchanged a look.

Before either of us let our thoughts fly into words, she patted his shoulder. "You did fine, officer. We'll get him." She said it with conviction. Then she grinned at me. "You did your best."

I saw Cressey's upper lip twitch. Then he relaxed, seeing who was being blamed. I rolled my eyes.

Eventually Lindstrom shooed them all away and led me into the house. "Hungry?"

I looked at her blankly, as though food were a foreign concept. "It'll be hours before my stomach unknots."

"Hmm. Could I have that in writing?" But her heart wasn't in the zinger. She disappeared into the den and came back with two legal pads and pens and dropped them on the kitchen table. "Let's review what we learned." Her tone was business-like but upbeat. She looked like Rebecca Lobo after a good half.

"I learned I have an old body."

She shot me a look, rather like Griff's to his buddy, dark beard. "Look, Darcy, for the first time I know this guy puts on his pants one leg at a time."

"To coin a phrase."

She ignored me. "I didn't get close enough to see him well, but you were closer. Stop being so negative. Loosen up a little. Let's list all the details you can remember. Maybe we can get a police artist to do a sketch." She was running on high, full of the possibilities.

I tried seeing it her way. He was no longer a disembodied voice. He had a definite physical body, and the body probably had fingerprints and a name.

"I already told you all the details I remember."

"Perhaps," she said amiably. "Let's walk through it again. How tall was he, do you think?"

She walked me through it bit by bit: five-foot ten, slender build, dark pants, dark tee shirt. Definitely white and a pale white at that. Not Latino. Maybe, outside possibility Asian. A hell of a runner. That might clear Krebs. Darkish hair, not quite black I thought, though I wasn't sure. Every time I paused, she pressed me with another question. She was easier on me than she'd been with Kathleen Clawsen, but her determination had its effect.

What we knew still seemed like a pitiably short list to me, but gradually my own curiosity served as a lure. "What about the answering machine tapes, the ones with his voice on it? Won't that help?" I asked.

"If we get a voice to match with it. Do you remember any voices like it?" she said.

"No. But he sounded a little artificial, not like a mechanical voice, but like someone reading for a play. A bad actor."

"You're saying we should check amateur theater groups?" She lifted a brow.

"No. Just what I think he sounds like."

She nodded. "That's what Neely says. The guy sounds like he isn't talking naturally, he's trying to spook me. Trouble is, it's worked. I can't hear him that objectively." For a moment her spirits dipped, but then she shrugged. "Did he say anything while you were running?"

I thought about it, shook my head. "Funny. It's like a silent movie chase to me. I know there were noises—traffic, market vendors setting up, but I don't think he said anything, nor did I, except to the dog."

"How would you describe his haircut?"

"Geez, I don't know. More short than long, not really as traditional as Walter's but not styled either."

"My impression, too," she said agreeably.

"Bad luck there. Krebs has white-blond hair with gray. Closer to

Aubuchon. Page is a skinhead or a redhead, depending."

"Maybe."

"What do you mean, maybe?"

"What you just said, depending. Imagine Walter bald."

"Oh."

She reached out and ruffled my hair, encouraging a slow fifth grader. "Yeah." Before my feelings got ruffled, too, she jumped up. "Let's go." She caught my questioning look. "To Clark Street. Mug shots."

"You know how to show a girl a good time."

"Don't give up on me yet."

CHAPTER THIRTY-FOUR

This wasn't my first trip to the Clark Street Police Station as Lindstrom's guest. The previous December she'd questioned me about the Brooks case. This time felt different. She told me that quite a few of the detectives were on the Arch Grounds, helping police the VP Fair. So she wasn't parading me in front of her entire group of colleagues on the fourth floor that Saturday morning, only a skeleton crew. And I came in as a witness, not as her girlfriend or a suspect. Even so I got plenty of scrutinizing stares, and none of them left me feeling stamped U.S.D.A. Grade A. I tried not to take it personally, knowing how suspicious of strangers cops tend to be, but I saw that Lindstrom's morning walk into the squad room could cause shivers in anyone, not necessarily someone afflicted with internalized homophobia. She kept a professional distance from me as we walked through and as she returned a few greetings. Some didn't say howdy, but that may have been the kind of guys they were. Maybe from embarrassment, maybe to put me at ease, she stuck me into an interrogation room and promised to return with mug shots and coffee.

She was as good as her word, bringing back a cup of pure caffeine that seemed to need F.D.A. regulation to be legal. A uniformed cop carried the heavy binders featuring the city's latest criminal celebrities. She thanked him and opened the first binder. "Sorry, no hazelnut today," she said, noting my wince after the trial sip.

"How many cups before the stomach lining disappears?"

"Oh, is that the connection?" Now that the door was closed, she patted my shoulder in a friendly way before taking a seat beside me so that we could look through the Clark Street yearbooks together.

A journey not without nostalgia. There was the killer from the Brooks case, who had, in fact, brought us together. And turned out we both knew Johnny Smart (terribly misnamed), Brenda Wyatt, Curtis Fowler, Billy Leigh, Gino Travelli, Stuart Kiwotzki. Lindstrom even unbent enough to regale me with the highlights of Stuart's capture, but she didn't lose her focus. She might permit a short diversion, even a pee break, but each time she brought me back. "Him? How about this one? Could this be him?"

I'd left the metal folding chair to take a stretching walk around the table when Johnson and Neely came in, looking like an updated Mutt and Jeff. The weather had forced them both into short-sleeved shirts. Each wore a sweaty shine on his face and half moons round his armpits. Johnson had loosened his tie and collar. Neely had pulled the knot of his tie half-way down his chest.

"Hi, Meg, hear you had quite a chase," Neely said. Without asking, Johnson pulled up a chair, and Neely perched his smaller rear on the end of the table.

"She found out she doesn't run as fast as she used to," Lindstrom said, and the men laughed agreeably.

This started Johnson onto a shaggy dog story about when he was a young patrolman, and we all listened with the deference due to a senior officer and laughed when his chuckle signaled the end. Still, I was encouraged. By his looks and manner he was treating Lindstrom as one of the boys, and he wasn't giving me the 'civilian as alien' treatment. You might think I'd have a few blue chips left over from bringing in the murderer of Mary Margaret Brooks, but I wasn't relying on it. Cops have a lot of loyalty to their own, but still, there's a whadda-ya-done-for-me-lately mentality that's understandable when you consider how much shit they have to shovel just to keep the city livable. And I wasn't one of their own, which meant no one counted on me to stay on their side.

After all the joshing, Lindstrom gave them a crisp report of 'the incident,' as the chase now became. She toned down her own response a bit, wasn't quite so insistent that this was a breakthrough moment. I couldn't read Johnson's shrewd eyes. He listened carefully, though, and Neely nodded at the end. "We'll get the slimewad yet."

"Could this be somebody else altogether? You know, some guy lookin' to smash and grab your cars again?" Johnson's tone was easy.

"Could be, sure," Neely said.

I didn't dare look at Lindstrom. That would be wavering.

Lindstrom cleared her throat. "Might be, sure. But I think it wasn't. Car thieves don't set off a box of fireworks as a distraction."

Johnson nodded. "Well, the patrol boys will still keep looking in case he isn't smart enough to change his clothes—and you never know. Even the smart ones do dumb things." An article of faith that gave him the strength to keep going.

"Amen," said Neely, though he'd heard it before. I thought he was maybe a bridge between his partner and Johnson, interpreting both gay stuff and boy stuff.

I decided to risk being noticed. "Have you heard anything about Page and the Kentucky Lake cabin?"

Johnson gave me a rather fierce look, as though startled to find me still there. But maybe that meant less than I read into it. He softened it with a smile, the kind that stretched his lips without changing his eyes much. "Well, you know how those white boys are down there, slow and easy. Sooner or later one of 'em will amble up there and check it out. Neely, maybe you can give a call down there and goose 'em. And we'll put a couple more officers on the St. Louis search for Page, too. After the Fourth."

Neely nodded, but regarded me carefully. "You leaning toward Page?"

"Joe Griff gave me a serious scare. This sounds like the kind of thing those guys are into."

Johnson shifted in his chair, put on his most serious face. "Sarah, are you sure we can't get you out of town? Just till after the Fourth?"

She looked at her feet. "I know manpower's tight. But I think we've stirred him up."

"Got that right," Johnson said. "Next time he might blow up half of Soulard." He chuckled to take the sting out.

I watched a slow flush creep up Lindstrom's face. "I don't want to get out of his way." I could see the concrete setting around her feet.

Maybe Johnson could, too. He glanced at Neely, who jumped in. "After Sunday, we'll be richer in man hours. Now everything from managing traffic to guarding against pick-pockets at the Fair—" He let it trail off. Her blue eyes were challenging him.

"If I leave town, we'll just have to start all over when I come back. Meanwhile, who knows what he's going to do with all that bad energy?"

None of us could argue that this guy wouldn't hurt anyone else. But Johnson said, "Depends on who it is, doesn't it? If it's Aubuchon, I think he'd wait for you."

"What about his Branson alibi?" Neely asked.

I kept my mouth shut. If Walter reported that the alibi didn't hold, then we could bring it up. In the meantime, I avoided pointless diversions. Lindstrom's silence seemed to agree.

Johnson shrugged. "If it holds—" He shook his head. "I just don't like his hangin' around. His wife is dead. He's got no reason to hang around you."

"We've requested a full time tail on him," Neely said.

"And we'll get it later," Johnson said.

"After the Fourth," Lindstrom said.

They nodded. Neely spoke. "Till then it's just more efficient to use the manpower on you. Where you are, he may be." He shrugged. "If we have any manpower."

"That's what I think. So maybe we could draw this to a head—after the Fourth, I mean." Her voice was steady, but I saw the glitter of the hunting cat in her eye. "Maybe we could entice him out to play and be ready for him."

"Surround him?"

"Yes." She was answering Neely, but checking Johnson's response.

"Why would he believe your guard dogs have pulled back?" Johnson asked. "Especially after this morning's stunt."

"For the reasons you've said. It's the Fourth. He doesn't have to be a genius to figure we're stretched thin with not even enough overtime cops to guard my house. Maybe I *will* stay away. Maybe at Meg's. Then, when I come back, we'll set the trap, but hope it looks like we think he's lost interest. No obvious guards."

"I don't like using you as bait," Neely said.

"I don't like being bait, but that's all I'll be until we catch him."

They were doing one of those eyeball tug of wars, strictly between them stuff.

Johnson broke in. "Is Meg's safe?"

How could we know?

Lindstrom pursed her lips thoughtfully. "We've heard nothing from him there."

"We haven't really tried to conceal my apartment." I thought of the times I'd driven straight from Lindstrom's place to my own.

"He won't be expecting us. He probably scouts around before he does his little stunts." Lindstrom spoke confidently. "We need only two nights there."

No one disagreed with her or pointed out she was guessing. Instead, Neely smiled at me. "Lucky you. You win the house guest."

I managed only a head shake and a limp grin. "Do we get a cop to go with her?"

They scowled in unison. "We'll try," Johnson said.

We ping-ponged a few more comments back and forth before Johnson heaved himself up, dismissing us. "I'm glad it was you-all out there running this morning," he said with a dramatic sigh. He nodded toward the open binders. "Let us know if you find him."

By this time we were edging toward nine-thirty, and my stomach, so terribly full earlier, was now threatening to bite. Lindstrom heard a growl and closed the books. "Time to feed you."

She didn't sound disappointed that we hadn't spotted him among the senior photos, nor that our exchanges with Johnson and Neely hadn't been so productive. I know a good part of homicide work is simply soldiering on, hoping you get lucky and he or she gets dumb. Somehow the adrenaline she'd sucked in during the morning's footrace was still stoking her optimism.

She asked me to name the place so I took us back to South Grand and to South City Diner, where I did some stoking of my own, shoving in their Breakfast Burrito and a side order of perfect breakfast fries and finishing her second pancake.

"Stomach better?" she asked over the real coffee.

"Don't alienate your supportive PI."

She looked at me squarely, giving me serious regard from blue eyes obviously drawn from some Norwegian fiord. "You're right, Darcy. Thanks for putting your life at risk to help me."

Well, that was too mushy to handle right in the middle of Saturday's breakfast. We were sitting at one of the tables in the center, too, and servers were squeezing by. Unlike Lindstrom to go too far. I didn't know how to get to my "aw, shucks" mode without a stumble.

Before I'd constructed my way out, she reached over, "If you joke now, I'll order another plate of eggs and dump them on your head."

Not even a lip twitched, though I think my brows lifted. In unison, of course.

When she saw that I wasn't going to stick a napkin up my nose or gargle my water, she continued. "Seriously. It's not in your job description, not for a PI or a friend or a—" She ran out of nouns.

"Don't stop. A what—?"

"—ever," she finished.

"Oh, that's lame."

She studied the syrupy remnants on her plate, looked up. "Yes. It is. But don't lose my point. You've done more than even my mother could ask for."

I'd never heard such an exaggeration from her before, but what it meant I didn't know. Maybe she had an Irish ancestor after all, one who knew a good story demanded more than a factual recital. But I'd never heard such a hint from her.

"Does this mean you're paying for breakfast?"

"Why not?" She caught our server on the fly and asked him for our check.

"What next? Do we give up looking at Krebs? Do you think we can do any more to find Page?"

"I work tomorrow at the VP Fair till five. I don't think you should do anymore with Page. Obviously his posse is too dangerous to stir up on your own—not that you didn't handle that well yesterday."

I bit hard on the compliment, but tried a nonchalant shrug. "Except for the driving."

"Except for. I need to go back to the cop shop and look at more mug shots. Maybe I'll recognize someone by the shape of the head."

I sighed. "I guess that means me, too."

She studied my face. "Yes. Not as much fun as playing dodge'em cars on Poplar Street Bridge or cops and robbers through Soulard Market, but," She sipped some water. "Why don't we stop by and see Harvey before we go back? We're in the neighborhood."

I was surprised. The last time she'd suggested we drop by my apartment had been at least six weeks before, and we'd ended up adding a chapter to the Kama-sutra. But I missed Harve and didn't question that she might miss him, too, short though their acquaintance had been. Normally I'd have preferred to walk back to my Arsenal apartment, but the heat made me grateful for the Toyota's AC, even on a short drive. When we climbed the stairs, I noted Patrick's MG was gone, which probably meant he was working at the bookstore and maybe we could have our regular Sunday brunch the next day. When we stepped inside, I found a series of post-it notes, a mix of mushy and teasing, from the lad himself and collected and read them while Harvey was greeting Lindstrom. I was grateful Patrick had straightened a pillow or two and cleaned up after Harvey, who has a tendency to toss kibble he's bored with. Best of all, Patrick had cranked up the AC, figuring no doubt that its whole purpose was to cool the cat. I was just thinking how friends are often better than lovers when she reached around me from behind, circling my waist and pulling me back against her. "Just how old is this body you're complaining about? Last time I saw it, it looked good to me."

I figured she was joshing. She still seemed keyed up from the chase and well, frankly, excited by the prospects of catching him at last, her belief that we'd lure him out again quite strong.

I wasn't feeling as upbeat. We'd chased him, but the fish got away. And I was tired of being aroused by her only to be turned aside.

I was just thinking how to say such things when she pulled me against her, still my back to her face, and, reaching around, pushed her other hand under my belt and down my belly and launched a thousand dream ships. Her other arm locked me to her, unnecessarily. She has the strong, long-fingered, good hands of a basketball player, and the first touch of them works every time. I don't need foreplay or fantasy or anything else but knowing it is she touching me there. I'm eager as a teenaged boy for the logical, inevitable, irrevocable, certain, sweet conclusion.

"Ah, you like that?" she mocked while my buttocks beat against her thighs. Her fingers fluttered inside me, and I chased them, trying to keep them just so, just there, but losing them in my own greedy grasping. But she's determined as a cat facing any form of "no." She kept finding there, kept tattooing it with butterfly-kisses from her fingertips while I knocked against her and lost all the rest of me: my ragged, humping breaths, my sweat-slick skin, the gurgling rasp of my pleasured self.

I struggled to turn around, to make it easier, quicker, to insure it, but she tightened her hold around my waist, kept me there, kept me chasing after her.

"Do you like—" The rest swallowed up because her mouth was against my back.

"Damn you." The microscopic focus was smaller and smaller. Just there, just that one spot contained the world.

"Ah, yes." Triumph. How did she know?

I bucked against her, felt her face bouncing against my spine, felt my rhythm ratchet up into a spasm, as involuntary as breathing, felt who I am fly away and rain down on the hand that ruled me.

When I returned, my arms were braced against the kitchen counter; she was curved around and over me. We rested like two spent swimmers who've been tossed ashore, saved in spite of themselves.

Of course, she never leaves well enough alone. I hadn't even steadied my breath before she started it again, and, as usual, she was directing traffic, pulling off pieces of my clothing, pulling me toward the bedroom.

"I haven't changed the sheets," I protested, wondering if Patrick had been that efficient.

"Good because you'll have to when we're through here." Smug. So damned smug.

I had only a moment to see Patrick hadn't and to rue the Snoopy as WWI Flying Ace design before she had me on those sheets, addressing all the same issues with all the same results and not a second of tedium in the repetition.

"I know your methods, Lindstrom. You think you'll leave me so wasted

I won't have the energy to get into your pants." An amazingly literate sentence considering my sorry state. She was sprawled, spread-eagle, on top of me.

I couldn't see her face; it was buried by my ear, but she sounded as though it carried a blush. "I'm not wearing pants." Indeed, she had shed all her clothes during our second dive.

"You aren't?" I grabbed for her buttocks, feigned checking.

She laughed. A good sign. It goes easier with Lindstrom if I can make her laugh.

The checking became massaging, became tickling, became her moving, spreading, squeezing, rocking, riding. We turned like synchronized swimmers, allowing me to swim over her. I talked to her nonstop unless my tongue was actively involved in other negotiations. I don't think she heard anything but the sounds of my voice, husky, intense, chanting meaningless monosyllables: yes, ha, now, hey, good, sweet, ripe, cop. Suddenly she grabbed my shoulder, and we clutched together while the bed squeaked and rocked and tossed us. I held on, while she crested, broke, crashed down, and we were lying on tangled sheets, struggling to remember our names.

I waited for some sign of connection from her because in all that great, chugging upheaval I wasn't sure if I'd touched her at all, or if, serenely, she'd used me and would discard me. Finally she opened one startling blue eye and smiled.

"You're funny, Darcy." Her voice sounded like a friendly ruffle of my hair.

"Funny?" As though the idea is terribly foreign.

"Who else says 'cop' in the middle of sex?"

"Yeah, well, it's like this: Cop a plea. Cop a feel. Please a cop." I started matching hand motions to the verbal cues. She laughed because she was embarrassed by 'cop a feel,' and embarrassment made her ticklish. And ticklish was the next-door-neighbor to you-know-what, and we started again.

Maybe this is what love is I thought while I still could think. I drank in great gulps of her: hair, eyes, skin. I wanted tiny sips, too; I wanted details— how her pubic hair waves rather than curls; how her very feet are lovely and lissome. But I had what I wanted; I was touching her, moving her, pushing her back into the waves. I had no time in the fury of the storm, no time to think.

***

My bedside clock said one-thirty p.m. when she pulled me close after the last time and said, "That was especially fine, PI Darcy."

"Damn straight. No, damn gay."

She was sinking fast. "Hold me. I want to sleep and sleep."

I spooned up. I didn't mention mug shot viewing. That world was far away. Soon her breathing came regularly. Harvey jumped up and claimed his spot on the pillow behind me. Between his purrs and her heartbeats I rocked in safety like a snug boat on gentle waves. She slept; Harve slept; I slept.

CHAPTER THIRTY-FIVE

My eyes fluttered open at four-twenty. The room was stuffy. I hadn't interrupted our ballet to switch on the fan I used to stir the cooled air around. I was crowded. I was still spooned around Lindstrom, who was soundly asleep, but Harvey had planted himself behind my knees, and I was locked in. I diverted myself by looking at Lindstrom, even risking a touch to sweep a few blonde hairs from her cheek, the better to see her with. The tenderness I felt may have been an emotional cliché; I didn't care. I wanted to protect her, keep her safe, shield her from harm.

I also wanted to move. I don't have claustrophobia, that would be a disease. I do get twitchy when cornered. I tried to push Harvey away, but he does this cat Zen thing where his eleven pounds gain density, and he's a white boulder dropped onto my bed. I felt sweaty and itchy and was sure I'd get a charley-horse in my left calf if I didn't move immediately. No alternative presenting itself, I scooped Harvey away, earning a plaintive complaint. Then I slipped away from Lindstrom, the bed creaking loudly, but she didn't move.

I dressed in two minutes and tip-toed out to my living room and kept going, just picking up my keys so I could lock behind me. Then I knocked on Patrick's door asking the goddess to let him be home.

"Meg!" He was in neatly pressed white Dockers and a navy tee.

"Are you going out?"

"No, I worked this morning, but I got the afternoon off. I just haven't changed. Want to walk down to Mokabe's?"

"No, Lindstrom is next door. Asleep."

"Ahhh," he said appreciatively. "Do I congratulate you now, sailor?"

Despite our long history of shared confidences, I felt the blush that didn't creep but ran up my neck to my cheeks. I walked past him too fast for a hug. "I need a favor, Patrick."

He could have said something about how long it'd been since we'd had quality time together. But when it's down to the bone, the boy has class and reserve wells of generosity. "So ask."

"Patrick, it's a long story, and I'm sorry I'm behind with the latest installment. But I need to go out, and I'm afraid to leave Lindstrom by herself."

"Don't worry, Meg. I've had bad sex many times, and it's never left me suicidal. Well, not enough to act on it." Okay, in the past I'd shared the fact that not every encounter with Lindstrom had been as blissful for her as for me.

211

"This is about the stalker."

"You mean the guy who killed Viv?"

"Yes. We don't know who it is yet, but we've had more scares." I hastily sketched in the incidents about my car window and the morning's chase through the market; his face grew grimmer with each detail. "I don't know if the creep knows we came here, but I think it's possible. Lindstrom hasn't had a good night's sleep since Viv was killed. I hate to wake her, but I don't want to leave her by herself while I go out."

"And you're doing your early Christmas shopping?"

"I want to ask someone some questions."

"Won't that be risky—going by yourself?" He gave me a close, scrutinizing look, one I swear he learned from Betty.

"No, really not, Patrick. But maybe I can find out something that will get us a bit closer to catching this guy." This was becoming our mantra.

"What do you want me to do?"

"Stay in my apartment with Lindstrom till I get back."

"Oh, that's adventurous." Periodically Patrick gets a yen for the excitements of real detective work.

"Please." Our code for no *buts*, no dickering, just do it.

"I'm coming, I'm coming," he said in what I hoped was mock irritation. Patrick's feelings about Lindstrom were no secret. She just wasn't good enough for me. She was jealous of him, too. I couldn't worry about it now.

"Thanks, you're a pal."

"Never forget it," he tossed over his shoulder. He locked his apartment behind us.

"I'll just look in and check on her," I whispered.

"In case she's turned into a werewolf while you're gone?" he whispered back.

"Patrick!"

He shrugged and occupied himself with Harvey, who'd ambled in to greet his favorite uncle and, of late, main source of both kibble and affection.

I tiptoed back into my bedroom. Lindstrom had pulled the sheet down, exposing shoulders that wrecked me, and she was hugging my pillow. For a moment I thought about telling Patrick I'd changed my mind, go home, I would entertain Detective Lindstrom for another couple hours. But I thought my chances of repeating the afternoon's delights were better if I got us out from under the killer's stare. And, delights or not, I wanted to free her from him.

I pulled her 9mm from her shorts, returned to the kitchen, and put her pistol on the table. Patrick looked as if I'd introduced a snake into Eden.

"This won't bite, Patrick. Pay attention." I quickly touched on the basics.

"You want me to carry this with me around the apartment?"

"No, Lindstrom will be pissed if she thinks you have messed with her gun. But just put it on the table beside you while you're sitting in there reading on the sofa." I stopped and acknowledged his look with a grin. "Right, I'm being a total control freak. Don't read if you don't want to. I've got crossword puzzles. Just something quiet so she sleeps."

"Damn, I was thinking of blasting away with the latest salsa. Disco's coming back, you know."

I patted his arm. "You don't have to touch it unless you need it, then you just point and shoot. It's got a serious kick."

"I love it when you talk dirty."

"Behave."

He threw up his hands. "All right, all right. You put it on the table." He's just totally phobic about guns. I don't know if even his therapist knows why. I won't have anyone thinking it's because he's cowardly. Patrick is one of the bravest men—one of the bravest human beings—I know. Not least because in spite of his fears, he was doing what I asked.

I moved the gun, ran over the basics one more time. He nodded impatiently, but he screwed his mouth around in that twist he gets when he's really listening to instruction despite the boring lesson; I figured he'd looked that intent during fifth-grade spelling tests.

To seal our bargain, I gave him a quick hug. He grabbed my arms lightly and said, "When are you coming back?"

"When you see me."

Another panic attack. "What'll I do if she wakes up?" He stepped back.

"Throw her to Harvey."

"I'm being serious here."

"Me, too. She likes Harvey."

"Not to be petty, but this is going to be a big debt, Meg."

I grinned. "Lucky her, waking up to find you here."

"Really big."

"Bye, Patrick. Lock up behind me." And I was gone before his objections entangled me.

***

A firecracker popped from my neighbor's yard just as I pulled open the door of the Plymouth. I grinned. Celebrations were indeed in order. A blast of heat poured out of the car, and I leaned over to roll down the window, grateful that Buddy had worked his magic in such a timely way. The plastic sections of the seat stuck to my bare legs and burned.

I wondered briefly if Page killed Viv. Might it still be Aubuchon harassing Lindstrom—punishing her for letting Viv get killed? Maybe Viv's real killer had just slunk away. But that didn't explain the note, or this morning's intruder. That wasn't Aubuchon. And I was pretty sure it wasn't Krebs either. No way he could outdistance me with a stiff knee, and it certainly wasn't his light-blond head. But I had to make sure.

I wanted to check the VCR repair shop first to see if Krebs was working before I tried talking to Sandi Bidwell again. The traffic on Grand was dense and the fumes nearly overpowering. But neither the carbon monoxide stink nor the stabbing rays of the sun could distract me. I was on my white horse again. Off to slay Lindstrom's dragons, the smell of her still radiating from me. I rummaged in the back seat at a light and found my tape case. A Heather Bishop kind of drive, I thought. For the first time this week, I felt sure we would catch the killer before he shattered our lives again with his violence. I grinned and sang along with "I Want to Be Seduced." At Wyoming, I got caught behind a Bi-State bus, and the traffic on my left flowed around me. I gave it up and admired the beautiful woman on the bus's rear billboard selling perms and relaxers with her devastating smile.

I pulled into a side street about a block from Advance to think about whether I wanted Krebs to know that I was still sniffing around him. I weighed the pros and cons and picked pulling his chain. It might be good for him to worry a bit. So I pulled back onto Gravois and parked right in front of Advance TV.

The shop's air-conditioner was running hard, and I pulled my shirt away from my sweaty back to enjoy the cool. A large white man in a plaid shirt hunched at the desk behind the counter, surrounded by his own cigarette smoke.

"Hi, is Terry Krebs here?"

"No, he's gone for the day. Can I help you?"

"I thought he generally worked on Saturdays."

The man scratched his head, which seemed very big and almost perfectly round.

"He opens up on Saturdays, usually. He goes home about two. He'll be in tomorrow. Would you like to leave a message?"

"No, thanks. Listen, did Terry work early on the 19th, Saturday before last?"

"Look, I don't know what this is about, but Terry's okay. He's trying to get his life back in order. The man made a mistake. A terrible mistake, but he's paid his debt to society; now I think you people should leave him alone. Let him be." This man's attitude was remarkably like Walter's about legitimate police business.

"Were you working with Terry Saturday morning on the 19th?"

"Part of the morning, yes. He was here at eight, same as usual. I came in at ten."

"How about the 23rd—Wednesday? Did he work that day?" The day of Viv's funeral, Lindstrom had received two calls.

"No. He's off on Wednesdays and Thursdays. We're open seven days here. I need Terry on Saturday and Sundays. He's a good employee. Very reliable. I'm sure he's not done whatever it is you all are bothering him about. He came to work here directly after he left the correctional center. Hasn't missed a day of work."

"What time does he leave on Friday nights?"

"Friday's his long day, eight to eight. Sometimes he doesn't get out of here right at eight. If we've got a customer or he's finishing up a repair."

"Thank you, Mr.—"

"My name's Duncan, George Duncan."

"Thank you, Mr. Duncan. I hope your faith in Mr. Krebs is well-founded."

I reluctantly left the cool shop for the white hot pavement. So Krebs didn't miss work the Saturday after Viv's murder. Still I wanted another talk with Sandi Bidwell. And if I couldn't find her, I'd follow up on Page.

***

As soon as Sandi opened her door, I could tell something was wrong. She was the picture of dejection. Her shoulders rounded forward, and her already grim face soured when she recognized me.

"You lied to me."

'Only a little' was the first response that came to mind, but I rejected it. "I'm sorry. I did mislead you about reporting to Terry's PO, but everything else was the truth."

"You told Terry you were a reporter."

"Yes, I did." I balanced my weight forward, ready to jump in case she was thinking of throwing a punch; instead, Sandi just sighed.

"Could we go somewhere and talk?" I suggested.

"Why should I talk to you?"

"Because I need your help, and it can't hurt. Either Terry's done something terrible or he hasn't. Our talking won't change the facts. If he's done what I think he might have, you certainly can't protect him." Sandi sighed again and stepped back into the apartment.

"Come on in."

"Is he here?"

"No, he's over at the gym. At least that's what he told me."

I waited for her to elaborate, but instead she turned and walked into the dark, hot room. I followed her through an open doorway into her bedroom. It was tiny, entirely filled with a double bed and a small dresser. We brushed the end of the bed as we walked through to the kitchen. High on the kitchen wall was what looked like half a window. I realized that some landlord had cut a small apartment into two apartments. Sandi pushed a rattling box fan to the side and turned back to me.

"Want a glass of tea or a Coke?"

"Coke, please." The apartment was stifling in the late afternoon heat. The brick building had absorbed the sun all day and would radiate heat all night. The only source of natural light seemed to be the half-window, so there wasn't even the remote possibility of a breeze.

"He was angry at you for talking to me?" I asked as she handed me an aluminum can of Vess diet cola.

"Huh, angry don't even begin to get it." She pushed her thumb into the thin aluminum of her can and let it pop out again. "I just don't know anymore. He's spooking me."

"Has he been acting odd?"

"Who are you, really?"

"My name is Meg Darcy. I'm a private investigator."

215

"This isn't about stuff being stolen."

"No, it isn't. It is about a woman being murdered, and I'm trying to keep another woman from being murdered as well."

"Did Terry know the woman who was murdered?"

"Not directly. But I'm pretty sure whoever killed Vivian thought she was this other woman."

"The woman you're afraid will be killed?"

"That's right."

"I don't know. I thought what happened to Terry's wife was just a fluke. He explained it so well. How he just got so mad when he saw her in bed with that guy. After he had given her another chance. He said everything just went red, and he didn't even know what was happening. The cops had to tell him his wife was dead. He didn't mean to kill her. But now... "

"Now he's saying or doing things that frighten you?"

"When he found out I'd talked to you, he was so mad. He pushed me down and screamed in my face. He said I'd end up like his wife if I wasn't careful." Tears welled up in Sandi's eyes, but she didn't let herself cry at the memory of his rage.

"He threatened to kill you."

"It sort of sounded like that. I don't know what he meant, really. He calmed down later. But since then I just can't get that out of my mind. It's like he's a different person to me now." She looked into my eyes for clues to Terry's potential violence. "What will I do if he really killed that woman?"

"You'll stay away from him until we get enough to arrest him."

"You don't understand. He'll be back over here this evening. I can't just tell him he can't come in because I'm not sure if he killed somebody or not."

"Sounds to me like Terry isn't a very good bet even if he didn't kill Vivian. No one should threaten to kill you."

Sandi looked miserably unresolved.

"Was he really with you all that Friday night?" I asked.

"He said he was going out to rent a video," she mumbled.

"He walked?"

"No, he took my car. The video store is only a couple blocks away. I was in the tub. I figured it was no big deal."

"When did he leave?"

"About ten-thirty. He got back about midnight. He had the videos. He said some guy was going berserk outside the video store and throwing garbage around. He got hit with a bunch of it and had to go home, shower, and change."

I leaned forward. Not only was Krebs unaccounted for during the crucial time, he had also had to shower and change. My heart started pounding. But I was pretty sure it wasn't Krebs that we'd chased through Soulard that morning. Could that have been unrelated? Surely it was too much of a coincidence to have been a different stalker lurking underneath Lindstrom's bathroom window in the early morning hours.

"Is there something wrong with Terry's leg?"

"He was limping the other day. He said he hurt his knee at work."

"What about last night, Sandi? Did Terry spend it here with you?"

"No. He never really spends the whole night here. Either I take him home, or he catches the bus."

"Has he ever mentioned Vivian Rudder or Sarah Lindstrom?"

"No, the only people Terry talks about are George and his wife and Jim, who works at Advance, too. And the guys at the gym."

"Has he said anything about getting even with a cop?"

She shook her head silently. "How will I know?" she asked, a tremble growing.

"I think you should stay away from him. Just avoid him until we know for sure."

"How am I going to do that? What will I say to him?"

"You don't have to tell him anything. Go away for a few days."

Sandi frowned at me and sat up straighter. "Don't tell him I talked to you again, okay? Just leave me out of this. Then if he didn't do it, everything will be all right."

I bit my lip to avoid giving more unwanted advice. "Thank you for telling me the truth, Sandi. I won't tell Terry anything." She nodded and lowered her head again. I let myself out of the airless apartment.

It was still rush hour, so it took me nearly thirty minutes to get to Krebs's apartment on Spring Street. I wanted a look inside his place.

The address Sandi had given me was an auto parts store at the street level. The apartment over it had mini blinds at the windows. I walked casually into the alley and around the back of the building. Sweat trickled down the side of my face as I looked at the wooden door that probably led up to his apartment. The back door of the auto parts store was a heavy metal one, painted gray-blue. A broken cinder block lay near it for propping the door open. Was Krebs really at the gym, as he had told Sandi, or was he outside Lindstrom's house watching and waiting? Or was he upstairs, planning how he might satisfy his urge to control through fear? I decided that when I did confront Krebs, I didn't want it to be in his apartment, with no back up, so I walked around to the front of the parts store.

"May I help you?" asked the spit-polished young black man behind the counter.

"Yes. I heard that the apartment upstairs was available. I'd like to speak to someone about renting it."

He looked puzzled. "I don't think so." He turned toward the back, through rows of metal shelves holding cardboard boxes of fuel pumps and spark plugs. "Hey, Tanner. Did that guy upstairs move?" We heard a muffled voice, but the words were indistinct.

"Hang on a minute." The young clerk headed back through the aisle and disappeared around a corner. I looked around. The whole store was antiseptically clean, very different from my mental image of an auto parts shop. I guessed times in the business were different now that they had to compete with the chain stores on every corner. The shop in my neighborhood was still a drop off station for dust and greasy grime. In a minute, my clerk was back with Tanner, a middle-aged white man, in tow.

Tanner spoke. "No, that apartment's rented. Has been for several months."

"Oh well, I guess my friend was mistaken. Do you think the current renter could be planning to leave?"

"I don't know, you could ask him, I guess."

"Is he home now?"

"I think so. We can hear his television from the back room. It's on now."

"Thanks a lot, guys."

They nodded agreeably and wished me a good day. I was frustrated about not being able to get in now, but Krebs was due back at work tomorrow morning, and the sign on the front door said the auto parts store would be closed on Sunday, so I'd have clear sailing then.

***

My apartment felt like a haven to me. It smelled like home, and Harvey trotted right into the den to greet me. I could tell he was nearly ecstatic to have Patrick and me home at the same time. Voices floated in from the kitchen, but neither Patrick nor Lindstrom seemed interested in greeting me. I walked straight through to the bathroom with only a wave. I wanted to wash the grime off my face and brush my teeth before I faced whatever tension those two had created in my absence. I tried not to imagine Lindstrom's reaction when she woke to find herself 'guarded' by Patrick. As I had my face buried in the towel, I heard Patrick's yelp from the kitchen. I rushed out the door and heard Lindstrom's hearty laughter.

"I can't believe it," Patrick wailed, "You discarded eights twice."

"What is going on here?" I asked.

"Canasta," Lindstrom replied, unable to keep the gloat from her voice.

"Subterfuge and sleight of hand. I had her, Meg, until that pile." Patrick pointed at the half a deck Lindstrom was gleefully sorting through, building her melds. "She was on the ropes. What a ruse, and I can't believe I fell for it." Patrick ran his hand over his very short blond hair.

Lindstrom had stopped giggling, as it seemed to interfere with her fierce concentration on her cards.

"Want to just fold?" asked Lindstrom in a flirtatious tone I rarely heard from her.

"Oh, no, you don't!"

"Patrick never folds," I offered. "And he'll keep score as well." I pulled up a chair and watched, fascinated, as Lindstrom sorted the wad of cards in her hand. "I didn't know you played canasta."

"I hadn't in years," she replied.

"It was that or have a huge fight about the danger you are in, Meg." Patrick patted my hand. "We decided on a less painful outlet for our various fears."

218

Lindstrom looked up sharply, but grinned when Patrick winked at her.

An alliance between Lindstrom and Patrick was the last thing I'd expected when I left him here to guard her. Lindstrom, still intent, discarded a black three.

"Oh, generous one, this card beggar humbles himself at your munificent gift." Patrick drew an ace and slapped it down on his meld of four aces and two wild cards. He plucked a black ace and put it on top, drawing the canasta into a neat pile.

"Hey, how about dinner," I suggested hopefully. "We could order some pizza."

"Wait until we're finished here," Lindstrom cut me off.

"After the game, we'll talk. Maybe we'll go out." Patrick discarded a four, and Lindstrom picked it up.

"You're never satisfied, are you? Just take and take and take," Patrick said.

As it seemed my company wasn't crucial to the party, I walked back into the living room and watched the late local news. They played two more hands before Lindstrom reached five thousand.

We went three rounds of 'where to eat' and finally settled on Pho Grand. Over spring rolls and curry, I caught them both up to date on my conversation with Sandi Bidwell. Lindstrom was intrigued by Krebs's sudden lack of alibi and his threats to Sandi. Then, as I hadn't see Patrick in a while, I had to back up and review my interview with Gregory Page's family and friends, and Aubuchon's weirdnesses. I went lightly over the being-chased-by-skinheads-in-a-pickup-truck scene to avoid worrying Patrick unnecessarily. But I did ask him to keep an eye out for pickups or other vehicles bearing the Confederate flag.

Lindstrom told Patrick about the arrival of Viv's pen. Lindstrom said she'd called Neely as soon as she woke up this evening and learned that the evidence tech had been unable to raise a single usable fingerprint from the pen or wrapper. Not even a UPS employee's. But Neely now knew the pen had been sent from the UPS office at 520 South Jefferson.

As we sipped iced coffee after our meal, I watched Lindstrom telling Patrick her version of our foot chase that morning. I wasn't sure if it were actually catching a glimpse of our stalker or sex with me, but she was certainly more relaxed this evening than I'd seen her since Viv's death. Her smile as she described my flying to the floor of the market lit up her eyes. Perhaps Patrick had worked some healing at the canasta table. I marveled at how well the two of them were getting along. Before we settled the bill, Patrick was advising Lindstrom to sleep at my place tonight. He thought the change might do us good and let our stalker know we weren't under his thumb. Lindstrom simply agreed with Patrick. He left us at my door with a kiss for me and just a grin for Lindstrom. Some things, at least, were in proportion.

I was undressing, happily anticipating a cuddle in my very own bed when the phone rang.

"Meg? Are you there? If not, I'll leave this message on the…"

I picked up. "Hi, Walter. What's happening?"

"I got us the deal on the theater. It will be a good contract for us, but we'll need to set a date to interview some people down here."

"Great," I couldn't believe he was calling me to chat about the security business. Walter doesn't usually need my praise to do his job.

"And I believe the cops were right about Aubuchon."

Oh.

"I found the bartender he yammered at after dinner till about 9:30, then the desk clerk at the Ramada is sure he staggered in at ten because they had a little talk about the news. She thought he was cute, but decided not to flirt when she smelled the beer. Her first husband was an alcoholic."

"Thanks, Walter. That clears the path a bit."

"So where are we now?"

Lindstrom came back in and sat on the bed, openly listening while I ran down Page's and Krebs's profiles for Walter. When I hung up, she seemed disappointed that it couldn't be Aubuchon, but oddly comforted by Walter's efforts on her behalf. Then she stretched and groaned and fell to sleep immediately.

CHAPTER THIRTY-SIX

I spent most of the night either chasing or being chased by shadowy, vicious men through long subterranean tunnels. A bottle rocket exploded in Tower Grove park at daylight and that finished my sleep. I tried to slip quietly out of bed, but Lindstrom stirred and sat up.

"Let's go back to the house," she said, wide awake in an instant.

"At this hour?"

"Yes. I want to check it. And it'll keep our schedule unpredictable. He'll never know when it's safe to come creeping around. Besides, I have to be at the Arch grounds by nine."

"I hope Neely and Johnson have been excused from guard dog duty."

Lindstrom grinned at me. "Sure, saving my life is important enough to get them off, just not me."

"Are you sure it's safe for you to be doing this?"

She sighed. "No, being a cop is never safe. Especially where the booze is flowing freely, but it'll be your ordinary drunk who shoots me today, not Viv's killer. He won't have any way to know I'm at the Fair and wouldn't dare try to take me on in that crowd if he did."

"The crowd might be perfect cover."

"Darcy, I appreciate your efforts, but this is my job, and I intend to do it. Let's go." So we got dressed and drove through the watery early morning light. The city was mostly asleep at this hour on Sunday, and we were quiet on our way to Soulard.

She went to get the morning paper. She claimed the front section and the Metro section, so I took general news and poured coffee. Twenty minutes later I waved good-bye as she left and hurried back into the kitchen to dial Patrick's number.

Surprisingly, he was already awake and perky. "Hi, Meg. Where are you? I just went over to your place to see if you wanted bagels before I go to work."

"We left at the crack of dawn and came over to Lindstrom's house. You have to work today?"

"'Fraid so. Ten to two."

"But, Patrick, I need you on a very important mission."

"Can't Lindstrom help?"

"It's illegal, so she wouldn't. Besides, she's playing cop at the VP Fair today."

"Oooh, poor girl. It's going to be a hundred in the shade down there today. In that case, it'll have to wait until two o'clock. How illegal?"

"Just a little breaking and entering."

"You're not thinking of messing with that skinhead's stuff, are you?"

"No, Krebs's apartment. I need a lookout. He gets off work at four. Maybe we can still do it. Can I pick you up at work, and we'll go straight over there?"

"I'm not sure, Meg. Can't Lindstrom get a search warrant?"

"She's not even supposed to be touching this case."

"Well, then tell what's his name. The man who is supposed to be investigating this."

"Patrick, I don't think we've got enough for a search warrant, and with the holiday, it may well take me two days to convince them to try. I just want a quick look around. Then if there's something there, I'll tell them, and they can get a warrant."

"Does she know what you're planning?"

"Patrick, really."

"Oh, all right. I'll be your lookout. But if he comes home and catches us, I swear I'll kill you myself and save him the trouble. Pick me up at two." He hung up.

I thought for a few minutes about trying to get another operative to back me up so I wouldn't have to wait until two. But Krebs was supposed to work until four, so we should have plenty of time to get in and out.

I drove by our office to check the machine. Still no calls from Page. I allowed myself time for four hands of solitaire on my computer, but won the third game and stopped while I was ahead. I got some latex gloves from the storeroom and checked to make sure my pick locks were in my bag in the back of the Plymouth. I typed up notes on the interviews with Sandi Bidwell and Joe Griff. It was only noon. I got on the Net and cruised around Planet Out.

Finally, when I could sit still no longer, I headed to the bookstore. I spent my extra minutes finding a book for my brother Brian's birthday. At ten minutes to two Patrick took mercy on me and picked up his empty lunch sack and apologized to his co-workers. They weren't too miffed as very few St. Louisans were spending their holiday shopping for books. We took Patrick's MG, hopefully unrecognizable to Krebs.

I babbled all the way over to Krebs's apartment. Despite my assurances to Patrick, I hated sneaking into places I was unfamiliar with. And I was scared witless about getting caught.

We drove to Advance, and Patrick walked in to inquire about buying a used VCR to insure that Krebs was where he was supposed to be and that he was the only one working, so theoretically, at least, he wouldn't be sneaking out early. We made a quick right and headed for Krebs's apartment. I made Patrick cruise the block twice looking for the perfect parking spot, not too far in case we had to make a fast break, not too close so if something went wrong, some nosy neighbor wouldn't associate the MG with Krebs's apartment. I crammed my revolver, two pairs of gloves, and my camera in the attaché case. I stuck the pick locks in my pocket. We rolled up the windows, and Patrick practiced his two-fingers-in-his-mouth piercing whistle. With my ears ringing, I took a deep breath and gave the signal to begin.

I stationed Patrick by the dumpster where I was pretty sure I'd be able to see him from Krebs's apartment window and reminded him that Krebs might be coming in Sandi's Chevy or on the bus. The heavy metal door to the auto shop was locked tight. So was Krebs's lighter wooden door. My palms were sweaty as I looked around and pulled the pick locks from my pocket. The only lock was in the doorknob. Krebs's landlord hadn't installed a deadbolt, saving me time and trouble. Unfortunately, I jimmied locks infrequently, so my performance would have embarrassed Kinsey Millhone. Nonetheless, and in spite of palms that were sweaty inside latex gloves, I finished the job in just under seven minutes. Patrick's eyes widened at the delay, but bless his heart, he refrained from commenting. I listened carefully at the bottom of the stairs, but all I heard was my own raspy breath. I moved up the stairs quickly and quietly and listened again outside the door for Krebs's apartment. I put my hand on the knob and could barely believe my luck when it turned easily.

The inside of Krebs's apartment was clean and neat as a barracks. The frayed green wing chair was at an exact right angle with the tan couch. The coffee table was precisely six inches from the edge of the couch and perfectly centered. No books in sight. A drum table beside the chair was my initial objective, but first I stole a look at my lookout. He was craning his neck to see as far as he could into the alley. I waited a moment until his eyes rose to the window and gave him an okay sign. He sent one back.

I kneeled in front of the walnut drum table and pulled gently on the brass handle. It opened easily to expose a stack of magazines. Old *Sports Illustrated* and copies of *Time* that looked like they'd been lifted from doctors' offices. A newer electronics magazine had Krebs's mailing label on it. The dining room was more of a passageway between the living room and the kitchen, but it held a three-drawer chest, and I started with the bottom drawer. I fingered through bank statements and official correspondence from the Department of Corrections.

My heart nearly stopped as the phone rang. I swallowed and found a lump in my throat I couldn't account for. Whoever wanted Krebs was persistent; the phone rang thirteen times before she or he gave up. I gave the next two drawers a quick flip through and found only dish towels and a few old western paperbacks. I stuck my head in the kitchen, but figured that was not as likely as the bedroom so I started in there.

His bedroom was on the front of the building, facing Spring Street. I had just opened the closet door when Patrick gave his piercing whistle. My knees went soggy, and my lungs sucked at nothingness. I dropped near the floor and scuttled for the door. I ran headlong down the steps and stopped at the outside door. I listened. Nothing. No footsteps, no voices, no sound from Patrick. What the hell was happening? I eased the door open a crack and saw the toe of Patrick's tennis shoe.

"Patrick," I hissed.

"Um, I saw an old Chevy, but it went on down the alley."

"What color was it?"

"Blue-green," he said.

"More blue or green?"

"Green, I guess."

I took a breath. "Can you see it now?"

"No. It's gone."

"Okay, I'm going back up. Try not to panic, okay, Patrick?"

"I'm not panicking, Meg. This is stupid and dangerous. I can't believe I agreed to do this. Are you almost done?"

"Almost." I knew no other answer would be acceptable. I ran back up the steps.

His small bathroom was off the bedroom, and like the rest of the apartment, tidy. I peered into the shower. Nothing there. On the wall, to the right of the mirrored medicine cabinet, were a few brown spots. I sniffed at them. Not blood. Chemical. I found the small waste basket near the sink. Tissues, Q-Tips, and an empty can of spray-in hair color. Terry Ray had suddenly had an urge to be a brunette. I tossed the wash-out color can back into the basket and rushed into the bedroom.

I was sure in my own mind now, but needed more to convince Johnson. I pulled open the closet door. There, pinned to the hollow-core door was a picture of Lindstrom and me on her back porch. The light was bad, and it had been taken from too many feet away for the camera's capabilities, but our shapes and the house were clearly recognizable. I squinted at it and tried to remember us ever sitting on her porch. It had to be the morning after Patrick and I had sat outside her house after Viv's funeral. My eye strayed to the other pieces of paper tacked on the inside of the door. The *Post* articles about Vivian Rudder's death were all there as well as a 3 x 5 card labeled Sarah Madeline Lindstrom with her date of birth, social security number, and license plate number. Under that, in a slightly different hand, as if he had written it after he pinned the card up, was Vivian's name. Under that was a blurred picture of Lindstrom getting out of her car at the Clark Street station. At the bottom was another 3 x 5 card headed Margaret Ann Darcy with my home and work phone numbers, the office address, and my date of birth.

My heart was pounding as I touched the doorknob. This was enough. Krebs was our man, and Johnson could arrest him with this and get a search warrant to find it legally. A white envelope above the other items caught my eye just as I started to close the door. I pulled its push pin out carefully and looked inside. I couldn't bring myself to touch the lock of hair he'd pulled from Vivian's head. It lay there, limp and silent. Dead. I wondered if this had gone on longer if he were planning to send that to Lindstrom, too, or was that his own special trophy to cherish?

As I dialed the Clark Street station, I started crying. I tried to stop because I knew they would never understand me if I didn't. I bit my lower lip until I tasted blood and just managed to spurt out, "Homicide." The dispatcher didn't ask for details; she just transferred me. A baritone answered and said Neely wasn't in when I asked.

"I can take a message for him."

"No, I need someone right now. Is Johnson in?" I strained to keep my voice steady.

"Hang on, he was here earlier." He put me on hold, and I slid to the floor and put my head on my knees. Ages passed. I looked at my watch. Three-thirty-five. I had to get out of there. I promised myself that if Johnson didn't come to the phone in sixty more seconds, I'd leave and call him from somewhere else. The baritone startled me.

"Nope, he's gone, too. Want me to leave a message?"

"No, page both Johnson and Neely. Tell them to call Meg Darcy immediately. And page Lindstrom, too. She's down at the Arch, at the Fair. Tell them all to call me as soon as possible." I hung up without waiting for his answer. Even with all our technology, it is harder than ever to summon the cavalry.

I stood shakily and returned to the bedroom where I closed the closet door carefully.

A minute later I was standing in front of Patrick.

"Meg, what's wrong?"

"It's Krebs, Patrick. Let's get out of here before he gets home."

"Did you lock the door?"

I stepped back to double check it, and we walked to his MG without further conversation. We headed back toward the bookstore. I told Patrick what I'd discovered.

"He had me, Patrick. That day I went to see him. He just played me."

"What are you talking about, Meg?"

"He faked that limp, then later dyed his hair. I feel so stupid. I should have gone into his apartment right away. We could have had him a week ago."

"Meg, let's go to the police station. They can go to the shop and arrest him."

"No one's there."

"What do you mean?"

"I called. Neely and Johnson are out. Lindstrom's at the Arch grounds guarding the Fair. I had them paged."

I found I could breathe and talk at the same time. I didn't cry, but felt as if my chest were going to blow wide open. I wouldn't be able to stay inside my skin until I saw Lindstrom again, alive and whole. Patrick's MG slid in beside my Plymouth. "I'm going back to Lindstrom's." I glanced at my watch. "She should be home soon."

"Shouldn't I go with you?"

"No, what I have to tell her will be hard. She'll be more comfortable if we're alone."

"I'll go home then. Maybe I'll just grab Harve and take him over to my place."

"Why? He's all right at my place. He'll commit murder and mayhem on Oscar and Quentin."

"I just feel creepy about this guy, Meg. You don't have a security system like Lindstrom. What if he gets in? Besides, I'll confine the terrorist to the bathroom."

He was right. Better safe than sorry. "Okay, Patrick. Thanks for being my lookout." I patted his knee, and he nodded.

"Call me after you've talked to Lindstrom."

"Sure, see you later." I wasn't looking forward to telling Lindstrom the grisly things I had to tell her, but I'd already decided that it had to be the whole truth, so she'd see that she had to get away with me, maybe to my mom's place until Krebs was safely locked away. Anything less than the details about the pictures in Krebs' apartment, any fudging on my part, and the stubborn homicide detective would want to stay around and 'help' Johnson and Neely collar Krebs. They didn't need any help from her. One look at Krebs' trophy collection, and the case would be complete. Lindstrom just needed to be out of harm's way so there wouldn't be any further violence.

I took a deep breath. This was going to be one of the most difficult conversations of my life. I fished my cell phone out of the back seat and turned it on. I needed my wits about me, but my stomach felt shaky, and I couldn't think of the envelope with Viv's hair without wanting to cry again. I drove grimly to Soulard.

CHAPTER THIRTY-SEVEN

Once inside at Lindstrom's, I couldn't sit down to wait for her. I paced through the kitchen and up and down the hallway. Bits and pieces of the last two weeks raced through my mind. I stared at my watch as though I could propel it forward.

The phone rang. I sprinted into the den and caught it mid-ring.

"Hello."

"Hello, Meg. Or should I call you Jennifer?"

I stopped breathing at the sound of his voice. No disguise this time. I reminded myself not to give anything away. We didn't have him safely in our clutches.

"What do you want, Krebs?"

"I'd like to talk to your girlfriend. Is she home yet?"

I tried to think. What would happen if he knew she was at the VP Fair? Would Lindstrom be safe there? I decided not to risk anything.

"Where she is is none of your business, Krebs."

"Oh, but you might change your mind about that. My plans have altered slightly, but I think I have something you want."

The next thing I heard chilled me.

"Meg, don't do it—whatever he wants. I'm okay." It was Patrick's voice, breathless but brave.

"Bad advice, Meg. But you get the idea. We're at your place. Bring Sarah. And if I see any cops, I'll hurt him bad before I kill him. I know exactly how long it takes to get here from there. So hurry."

Krebs slammed the phone down, and I stared at the receiver. I quickly hung up and picked up again to dial my number. He picked the phone up and immediately dropped it into the cradle. He didn't want to talk to me anymore on the telephone. Okay. He wouldn't play. I'd go. Before I did, I recorded a new outgoing message on Lindstrom's answering machine. "This is Meg Darcy. Krebs has Patrick at my apartment. I'm going there now. It's four-forty p.m." Now when Johnson or Neely or Lindstrom called in, they'd come to get us. I grabbed my gun and raced through the door without setting the alarm. I desperately hoped Patrick and I would both be in one piece when the troops finally arrived.

I noticed nothing on the way to Arsenal. Anxiety for Patrick consumed me so that I was startled to find myself at the apartment. I pulled in two doors down, out of eyesight from the windows. I didn't want Krebs knowing exactly when I arrived.

I approached the house from behind, willing my heart to slow down so my brain could function. I slipped in the back door and stepped warily to the far right side of the stair case. Each step was a trial—the old wood was inclined to creak at every footfall. Halfway up I reminded myself to breathe. My thoughts were tumbling, but I was beginning to see a plan of attack. At the landing I listened. No sound from either apartment. I unlocked Patrick's door.

Inside his apartment I tried to move quickly and quietly. I gathered screwdriver, step stool, and Patrick's good carving knife. My pockets were too shallow for the screwdriver and knife, and I'd need my hands. I opened the junk drawer again and fished out the duct tape. Hurriedly, I held the knife and screwdriver against my thigh and wrapped the tape snugly around the leg of my pants. That would have to do for a temporary tool belt. I carried the four-step stool into Patrick's bedroom and opened his closet door. Oscar looked up from his curl on the bed and yawned.

I climbed up the stool and scrambled onto the shelf at the top of Patrick's closet. I pushed at the square plywood board that serves as an attic door; it fits snugly into a two-by-four frame like a lid on a pan, and its twin opens into my closet. I pushed against it with the heels of my hands. The lid moved up into the attic. I set it aside, gently, trying not to generate even the slightest noise Krebs could interpret as an invasion.

I hoisted myself up by my elbows, scraping an arm. The light was dim. Thin sheets of plywood lay over the joists. It was at least a hundred and twenty degrees in the still air of the attic. Sweat trickled through the dust on my face.

When I stood, I had to duck to avoid hitting my head. I moved carefully across the plywood to the square frame in the floor that would open into my closet. Just as I pulled the long screwdriver from my improvised tool belt, I heard a noise from below. Someone was knocking at my apartment door. I crouched, perfectly still, over my bedroom closet. I had expected the phone to ring. Surely the police department would contact Krebs by phone. Someone was stumbling into this.

I pushed the screwdriver in between the two-by-four frame and the door that fit into it. Humidity had sealed this one tight. No handle to lift the lid. Obviously anyone coming down from the attic would first come up through this door. I heard Lindstrom's voice, muffled, far away.

"Darcy, it's me. Are you in there?"

What on earth was she thinking? Her voice was cheerful. She hadn't gotten my message. She must have come here first. Where were Neely and Johnson?

The screwdriver skidded from my sweaty hand. I heard thuds and voices from below like the sound effects of an old radio drama—my racing mind supplied the visuals. I lunged for the screwdriver, began prying around the edge of the door, trying for the leverage to lift the wood. All I needed was an inch, a small space under the lip of wood, something to tug. Sweat ran into my eyes. The door suddenly pulled free; I heard Patrick shout "No!" from below, accompanied by more crashes and thuds. I thought I heard the thread of her moan amid the tangle of grunts and curses.

I dropped down onto the closet shelf and pushed myself over the edge onto the floor, cracking my head on the doorjamb on the way down and noticing a startled Harvey wedged into a corner pile of my shoes. I took less than a half second to shake the sweat from my eyes and pull the .38 free, then threw the closet open wide and ran headlong through my bedroom into the living room.

My eye took in more detail than I could immediately process. Patrick was duct-taped to one of my kitchen chairs, which was in the middle of the living room. Right behind him Lindstrom, still in uniform and cradling her left forearm, was scrambling to her feet, a rage possessing her face. Blood streamed from a cut over her left eye, and she looked pale. Krebs closed in on her, wielding an aluminum bat. The look on his face told me he wasn't sure that was enough of an advantage if she got to her feet again.

Gun trumps bat.

"Hold it, Krebs! Drop the bat!"

But they were too close together from their struggle. And he was quick, mind and body. He slid around behind her while she was still on one knee and used the bat like a baton under her jaw, tilting her chin, and forcing her body upward. "I'll snap her neck." Her broken arm dangled at an impossible angle.

Her eyes ordered me to shoot the bastard, but I was stuck. Her torso sheltered his.

He looked more sure of himself. "*You* drop the gun."

I had maybe a split second to decide if I could make the head shot without signaling my intention.

Without warning, Patrick screamed some kamikaze screech and threw himself and the chair backwards into Krebs. The bat clattered to the floor, and Lindstrom lunged for it. Krebs pulled back, trying to free himself from the tangle of arms and legs. He pushed Patrick and his chair, slamming Patrick's head on the floor. I stepped in and held my .38 to Krebs's temple. "Don't move a single muscle," I said. I saw only a silvery blur from the corner of my eye as she swung the bat with her right arm. I heard the sickening crack of his elbow snapping, and Lindstrom's own grunt of pain. Krebs's body crashed sideways from the impact. My stomach churned.

I thought it was over, but she towered above him, her eyes intent as, one-handed, she raised the bat for another blow.

"Lindstrom! Stop!"

She glared at me. Then, slow-motion, she lowered the bat to her side. "Where's my gun?"

Maybe she was in shock. I rose from my crouch and, keeping my gun on Krebs, edged toward her. "Give me your cuffs."

"Cuff him in front. Don't pull that arm behind his back." She spoke quite calmly, as if she hadn't just deliberately shattered that arm.

"Help me up. I can't see a damn thing," Patrick said.

"Hang on, let me get him cuffed."

I gave Lindstrom my .38. She kept it pointed at Krebs while I cuffed him and then pulled Patrick upright. His forehead was cut and bleeding profusely. "Tie his feet. The tape's on the desk," Patrick said. I took his advice.

Absurd as it sounds, Krebs looked relieved to be out of the fray; he had the inward look of one concentrating on how much he was hurting. The few curses he directed toward me sounded perfunctory. I could hardly comprehend it—this creep who had menaced us for so long lay like a limp sack.

Only then could I tend to them. I turned to Patrick and cut his hands and feet free.

I swiped some of the blood from his face. "Can you call for help? Tell them a cop is down—that'll get 'em here. Also that we need two ambulances." He nodded and hobbled toward the phone in my bedroom.

"I'm not down," she said. She sounded like a crabby little kid denying sleepiness. She was standing but barely. I took her good elbow and steered her toward my sofa, which in the fray was now shoved liked a diagonal slash across my living room. I eased her onto it before she passed out. "My gun," she said.

I thought I understood. A quick search revealed that Krebs' weapon—a cheap little .22—had landed in the entrance hall. Lindstrom's 9mm had somehow skidded under the desk. I know all about leaving crime scenes intact. I lay down on my belly and reached back and retrieved the pistol. She was quite pale by then, her face streaked with blood, a skim of sweat beading her upper lip. But, when I handed the department issue weapon back to her, a smile flitted across her strained face; then she leaned over the edge of the couch and vomited on the floor. She was human after all. I swiped it up with one towel and used another, only slightly damp, as a makeshift sling.

I glanced at Krebs. He had lost consciousness. A quick check showed he still possessed a pulse and breath. Just touching him sent a shudder across my skin. Part of me was still afraid that as in a horror movie he would rise and slay us yet.

I heard Patrick's voice rising in the bedroom, a sign I interpreted as his encountering bureaucratic resistance.

"Did you tell him to order an ambulance?" she asked.

"Yes. That arm is swelling. Do you hurt badly?"

"Um, sure. But the ambulance is for Krebs. We can't book him until that elbow is set."

I hesitated, then plunged. "Why did you do it? I had him down."

She looked at me steadily.

"Did he hit you with the bat?" I asked.

"Three times, but that wasn't why I broke his arm."

"Why, then?"

"For Viv."

CHAPTER THIRTY-EIGHT

Cops poured into the apartment, led by Neely, closely followed by paramedics and Johnson. I noticed all the extra players buzzed, like Willie McGee had hit another long one to save the day. Neely went directly to Lindstrom, and his face pretty much matched mine when I first saw what Krebs had done to her, but nothing could lessen Neely's relief that she was alive and, if not well, not mortally wounded. Neely seemed a man who knew personally that you could live with wounds.

By the time the paramedics revived Krebs, he began whining, "The bitch deliberately broke my arm," a statement Johnson and every other cop seemed unable to hear. But I noticed, and so did Neely, that Lindstrom was developing a defensive wince, and he solved it by asking her if she felt able to move to the kitchen, leaving Krebs to the tender glances of the twenty-year veteran Neely had tagged to meet him at the scene. In minutes the medics had finished splinting Krebs's arm and strapping him to their stretcher, and Johnson joined us in the kitchen.

Right away Johnson moved up a notch on my Christmas list by the way he questioned Lindstrom, an artful mix of gruff cop talk sprinkled with sympathetic 'um-ums' and 'my-mys' like someone's mama bandaging a scuffed knee. Two more paramedics came into the kitchen and began taking Lindstrom's blood pressure; it had not gone unnoticed that she'd waved the first set off so that they could attend to Terry Ray Krebs and Patrick. Neely and Johnson seemed to take it for granted that a cop would always put her welfare last. But the paramedics and I were tending to fuss, and I, at least, was tempted to force her to let them look at her obviously broken arm and the cut on her face.

Eventually, the cops got around to taking a formal statement from Lindstrom, and she told it like it happened and in the usual cop jargon that obscures blood and piss. When she got to the critical part, she said, "And, as I was applying necessary force to subdue him, I heard a snap. I suspected a fracture had occurred."

I strained to listen, afraid the cops would somehow pluck the truth from thin air. Johnson gave one of his raspy chuckles. "You didn't kick him in the head?"

"No."

"Shame."

Gallows humor. Why did I feel a sense of complicity?

I ducked out of the kitchen. She should tell it her own way. I needed a moment to think. And I needed to go out and help the paramedic insist that Patrick go to the hospital. I thought he needed his forehead stitched.

When I returned to the kitchen, Johnson looked at me and tilted his head to indicate "follow me." He led me into my bedroom where an evidence tech was peering into my attic in puzzlement. "I came through there, not the perp." She smiled in relief at not having to dust the inside of the closet and the attic for prints.

"What's on your mind, Darcy? You're as antsy as a kid with stolen candy," Johnson said.

"Will Lindstrom get into trouble for breaking Krebs's arm?"

"You heard the detective. She used necessary force. Isn't that what you saw?" I had his full attention now, but he wasn't leaning on me with his question. I saw in his face merely a neutral curiosity despite his wording. He'd seen everything in his years on the force, and seeing one thing more wouldn't stun him.

I took a beat to run it by. I'd never forget the snap of Krebs's bone, but it happened so fast. I remembered the feeling I'd had watching him slam Patrick into the floor. I thought of all the days he'd seemed superhuman to us in both elusiveness and power. "That's what it looked like to me," I said. But the certainty I put into my voice didn't spread all the way through me. A small niggling doubt lived.

Maybe he sensed it. "I've never worked with Lindstrom, but Neely has. I know Neely. He uses velvet gloves on perps, and my understanding is that Lindstrom does, too. And anyone who knows her a half-second knows she tells the truth. So, if she says it was necessary force, that's biblical. Don't worry, Darcy."

I must have looked convinced because he patted me on the shoulder and then strode into the living room to check on progress. A procession was moving from the kitchen down the stairs, and I realized they were finally taking Lindstrom to the hospital. Not surprisingly, she was walking to the ambulance under her own steam while annoyed paramedics escorted her. They were followed by Neely and the twenty-year veteran who'd been watching Krebs; their silly grins indicated I'd missed a witty exchange. Lindstrom's face was drained of color and beads of sweat pearled her upper lip. She ignored me in the heart-wrenching way of a loved one absorbed in her own pain, and I fell in line at the end of the parade.

I heard the veteran mutter to Neely, "She's a feisty one." Had she threatened to deck a medic?

A third ambulance had come, the first having already moved Krebs away, and a paramedic was closing Patrick into the second. I grabbed the paramedic and instructed him to go to Barnes. I wanted all my chicks in the same coop. Lindstrom now had a small audience in a semi-circle around the open doors of the ambulance because a few uniformed officers had drifted over with us to watch as the medics tried to assist her up the step into the ambulance. Things were awkward, since they could touch only one of her arms to help her, and I heard one unforgiving medic mutter, "There's a reason we use stretchers."

But at last she was settled, and the taller medic leaned out and asked, "Who's riding with the patient?"

Neely and I exchanged looks, and I realized Johnson had come out to see her off. I didn't know police etiquette. Did police partners ride with their wounded? If I jumped into the ambulance now, would Lindstrom be embarrassed by this open acknowledgement of our connection? Neely leaned toward me. "Go on, Meg. You've been through all the rest of it with her. We'll drop by the hospital when we finish here."

Sounded like an invitation to me. I jumped in and settled myself on the seat and stayed out of the way till the medics seated themselves, too, and we were moving. Lindstrom had closed her eyes, but she opened them when I took her free hand.

"It's over," she said from a distance.

I didn't think so, but I nodded anyway.

***

Three hours later Johnson and Neely joined me in pacing outside the operating room because the free-for-all had turned a clean break into a nasty one requiring pins and surgery. Before she was in the recovery room, Johnson was called away because a Kentucky sheriff had found Gregory Page at the Strickland cabin, but Neely hung in there two more hours before he could slip in and bring comfort to his partner. "Are you going back in?" he asked me as he came out.

"For a while."

"You look like you could use some sleep."

I nodded. "If she drifts off."

"Better hurry and say good night, then." He looked at me speculatively, maybe considering a hug. But what he said was, "She has a lot to thank you for. We all do."

"She saved herself."

"She couldn't have done it by herself. That's what she says, and I believe her."

He must have seen how much I didn't want to talk about it then. "Well, Johnson and I still have things to do. He seemed reluctant to go. "Take care of her, Meg."

The lightning struck, and I realized in these liberated times a dyke could make the first move. I gave him a quick hug that grew. "Thank you, Neely."

Shortly after, Patrick was released. A velvety night met us as we left the medical complex. Barnes was lit up, the proud flagship of the Kingshighway hospitals.

Our police driver was a rookie, a skinny white woman, tightlipped with nervousness. For once I didn't take such shyness as a personal Darcy challenge. Patrick was quiet, too, for a block or so. We were sitting together in the back. When he spoke, his voice was so low I had to lean toward him to hear.

"I feel so stupid, Meg. He was waiting for me at the top of the stairs." Patrick shook his head. Stitches closed the cut which had bled so dramatically.

"That's one of the worst things about these perps, Patrick. They leave us feeling to blame. Like it was your fault."

"He put the gun to my head and told me to unlock your door. Then he tied me up and left and came back with the bat." His voice wobbled a bit at the end.

After the fact, all the feelings rush in.

I reached for his hand. "You were terrific, Patrick. You saved the day with your chair slam."

A silence. Then just a tad of pride as he said, "I knew a lifetime of 'B' movies would pay off."

"Is that where you got that howl?" I squeezed his hand.

"Oh that. In eighth grade I was in a play, and I had to scream. Typecast even then. Only a supporting part, but I was the star of the school for weeks."

Actually I recognized this story, but his retelling of it comforted me. Patrick interrupted himself. "Have you seen Harvey?"

"He's fine. We may not get him to come out of the closet, though."

"I didn't tell him anything, Meg." I knew he wasn't referring to Harvey.

"You were brave, Patrick."

"What happened when Lindstrom came?" he asked. "I could hear, but I couldn't see into the hallway." A pause. "I was too terrified to scream a warning. I thought he might just open the door and shoot her."

I heard the guilt, the seed of all the 'if onlys' he could torture himself with if we didn't stomp that seed now. "You thought right. Guys like Krebs are hair-triggers."

I was just saying what he needed to hear. We'd all have to replay and sort it.

"But how did she get the gun away from him?" Patrick returned to his question.

"She told Neely and Johnson that Krebs had her covered when she opened the door. Krebs ordered her to hand over the gun. She pulled out her 9mm and acted like she was handing it to him, grip first. She swung it up against his wrist and knocked his pistol out of his hand, but lost hers from the blow."

"God, she's ballsy!" Sounded like uncomplicated admiration.

"Brass ovaries." I patted his hand. "Then they had a wrestling match, but Krebs got back to the living room and the bat."

"I saw that."

He needed some minutes to think about that part, and before he was ready to speak again, the driver had pulled up in front of our apartment building.

I knew my place wasn't as wrecked as that of many crime victims. A misplaced sofa, a few splatters of blood, lots of fingerprint powder. If I didn't climb back on this horse now, I risked leaving Krebs the ruler of my castle.

"Let's go find Harvey," I said.

But he met us at the door and had complaints to make about the loud and unruly crowd who'd invaded his space that afternoon. I sat Patrick down at the kitchen table while I made him a cup of tea to accompany his Tylenol with codeine. He spent the time soothing the indignant Harvey, and in that process I heard Patrick's healing begin. Betty often says looking after someone else is the best way to reduce your own troubles, and sometimes she's right.

Now both of us were too whooshed to talk more.

"I'd better stay here tonight," he said.

I was too weary and too grateful to fret about who was protecting whom. Comforting whom.

"If you take the bed, I'll have to change the sheets."

"The couch is fine."

I slept like a baby in smelly sheets; Patrick, less comfortably, on my couch, even though his own bed was only a few yards away. Just before I sank under, the vacillating Harvey decided his Uncle Patrick needed him more.

***

I didn't get back to the hospital till Lindstrom had had her first breakfast, but I did get to watch her struggle with her lunch. Her cast extended above her elbow on the left arm. The soup was easy, but one-handed jello is a challenge. I offered to feed her bite by bite; she waved me away.

Her color was back, but her eyes stayed distant. I decided to start with a safe subject.

"Harvey sends his greetings. Patrick, too."

Her attempt to smile looked so physically painful I nearly winced. The cut on her forehead had required stitches, and her lips looked a size larger. I didn't want to think about why.

She wasn't willing to stay on the surface, though. "I feel stupid, Darcy. I just walked into it. I wasn't thinking about him at all."

"What happened? You weren't supposed to get off work until five."

She tried a shrug, grimaced. "There was a fight at the Fair. I cuffed some kids and took them down to booking. My supervisor said to take a break and come back. So I swung by your place on the off chance you'd be there."

"To go to dinner?" I coaxed.

She flushed a full-throttle rose—an interesting effect with all the stitchery and swelling. Before I could tell her, she said, "I was thinking of something else."

I got it. I grinned.

"So I wasn't thinking about him at all. I knocked twice, then used my key to open the door, and there he was."

"But then you thought fast and fought like a champ."

She looked away, not ready to hear it. I tried to steer toward safer ground. "When can you leave this pop stand?"

"This afternoon." She saw my look. "HMO. No coddling."

I thought I'd need to slip away and wash sheets and towels. To her I said, "What can I get from your place to make you comfortable at mine?"

She didn't argue a second. I thought I saw tears well up, but she looked away. I couldn't imagine what she'd had to endure as nightmares last night.

"I think you saved my life," she said, her voice mostly steady.

"You saved your own." I was tired of this debate.

"Listen for a change." She puffed air through her swollen lips. A silence. She left it hanging. In a flash I saw that we'd have quite a few mornings discussing horrors over our bran flakes before we rid our lives of them.

"This time I want you to listen to me, Lindstrom. I think you ought to see someone about all this."

Another silence. "I can't talk to you?"

I was surprised. "Sure, you can. I didn't mean that. I just meant—in addition to me, someone who knows more."

"Someone to fix me." She sounded sad about it.

"No. Someone to listen who isn't confused herself." I moved closer to the bed, thinking to take her hand, but all that happened was that she looked up with unhappy eyes.

"You think I went too far, don't you? You won't forget it."

'Her fury *had* scared me. Because it was my own as well. In a flash I realized either of us could have killed Krebs. I could not only see the scene but feel the heat of righteous rage roaring through me. Justified or not, that firestorm had shaken me.

"What's going on?" she asked.

"Something terrible happened to both of us. We'll need some time to put it behind us."

She looked away, thinking about it. Then she said, "I might have a permanent scar over my eye. Will that bother you?"

"I didn't fall for your beautiful face," I lied. I had—her face, her proud carriage, her insufferable arrogance. All the wrong reasons. And I wasn't sure that was enough to see us through.

"What then?"

Well, that was an unfair question.

Before I could answer, she asked another. "You think we can't make it?"

Suddenly I was in a panic. What *did* I feel? "I don't know, Lindstrom. Maybe we're trying too hard."

She considered, then motioned me closer, grabbed the front of my shirt with her good hand, and pulled me down nose to nose. "No halfway measures," she said, and, ignoring the pain and public display rules, kissed me.

236